Wicked Magic

CHEYENNE McCRAY

St. Martin's Paperbacks

This is a work of fiction. All of the characters, organizations and events portrayed in this novel are either products of the author's imagination or are used fictitiously.

WICKED MAGIC

Copyright © 2007 by Cheyenne McCray.
Excerpt from *Moving Target* copyright © 2007 by Cheyenne McCray.

ISBN: 0-312-94957-X
EAN: 9780312-94957-0

Printed in the United States of America

St. Martin's Paperbacks edition / September 2007

St. Martin's Paperbacks are published by St. Martin's Press, 175 Fifth Avenue, New York, NY 10010.

10 9 8 7 6 5 4 3 2 1

To my three sons, Tony, Kyle, and Matthew.
You guys mean the world to me.

ACKNOWLEDGMENTS

Monique Patterson, who lives to torture me (even though she claims she doesn't. Ha!)

As always, thanks bunches to my crit partners, Annie Windsor, Patrice Michelle and Tara Donn.

Thank you to my agent, Nancy Yost, one of the most fun and savvy people I know.

To the people of San Francisco, my favorite city in the USA. Thank you for allowing me the creative license I have used in your wonderful city, including dates, times, and places.

To every one of the folks at St. Martin's Press, you rock!

And a very special thank you to Craig White and Olga Grlic for the most awesome cover ever. I'm in love with you both!

Chapter 1

The vision came quick and strong and Rhiannon Castle's heart beat so hard her chest ached.

She dropped to her knees on her apartment floor and tried to breathe as the vision swam before her eyes.

Ceithlenn. The evil goddess from Underworld.

Her hair literally flamed and her eyes were a deep red. She had fangs, claws, and huge leather wings.

The goddess was terrifying and fascinating all at once.

Rhiannon felt the force of Ceithlenn's hunger as if it were her own belly that rumbled painfully. The knowledge that Ceithlenn hadn't fed in the three days since she'd left Underworld flowed into Rhiannon through the being's thoughts. Darkness was Ceithlenn's friend as she swooped through the San Francisco skyline searching for a victim or two.

The goddess dropped silently in a crouch behind a man with a pink Mohawk. She watched him for a moment, perching on the cracked sidewalk with her clawed hands resting between her thighs. In Underworld there had been no humans to dine on . . . and they looked *delicious*.

Rhiannon's stomach churned.

Ceithlenn extended her sharp claws as she moved her hand to the side. She slowly scraped her nails across the cement, a deep, ominous sound.

It came to Rhiannon, then. Ceithlenn was waiting for her

victim to acknowledge her. She wanted to experience the delight of the man seeing death staring him in the face. She studied her prey intently and swiped her tongue between her lips before giving a low roar like a tiger.

The moment Ceithlenn growled, the guy came to a stop. From out of his jacket sleeve he flipped open a switchblade and whirled to see what or who was behind him.

His eyes widened at the sight of the goddess. "What the fuck?"

With one flap of her great wings Ceithlenn leapt onto the man, slamming him to the concrete.

His knife skittered across the sidewalk. He started to shout but she sank her fangs into his throat before a sound could leave him.

Rhiannon nearly screamed as blood spurted. She felt the warm fluid in her mouth; experienced the thick, metallic taste as it flowed down her throat. She sensed Ceithlenn's thrill as she dined on the human's flesh.

And then *power*. Ceithlenn sucked up the dying man's soul, drawing it into her until his final death rattle. The potency of absorbing the human's soul was electrifying. The burst Ceithlenn felt in her magical strength was unreal.

As realization dawned so did her delight . . . she could absorb a *human's* soul and magnify her own powers. That was something she had never been able to do with any other living creature or being.

Rhiannon trembled and almost threw up as the vision held her captive and Ceithlenn dined until filled. Until all that was left were bones with bits of meat clinging to them.

Rhiannon felt the goddess's satisfaction and triumph— and the thrill of her discovery.

Souls. She needed more human souls.

For a moment Ceithlenn scowled. Looked around her, then sniffed the air.

Rhiannon recoiled.

Was Ceithlenn feeling Rhiannon's presence?

Ceithlenn scowled again then took to the air, flapping her great leather wings. Rhiannon felt Ceithlenn's rush of ecstasy as she circled the city. Sated for now and satisfied with her discovery, the goddess headed to her lair.

Ceithlenn glanced over her shoulder, as if she were looking directly at Rhiannon, and growled.

Rhiannon felt the darkness then, the recognition of the Shadows buried deep inside her—

And knew that the goddess recognized it, too.

Rhiannon cried out as she jerked back to reality. Her eyelids popped open to see that she was in her own apartment.

Her sight blurred and she could hardly breathe. Bile rose in her throat as she tried to ignore the tastes still in her mouth, but she couldn't handle it any longer.

Rhiannon scrambled up from the floor of her living room and fled for the bathroom. She fell to the linoleum, hit her knees, and puked into the toilet until nothing was left. It felt as though her stomach would come up her throat.

She spit the acidic taste from her mouth and found she no longer felt or tasted flesh and blood on her tongue. But the thought caused her to dry heave so that her sides ached from it.

When she stood to rinse out her mouth in the sink, she caught a glimpse in the mirror of her moon-white face. The usually pale scars slashed across one cheek by the queen of the Fomorii demons stood out like red trails. Sweat on her forehead glistened in the bathroom light. She looked away from the mirror, washed her face, swished water in her mouth, and brushed her teeth.

Her mind was a jumble as she staggered from the bathroom into her bedroom.

Had Ceithlenn seen her?

Worse yet, had the goddess seen the *Shadows*?

Before Rhiannon reached her bed, she dropped to the carpet, and passed out from exhaustion.

And fear.

Chapter 2

Keir laced the leather ties of his breeches as Lise lay curled up on the bed, watching him. His Pleasure Partner's elbow pressed into the mattress, her head resting in her palm. She gave him a sultry and satisfied smile, telling him she wanted more.

Keir had far more pressing matters to be concerned with than the beautiful, naked woman on the bed.

While he had been training more Tuatha D'Danann warriors, he had not been to the San Francisco Otherworld for three months. Time had run out and now he must return with his warriors to the city come morning.

The blond curls between Lise's thighs matched the shade of her long hair. Her lush breasts with their large pink nipples were tempting enough that for a moment he considered climbing back into bed with her.

Pleasure Partners like Lise willingly chose to serve in Pleasure Houses designed to fulfill the fantasies and needs of all comers. Keir did not mess around with fantasies. What he wanted when he came to a Pleasure House was a good fuck.

"Sure you are not ready for another round?" Lise said in a voice that came out in a purr. She pushed herself to a sitting position and lightly ran one of her fingers down his biceps as he yanked on one of his boots. "I want to take you again, warrior." Obviously Lise had decided to drive him out of his mind by bringing his cock back to full attention. But he did not have time to indulge in bedding her again.

"I have business to attend to, woman," Keir said gruffly, yet it did not deter Lise.

Her warm vanilla scent wrapped around him as she pushed his shoulder-length black hair aside and pressed her lips to his neck while he pulled on his other boot. "Your reputation as a lover was not exaggerated. Despite your show of roughness, you are one of the most incredibly passionate partners I have had. It is no wonder all the women in this Pleasure House would willingly spread their legs for you." She sighed. "Bastard son or not, any lady, from highborn to Pleasure Partner, would love to have you between her thighs."

Keir scowled, feeling the familiar rise of anger at the mention of his parentage. Not that anyone but the man who fathered him cared about Keir being a bastard. Between Keir and his half-brother Hawk, he had definitely not been the favored child—as his stepmother was quick to remind him. It had created a bitter rift between him and Hawk—the son of a true union. A rift that had lasted to this very day, centuries later.

Keir had learned as a boy not to form sentimental attachments of any kind. Even his blood mother had abandoned him.

The only ones he trusted were his D'Danann warrior brethren. He trusted them in battle and with his life. It was ironic that Hawk was counted among the brethren.

"You are a mystery. A puzzle to be solved," Lise said.

He jerked on his leather tunic, forcing her to move away from him. Before she could touch him again, he stood and strode to a chair where he had flung his weapons belt before taking the Pleasure Partner to bed. The room was too frilly for his taste. Pastels with wildflowers and white furnishings—a woman's room. Vanilla-scented candles flickered on every surface, and the smell mingled with the scent of their sex.

Keir fastened his weapons belt around his waist and did not bother to look at Lise again. They had gone three rounds and yet she was begging for more. The thought should have given him some measure of satisfaction, but as usual he felt nothing more than the easing of his needs and the desire to go back to the training yards.

"I wonder what kind of woman it would take to tame you?" Lise said casually.

The comment caught Keir off guard and he cut his gaze to Lise. Her lips were pursed and she looked as if she truly was interested in her own question.

Keir did not bother to answer. No woman would tame him.

He pulled more than enough coins from a pouch in a pocket of his breeches and dropped them on a table beside the bed. The coins clattered across the surface and one rolled to the edge.

Lise caught it with a delicate sweep of her hand and closed her fingers over the gold. "Trust me," she said with a quick grin. "One day you will meet that woman and she will have you on your knees."

Keir gave a slight bow from his shoulders. "Madame Lise," he said before turning away. His boots thumped on the wooden flooring as he headed out of the bedroom and closed the door behind him.

Women.

He would need to return shortly to San Francisco with the younger Fae warriors he had been training in the skills needed to defeat Fomorii demons. Unfortunately, none of them could be trained to fight Ceithlenn until the D'Danann were able to discover her weaknesses. And Keir would be damned if he did not find a way to determine what those weaknesses were.

Keir strode from the well-kept Pleasure House toward the training yards. Dust swirled around his boots on the dry path and sunshine warmed his bare arms. The clang of swords rang through the air, becoming louder as he approached the yards.

Word had come to him only yesterday that Silver Ashcroft, a witch and Hawk's mate, had scried with her cauldron that Ceithlenn was, as feared, in San Francisco. Another witch he had not met had experienced a vision that spoke of foul deeds this evil goddess had already committed.

When Keir reached the yards he noticed with satisfaction that his new warriors looked fit and ready for battle. He would only be taking ten more D'Danann with him to fight the Fomorii and Ceithlenn, but this contingent would have to be enough. They would join the other warriors currently stationed in the city. The Chieftains would allow no more to pass through the veil. As it was, their leaders did so grudgingly, since crossing to an Otherworld like San Francisco required the aide of Elves or those with Elvin blood.

Prejudices between the Elves and the Fae ran deep, and it was a wonder that any form of agreement had been reached for travel between worlds. The rivalry extended back over millennia.

The rivalry stemmed from arguments on whether travel or contact to old Otherworlds should be allowed, and the Fae believed the access points should be sealed. Being more neutrally aligned, the Fae had always been more clannish and territorial and less "for" traveling to old Otherworlds.

On the other hand, the Elves had always been more arrogant, less territorial, more for freedom and remaining uninvolved. They were also neutrally aligned, however, and on occasion would step in on the side of right and justice.

The Elves were ultimately responsible for the whole mess in Otherworld. If not for them, the access points would all have been sealed, and no being could have gone to the San Francisco Otherworld. Now that they had created the mess, the Elves had not even stepped up to fix what they had caused.

Keir folded his arms across his chest as he watched two of his warriors spar. The pair battled at the center of a small circle of D'Danann Enforcers who cheered them on. Rhona was lighter on her feet and quicker with her sword, but the young man Tegan was gifted with the speed of flight.

Rhona and Tegan clashed swords and for a moment were locked in a battle of power and will. She whipped her sword around his and shoved Tegan away. In a beautiful display of strength and agility, she performed a quick backflip, landed in a crouch, and swept her sword at Tegan's knees. Tegan had already unfurled his great gray wings and rose to easily dodge her blow. He attacked from the air, but Rhona rolled on the dusty ground, out of his reach, sprang to her feet, and released her own pair of beautiful russet wings that matched her hair.

Pride filled Keir's chest at the sight of his warriors.

These days, the D'Danann Enforcers rarely left the Sidhe, usually only to answer calls for aid from other beings in various Otherworlds—if approved by the Chieftains. Now that the damned Fomorii demons had escaped their purgatory, it was the duty of the D'Danann to take them out.

Fomorii were demons from Underworld that could kill a human by taking over his or her body. The demon then became that person—at least in appearance—and took over that individual's life. Fomorii could morph from demon form to human form at will. Most of the demons had infiltrated the city's government and several wealthy individuals.

But before those beasts could even be routed, the D'Danann and the San Francisco witches had an entirely new threat to deal with.

Ceithlenn.

The goddess who had been imprisoned in Underworld with her husband Balor all those centuries ago. This time Ceithlenn's evil soul had taken over the body of a young, powerful, female warlock.

Keir had seen it for himself during their last battle, before the door to Underworld had been shut. The threat was unmistakable, yet it was unknown how the D'Danann and witches would fight this new being.

Rhona and Tegan continued to spar in the air, a perfect dance of power and grace. But not fierce enough to suit Keir. He had to ensure they would be prepared to battle anything they faced. The loss of even a single life was one too many, and he would not see one of his brethren fall if he could help it in any way.

He spread his great black wings at the same moment he unsheathed his sword and in two wing thrusts was at the center of the mock battle.

"You must be ruthless," he growled as he blocked sword blows from both Rhona and Tegan, who now worked as a team against him. "The Fomorii will not spar with you." He drove his sword at Rhona's midsection. She barely blocked it, and the power of his stroke was so great that she grunted with the effort.

"With one swipe of their claws," Keir continued as he spun in the air to parry with Tegan, "the demons will bring you down. Never forget that many of the Fomorii tip their claws with iron now, making them poisonous to Fae.

"Show them no mercy." In two swift blows, Keir had both Rhona and Tegan dropping from the air to land on the dirt of the training yard. "You can expect none from them."

The two warriors looked chagrined as Keir touched down between them, sheathed his sword, and folded his wings away. Rhona's and Tegan's hair were plastered to their foreheads, the sides of their faces glistened with sweat, and they were breathing heavily as they folded their wings away as well. They must have been sparring for some time before Keir arrived because it was difficult to exhaust one of the D'Danann.

"Come." He slapped both Rhona and Tegan on their backs. "It is time for food and ale. In the morning we go to war."

The other warriors laughed and began joking with one another good-naturedly, and Keir felt a strange warmth in his chest. The D'Danann warriors were his family. The only real family he had ever known. He respected them, relied on them in battle, and had confidence they would watch his back. No matter his rivalry against his brother, Keir trusted Hawk in war.

Outside of war and training, Keir tended to keep to his own, but not when these warriors needed him to be the glue in their camaraderie and in battle. They were young and required the spirit of teamwork in every way.

After a fine meal of fresh cornbread drizzled with honey, roasted chicken, spinach, potatoes, and bread pudding, Keir made his way to his cabin in the woods outside the village.

Rather than living in the barracks with many of the D'Danann warriors, or in a treetop home, and certainly unlike members of the court who resided in their great mansions, Keir had long ago chosen a simple cabin in the woods. It was difficult to be away from all the other D'Danann, but he chose to ignore the Dryads, Pixies, Faeries, and any other beings that might be nearby.

Sometimes that was not so easy to do.

Tonight, though, he thanked the gods the Pixies were not up to mischief around his home, decorating it with flowers or some odd nonsense. Not one of the mischievous Fae had dared to *enter* his sanctuary, but they had no compunctions about the area around his cabin.

Wood scraped wood as he opened the door and then slammed it shut behind him. The three-room cabin was large and airy. He didn't require much . . . just an open-beamed great room, a bedroom, a place to take a piss and a bath. All the furnishings were large, comfortable, and made for a man.

He strode to his bedroom and grabbed his haversack, intending to pack some of his own supplies. The last time he was in the San Francisco Otherworld, he had been forced to use the perfumed soaps and shampoos of the witches.

The moment he opened his pack, a tiny Faerie poked her head out.

"Godsdamnit, Galia." Keir scowled and opened his pack wider, releasing her lilac scent.

The blond Faerie rose out of his haversack with a mischievous expression on her perfect face. Pink Faerie dust sparkled in the air from her wings. She was no longer than his hand from the tip of his middle finger to his wrist, and her long blond hair reached past her knees, covering both her naked ass and her bare breasts. "What in the Underworlds are you doing here?"

She fluttered up to his eye level and grinned. "I thought I would come for a visit."

Keir turned away and stomped to his bath chamber. "Out of my home."

Her laugh was like tiny bells. She darted ahead of him and landed on a cake of soap. It slipped and she giggled as she skated on the soap the length of the wooden shelf. She wove in and out of his bath items, barely missing his body gel and shaving gear, but knocking off the brush he used for his teeth. When she reached the end of the shelf she placed her palm out and threw up a shield to keep herself from sailing off and onto the floor.

"Galia!" He jabbed his finger in the direction of the doorway. "Out!"

After coming to an abrupt stop, the Faerie hopped off the cake of soap. "Are you going back to that Otherworld? The one called San Francisco?"

"In the morning." Keir grabbed the brush from the floor and jammed it and the other bath items into his bag. "Now, leave."

She fluttered after him as he packed extra clothing and weapons. Pink Faerie dust glittered wherever she flew, and she darted just about everywhere, exploring his cabin despite his orders for her to leave.

When he finished shoving items into his haversack, he tossed the bag by the front door. He yanked the door open and pointed out into the growing darkness. "Back to your Sidhe. Now."

Galia fluttered up to his face and startled him as she kissed his cheek with a feather-light touch before using her delicate wings to back away. "Such the big, bad warrior. You need to have a little fun."

"Out," he growled when for some reason he wanted to smile. That thought had him scowling again.

The Faerie giggled, then swooped out of his home and into the twilight, pink sparkles and the scent of lilacs following in her wake.

Keir shook his head. Galia had teased him often outside of his cabin, but like other Fae she had never been in his home. What made her trespass today? Apparently her desire to go to the San Francisco Otherworld.

Pink dust. Damn. It would be weeks before he got the female-smelling lilacs out of the air.

But he had far more pressing matters to be concerned with than one of the mischievous Fae.

Ceithlenn.

Keir was tempted to rouse his warriors and head to the

San Francisco Otherworld tonight, but his men and women needed at least one good night's rest before they went to war.

After removing his weapons belt and setting it on a table, Keir went to a small corner of the great room to a chair positioned by the window where carved wooden figurines perched on the sill. Among the small figures were an elk, a squirrel, a hawk, and a raven. Keir settled into the chair, leaned forward, and reached for the box where he kept his tools.

When he was but a boy, a Dryad had shown him how to bring the creatures to life that "lived" in the wood. No one, save for his Dryad teacher, was aware of his aptitude for this art form. It was simply something he chose to do to relax.

Keir removed a large piece of cedar from a pile of assorted wood the Dryads had given him, grabbed one of his carving tools, and slid the metal into the cedar. He concentrated on bringing it to life.

Only this time, for the first time, it was not an animal he carved, but a face. As the features formed he found himself shaping the head and shoulders of a woman he had never met.

He couldn't seem to stop himself. It was as if the face had to be released from the cedar before he left in the morning.

When Keir was finally finished, the wood polished until the features shone in the dim candlelight, it was late into the night. He blinked his tired eyes and stared at the face for a while. He stroked the cheek with his thumb, the polished wood as smooth as a woman's skin.

Why had he carved a face? The face of a woman he did not know?

He shook his head, put away his carving tools, and set the face on the windowsill before heading to his bed. Despite the urgency he felt, he needed what rest he could get before leaving come morning.

They were going to war.

Chapter 3

SAN FRANCISCO

With a grunt of exertion, Rhiannon helped Sydney physically move a long table from one end of the once closed-off common room to the other. They set the table down with a loud thump and Rhiannon put her hands on her jean-clad hips, rolled her shoulders, and moved her neck from side to side to relieve some of the stress. Her chin-length auburn hair swung as she moved her head.

It was only the night before last that she'd had the vision of Ceithlenn and the images still turned her stomach and caused the Fomorii scars on her cheek to burn.

The common room was filled with the chatter of witches, warriors, and Paranormal Special Forces—PSF—officers all working together. As much as she wanted more D'Danann to get here and get here quick, she had no idea where they were going to put them. They'd probably have to sleep on the floor of their shared apartments until more rooms were ready. She and the others would have to make the basement into a living area.

Yeah, they needed more space. Never mind the friggin' grocery store and cookie factory they needed to buy to feed the warrior Fae. Thank the goddess for the wise investments most of the witches had made over the years.

Dirt streaked Rhiannon's cheeks and sweat rolled down the side of her face. But she felt the satisfaction of a job well done as she gazed around the room where everyone was working to move out old furniture, boxes, and assorted other items.

Jake Macgregor, the PSF Captain, had inherited the apartment building, which was in the Haight-Ashbury district, and had opened up the common room just today. The witches and D'Danann had used a combination of magic and muscle to set the room to rights in record time. With all the additional D'Danann warriors on the way from Otherworld, plus the warriors, officers, and witches already stationed in the building, they needed the space.

"*Much* better," Rhiannon said to Sydney. Spirit, Rhiannon's cocoa-colored cat, jumped onto a nearby couch. Her familiar gave a loud meow, perhaps agreeing, perhaps not.

"Just a few things to take care of." Sydney leaned one hip against the table and adjusted her chic glasses. "Hopefully we'll be done before the new bunch of warriors arrive."

Sydney had gorgeous raven hair and violet eyes that were only partially hidden by her glasses. She was the CEO of an advertising agency on Market Street in downtown San Francisco and usually wore fitted suits. Today was Saturday and she still managed to look great, dusty or no, in a pair of designer jeans and a lilac polo shirt.

Next to her, Rhiannon felt frumpy in her snug purple jeans and her bright yellow "I heart San Francisco" T-shirt. It had been a little warm today, the sun out from behind the fog, and her skin was a bit red from having been in the sunshine. She was so fair that the slightest exposure to sun went a long way.

She wiped her palms on her jeans and gave a big sigh. So much done, so much more work to do. Other rooms needed attention, and she was certain they weren't going to get it all done before the additional D'Danann Enforcers arrived. There was no way they'd be able to use the kitchen of Enchantments, the metaphysical shop they owned that was next door, as a meeting place any longer. They'd been pushing it as it was.

Sydney's Doberman familiar, Chaos, bounded into the

room, headed straight for Sydney. The moment he reached
her, he jumped up and planted his front paws on Sydney's
belly, leaving two dirty prints on her shirt. She laughed and
rubbed the big lug behind his ears.

Spirit hissed, laid back his own ears, and arched his back.
"Oh, get over it." Rhiannon shushed the cat, who had never
taken to the Doberman. Much like he wasn't crazy about Janis Arrowsmith's mouse familiar, Mortimer. Rhiannon had
been concerned more than once that Spirit would forget the
"familiars don't eat familiars" rule when it came to Mortimer.

Chaos was harmless—but unfortunately lived up to his
name. Well, he was harmless unless his mistress was threatened in any way.

A cheer rose up as Cassia strode in with trays of food
followed by Copper and Silver, who were laden with platters
as well.

The Doberman loped toward the witches carrying the
food. Sydney groaned. "Pain-in-the-ass familiar," she said as
she went after him, leaving Rhiannon alone.

Rhiannon grinned as Tiernan, one of the D'Danann, took
the tray Copper was carrying despite her insistence that she
could do it herself. He was having the hardest time getting
her to take it easy and stay off her ankle cast. The copper-
haired witch had broken her ankle in Otherworld when she
went to battle to keep a door to Underworld closed.

Tiernan ignored Copper's protests and carried the platter
to the table that Sydney and Rhiannon had just moved.

Copper hobbled after him, her long braid slipping over
her shoulder. "Dammit, Tiernan. I was doing just fine." After
he set the tray down he kissed her soundly and Copper melted
into him.

A twinge of envy gripped Rhiannon before she brushed it
aside.

Nothing lasted forever. People left. They left all the time.
Her birth parents had abandoned her on Aunt Aga's doorstep
when she was only two. Growing up, she had learned almost
nothing about them, let alone how she had inherited her

Elvin blood. Aunt Aga was her mother's much older sister, and she had made it very clear that she resented the burden of raising her niece.

Rhiannon leaned her hip against the table laden with food and sighed.

When Rhiannon's strange ability had appeared, Aunt Aga had been so horrified, Rhiannon knew that the power was something bad. Maybe even something evil. When she turned eighteen, Aunt Aga had been only too happy to tell Rhiannon that she had to leave. Rhiannon had been able to move onto a houseboat owned by a nice elderly couple she had befriended, until Silver gave her a job at the Coven's metaphysical shop.

Over the years, Rhiannon had dated here and there and had had two serious relationships. One had ended with her catching the guy with another woman. The other ended with the man leaving her for a woman who had kids. The only thing in her life that had seemed to last was her love for her Coven sisters and their love for her . . . Well, there was an exception to the rule, Hannah. That witch rubbed her the wrong way. Always invading her personal space—her "little box," as Hannah liked to call it.

Her Coven sisters loved her in return, but what if they found out about Rhiannon's ability? She looked around the room at her friends. She had worried about that more than once.

It was one thing to turn to dark magic.

It was another thing to carry the darkness inside.

What if they found out about the Shadows lurking within her? Would her chosen family still feel the same or would they react with disgust and horror the way Aunt Aga had?

Rhiannon never intended to find out.

Her stomach churned at the thoughts. She couldn't begin to summon an appetite, no matter how good the food smelled on the table beside her.

She shook her head as all the D'Danann and PSF officers dug in to the food. Trays of turkey sandwiches, huge bowls of Boston baked beans, potato salad, and macaroni salad. Platters of deviled eggs, fresh-baked rolls, large arrangements of assorted vegetables and dip, bags of potato chips, pitchers of iced tea, soda pop, and orange juice. And not to forget the dessert—chocolate, red velvet, and marble cakes. Oh, and the witches never left out the chocolate-chip cookies, a huge favorite of Hawk's. Cassia was having to cook full-time these days.

Yeah, the D'Danann warriors definitely lived up to their legendary appetites. Now, if they would only find their Cauldron of Dagda, the witches wouldn't have to fear going bankrupt trying to feed them. The god Dagda obtained a cauldron from the city of Murias and used it to feed his army of Tuatha D'Danann. The food in this magic cauldron never ran out and it had healing powers, as well as restoring the energy and strength of anyone who ate from it.

Damned if they couldn't use that all the way around.

A large commotion started at the doorway to the common room and Rhiannon looked casually over to see a new group of leather-clad warriors entering the room. The D'Danann already stationed in San Francisco greeted the men and women with slaps to their backs and the kind of handshakes people used to do way back when—hand to elbow grips. Rhiannon liked the way they spoke with unusual accents, mostly thick Irish brogues.

"Godsdamnit, Keir, what took you so long?" Hawk growled when he strode up to one of the warriors Rhiannon had never seen before. Her heart thumped a little more than usual when she looked at the stranger. "You should have been here two days ago."

"Always jumping into the fray without preparation, *brother*." Keir's scowl and the way he fisted his hands told Rhiannon the term "brotherly love" might be a bit lost on these two. He tossed a worn leather pack against the wall and Rhiannon thought she heard a faint "oof." She shook her head as she swung her attention back to Keir, who was saying, "Seems you have yet to learn your lesson about planning."

Silver came up beside Rhiannon, carrying her full plate. "There they go again," Silver said.

Rhiannon glanced at Silver before looking back at the arguing men.

"He had to ensure these warriors were ready." Tiernan pushed his way between Keir and Hawk. Tiernan had selected a couple of sandwiches and placed them near a pile of potato chips on his plate. Having been born to a high D'-Danann Court, Tiernan's Irish accent sounded more refined than the others. "This group is young," he added.

Hawk grumbled something Rhiannon couldn't make out and then he turned his back on Keir. She hadn't known Hawk had a brother. Or maybe it was just one of those things—all the D'Danann called each other brother and sister. But it was the way Keir had said the word *brother* that made her think there was more to the situation.

She wanted to turn and ask Silver if they'd figured out where all these men and women were going to stay, but she couldn't quite take her gaze off the new warrior.

And then, for some reason she caught *his* attention.

Their eyes met and she couldn't even blink, she was so mesmerized. A connection sizzled between them that made her heart beat even faster.

The man studied her in a way that made her feel like he was stripping off her clothing layer by layer. Her cheeks heated as his gaze slowly perused her from head to toe and then his eyes met hers again. He had the deepest, darkest eyes she'd ever seen.

His black hair reached his shoulders, and goddess, what impressive shoulders he had, not to mention that broad chest. His sleeveless leather shirt showed his finely carved biceps and his forearms had a light scattering of black hair that led down to strong hands. What could he do with those hands . . .

Rhiannon's belly did a little flip.

Like the other warriors, he was clad in leather pants and wore a weapons belt with a sword on one side, a dagger on the other. His snug pants, showing muscled thighs, were tucked into scuffed leather boots that reached his knees. And what an impressive package was outlined against those leather pants.

When her gaze met his again, she saw that his expression was fierce, proud, and arrogant. Definitely arrogant. He wasn't what she'd call handsome. He was rugged, unruly, untamed-looking. He had a scar that slashed one cheek and reminded her of her own scars.

This warrior was a bad boy. Definitely a bad boy.

Rhiannon tried to think of other things—like playing her favorite video game and killing spiders with little blue swords. And tried really hard to *not* think about how hot that guy was. But for a long moment they held each other's gazes. Rhiannon couldn't breathe. Her nipples tightened beneath her grubby T-shirt and she felt a shaft of desire shoot straight down through her belly to the place between her thighs.

With a tremendous effort, she cut her gaze away from the warrior's and was able to suck in a deep breath. She was positive he was still staring at her—her entire body burned.

Rhiannon cleared her throat. "I don't suppose you know who that guy is with the scar? The one Hawk called Keir," she said to Silver, who was still standing beside her.

Silver pushed her long, silvery blond hair over her shoulder. She was "eating for two" as she said, now that she was pregnant. She'd already eaten half the food that had been stacked on her plate.

Silver and Hawk had recently gone to Otherworld to be soul-bonded in the D'Danann tradition. At the same time, Silver's blood sister, Copper, had bonded with her D'Danann husband, Tiernan. Rhiannon wished she could have attended, but with the battle against the Fomorii, it wasn't possible for the other witches to take any chances and leave.

"Keir is Hawk's half-brother and the two have *never* gotten along." Silver glanced in the direction of the warriors then raised one eyebrow as she turned back. "Keir looks like he wants to eat you whole, honey."

"He's new?" Rhiannon could still feel the intensity of his stare, but she tried to sound casual as she spoke. "He hasn't been around since I got back."

"That's right." Silver cocked her head. "You were off trying to get aid from the other Covens when he arrived around Samhain. You missed the battle, and before you returned he went back to Otherworld to train some of the younger warriors who'd never fought Fomorii before."

"Oh." Rhiannon wasn't used to being at a loss for words. Nor was she used to being stared at like she was a rich chocolate dessert. The heat of his gaze made her feel more like chocolate icing sliding down the side of a cake as it melted.

"Uh-oh." Silver glanced back in Keir's direction, then to Rhiannon. "Looks like you're going to get to meet him."

"What—" Rhiannon started but Silver slipped away into the crowd of people in the common room.

In the next moment a shadow fell over her and she caught the rich musk of male along with fresh air and forest breezes. She slowly turned to face the man who now stood just inches from her. Invading her "little box," as Hannah would say.

She took a step backward and found herself with her heels against the baseboard of the wall behind her. He moved in closer. She tilted her head to meet the warrior's dark eyes and she drew herself up to her full height of five eight. Dammit. He was still a good eight inches taller.

"Mind giving me a little space here?" she managed to say, even though her heart was thumping like crazy.

He said nothing, but braced one hand on the wall above her head, making her feel caged. And hot, definitely hot, in more ways than one. He reached up and trailed one finger down her arm, causing goose bumps to rise along her skin.

"Stop it." She tried to shrug away from him as he stared at her. "What do you want?"

"You." He moved his hand from her arm to her hip as if he owned her and pulled her a few inches closer to him. "And I always get what I want," he said in a deep, sexy brogue.

This time a different heat slid through Rhiannon's veins. She gritted her teeth and shoved his hand off her hip. "I don't know who the hell you think you are, but you're hitting on the wrong female. I don't like men who think with their dicks instead of their heads. Been there, done that."

She tried to move away from him, but he captured one of her wrists in his big hand. "Tell me your name," he demanded.

Oh, no way was he going to treat her like this.

She attempted to jerk her wrist away, but he held her tight. "Your name," he said again.

Rhiannon yanked harder. "Screw you."

"I would like that," he said and gave her a smile so wicked a feeling like spellfire went berserk in her belly.

Rhiannon clenched her jaw and tightened her resolve. "You'd better back off or you're going down, big boy."

An amused expression crossed his features. "One so small as you could best a warrior like me?"

Small? That was something she'd never been called. "I'll give you two seconds and if you don't release me, believe me, you'll be more than sorry."

Keir gripped her wrist tighter and moved his hand from the wall above her head to reach for her other arm.

Rhiannon let loose a burst of gold spellfire straight at his groin.

The expression on his face was priceless. Shock followed by pain followed by shock. The big bad warrior dropped to his knees and braced his hands on his thighs. Despite the fact he was clenching his jaw, a groan squeezed from between his tight lips and he fisted his hands.

Rhiannon smiled and stepped around him, wiping her hands as if dusting them off. "My work here is done."

Keir had been kicked in the balls before, hard enough to damn near drop him to the ground. But this—this witch had done exactly that with a flick of magic from her fingers.

Lise's comment yesterday, about a woman driving him to his knees, chose that moment to enter his mind and he gave a low growl.

Keir ground his teeth and forced himself to his feet.

Gods, he could not even begin to walk across the room. He probably would not be able to fuck for a week.

He took a deep, slow breath. That was exactly what he was going to do with that witch. He had no doubt she wanted him, and he was going to make sure she enjoyed every minute of it. He would never take a woman by force. It would be just a matter of time before she admitted to herself that she desired him as much as he desired her.

Godsdamn.

Was he out of his mind?

She'd tried to fry his cock, for the love of Fae.

But he still wanted her.

From the moment he had seen her across the room he had known he had to have her. He had never felt such an intense need to possess a woman as he had in that fraction of time. He had seen her nipples grow into taut nubs beneath her shirt and the way her eyes had widened and her pupils had dilated told him she wanted him.

And she had seemed familiar . . . something about her face . . .

The face in the wood. The image he had carved last night had looked almost exactly like this witch. *What in the name of Underworld?*

When he finally managed to stand, he braced one hand on the table and straightened to his full height. Gods, the pain. He looked at the sea of faces in the room. Damnation, he could barely focus. Just about everyone had stopped what they were doing to stare at him.

The warriors, witches, and human PSF officers looked away and started talking again, most grinning. There was the unmistakable sound of laughter from a few. He saw Hawk's amused look and wanted to slam his fist into his half-brother's jaw.

The pain in his groin would not let him take the steps needed to do so.

Keir took a deep breath and focused on trying to speak as he turned to face Copper, who was now standing beside him. Copper looked like she was trying not to laugh, but fortunately for his pride she managed to keep her expression straight.

"Who was that wench?" he asked, finding it harder to talk than he had thought.

"Er, 'wench'?" Copper grinned. "Damn, Keir. Your balls might just get another blast if she hears you call her that."

The mere thought brought a fresh round of pain and he could barely keep from wincing.

"Rhiannon." Copper cocked her head to the side. "What did you do to piss her off like that?"

"I simply told the woman that I planned to bed her."

Copper released a burst of laughter. "Really? You're lucky a zap to your nuts was all she did."

Keir nearly growled. "I am hungry," he said, even though at this moment he was not sure he could eat. Doing his best not to limp, he grabbed a paper plate and started spooning what was left of the baked beans onto it.

Chapter 4

Darkwolf was having an increasingly difficult time keeping his emotions hidden from Ceithlenn as she paced to and fro in the penthouse.

The manipulative bitch had been there five days and he wanted to kill her. She ordered him and every other being around and forced Darkwolf to bow to her when she was in the mood to be worshipped.

Goddamn but that pissed him off. Her magic was too powerful for him to stop her from forcing him to practically kiss her boots. He gritted his teeth and kept his thoughts masked behind steel walls in his mind that not even the essence of Balor had been able to penetrate.

He'd become very good at masking his thoughts from Ceithlenn, as well as Balor's essence.

If only Darkwolf's Balorite Clan had not been destroyed by Ceithlenn, Darkwolf could have gathered the warlocks. Together could they have used their black magic against the goddess? Perhaps a banishment ritual that would have sent her back to Underworld?

Why he even traveled that vein of thought was a waste of time. Ceithlenn had murdered most of his Clan and the rest had fled the city when she arrived.

For the first time Darkwolf cursed the day he had found Balor's eye on the shores of Ireland. He had been a white witch then, known as Kevin Richards. But the moment he picked up the stone eye, it had fed on desires already buried deep within him. His heart had been filled with black witchcraft and he'd become among one of the most powerful and feared warlocks in the world.

All because he had found Balor's eye. The eye that now dangled from a thick chain around his neck. Thankfully, the eye was quiet. When Balor chose to make his presence known, the pain in Darkwolf's head was excruciating and he had little choice in his actions.

Darkwolf reclined on one of the couches in the sumptuous penthouse he and the Fomorii now controlled.

And Ceithlenn. He couldn't forget her, now could he?

Ceithlenn had sent Junga, the Fomorii Queen, and a few of the other demons on some kind of errand.

Darkwolf watched Ceithlenn continue to pace from one end of the spacious great room to the other. She remained in Sara's human form when not on the prowl, thank the gods. Sara was a white witch whom Darkwolf had converted to dark magic. But then she had betrayed him and had absorbed Ceithlenn's essence when the door to Underworld was cracked open.

Ceithlenn-Sara's punk-red hair curled in a soft bob around her face and her eyes were fascinating. They were ever-changing, shifting colors like sunlight on a pond—brown to blue to green to silver. She wore a black leather catsuit with a V neckline that dipped to her navel—the leather barely covered her nipples before the V grew smaller. The suit, interestingly enough, had a zipper that ran from below her belly button all the way down her crotch and up past her ass.

Despite himself, Darkwolf wondered what it would be like to fuck her and his cock hardened. Would he be able to sexually control her like he controlled the demon-woman Junga when she was in her human form?

"I need more souls," Ceithlenn-Sara said, and he startled at the sound of her voice. "The first one I devoured filled me with power, but not enough."

"Enough to do what?" he asked before he could stop himself.

She whipped her gaze to him. "To bring my husband to me, of course."

Darkwolf chose not to respond and simply watched Ceithlenn.

"I have had visions." Thankfully she continued her pacing. "I must start little by little. Two souls next, then perhaps four. Next a small crowd and then a larger one. I do not have to eat their flesh, no. I must simply kill them and draw their souls to me as they die."

Morbid curiosity filled Darkwolf. "Why do you have to start with a few souls at a time?"

The goddess snapped her head to look at Darkwolf and he nearly recoiled from her hideous smile. "I do not have the strength yet. My power will gradually increase with every soul I consume until I can take multiple souls at a time."

Darkwolf frowned. "How will you do that?"

Ceithlenn-Sara pursed her lips. "As I grow in power, I will be able to kill by perhaps causing an enormous sign to fall and land on several people. Or I might force a landslide where there are hikers. Possibly then I will be strong enough to cause a great wave to crash into part of the city and I will devour those souls." She stopped and her smile grew almost ecstatic. "When I take enough souls, I will have the strength to call forth my husband."

Darkwolf's scalp prickled at Ceithlenn's cold words. But even as his mind rejected what she was saying, Balor's essence took over his thoughts, his entire being. Pain shot through his head but he forced a smile and the eye at his neck grew brilliant red.

Ceithlenn smiled in return and walked to where Darkwolf reclined. She reached out her hand and grasped the eye in her palm. "My love," she murmured.

The power of Balor gripped Darkwolf and he stood to tower over Ceithlenn. She wrapped her arms around his neck, brought his head down to hers, and pressed her mouth to his. Balor's hunger for her taste, her body, was too great for Darkwolf to control. He caught Ceithlenn's burnt sugar smell and a hint of Sara's jasmine scent.

Ceithlenn drew away from the kiss, her eyes no longer shifting but now crimson. "On your back on the floor," she commanded.

There was no way for Darkwolf to fight the magic of Balor's essence and Ceithlenn in the flesh. In moments he was flat on his back. She flicked her fingers. His jeans unfastened and his erect cock sprang out.

Ceithlenn licked her lips and somewhere in the back of his mind Darkwolf was grateful she hadn't changed into the flame-haired being. Gods he hoped she wouldn't.

At the same time he was disgusted with himself for wanting this. For wanting to fuck this human version of Ceithlenn.

The agony in his head grew more intense as Balor's desire caused his erection to become painfully large. Ceithlenn brought her hand to her navel, slowly drew the zipper down and exposed her shaved mound, then the glistening folds of her pussy. Her musk was strong as she sank to her knees and grabbed his cock.

"Balor," she said as she positioned the head of Darkwolf's cock at the entrance to her core. "Until you can be here, my love, I will make love to you through this human."

She sank on his cock, sheathing him so tight he thought he might come. Now. It felt so goddamn good. But Balor's and Ceithlenn's magic held him back. As she slowly rode him, she brought her hands to her chest, pulled at the catsuit, and let her large breasts fall free of their confines. The power of Balor's lust was so great that Darkwolf found himself slamming up to meet Ceithlenn with every stroke.

She rode him harder and harder, pinching and pulling her nipples. "I remember, my love. It will be so again."

With her scream of triumph he felt her channel clamp down on his erection, her contractions so fierce that his cock ached even more. Her red eyes met his and she gave a wicked grin. "Come for me now, my love."

A groan tore from Darkwolf as his climax rocked his very being. His entire body throbbed. The power of his release combined with Balor's triumph made him cry out again. He couldn't see, couldn't think, could only feel the magnitude of his orgasm.

When his vision was no longer hazy and he could see Ceithlenn clearly, he realized the pain in his head was gone and it was now only this woman—the Sara part of her—and him on the floor. And she was dominating him.

She gave another wicked grin and pressed her lips to Darkwolf's. She tasted different. No, it was that he was tasting her with his own senses and not through Balor's possession of him.

Ceithlenn-Sara's eyes were again those ever-shifting colors and she started rocking on Darkwolf. His erection grew hard inside her and he cursed himself for wanting her, wanting this.

"Now I'm fucking *you*, Darkwolf." She ran her long fingernails down his chest. "And I have you exactly where I want you."

Chapter 5

Keir's balls still ached and he cursed aloud a certain witch as he stomped up the concrete stairs that led to a utility room. He had chosen to take any living space that would allow him peace and satisfy his need to be alone when he required rest from search or battle.

Despite the pain in his groin and the amused grins of his comrades, he had forced himself to stand in the common room and eat as much as he could get down considering the pain in his balls.

Now he could use that moment of peace.

Bedroll under one arm and haversack over his other shoulder, Keir reached the room and turned the knob. The moment he opened the door, dust attacked his senses and he sneezed, causing more dust to whirl in the dim light coming through the small window.

He tossed his haversack onto the concrete floor as he surveyed the cramped space.

An "oof," then a small, muffled sneeze came from his pack as soon as it hit the floor.

Keir narrowed his eyes as he dropped his bedroll and glared at the leather pack. Even as he picked it up he knew exactly what he would find.

"Galia!" he roared as he opened the haversack.

The tiny Faerie zipped out and away from him before he

could catch her. Sparkling pink Faerie glitter swirled with the room's dust, along with a hint of lilacs.

"Is this what the San Francisco Otherworld is like?" She grimaced as she darted out of Keir's reach when he grabbed for her again. "If it is, I do *not* like it."

"Godsdamnit, Galia." He clenched his teeth. "What in the Underworlds—"

"I wanted to see this Otherworld." She sneezed again, an indelicate sound for one so small. "Please tell me this is not what it looks like everywhere. If so, it is no wonder the Fomorii want to live here. It suits them."

Keir nearly roared with frustration as he glared at the normally exuberant Faerie. Instead he grabbed his bedroll, untied it, and flung it onto the floor. A larger cloud of dust billowed throughout the room.

He sneezed and swiped dust away from his face with one of his hands. "I will have one of the part-Elvin witches take you home, where you belong."

"If you can catch me." Galia's laughter tinkled like little bells and he knew she was back to her usual mischievous humor.

The Faerie was so tiny he could grasp her in his hand and only her head and feet would show. He pictured himself clasping his hand around her, stuffing her back into his haversack, and sending her away.

The blond Faerie hovered just out of his reach, her tiny wings sprinkling pink dust that was bright enough to help light the room.

Jake had not overstated the smallness of the place, nor the fact that it needed a good cleansing. The one small window had glass blocks that let in just enough sunlight to see. Several rusting metal boxes lined one wall. Jake had told Keir it was an electrical room and warned him that it was not suitable for a living space.

Yet Keir would rather stay in this place and have his peace and quiet when he required it.

Now to rid himself of a certain Faerie . . .

"Galia." Keir tried to keep his voice and his temper in

check. "You cannot stay here. You *will* return to our Other-world."

The Faerie snorted and crossed her arms over her naked breasts. Her knee-length blond hair managed to look clean despite the room's dust. "Make me."

Keir braced one palm on the door frame, his other hand on the doorknob of the open door as he glared at Galia. "My pleasure," he said as he stepped back and slammed the door shut, locking the Faerie in the room.

"Keir!" He barely heard her muffled voice through the metal. "Let me out!"

He studied the door for a moment as tiny pounding noises and cries met his ears. No gaps at the floor or anywhere else he could see and he doubted her magic was strong enough to turn the doorknob *and* pull the heavy metal door open in order to escape. The window's glass blocks were so thick it would likely take a battering ram to get through.

With a feeling between exasperation and satisfaction, Keir turned away from the door and strode back down the stairs.

Rhiannon sat in the common room with the other witches, along with Jake and several PSF officers. They waited for the D'Danann to get the newly arrived warriors settled. A lot of doubling up was needed and it would be a tight fit until they cleaned up more space. The basement was a possibility.

A good hour had passed since Rhiannon zapped Keir in the nuts. She'd left the common room and marched up to her room and attempted to kill off a bunch of spiders with Frodo on her *Lord of the Rings* video game, but ended up almost throwing a fireball at her television screen instead. She'd tossed down the game controller, then took a long, hot shower. When she finished dressing, she returned to the common room to be in on the planning phase of what they would do next.

It pissed her off how she couldn't get that Neanderthal of a warrior out of her mind. Despite the fact he'd cornered her, invaded her personal space, and acted like he owned her.

She doubted *that* would ever happen again.

Yet she couldn't get rid of the images of Keir caressing her body with those strong, callused hands. Just the way he'd made her feel the moment their eyes first met had set in motion a heated whirling sensation in her belly that refused to die down.

Bless it!

Rhiannon ground her teeth while she stroked Spirit. He stopped purring beneath her touch and started to twitch his tail near her elbow. Guess she'd been petting him a little too hard while thinking about that ass of a warrior. She softened her touch and Spirit started to purr again.

After being in her grubby T-shirt and jeans, she'd felt a need to dress exceptionally bright to pick up her mood after she'd finished her shower. She wore a vivid pink blouse along with a short skirt of royal purple in the same cottony material. The skirt was in the style she favored, softly draping from her waist to just above her knees.

The moment Keir walked into the common room, Rhiannon sensed it. Hair prickled at the nape of her neck and goose bumps slid across her skin. She took a deep breath, forced a haughty expression on her face, and turned to look directly at him.

He was staring at her from across the room as if he might eat her up—that or kill her. After what she'd done to him, it would be a wonder he *didn't* want to kill her.

Yet there was some kind of electrical charge to the air as their eyes met. She was so sexually aware of him that her heart pounded and her mouth went dry.

She forced her gaze away and raised her chin as she watched other D'Danann warriors fill the room, along with a few more PSF cops. When everyone was accounted for, Rhiannon stood, leaving Spirit on the couch.

The room went quiet as she took her place at the front of the room. "Ceithlenn is somewhere in our city," she said as she swept her gaze from one end of the half-moon-shaped crowd to the other. She took great care not to meet Keir's eyes. "Night before last I had a clear vision of her." Rhiannon swallowed as the images and the tastes came rushing back and bile rose up in her throat. "She is a flesh-eater and a soul-stealer. She'll grow stronger with every soul she takes."

"What makes you so certain this is true?" came Keir's deep, mocking voice as he folded his arms across his chest.

Spirit hissed loud enough to be heard through the room.

Heat flared beneath Rhiannon's skin as she met Keir's gaze. "I *know* it's true." She didn't pause, didn't allow herself time to feel any more revulsion from the vision. "I can still taste the blood and the flesh of the human she ate. I can still feel the satisfaction in her full stomach. I can still sense the power flooding through her as she stole that human's soul. I can still hear her thoughts. She plans to take more souls to make herself strong enough to bring back her husband, Balor."

She could also still feel Ceithlenn's recognition of Rhiannon's hidden powers.

The *Shadows*.

And now the Shadows were responding to her anger at Keir, trying to burst from within her and take him down. It would feel so good to set them free—

Goddess! How could she have such dark thoughts and even darker magic inside her? She was a gray witch, not a warlock.

She inhaled and battled back the Shadows. Fought them and locked them deep inside.

Rhiannon clenched her fists at her sides and clenched her teeth just as hard as she stared at Keir's unyielding expression. When she spoke she raised her voice enough to carry throughout the room. "Whether *you* choose to believe me or not doesn't matter. What does matter is that the rest of us make plans and do whatever we can to track that goddess and put her away. For good."

Soft murmurs spread throughout the room. When Rhiannon could tear her gaze from Keir's she proceeded to describe her vision, sparing no details.

"The first problem is obvious," she said when she finished. "We need to track her down. My fellow Coven sisters and I"—she gestured to the other witches—"have so far been unable to use divination to figure out where she is."

Sydney stood and stepped beside Rhiannon, taking her

turn. Chaos took his place next to his mistress. In her matter-of-fact manner, Sydney said, "But yesterday, through our various forms of divination, my Coven sisters and I *were* able to determine that several Fomorii have infiltrated positions of power. They have taken over host bodies of politicians, law enforcement officers, and wealthy citizens."

Sydney's long black hair gleamed in the common room's yellow lighting. She explained what the witches had discussed as a way to discover where the evil god-wife was. "We find one Fomorii at a time and track it. Hopefully, one of the demons will lead us to Ceithlenn's lair. Now we need to determine how to do that." She looked at Jake Macgregor and added, "Perhaps some kind of homing device."

Jake got to his feet. He was six-four with dark hair and gorgeous baby blues, well-muscled and broad-shouldered. "We've got the means," the PSF cop said, "but we'll have to get up close and personal with these sonsofbitches. We just have to figure out how to do it."

"We"—Sydney gestured to the other witches grouped together on a pair of couches—"can search for the demons and tag them with Jake's technology. That'll allow any of us to follow a demon, hopefully to wherever Ceithlenn is hiding."

Her statement started an argument that was enough to give Rhiannon a pounding headache. *No,* the warriors wouldn't allow the witches near the Fomorii no matter what form the demons were in. *Yes,* the witches insisted they damn well would help.

"Enough," Hannah said in her cultured but authoritative voice, loud enough to be heard over the din. She brushed a shock of blond hair to the side of her face so that it rested against her otherwise dark brown locks. Surprisingly, the group went quiet.

"We have consistently proven ourselves in battle," she continued, "and you still treat us as if we can't cast a spell without your aid, for Anu's sake." Her chocolate brown eyes scanned the faces of the crowd. "We *will* assist in the search for the Fomorii and Ceithlenn, and that's the end of the discussion."

The men started to grumble but Rhiannon stated in a loud, clear voice, "This is bullshit. We work together on this, and *that's* final."

After more discussion and a lot of planning, everyone gradually left the common room until Rhiannon was alone. She needed alone right now.

She curled up on the couch, braced one elbow on the padded armrest, and rested her chin in her palm. Spirit silently jumped into her lap and rubbed up against her belly. With her free hand she scratched behind his ears and he rumbled his approval in his deep purr.

Rhiannon couldn't stop thinking about what had happened earlier. The fact that the Shadows had reacted to Keir when she'd been angry at him was like a toothpick poking at her mind.

She hadn't had to fight against the darkness for so long she couldn't remember the last time. Certainly not since she was very young. She'd kept control over the Shadows, mentally locking them in a box inside her, the key thrown away.

But now . . . it was as if the key had been found . . . and the box opened.

How? Why?

Ever since Aunt Aga had caught Rhiannon playing with the Shadows as a child, she'd known they were something horrid that had to be kept hidden.

Aga had screamed at Rhiannon. Had yelled about the demons inside her and how she should be thrown onto the street even though she'd only been five years old at the time.

One of the Shadows, reacting to Aga's screaming, had jumped on her and tried to throttle her.

Aunt Aga had choked and wheezed. Her face turned purple and her eyes bulged.

As that innocent little five-year-old, Rhiannon had cried and begged the Shadow to stop. After a few moments, the Shadow paused, then dropped Aunt Aga, who'd collapsed like an unwatered plant withering in the sun. The Shadow shot back inside Rhiannon, along with the other four Shadows she'd been playing with.

At that time, the Shadows didn't hurt when they were inside her. They felt warm and comfortable, just like when she hugged her favorite rag doll.

But she'd learned an important lesson that day that she never forgot. The Shadows were inside her, but she could never let them out again.

For a while, when she was still young, one would escape now and then and her little heart would pound as she demanded it to go back to sleep. Finally, she became so strong magically that no matter how hard the Shadows tried to come out, she'd been able to keep them tucked away. Locked inside that small box with no key.

Rhiannon swallowed hard. Somehow the key had been found and the box opened.

And she had a horrible feeling it had something to do with Ceithlenn.

When Keir reached the door to the electrical room, he paused. *By the gods.* He had been so focused on the situation at hand, and on that witch, he had forgotten about Galia. He had meant to ask the half-Elvin witch Cassia to help him send the imp of a Faerie back to Otherworld.

He paused, his hand above the doorknob. Galia would no doubt be ready to fly past him the moment he opened the door—if he gave her a chance.

With his gaze he measured the door. He was tall enough that his head nearly reached the top of the door frame. All he had to do was open the door wide enough for his body to slide through and then slam the door behind him.

Keir shook his head. This was absurd.

He opened the door in one quick motion, slipped through, and slammed it behind him.

His jaw nearly dropped in surprise.

Not a smudge of dirt or hint of dust remained in the room. It smelled of lilacs.

He searched the room with his gaze and found Galia sitting on one of the metal boxes against the wall—a box that was no longer rusted, but looked new. Everything in the room looked new.

The little Faerie sat on the edge of the box with her hands braced to either side of her and her legs crossed at the ankles. Her long blond hair hung over her breasts and her green eyes were clear and bright.

"Well?" She tilted her head, obviously expecting some kind of praise.

Keir wanted to be gruff with her, but this was not the moment to yell at the imp. He was not enthralled by the smell of lilacs, but the clean room was a pleasant surprise.

"Thank you." His voice was rough despite his attempt to sound grateful.

Galia pushed off from the top of the metal box and fluttered right in front of his face. She crossed her arms over her chest as though she expected a better response.

Then her face brightened as she giggled and swooped around the room. "It looks much better, does it not?"

"Aye." Keir gave a curt nod. "I am grateful, little wench."

"Wench?" Galia snorted, then stopped fluttering to hover close enough for him to reach. She wrung her hands and gave him a pleading expression. "You would not send me back now, D'Danann, would you?"

Instead of grabbing the Faerie, Keir sighed and rubbed his hand over his face. "Godsdamnit. I cannot have you staying with me—it is dangerous for you here. You must return."

Galia rolled her pretty green eyes. "My magic is enough to protect me." She gestured to the room. "Cleaning this place is only a small measure of what I can do." She fluttered closer. "I am not as silly as you think I am."

At that absurd statement Keir crossed his arms. "The ability to clean a room with your magic will not protect you from what is out there. A being beyond evil exists in this city, a being that would swallow you whole in the time it would take you to throw up a shield. A shield that would never be powerful enough to protect you in the first place."

"I will stay out of the way." Galia's sad expression touched his heart in a manner he had not expected. "Please?"

With another sigh, Keir scrubbed his hand over his face again. For a moment he studied the mischievous Faerie. "For a short time." He could not believe the words were coming from his mouth. "I will allow you to see this Otherworld, and then you must return home."

Galia's face lit up and she swooped around the room, giggling and leaving pink dust and the scent of lilacs in her wake.

When she came to a stop she was smiling and excitement shone in her eyes. "I want to see it now. Can I please?"

Keir braced one of his hands on a wall and looked down at the floor before looking at the imp again. "If you stay out of sight and obey me. If I tell you to hide, you will comply. You must avoid Ceithlenn and the Fomorii at all costs." He shook his head. "Do not let the other D'Danann know you are here."

His comrades would never let him live it down if they knew a Faerie had crossed the veil to San Francisco with him—and he had allowed her to stay.

"Can we go now?" She bounced up and down in the air so fast it almost made Keir dizzy.

He shook his head with exasperation and dug into his haversack. He pulled out a long, black coat that he wore to hide his weapons when out among the people of this city. "In my pocket," he said after he shrugged into the coat. "Stay out of sight until we are in the air."

Galia laughed in obvious delight and in a flash was in his right pocket. Her little hands clung to the edge of the material as she peeked out.

"Down," he ordered and she immediately disappeared from sight.

Keir stalked out of the now spotless electrical room and shut the door behind him. His sword banged against his leg as he headed up to the rooftop.

When he reached the small garden area, cool air brushed his face along with the scent of the ocean mingling with the city's countless smells.

Keir's black wings magically pushed through the coat, unfurled, and spread wide. He flapped his large wings and took to the air with the ease of his people, and vanished from human sight.

"Now?" came Galia's muffled voice from his pocket.

"Aye," Keir said as he soared over the city.

He glanced down and saw the Faerie peek her head out of his pocket as he flew from the Haight-Ashbury district toward the bay.

"In all of Otherworld, I have never seen such incredible sights as these," she said with wonder in her voice. Her eyes were wide and filled with delight and she wore a broad smile. "May I fly with you?"

Keir found the corner of his mouth twitching and he had the absurd desire to laugh. He forced the feelings back. "Can you keep up?"

In response, Galia flew out of his pocket and zipped along beside him, pink Faerie dust in her wake. "This is amazing," she said in a breathless voice.

Keir turned his attention to his task. "We must attempt to scent out the Fomorii. They have a rotten fish stench when in their natural form."

He glanced at the Faerie and saw her wrinkle her nose.

He almost smiled again, then gave a low growl. What was the matter with him? First he was obsessing over a witch who had literally driven him to his knees, and now he was almost enjoying Galia's company.

Choosing to ignore her, he swept low over the city, focused on scenting out the demons. Unless the Fomorii had all taken over human host bodies, he and his comrades should be able to track them down—unless something blocked their odor.

Keir frowned and swooped lower, weaving his way around buildings and above vehicles, and avoiding the wiring that crisscrossed Market Street. When he reached the bay, he drank in the scent of brine and felt more moisture against his face from the fog rolling in.

The entire time Keir searched for the demons, Galia chattered and giggled so much that he was tempted to shove her back into his pocket and keep her there.

Chapter 6

This had better work.

If not, she was going to kill Mackenzie.

Rhiannon tugged down on her *very* short skirt and prayed she wouldn't wobble in her obscenely high heels when she was summoned. She was used to wearing her comfortable and colorful clothing, not a pastel pink button-up blouse that was too snug and gaped to allow a view of her ample cleavage. Not to mention a matching tight miniskirt that molded to her curves and darn near showed her underwear when she sat down. She liked short, but *give me a freaking break.*

She kept her knees pressed closely together and raised her chin as she sat in the waiting room to be called in for the interview.

To make sure she wasn't recognized, Rhiannon's chin-length auburn hair had been spelled black, her scars hidden by a thick coat of makeup that was driving her crazy. She never wore makeup and it felt like her skin was suffocating.

Witches healed faster than normal humans, but in this case, the scars wouldn't go away. The iron on the claws of the demon queen and the scars they had left on Rhiannon's cheek had proven she had Elvin or Fae blood in her. Iron could be deadly to both races.

Cassia said Rhiannon was Elvin, and Cassia knew a lot more about such things than anyone had ever realized or expected in the past. Rhiannon still couldn't get used to the idea that she was part Elvin.

She let out a sigh and thought about her birth parents. Which parent had been Elvin? Which one had been a D'Anu witch?

It didn't matter how pissed Rhiannon was at her parents for abandoning her, a part of her wanted to know more.

Once again, like so many times before, a flash of a woman's scream and the vague outline of a face came to Rhiannon. Then a sense of stumbling away from a great ball of fire. Why did she have this vision every time she thought about her birth parents?

Rhiannon shook her head and forced away thoughts of her parentage and looked at her fingers. *Get your mind back on the job, Rhiannon. You're here to tag a demon, not go down memory lane.*

She had left all of her jewelry back at the apartment, except for an obsidian and gold ring she wore for protection and to deflect negativity. It didn't have a pentagram on it. She didn't want to provide any hints of who she really was, but she felt naked without the rest of her jewelry.

Two days had passed since the meeting in the common room and Rhiannon getting this job interview had been the witches' first break. It was still early morning, so even *when* she tagged the bastard, they wouldn't be able to track him until the end of his business day. Hopefully he didn't have an event planned for the evening and would go straight to Ceithlenn's lair.

While she waited, Rhiannon looked up from her hands and glanced around the lobby. It was certainly impressive— all marble, mahogany, and glass, with porcelain sculptures of birds in flight. Hard to believe that the congressman with all this wealth and power no longer existed.

Only no one knew that yet.

This Fomorii they had tracked down through Sydney's talent. She was able to divine things by allowing melted wax to drip into a pewter bowl of consecrated water and then could "see" whatever it was she was attempting to visualize.

She always chose wax of different colors and scents appropriate to the situation.

The ever-so-friendly (*not*) receptionist came through the heavy wood door of Congressman Dentworth's office and gave Rhiannon a false smile. With her short brown hair and fresh-faced appearance, the woman looked like a soccer mom but had the manners of a real bitch.

The receptionist examined her long, manicured nails. "You're up, cookie."

Rhiannon forced a fake smile of her own. Just a little flick of her fingers and she could seriously hose the secretary's computer for a while.

Instead, Rhiannon rose from her seat in the waiting room as gracefully as she could and tugged down the skirt with one hand. She wobbled in the unfamiliar spike heels as they clicked across the marble floor. She was positive high heels had originally been designed by a male as a torture device for females.

Cookie Woman held the door open for Rhiannon, then closed it behind her. Rhiannon entered a beautifully appointed office, also of mahogany, marble, and glass, but with thick forest green carpeting. Through a large window, she could see an impressive view of San Francisco's skyline.

Rhiannon clutched the stupid little pink purse in her left fist as she approached the blond man who crossed the office, his right hand extended. He had a friendly, easygoing expression. She'd always considered him to be a good congressman. It really sucked that he'd been killed and his body now hosted a power-hungry, butt-ugly demon.

"Welcome, Ms. Smith." The supposed Congressman Dentworth clasped her hand.

The moment Rhiannon touched his hand, she felt a rush of bile climb her throat. When he released her, she fought back the urge to turn him into a pile of dirt right there in the office. One good-sized fireball and he'd be toast.

No killing . . . no killing . . . it wouldn't be as fun as I think it would be . . .

No, she would never cross that line.

But the D'Danann would.

It was all she could do to smile again, and take the seat in front of the desk while the demon moved into the plush leather office chair on the opposite side. It was obvious the demon had taken over this host body efficiently. From what the witches had gathered from their divination, some of the Fomorii apparently had difficulty assimilating into the world their particular host had occupied, but this one was smooth.

Fomorii demons normally smelled like rotten fish, but whenever they were in a host body, they simply smelled like the human who had formerly inhabited the body.

"You are here for . . ." He rifled through papers on his desktop as he casually glanced at her cleavage. ". . . the administrative assistant position."

"Yes." Rhiannon struggled to keep her voice pleasant.

While the congressman began to grill her on her qualifications, Rhiannon eased the clasp of the purse open and withdrew a small, clear, sticky patch, keeping it stuck to the end of one finger. She did her best to flub the interview so he'd cut it short, but the bastard's eyes kept landing on her breasts. Apparently this demon had a thing for women with big boobs.

When he finally rose to walk her out of the office, Rhiannon stood and let her purse tumble off her lap and onto the floor. It landed with a thunk on the carpet and the contents scattered everywhere. A tube of lipstick—which she never wore— rolled under the desk. A wallet and coins scattered everywhere, along with other things Mackenzie had shoved into it to give Rhiannon enough time to do what she needed to do.

Great. That . . . *witch* had stuck a condom package and a tampon in the purse as well.

Predictably the man squatted down to help her pick up the items, and she saw the quirk of his mouth when he spotted the condom. Rhiannon snatched it up and stuffed it back into the purse. Oh, great. Just how low could things go before this mission was complete?

As she leaned down to grab the tube of lipstick from beneath the desk, he shocked her speechless when he "accidentally" brushed one of his hands against her nipple.

Well, all the better. Rhiannon choked back her anger, leaned into him, and grasped his arm as if to steady herself. She planted the patch on the sleeve of his suit jacket with one press of her finger.

Rhiannon gave him a seductive smile. "So sorry," she said, easing to her feet with the now refilled and tightly closed purse. She nearly fell against him when she wobbled in the freaking stilettos.

He rose up to meet her and was standing close, waaaaaay too close. "The job is yours, Ms. Smith. When can you start?"

Rhiannon took a couple of steps back. She hadn't expected *that.* "I—I'll need a few days."

He'll be dead within one.

"Monday, then." He took her hand, held it between both of his, and she shuddered.

Her skin crawled and she pictured him as one of the many demons who had kept her in captivity until Silver, Hawk, and Jake had saved her.

She yanked her hand back and he gave her an odd look.

Rhiannon regained her composure and tried to appear pleased. "Sure. Monday. Thanks."

Rhiannon moved across the office to the door on her unsteady heels, but the demon beat her to it and held it open. She managed a half grimace, half smile as she hurried past him, calling out another "Thanks" over her shoulder. Wouldn't do to have the demon suspect her.

As she passed through the reception area, Cookie Woman gave a condescending look over her computer monitor.

Rhiannon couldn't resist a small flick of her fingers.

The last thing she heard as she walked out the lobby's glass doors was the receptionist's cry of dismay as her computer screen fizzled.

It was good to be a witch.

◆ ◆ ◆

"What in the Gods' names?" Keir nearly roared as he tried to stare Mackenzie down, his hand gripping his sheathed dagger. "You allowed her to go to the demon? Alone?" Blood pounded in his veins at the thought of Rhiannon so close to one of the Fomorii.

The petite blond's blue eyes appeared thoughtful as she studied him. Mackenzie was sitting in the apartment building's common room, where she'd been thumbing through what he had learned was a New Age magazine.

"You've really got to get over yourself." Mackenzie shifted her gaze back to the magazine and flipped another page. "Goddess knows you've got the hots for her, but she sure doesn't seem to want anything to do with you."

Keir gave another low growl.

Rhiannon sailed into the room and Keir's scowl deepened. Her hair was black instead of the usual dark shade of red and she had some kind of paint on her face, hiding her beautiful freckles.

But what she was wearing—a formfitting skirt and a blouse that nearly bared her breasts—made his cock hard and his blood boil. The idea of any other man seeing her body like this infuriated him.

"Hey, Rhi." Mackenzie dropped the magazine and rose to her feet. "How'd it go?"

Rhiannon barely spared Keir a glance but gave Mackenzie a smug look as she circled her hand above her hair, changing the deep black shade to auburn again, then made the same circular motion in front of her face, causing the makeup to vanish.

"Tagged the bastard," Rhiannon said with a grin as she tossed her bag onto the couch. "Definitely Fomorii."

"Hot damn." Mackenzie raised her hand and the two witches gave a "high five" to one another. Mackenzie jerked her head toward the stairs. "I'll tell Jake. A group can track the demon tonight." She turned and left, her shoes making sharp taps as she trotted up the steps.

"I do have a score to settle with you, Mackenzie," Rhiannon yelled after her, but the other witch had already disappeared upstairs.

"What in the gods' names did you think you were doing?" Keir bellowed at Rhiannon, jerking her attention to him. "Going to a Fomorii. Alone."

Rhiannon marched up to him and pointed her finger at his face, her cheeks flushed and her eyes sparking green fire. "I don't answer to you, Keir. You'd better get that straight and now."

"Fool of a woman." He pushed her hand down so it was no longer in his face. "You never should have gone alone."

"Oh, sure." She looked pointedly at his clothing, his sword and dagger. "Like I'm supposed to take someone who looks like a reject from a Renaissance fair."

Keir had had enough. He took her by the wrist. "You will never go near a Fomorii alone again."

"Bite me." She tried to turn away from him, but he kept his grip firm. "You'd better let me go," she said, her jaw tight with anger. "Or I'll spellfire your cock again."

With a quick movement, he caught her other wrist and pinned them both behind her back so she couldn't use her magic if she tried.

He pressed his body tight to hers and outrage flashed across her beautiful face. Her light citrus scent combined with her natural musk nearly sent his head to reeling.

"Whoever hurt you should be gutted," he said in a rough voice and her eyes widened in surprise. "Tell me his name and I will do it myself," he added before he captured her mouth with his.

Rhiannon gasped as Keir kissed her, and lightning zinged from her belly to her now-damp folds. The fact that he had recognized her pain from past relationships made her head spin nearly as much as his kiss did.

He thrust his tongue through her parted lips and took her in a thoroughly possessive kiss. Every inch of his hardness pressed against her through his leather tunic and pants, from his heavily muscled chest and abs to the rigid erection between his thighs.

She struggled against his hold, tried to tear her mouth from his, but he wouldn't relinquish control.

And suddenly she didn't want him to.

Before she even realized it, she was kissing him with the same intensity. Hard. Rough. She cried out her passion when he nipped her bottom lip. He smelled of leather and male musk, of something wild and untamed as he was. Something that made her crazy for him.

This is nuts, Rhiannon!

But she couldn't stop.

It was crazy—all wrong. He was a big, hulking Neanderthal.

But, goddess, could he *kiss*.

The next thing she knew he had her back to a wall, his body snug against hers. He kept her wrists pinned behind her back with one of his hands, his other was free. Her entire body trembled as he stroked her curves with his fingertips.

She squirmed, yet arched into his touch at the same time. It was only then that he relinquished his hold on her mouth, but didn't release her wrists. All she could do was moan. She struggled, yet that only made her even more filled with lust.

"You are wet for me, little one," he said in a low rumble, his rich Irish accent sending more thrills through her body. "I could fuck you against this wall and you would scream my name."

Between panting breaths she said, "Arrogant bastard."

His sinfully dark eyes held hers captive. "You want me."

She could picture his naked muscled body. His hips between her thighs and his erection thrusting in and out of her pussy. His powerful chest would chafe her nipples and his long black hair would tickle her cheeks as his tongue plundered her mouth.

This is insane!

But her body was betraying her. Right now she wanted

nothing more than to wrap her thighs around his hips and
take his cock deep inside her right up against this wall.

The fantasy only made her want him more.

From some distant part of her mind she heard voices and
the real world came crashing down.

Keir jerked his head up.

"Oh, crap." Rhiannon had totally lost track of time and
place. Her already hot body flooded with more heat.

"Maybe we should leave," came Sydney's amused voice.
"I think Keir and Rhiannon are a little busy."

Alyssa giggled. "Looks like Hannah won the bet."

Laughter followed the sound of shoes hurrying up the
stairs as the pair left the room.

Keir had his hands braced against the wall to either side
of Rhiannon's head, and he was looking at her like he didn't
care that they'd been caught on the verge of some very hot
sex. She could smell her scent mixing with his, and it was
driving her wild.

"I can't believe this." Face still flaming, Rhiannon tried to
duck under his arm, but he pushed her against the wall again
with his hard length, his erection pressing into her belly. She
felt an instant spasm in her core. She ached so badly to have
him inside her, but she wasn't about to let him know that.
"You can't have forgotten that spell this fast."

He gave her one of his supremely arrogant looks that
made her want to slap him. "Your room," he commanded in
that deep brogue. "Now."

"When witches can fly broomsticks, or Underworld becomes a theme park attraction, whichever comes last." This
time Rhiannon slipped beneath his arm.

Before she had a chance to escape, Keir whirled, caught
her by one arm, and jerked her backward. She stumbled and
fell against him, her soft body along his once more, his erection pressing her back.

He brought her around to face him. "Another man may
have hurt you, but I will not."

She opened her mouth, but again he had surprised her.

How could such a—a barbarian have that kind of insight when he didn't even know her?

"We will finish this," he promised, and she went from shocked to pissed as he spoke. "I will be inside you. And you will beg me to fuck you."

Rhiannon yanked her arm away from him, and this time he let her go. Her cheeks were red with fury and her green eyes flashed. "You—you—oooh!" She spun around and marched across the common room's wood floor and up the stairs.

By the gods, she was even more beautiful when she was angry.

Keir's cock ached, but he still felt some satisfaction. He had broken through one of her barriers and he intended to knock them all down.

Rhiannon's heels clicked on the stairs and she gripped the handrail to keep herself steady. She could just see herself falling down the steps and back into Keir's arms.

Both anger and desire flooded her body, but it was the desire that infuriated her. The thought of him fulfilling his promise made her underwear damper and her nipples harder and tighter than they were before.

When she reached the second floor, she strode down the hallway and into her apartment. Right now she needed some time alone to cool off. She slammed the door shut behind her and sagged against the wood, closing her eyes.

Oh, my goddess. She couldn't believe how easily her body responded to Keir's touch, his mouth. She could still taste his unique masculine flavor on her tongue, could still feel the chafe of his stubble against her sensitive skin.

She needed to climax now. Needed to take care of the ache deep inside. She slid one palm up her thigh, and moved her other hand into her blouse and then into her bra to tug at her nipple.

She slipped her hand into her satin panties, and pushed her finger into her folds.

A moan escaped her lips as she began pinching her nipple and circling her clit. With her eyes closed, Rhiannon imagined Keir's fingers plunging in and out of her pussy, his hot mouth on her nipples. And his cock—considering how long and hard it had been against her belly—would fill her completely.

Rhiannon let everything around her fade as she imagined Keir taking her up against the wall, as he thrust in and out of her, hard and fast. Nothing about him would be gentle. He would be fierce, intense, *wild*.

Her fingers circled her clit faster and faster. She could picture his features, that look of arrogance that made her want to slap him and fuck him all at the same time. His scarred and rugged face, his deep black eyes, and his well-defined body.

She came closer and closer to climax as she pictured what the man would do with her. *To* her.

With a low cry Rhiannon came, her orgasm fast and furious. Her mind spun and her body rocked against her hand.

She opened her eyes and slid down the door until she was sitting on the floor, her knees bent, her chest rising and falling with the heaviness of her breathing. She released her nipple and braced her palm on the wooden floor. She slipped her other hand from her panties and brought her fingers to her nose to catch the scent of her musk.

It was the first time she'd let any man kiss her since she'd caught Derrick with his pants down, getting a blow job in his office from one of his coworkers.

Rhiannon shook her head as she pushed herself to her feet. She couldn't believe she'd let Keir kiss her. And now she'd given herself an orgasm while fantasizing about sex with him.

She was definitely losing it.

Chapter 7

From behind the wheel of Jake Macgregor's black sports car, Rhiannon watched Jake check his homing device as they waited for "Congressman Dentworth" to leave his office for the day. Jake had positioned himself outside the revolving glass doors to the building. Keir, Tiernan, and Sheridan were perched atop the building, waiting for their mark.

It was a dreary gray day—in other words, a normal day for San Francisco. A light mist coated the car's windshield and the fog lay low and heavy. Like the others, Rhiannon was dressed all in black.

Rhiannon was incredibly aware of Keir, no matter that he was so far above her. Heat rose to her cheeks at the thought of the kiss earlier.

What had Alyssa meant by saying Hannah won the bet? Rhiannon had toasted Keir's nuts. Why would anyone think she'd let him kiss her? Especially Hannah?

Why *had* she let him kiss her?

Because he's totally hot and I haven't had sex in way too long.

Rhiannon banged her head against the steering wheel and closed her eyes. She had to get the memories of his kiss and his promise of exactly what he planned to do with her out of her mind.

A promise her body was primed to help him keep.

With a groan she raised her head, opened her eyes, and forced her attention back to Jake, who was still positioned by the front doors. She fiddled with the earpiece she would use to communicate with him and the other D'Danann.

Rhiannon reached up and touched her cheek when she felt a twinge of pain from just thinking about the demons.

"The congressman is moving." Jake's voice came through the earpiece loud and clear. "I'm picking him up on the scanner. He's pretty close."

"There he is." Even though Jake couldn't see her, Rhiannon gave a quick nod to the man just exiting one of the huge buildings on Market Street. "He's carrying a black briefcase, wearing a striped black and red tie, and he's blond."

"Got him." Jake started following the man through the crowd of people leaving work for the day.

Rhiannon knew Jake had tucked a gun and a sheathed dagger at the back of his jeans. He wore a loose black shirt over his black T-shirt—the shirt also hid the body armor he'd chosen because it was designed to be good in a knife fight. Fomorii claws and knives were close, but Fomorii claws were definitely deadlier.

Bullets had proven to be almost worthless against the demons, unless they were still in human form. Daggers and swords were the most effective for decapitation and carving out the Fomorii hearts. Otherwise the demons healed almost instantly.

"What the hell? It looks like he's taking BART," Jake said as he began to follow the Fomorii man down the steps to where the Bay Area Rapid Transit trains would take its passengers all over the city and the Bay Area. No telling if the demon was going to where the congressman had lived, or if he was meeting with other Fomorii.

In San Francisco traffic, it would be impossible to follow the man with a car. When Rhiannon had first dropped Jake off, she had to circle the building several times to find a parking spot. She finally settled for parking illegally in front of a fire hydrant, and had to use her magic against two different policemen to avoid getting a ticket.

Rhiannon tapped her fingernails on the steering wheel. *Bless it. Why is the demon taking BART? As a "congressman" wouldn't he have a personal driver?*

"He's getting on the transit headed north," Jake said, his voice crackling through the receiver. "I'm going after him."

"We'll follow." Keir's clipped words came through the communication device and a shiver trailed Rhiannon's spine. "As soon as he disembarks, we will be ready," he added.

Rhiannon decided to sit tight until Jake told them where the demon was going. She hoped it was close. After her little run-in with Keir today, she could use a good battle. Letting loose a few blasts of spellfire would relieve some of the frustration inside her.

Keir had studied multiple maps of San Francisco, including its transportation routes. He had an excellent memory and knew the location of each BART station in the Bay Area.

He used his magic to unfurl his wings through his leather tunic. He flexed the muscles in his back as he spread his wings wide before lifting himself from atop the building and into the foggy sky, invisible to human sight.

On one side of him traveled Tiernan. The warrior had been a lord of the court before he gave everything away for the human witch Copper. Keir was not sure a woman was worth such a price, but he had great respect for Tiernan, who had given up much for what he desired, for the one he loved.

Love. Keir shook his head at the thought of such nonsense.

Sheridan flew to his other side. Her wings were as blue as her eyes. The beautiful blond warrior Fae favored the sword. She had the ability to solve disputes with a few calm words—but if someone were to anger her, she could, as the cop Jake would say, "kick some serious ass."

Soaring northeast, Keir enjoyed the rush of wind over his body, the moisture from the fog coating his face, the feel of his wings pumping. Blood lust raged through him at the thought of taking down another Fomorii.

But inevitably his thoughts returned to Rhiannon. She

vexed him like no other woman or Fae being ever had. Keir was used to having any unattached female he chose and he always found new partners regularly. He enjoyed his freedom far too much to obsess on one woman.

This witch, though . . . He wanted her like he'd never desired a woman before. After he had driven them both crazy with his kiss, she had fled. He'd had to slip into the men's restroom, where he stroked his cock and visualized taking her hard and fast. He had managed to climax, but afterward he realized that the whole incident only made him want her more. Perhaps once he bedded her, he could get the wench out of his system.

He would have to do something soon. He was so frustrated that his muscles remained tense and his jaw ached from clenching it so tightly.

Keir pumped his wings harder. Like other women in his past, Rhiannon, too, appeared to have no interest in a long-term relationship. Why then did she resist him?

While he and his comrades circled over the piers and back to the Embarcadero BART station, another thought came to Keir. His frown deepened.

Why was it so important to *him* to bed this witch? To pull down her emotional barriers? Why did she intrigue him in ways no other woman ever had?

Because Rhiannon was like no other woman in his past.

Something about her drew him in, made him want more.

Absurd. He shook his head and focused on the city as he circled, waiting for Jake's report.

Keir's gut told him Embarcadero was the right place. As former sea gods, the Fomorii would be close to water if it were possible.

Within minutes Jake's voice crackled in the earpieces he had given each of them, and confirmed the correct location was the Embarcadero station. "He's on foot, so I'm after him," Jake said.

"I have him in sight." Pleasure at the thought of battling the Fomorii filled Keir as he flew above the blond demon who was working his way through the crowd at the end of the station.

Unfortunately they had to track rather than kill this one—but the night was young.

The demon headed away from the station toward a group of buildings. Keir sailed high over the Fomorii. Keir and his comrades were invisible to humans but not magical beings. The demon paused for a moment and looked around as if he thought he was being followed. Fortunately he did not glance up.

Just as the man started walking again, Keir cast a look over his shoulder. His heart stuttered and then his blood set to boiling. Rhiannon was hurrying to catch up with Jake and they were just outside the demon's range of vision. The witch had not gone back to the apartments as he expected her to. As a matter of fact, he had demanded it of her before they had left. She had said something about "ripping him a new one" if he did not back off. Whatever the Underworlds that meant.

The demon continued making his way along a series of streets until he stopped in front of a circular piece of metal in the concrete, what Keir remembered to be a manhole cover.

After taking a quick look around, one of the demon's hands and arm began to shift into a malformed long green appendage with claws that were clearly tipped with iron.

The demon easily hooked his claws in the holes of the manhole cover, raised it, and set it aside. A blast of sewage and the rotten fish stench of the Fomorii flooded Keir's nose. The demon climbed down the ladder and shifted to its Fomorii form as it moved and pulled the manhole cover over its head.

Keir, Tiernan, and Sheridan touched down, so quiet their boots made nary a sound. They each folded away their wings, which slipped into their clothing and inside their backs. The trio became visible again to humans as soon as their wings vanished from sight.

Jake and Rhiannon crested the small hill to the right.

"You're not protected well enough." Jake kept his voice low as he spoke to Rhiannon.

"My magic is more than enough protection." She glared at Keir when she and Jake reached the D'Danann. "Don't you start, either, Keir."

A low rumble rose up in his chest.

Sheridan and Tiernan flashed each other amused glances before turning their attention to the manhole cover.

"The stench is strong," Sheridan said as she crouched and used her strength to remove the cover.

Rhiannon scrunched her nose. "Gross."

Since he could not dissuade the witch from joining them, Keir insisted on climbing down first, followed by Tiernan, Sheridan, Rhiannon, and Jake. The cop was determined to watch Rhiannon's back, which won him more favor in Keir's eyes.

The hair on Rhiannon's scalp prickled when they all stood at the foot of the ladder. *Gross, gross, gross*, she thought as sewage swished over her boots and the smell clogged her senses.

The only light came from the open manhole cover. "Damn, it's dark in here," Rhiannon said.

"D'Danann do not require light to see," Keir said in his arrogant tone and Rhiannon wanted to slug him.

"Well, humans and witches do." She held her hands up and with her magic cradled a dancing gold light in her palms.

"Works for me," Jake said.

Keir started walking in the direction of the rotten fish smell.

The Fomorii stench grew stronger and stronger as they made their way along the tunnel, through the sludge. The curved walls were not made of metal, but of brick, showing the age of this part of San Francisco's sewage drains. Much of the city's sewage systems were more than seventy years old, and other parts had been around a hundred years or more.

They had to crouch as they worked their way down the tunnel, passing an occasional metal drain as they crept along.

Keir raised one of his hands and brought them all to a full halt. *"Extinguish the light, little one."* Keir's voice in Rhiannon's mind almost made her yelp in shock.

Instead she let the small light fade until it was completely dark. For a moment silence reigned and then Rhiannon heard it—grunts, snorts, and growls from somewhere ahead.

In the darkness, Sheridan found Rhiannon's fingers and

squeezed. "Hold tight, Rhiannon," Sheridan said. "Take Jake's hand in yours."

Rhiannon fumbled behind her until her palm rested on Jake's chest. He took her hand, just as Sheridan started guiding them forward.

"*Stop,*" Keir said in Rhiannon's mind. She felt like tilting her head to the side and smacking her ear to get rid of his voice. "*I will scout ahead to determine the number of Fomorii and if Ceithlenn is there. The human transmitters may be too loud to use. Tell Jake what I am going to do, as I cannot mind-speak with someone who is not magically inclined.*"

After allowing Keir's words to take a moment to register, Rhiannon whispered the message to Jake, who gripped her hand tighter in response.

Rhiannon focused on her powers, letting the gray magic build inside her. But she kept the Shadows buried deep.

Keir's heart thundered with blood lust as he left the others behind. He crept forward until he reached a fairly large chamber where several sewage drains came together to flood into one larger tunnel. There was enough space for them to take on the demons here if they had to.

In the darkness he could clearly see at least ten Fomorii in their deformed shapes and varied colors.

No flame-haired goddess. He had witnessed Ceithlenn's transformation in the battle at the gate to Underworld, a sight he would never forget.

He relayed his observations through mind-speak to his comrades. "*Damnation,*" he added when he saw what slid in from another tunnel. "*They have a Basilisk.*"

The only thing more deadly to Fae than iron was a Basilisk's poison.

Keir stilled his breathing as the Basilisk raised its head, flicked its tongue, and scented the air.

Garbled noises came from the Fomorii, but from the way they were looking at all the tunnels, Keir had a good idea what the beasts were saying.

He kept himself pressed against the brick wall of the sewage tunnel as one of the Fomorii looked his way. *"It appears we are in for a fight,"* he told his comrades in mind-speak. To Rhiannon he said, *"Stay clear. It will be dangerous."*

He thought he heard her respond, *"Bite me,"* and he would have smiled if the situation were not so dire. As it was he wanted to protect her, to keep her from harm.

By the gods! This obsession was going to kill them all if he did not get his mind on the pressing matter at hand.

The Fomorii and Basilisk turned to face Keir and his comrades. The heat that always came before battle flooded his body and his energy doubled. Tripled.

"On my command," he said in mind-speak. The eyes of the Fomorii glistened as they moved closer. *"Now!"*

Tiernan was at his side in an instant. As one they drew their swords and charged the demons, giving the D'Danann battle cry.

Keir cut his sword in an arc and decapitated the first Fomorii he reached. The demon crumbled into dust to be swept out with the sewage. A bright ball of light appeared above them, illuminating the chamber. *Rhiannon.*

The light distracted the next Fomorii and Keir easily took its head with his sword. While he battled, he was aware of Sheridan and Tiernan fighting beside him.

Shouts and cries filled the large chamber to the point Rhiannon's ears rang. Her heart pounded as she flung a spellfire ball straight into the chest of a demon next to Keir.

The moment Rhiannon threw the spell, the Shadows threatened to burst from her. She caught her breath and nearly screamed from the power trying to push its way forward. She could barely focus on the fight for a moment, as she struggled to keep the Shadows tight inside her. With all the effort she could muster, she slammed the Shadows back. She wavered for just a second, then regained her concentration on the battle. Why now? Why would they come forth when she'd always kept them locked away? Controlled?

Rhiannon saw that Keir was too close to swing his sword at the burning, screaming Fomorii that her spellfire ball had hit. Instead, he lunged with his dagger and carved out the demon's heart.

The Fomorii dropped. As it became silt the demon's remains were swept away with the sewage.

The Basilisk raised high above the fray and hissed. Green poison gleamed from its fangs. It darted its head toward Keir.

Rhiannon's heart raced even faster. Keir raised his sword. Too slow!

Gunshots reverberated in the chamber from Jake's handgun. Blood squirted from both of the Basilisk's eyes. It reared with a scream, tossing its head back before diving blindly forward.

Rhiannon followed the shots with a fireball that slammed into the Basilisk's nostrils, causing it to shriek again.

As Keir raised his sword to behead the Basilisk, another demon charged him. The Fomorii lashed out with its massive claws, but Keir backed into the wall, dodging the strike.

He grasped the hilt with both hands and swung. The demon skillfully avoided the blade and charged.

Keir tried again to swing his sword at the Fomorii's neck, but the beast rammed him against the wall. Pain burst through Keir's head as it struck brick, but he ignored it as he raised one booted foot and shoved the demon away—but not before the beast raked its claws across his neck.

The pain ripping through Keir was enough to infuriate him even further. He sliced his sword toward the demon, but missed the beast's neck. His blade bounced off the demon's thick hide.

Again the beast shoved Keir up against the wall, only this time with its terrible jaws open, jagged teeth prepared to rip flesh from Keir's neck.

Keir was ready for it. He drew his dagger again, and in a lightning fast motion he sliced it deep into the roof of the demon's open mouth.

The Fomorii staggered, black blood pouring from its mouth. The beast had fallen far enough back that it was in sword range. Before it had the opportunity to recover, Keir beheaded the demon with one clean sweep of his blade.

The demon crumbled into the sewage.

While battling the Fomorii, Keir heard shots and more screams from the Basilisk. When he turned his attention back to it, Jake was closer, firing bullets into the Basilisk's skull.

Rhiannon hurled one spellfire ball after another into the Basilisk's face until its tough hide was charred, almost peeling from its body.

Holding the hilt of his sword with both hands, Keir swung and sliced through the burning hide of the Basilisk.

Its head tumbled into the sewage at their feet. Its headless body weaved from side to side then slammed into the wastewater before its body melted from existence like those of the Fomorii.

Sewage splashed up in the air, coating Keir and no doubt the other members of his team.

His sword at the ready, he whirled to face a new opponent—only to find none. The Fomorii were gone.

Keir had nothing to clean his weapons on, so he sheathed his bloody sword and dagger. His breathing was even despite the battle and the burn on his neck. He felt like he could take on a dozen more Fomorii.

Nothing like a good fight.

With satisfaction, he slapped Jake on the back, as he did with his comrades. When he came to Rhiannon they both looked at each other. She was just as drenched as he and they both smelled of the sewer, but she was still beautiful.

At the same time he wanted to yell at her for following them into battle, pride warmed his chest at how well she had handled herself.

"You did well," he said in the tone of a captain addressing his legion.

The witch folded her arms across her chest. *"Duh."*

Chapter 8

Ceithlenn's fury was a palpable thing. Darkwolf leaned casually against the penthouse's wet bar. He felt anything but casual. Tension crawled along his forearms to his shoulders and his neck.

He gripped his glass of whiskey—straight up—and brought it to his mouth. He tossed back the amber liquid, letting the slow burn of the alcohol travel from his throat to his belly. He'd never been one for drinking until this bitch came into his life.

The Fomorii Queen, Junga, had morphed from her demon form into her Elizabeth body. Darkwolf sensed her own rage at having lost some of her Fomorii foot soldiers to the witches and D'Danann tonight. One of the demons had witnessed the carnage—the creature happened to have been in one of the tunnels when the attack had occurred, but out of sight. The demon had scurried away to inform its superiors of the carnage.

Ceithlenn had almost roasted it on the spot. "Are you *sure* you were not followed?" she had demanded.

The demon had scraped the floor with its hideous face as it prostrated, shaking in obvious terror. "No one followed me," it said. "Of that I am certain."

"Fuck!" Ceithlenn had shouted, and Darkwolf could hear Sara's voice ring out with Ceithlenn's. "Thanks to their deaths, tomorrow eleven prominent men and women will have gone 'missing' and we have lost those important contacts. *And* one of my Basilisks," she hissed.

Ceithlenn-Sara sent the Fomorii back to the sewers to inform one of the legion leaders to select several demons that would need to take on human shapes and come to the penthouse. They then would have to be assimilated into positions of power within the city to replace the other contacts.

Now she raged in the penthouse's living room, her hair alternating between punk red to flames. "I want far more Fomorii to infiltrate the government," Ceithlenn said, "especially law enforcement. I need to know if we are discovered in any way. Including the lair where we keep our army."

Her hair flamed higher. "I will seek revenge on those who have dared to destroy what is mine."

She whipped her gaze to Darkwolf and Junga. At the look in her shifting eyes, Darkwolf almost choked on his last swallow of whiskey. He set the glass down on the wet bar but never took his stare from the goddess's. She might be more powerful than him—an understatement—but he refused to let her intimidate him. He wouldn't bow down to her unless she forced him to with her magic.

Even though Elizabeth-Junga also served the goddess's husband, Balor, Darkwolf sensed the same resentment in the Fomorii Queen that he felt against Ceithlenn. Elizabeth-Junga's anger rose up from her like waves that she barely kept from unleashing at the goddess. Although they hadn't had any opportunity to discuss it, he knew the Fomorii Queen would gladly kill Ceithlenn, just as he wanted to.

Unfortunately, when he and Junga had attempted to free Balor at the gate to Underworld, they'd let loose this bitch goddess, Ceithlenn, instead. Balor had made promises to Darkwolf and the Fomorii. Power, wealth, but power most of all. With Ceithlenn, they only had torment.

"I have plans for you two," Ceithlenn said in a low, ominous voice. "But not yet. *Not yet.*"

At that, Darkwolf's heart beat a little faster. What the hell did she mean?

Ceithlenn clenched and unclenched her fists, her long dark nails digging into her flesh so hard that Darkwolf saw the half-moon indentations her nails left.

She turned her back to them and faced the window. Would she die if he took a blade to her and rammed it between her ribs? What if he drove a silver stake through her heart? Sometimes she looked like a vampire. Maybe she would die like one.

Ceithlenn whipped around and looked at Darkwolf again. His gut clenched as he wondered if she had heard his thoughts. But he had learned to erect such powerful mental walls he doubted it.

Her gaze rested on the stone eye that hung from the chain around his neck.

Stabbing pain almost drove Darkwolf to his knees as Balor's essence flooded him. The stone eye glowed a brilliant red. Every time Ceithlenn called to Balor through the eye, the pain grew greater in Darkwolf's head, and the eye became even brighter.

He would take the damned thing off, but when he had attempted to, the chain and eye became supernaturally heavy. His one hope was that Balor would return and give Darkwolf the power that he had always craved—and that had been promised to him.

Ceithlenn-Sara reached Darkwolf, brought her hand to the eye, and caressed it. The pain in Darkwolf's head was so great he almost couldn't see. It was all he could do to keep his face a blank mask and not let Ceithlenn witness the crushing pain he experienced every time Balor took control.

"What shall I do, love?" she asked the stone eye as she continued to caress it. She clasped her fingers around the eye and the red light pulsed through her fingers. She lowered her lids as if in a trance.

When she opened her eyes, she released the stone eye to

rest against Darkwolf's chest again. The pulsing red dimmed and the pain in his head began to recede. He almost gave a groan of relief, but managed to keep it in check.

Ceithlenn looked at Elizabeth-Junga as she stepped away from Darkwolf. "Prepare your warriors so they will be ready to attack when I am."

Darkwolf studied Elizabeth as she kept her own face a mask of indifference and gave a bow from her shoulders to the goddess. Her eyes, though . . . her eyes still had that fire they always had, before Ceithlenn's arrival. He actually missed the times when he and Junga would spar when she was in Elizabeth's form. And then he would fuck Elizabeth, dominate her, let her know who was the *real* master.

Now who was master?

"Yes, Ceithlenn," Elizabeth-Junga said as she rose up from her slight bow. "The Fomorii will be prepared."

The goddess waved her hand toward the door. "Go then. Wait for my command."

Darkwolf recognized the tightness in Elizabeth's jaw as she turned away and strode to the front door. No doubt unconsciously, her ass swayed beneath the short skirt. As Elizabeth, she had long, striking legs, beautiful features, and luxurious black hair.

When she was in demon form—he hated the thought of what she looked like. A horrible blue demon with arms as long as an ape's and needle-like teeth and the stench of the Fomorii.

He'd always managed to mentally keep the two beings separate. When he fucked her, he was fucking Elizabeth.

Only now he was being screwed by a goddess-bitch, and *he* was the one being dominated.

Ceithlenn captured his chin in her hand and forced him to look at her. The sight of her ever-shifting eye colors never ceased to set him on edge.

She released his chin and planted both hands on her hips. "I want to know which D'Danann and witches are responsible for the attack, and I want to know *now*."

Darkwolf clenched his teeth as he inclined his head. "I'll

scry in my cauldron and come back to you with the information."

Ceithlenn narrowed her gaze. "See that you do so—at once."

He inclined his head again. "Of course." *Your fucking goddessness.*

Chapter 9

Rhiannon waved dust from her face as she stepped on the stairs leading into the apartment building's basement. Spirit delicately bounded down the stairs while Rhiannon followed the prints he left behind in the dust. When she reached the concrete floor she propped her hands on her hips and surveyed the room.

It was a mess, but it had possibilities. A good solid cleaning and the area could be used as another place for the D'-Danann to sleep.

She rolled her shoulders to relieve the ache in her upper back. It was the morning after the fight with the Fomorii. She'd had a hard time falling asleep last night—after a very long, hot shower to wash off all that gross sewage. Even now she still had too much adrenaline rushing through her veins.

And thoughts of Keir and his kiss before they'd gone on their mission weren't helping matters.

The memories of the Shadows trying to escape from her again was like a punch in the gut, and she held her hand to her belly. They seemed to be getting stronger. What was wrong? Did it have something to do with Ceithlenn?

She held her hand tighter against her belly as if that would help get the queasiness under control. At the same time she did her best to turn her thoughts elsewhere.

This morning she had showered again and doused herself

in her favorite citrus body splash. As always she dressed as colorfully as she could. She wore a turquoise blouse and hot pink skirt and sandals. After breakfast in Enchantments' café, Rhiannon decided to check out the apartment building's basement. So much had gone on the past couple of days, the witches hadn't had a chance to do anything with the place.

A quick scan of the basement revealed rotting wooden shelves that held empty jars and rusted thin cans. Crates were stacked haphazardly around the cellar, along with numerous other items. A ratty mattress was propped up against one wall next to old garden tools.

Yup, the basement had possibilities. She'd get every available hand to help and they'd make this room livable in no time.

Spirit gave a loud meow, and Rhiannon startled when the cat chased a mouse across the concrete floor.

"Okay, so you're going to be doing your share, too," Rhiannon said with a shake of her head.

Heavy footsteps pounded on the wooden stairs. She cut her gaze to the old staircase to see Keir coming toward her.

Rhiannon's heart rate picked up, but she took a deep breath and forced herself to maintain her calm. He was just a man, and when it came to women, men only thought with their *little* head.

She glared at Keir and pointed her finger at an old wooden crate. A stream of magic shot from her. The crate flared then crumbled into a pile of cold ashes. "Just in case you need a reminder," she said.

He reached her and gave her a deep, penetrating stare. She swore the man never smiled. He was so intense about everything. "I want you," he said in his deep Irish brogue.

Rhiannon's hair brushed her chin as she pushed it behind her ear. She hoped he didn't notice her slight tremor. "When are you going to get it through your thick head that *I don't* want you?" *Bless it.* Her voice trembled, too.

He brought his hand to her hair and caught a lock of it between his thumb and forefinger. His callused palm brushed her cheek as he let the strands slide through his fingers.

Rhiannon raised her hand to push his away, but he captured

her wrist and drew her toward him. She gasped when she fell against his broad chest.

He smelled of tea tree oil, marigold, comfrey, and magic that had been used over the purple slashes he'd gotten in last night's battle. Because he was Fae, and the Fomorii tipped their claws with iron, it was likely those slash marks would never fully heal.

Cassia had probably doctored him up when they returned. As arrogant as Keir had been with Rhiannon from the moment they'd met, she sure wasn't going to stick around to watch or help. He could bandage himself up for all she cared. It hadn't been like he was mortally wounded.

But right now he held her so close she almost whimpered at the delicious feel of his body against hers. Her heart stuttered. She placed her palms against his chest and pushed, at the same time tilting her head. She'd let him have it with one of her cutting remarks for pulling her up against him like this.

He gripped the back of her head in one of his hands and his mouth came down on her fast and sudden. She struggled in his tight embrace while he kissed her with as much passion and intensity as he had after she returned from the congressman's office.

Goddess, his mouth, his lips. It didn't matter how hard he was kissing her, how hard he was holding her—it was one of the most incredible kisses she'd ever had in her life.

She stopped fighting and started responding. Her head was spinning, her mind and body spiraling out of control.

It was an unearthly, almost Otherworldly kiss.

She slipped her palms up his chest, tangling her fingers into his long hair that was slightly damp, probably from showering. He growled and at the same time she moaned. She couldn't help it. The sound of desire just slipped out.

His stubble chafed her skin as he kissed her harder, impossibly more urgent. His tongue did magic with hers and he tasted so good. Of something primal and wild . . . of Keir.

Shocking her with his boldness, he slid one of his hands up her bare thigh and under the short skirt. When his fingers moved inside her panties he slipped them into her wet folds, causing her to moan into his mouth at the exquisite sensation of his rough fingers against her clit. Moisture lubricated his hand as he thrust two fingers deep inside her core.

It was only then that he relinquished his hold on her mouth, but she kept her arms wrapped around his neck, afraid her knees would buckle. All she could do was moan. No words would come to her as he pumped his fingers in and out of her. He brought his other hand from her hair and moved it to squeeze one of her nipples.

"You are wet for me, little one," he said in a low rumble, his rich Irish accent sending more thrills through her body. "I could fuck you right now."

She couldn't answer, couldn't say anything. All she could do was feel. Before she knew it, he popped off the top two buttons of her blouse and they clattered on the concrete flooring.

He yanked down her bra and freed both of her breasts. When he ducked his head to lightly bite one of her nipples before sucking it, she nearly screamed at the incredible feeling of his hot mouth taking her.

At the same time, he continued to pound in and out of her core, her hips moving in rhythm with his hand. She came closer and closer to reaching an orgasm that would put all other orgasms to shame. With a groan, she tilted her head back, letting go, enjoying the sensations. She was almost there . . . almost there . . .

"Keir!" A tiny feminine voice sliced a path through Rhiannon's awareness.

Rhiannon gasped, bringing her hands from around Keir's neck to try to cover her breasts. He slipped his fingers out of her folds and shielded her body with his. He backed up just enough to allow her to stuff her breasts back into her bra.

Anger replaced passion when she realized she couldn't button up her shirt, thanks to Keir popping off a couple of them.

"Galia!" Keir roared as he turned, keeping Rhiannon behind him.

Galia?

Rhiannon tried to move, but Keir's arm blocked her from coming forward. The best she could do was peer around one of his broad shoulders.

To see a dainty, naked blond Faerie.

A very pissed-off-looking Faerie.

Arms crossed over her tiny breasts, she tapped her little foot in the air as if she were doing it on a hardwood floor, sending poofs of pink dust along with the smell of lilacs into the air.

"What are you doing with this—this *human*, Keir?" the little Faerie called Galia said as she hovered in front of him.

Rhiannon raised her eyebrows. If she wasn't mistaken, the tiny twit was jealous. She frowned. Maybe Galia could grow into a full-size Fae and she and Keir had a thing going? At that thought, Rhiannon's cheeks heated. The ass wouldn't have been after her if he had another woman—Faerie, whatever—would he? Two-timing them both?

Been there. Done that. Had the scars on her heart to prove it.

Keir cut into her thoughts. "Go to our room before I send you back to Otherworld," he commanded.

Rhiannon blinked. *Our* room?

She tried to back away from Keir, but he had a hold on one of her wrists. Maybe a good blast of spellfire to his ass was in order.

The Faerie's angry expression vanished. She bit her lower lip and Rhiannon swore she saw tiny tears glistening in her eyes.

"Please don't send me back." Galia wrung her hands and her hovering became more erratic. She looked at Rhiannon and raised her little chin. "But what are you doing with a *human*?" she said, as though being human was lower than being a Fomorii.

Keir released Rhiannon's wrist and scrubbed one of his hands over his face. "Damnation, Galia. You do not belong here. I should have sent you home as soon as I found you in my haversack."

The memory of the small *oof* sound came back to Rhiannon when she thought about Keir slinging his pack into a corner when he'd first arrived. So this Faerie was a little stowaway, was she?

"Excuse me." Rhiannon pushed past Keir so that she was between him and the Faerie. "So nice to meet you, Galia," she said in a sweet-as-honey voice before she turned and headed up the stairs. "This human *witch* has other matters to deal with."

She cast a glance over her shoulder and saw Spirit sitting below the Faerie, staring intently up at her. His tail twitched as if he were about to leap for a succulent treat.

"Come on, Spirit," Rhiannon said. "Isn't one rodent a day good enough for you?"

Keir had never seen Galia's cheeks so red as she stared after Rhiannon's retreating backside. The imp looked like she could breathe fire. He frowned. For all he knew she *could* breathe fire. All Fae had different talents and abilities.

"Galia," he said in his harshest tone possible, drawing her attention back to him. "When I let you out of the room today, you promised to stay out of sight unless I gave you leave."

The Faerie's shoulders slumped and her coloring returned to normal. "But I was so *bored.*"

"I think it is time you returned home." Keir braced one hand on the end of the stair railing. "You do not belong here. You need to be back with Fae of your kind."

Galia fluttered out of his reach. She glanced around the basement and back to him. "I could clean this place, like our room. I'll make it look just as nice."

And make it smell of godsdamn lilacs while she's at it.

"No." His body still raged for Rhiannon, and he was none too happy with Galia for interrupting what was sure to have led to far more than touching and kissing. He could probably have had his cock inside the witch, taking her until they were both sated. Then he would have taken her a second time. And perhaps a third.

"Keeeeiiiirrrr." This time Galia's voice came out as a whine. She gave a distasteful look at the stairs. "I promise I will not interrupt you and the human again."

"That is for certain," he growled. "You will not have the opportunity."

"Look." A small glittering pink arrow appeared in her hand and she flung it at the stairs. For one moment Keir thought she was going to burn it down. Instead, her magic hit the stairs and exploded into of puff of pink sparkles that engulfed the staircase and gave off the strong smell of lilacs. When the sparkles vanished, the staircase was spotless and freshly polished. "See?" she said. "I am useful."

Keir rolled his eyes to the rusty exposed pipes in the basement's ceiling. Rhiannon and the other witches *had* been talking about cleaning the basement for the D'Danann. Galia would make that task much easier.

He blew out a huff of air and brought his gaze back to the Faerie. "What about your promise to remain out of sight?"

Galia nodded with such vigor that her hair floated around her shoulders. "I promise."

"Do not show yourself to D'Danann, witches, or humans," he said, unable to believe he was allowing a compromise.

Her chest rose and fell and disappointment colored her pretty features. "I understand."

Keir felt a twist in his gut and he wanted to thump himself upside the head for feeling bad about forcing the Faerie to hide.

"Thank you," he said, with a slight incline of his head, "for setting this room to rights for the D'Danann. I will take you out with me again to see more of this Otherworld."

Galia gave a delighted giggle and bobbed up and down in the air. "Now?"

"Later." Keir turned and headed up the stairs. He paused and glanced back at Galia. "What would you prefer to eat?"

The Faerie grinned. "Anything you think I would like."

Keir nodded and started up the stairs again. "I will see you shortly."

Rhiannon sat on a couch in the common room, her legs tucked up beside her, Spirit at her side. The cocoa-colored cat had stayed closer to her ever since she had been kid-napped just a few short months ago by the Fomorii. She'd been saved by Silver, Hawk, and Jake and a few of his officers, but so many witches hadn't made it.

At this moment the room was filled with D'Danann, PSF officers, and witches, discussing how to get to Ceithlenn and the demons. They had come to the agreement that the goddess must be near the location where they had battled the Fomorii and the Basilisk.

The chattering around Rhiannon became nothing more than a low drone as she petted Spirit and pushed all thoughts from her mind. Especially of a certain D'Danann warrior whom she'd almost had sex with in the basement.

Bless it! She didn't even know the man.

As she reached deep inside her for some semblance of calm, she began to feel light-headed. Her vision blurred and her ears felt as if they were stuffed with cotton. Her hand stilled in Spirit's hair.

Everything went hazy and she felt as if she were being transported out of her body, traveling, traveling. And then she stopped.

Rhiannon found herself in a large and sumptuous penthouse room. She looked at her hands then ran them down her skirt and felt the soft brush of her palms against the material. Her sandals sank into plush carpeting and she felt her chest rise and fall with every breath.

It smelled strange. Like burnt sugar and jasmine.

When Rhiannon raised her head, she saw the vivid image of a woman pacing before a window. Unfortunately, the wooden blinds were drawn so no view could be seen.

The woman turned and Rhiannon gasped.

Sara.

But not. Sara had been a white witch in the D'Anu coven who defected to serve Darkwolf, a Balorite warlock who practiced black magic. Copper had told Rhiannon how Sara had absorbed Ceithlenn's essence when the door opened to Underworld.

Sara was even more beautiful with red hair. It wasn't a

natural shade, but it suited her. She now had the most interesting eyes—they seemed to shift colors like a wavering mirage. A revealing leather catsuit barely covered her nipples or her crotch.

Just like the flame-haired being.

Rhiannon's heart beat faster.

She felt as if she were drifting, dreaming, yet still there, whole, in the room.

Ceithlenn. The name rolled through Rhiannon's mind and her heart moved into her throat. Sara was the goddess's human form.

Something stirred in the corner of Rhiannon's vision and she gave a soft gasp of surprise. Darkwolf. She ground her teeth from thoughts of what the evil bastard had done. If it wasn't for him summoning the Fomorii, *none* of this would be happening.

Not far from him was Junga in her Elizabeth form. The sight of her made Rhiannon want to throw up. That bitch had given Rhiannon the scars on her cheek.

She looked back to Darkwolf, who was staring at Ceithlenn. His handsome features were blank. The stone eye Rhiannon remembered seeing when she'd been captured by the Fomorii was still resting on Darkwolf's chest. But it was cold and lifeless, not the throbbing red that it had often become.

Tension suddenly crackled in the air and Rhiannon's attention snapped back to Sara . . . *Ceithlenn*. She was sniffing the air, her gaze slowly sweeping the room.

Then her eyes focused directly on Rhiannon.

As if Ceithlenn could see Rhiannon there, in the room.

Suddenly a sensation like invisible fingers digging into her brain caused Rhiannon to cry out and drop to her knees.

Ceithlenn's power grasped at the Shadows deep inside Rhiannon, driving into the places no one should have been able to touch.

Rhiannon screamed from the pain and clasped her hands to her chest as she fell from her knees to her side.

Ceithlenn growled and extended her hand, palm first.

Rhiannon's heart felt lodged in her throat as she writhed on the floor.

The room seemed to billow. Expand.

A tremendous *boom* shattered her ears.

A great force slammed into her chest.

Excruciating pain filled her mind, her body.

She screamed again before everything went dark.

Rhiannon's scream tore across the common room just as Keir walked through the doorway. His heart thundered. He reached her before anyone else and caught her in his embrace as she slumped forward on the couch.

Spirit jumped onto the floor but staggered, as if also affected by whatever was wrong with Rhiannon.

Keir felt the pulse in her neck and relief surged through him to find it sure and strong. Her breaths were so shallow he had not seen her chest move. He ignored everyone as he swept her up. Rhiannon remained limp and pale in his arms.

"What's wrong with her?" Keir asked Silver as she came to his side.

"She must have had some kind of vision." Silver pushed a loose lock of Rhiannon's auburn hair away from her smooth cheek and placed the back of her hand to Rhiannon's pale skin. "I just happened to glance up from across the room and saw that she was in some kind of trance—I've seen that same expression many times." Silver's eyes met Keir's, a look of fear on her face. "But then she jerked back like something had slammed into her and screamed. That's never happened during any of her visions before."

"Where is the healing witch?" Keir demanded, then saw the half-Elvin witch, Cassia, pushing her way through the crowd.

"Up to her room." Cassia gestured toward the stairs, to the upper-level apartments. "We'll get her to bed and then I'll take care of her."

Keir still could not explain why he felt the tremendous need to protect this woman, or why he wanted her so badly. But right now all he could think about was getting her safe and well.

Holding Rhiannon tightly in his arms, he followed the Elvin witch up the stairs to Rhiannon's apartment. When Cassia unlocked the door with her magic, it swung open and he caught the light citrus scent he had come to associate with Rhiannon. Cassia flicked on the lights, revealing a room as bright and colorful as Rhiannon herself. Splashes of reds, yellows, greens, blues, and purples greeted him from lamps and framed pictures, to couches and chairs, to kitchen canisters, towels, and potholders.

Cassia led the way to the bedroom and pulled back the sheets and Keir laid Rhiannon on the bed. Even her sheets were a bright shade of yellow.

Keir took her small hand and gently stroked her fingers as Cassia held her palms over Rhiannon's chest.

Iridescent sparkles glittered over Rhiannon's body as Cassia moved her palms above the witch. She looked startled for a moment. "It's worse than I thought—some kind of blackness is inside her."

Cassia removed her hands and the sparks vanished. An expression of deep concern was on her face. "I need to get a few things. You leave and let Silver take care of her while I run to my place," she said, hurrying from the room.

"I will not leave," Keir growled as he gripped Rhiannon's hand tighter and leaned over to see her beautiful face.

"Out of the way, you big numbskull," Silver said as she tried to push past him.

Before he could respond or move, Rhiannon's eyelids fluttered open. For a moment her green eyes met his, her expression going from puzzled to pleased to very displeased.

Keir gripped her hand tighter. "You will be all right, little one," he said in Gaelic before he allowed Silver to gently push him out of the way.

He sat in a chair beside the doorway, arms folded over his chest and his legs crossed at his ankles. He did not know why it was so important to ensure that Rhiannon was all right, but it was, and he had no intention of leaving.

Chapter 10

A force so powerful that it almost flung Darkwolf to the floor rocked the room. Elizabeth-Junga's shocked cry could barely be heard when a sound like a cannon burst in the air. The walls fluxed in and out, wavy as if made of water. Then everything cleared.

Fury on her features, Ceithlenn stood with her palm out, facing the wall across the room from her. Her hair nearly stood on end and her body reverberated with her anger.

Darkwolf automatically tensed. *What the hell?*

"That witch won't get in *my* head again," Ceithlenn growled.

"Who?" Darkwolf asked, trying not to sound too interested. He'd been a bit obsessed with the witch named Silver from the moment he'd met her, and hoped she wasn't centered in Ceithlenn's sights.

"The one you scried in your cauldron. The witch called Rhiannon." Anger shimmered in Ceithlenn's eyes. "The bitch dared to invade my thoughts—twice. I felt her the first time I dined on human flesh and absorbed that human's soul. But I didn't *see* her until she visioned us in this room. Right now."

Ceithlenn's scowl deepened. "I had the opportunity to read *her* mind, and you were correct—the witch was one of those who destroyed part of our forces."

Then she gave a wicked smile that turned Darkwolf's stomach. "I know the secret she guards so well," the goddess murmured. "A secret that will be her ruin."

Darkwolf narrowed his brows. *What did that mean?*

Ceithlenn-Sara approached Darkwolf with that look in her eyes he recognized only too well. She was horny again—and pissed. He didn't know how much more he could take of her.

He didn't want her.

He wanted her.

It was slowly making him crazy.

This time Elizabeth-Junga stayed in the room with them as Ceithlenn-Sara pressed her body against Darkwolf's. Ceithlenn's burnt sugar smell and Sara's jasmine scent almost made him scowl. She bit his lower lip, *hard*. His damned cock came to full attention as she rubbed her body against his.

"That bitch." Ceithlenn's fury obviously hadn't cooled as she bit Darkwolf again. "She was the one who instigated the invasion and she has paid. And will continue to pay."

With the power of her magic, she slammed him to his knees hard enough that pain shot through his legs. He ground his teeth to keep from shouting from the agony. She fisted his hair in her hands and yanked him close to her.

"So how does it feel?" She smiled, an eerie light to her eyes, and he knew it was the Sara part of her that spoke now. Sara, a warlock he had dominated much like he'd dominated Elizabeth, before Sara had joined with Ceithlenn.

Could he kill her in her Sara form? He would do it in a heartbeat.

"Tell me," Ceithlenn-Sara urged. "How does it feel to be the one at someone else's mercy?"

Chapter 11

Rhiannon blinked, then had to clench her eyes tight against the light coming in through her curtains. Dear Anu, her head ached and she thought she might puke.

Despite that, she felt somewhat comfortable, which was a strange contrast. The cool sheets hugged her, the mattress soft beneath. Spirit was curled up against her side and rubbed his head on her arm, acknowledging that she was finally awake. Scents of sandalwood and cypress hung in the air and she felt as if oil had been rubbed on her chest, belly, arms, and legs.

Something had happened . . . but what? She couldn't quite grasp it . . . Whatever it was perched on the edge of her thoughts and stayed just out of reach.

She finally managed to get her eyes open and squinted to try to ground her vision. Her whitewashed vanity table and purple dresser drawers came into view, although they seemed to swim a bit. The yellow wall behind them was almost too bright. She blinked again and saw that her bedroom was much cleaner than normal. She wasn't exactly the world's neatest person.

How had she ended up in bed?

And jeez, where did this headache come from? She was a witch, for Anu's sake.

Her skull hurt as she turned her head to see the rest of the room. The open doorway came into view next and then she lowered her brows.

Keir sat in one of her chairs beside the door. His arms were folded and he was looking directly at her.

She blinked. Instead of a leather tunic and pants, he wore a black T-shirt that hugged his muscled chest and a pair of snug jeans that looked so good on him her mouth watered.

Okay, there had to be something *seriously* wrong with her.

"What are you doing in here?" she asked in a voice that came out rough and dry. Goddess, she needed a drink of water.

Keir leaned forward as he uncrossed his legs and bent his knees. He rested his forearms on his thighs as his gaze held hers. "Are you all right?" he asked. He didn't sound as gruff as normal and it threw Rhiannon off balance.

She pushed herself to a sitting position and dizziness caused her eyesight to blur again. The sheet fell away and she looked down to discover she was in one of her robes. A royal blue satin one that gaped at her breasts. She hurried to tighten it while she avoided Keir's eyes.

When she looked back at him, she took a deep breath. "I'm fine."

"What happened?" His look intensified and his manner returned closer to what she was used to. Commanding. Authoritative.

This Keir she could deal with.

She scowled. "What are you doing in my room?"

"What happened?" he repeated, his voice growing in strength and his dark eyes narrowing.

Truth was, she didn't know. But she wasn't about to let him badger her. "Take a hike."

He frowned for a moment, then realized what she'd just told him. "I am not leaving until you are well."

"Oh, yes, you are." She pushed back the covers, and swung her feet over the edge of the bed. The moment she got to her feet she knew she'd made a big mistake.

Her head spun and her knees gave out. Just as she started to drop, Keir was there. He caught her to him, holding her tight and keeping her from falling. For a moment she allowed herself to sink against him, her cheek against his chest. She felt boneless, like she didn't quite have a grasp on reality.

He smelled so good. Woodsy and male, and the scent of the clean cotton T-shirt. With his hard body pressed to her softer one, that burning, spellfire sensation in her belly traveled between her thighs and up to her nipples. The roughness of his jeans and his hard chest rubbed against her through the satin of her robe.

"Let me go," she finally managed to get out. She didn't dare look up at him in case he took that as an invitation to kiss her like he had last time.

But he clasped her chin with his callused fingers and tilted her head back. Instead of a hard, possessive kiss, he just brushed his lips over hers in a touch so light it surprised her. His breath was warm against her lips and she almost moaned. She ached for more. Wanted more.

While she was still looking up at him in surprise, he eased her onto the bed so she was flat on her back. He tucked her in like she was a child. At that moment she didn't have the strength to argue or spar with him.

"Why are you wearing jeans and a T-shirt?" she asked instead. "What happened to your leather gear?"

Keir scowled. "Your law-enforcement officer, Jake Macgregor, insisted we look more like the people of your world to 'blend in.'"

Rhiannon couldn't help a small smile. "What about your weapons?"

Keir gestured to a chest draped with his long black coat. "My weapons are inside. I wear the coat over this new clothing."

"You look good," Rhiannon found herself saying. But then he looked good in leather, too. And most likely he would look good in nothing at all.

That line of thought had her *gently* shaking her aching head.

Keir sat in the chair, leaned forward, and rested his forearms on his thighs again. This time he spoke gently, "Tell me what happened, *a stór*."

Rhiannon wasn't sure what to think of this different Keir. She paused, then decided to answer his question. "I remember sitting in the common room and I was petting Spirit." She concentrated hard, her head aching with the effort. "But nothing else until I woke up." She studied him. "How did I get here?"

"I carried you," he said.

Heat crept up her neck to her cheeks. "Who changed my clothing?"

"Silver and the healing witch, Cassia," he said.

"You didn't watch, did you?"

He shrugged and her cheeks grew hotter. She pushed herself to a sitting position again, this time crossing her legs Indian-style. At once her vision swam. She placed her head in her hands until the dizziness passed. It was as if something was in her mind, taunting her, making her feel as if she were being watched—and not just by Keir.

And the darkness in her mind and her body—it wanted to come forward and she had to fight it back.

The bed dipped and springs creaked as Keir sat next to her. His hand enveloped one of hers and she raised her head. "I should get the healing witch now," he said. He was so close to her she noticed the purple marks on his neck from the fight with the Fomorii.

Rhiannon took a deep breath and let her hands fall to her lap, but he still kept a tight grip on one of them. "I told you, I'm fine."

She just couldn't remember a blessed thing and that was ticking her off. So were the dizziness and the weakness. Had she come down with some kind of virus? Since she was a witch it was unusual for her to catch anything a normal human would.

"So, how long have I been asleep?" Rhiannon glanced at the curtains. It looked like it had to be late afternoon.

He squeezed her hand. "Two days."

Shock flooded Rhiannon, causing her skin to tingle. Her jaw dropped as she stared at him. "You're screwing with me."

Keir maintained his steady gaze. "You were in the common room. You screamed and fainted. That was two days ago."

For a long moment she looked at him, his words not quite sinking in. "This doesn't make sense."

"Silver thought she saw you in a trance, as if you were having a vision."

Flashes came to Rhiannon at his words. Punk red hair. Catsuit. Darkwolf.

Stabbing pain.

Nothing.

"Bless it." Rhiannon took her hand from Keir's and pressed all her fingertips to her forehead as she lowered her head. "It's there. Not quite, but I can *feel* it at the edges of my mind."

Memories of pain accompanied by a fresh bout of real pain made her stomach churn. She grasped her hands to her belly and looked up at Keir. "Were you sitting in that chair very long?"

"Most of the time." He reached up and brushed her hair from her face. "I could not leave you."

"Why?" Her heart beat a little faster at his touch and the sincerity in his expression. "I don't get it."

Keir trailed his fingers from her hair to her cheek in a featherlight brush that made her shiver. "I was concerned for you, *a stór*."

Rhiannon swallowed and drew away from his touch, which was doing crazy things to her body. "You keep calling me that. What does it mean?"

He looked almost embarrassed as he said, "My treasure."

Heat rushed through Rhiannon and she barely kept from putting her hands to her burning cheeks. She felt like she'd just landed on another planet.

Keir, looking embarrassed and saying sweet things to her?

Who is this guy? What happened to the real Keir?

"Has it honestly been two days?" she asked as she forced herself to think of other things than the way this man was working his way under her skin. Her voice rose as it occurred to her that she hadn't asked the important questions. "What's been going on with tagging the demons? Any sign of that goddess?"

"It has been quiet since the day you took ill." Keir leaned closer and stroked the back of her hand with his thumb, causing her to shiver. "After the last battle, we felt it best to wait a short time before tracking the next Fomorii as they are sure to be more aware of us now. We have still kept to the skies in search of signs, but have found nothing."

She shifted from sitting Indian-style so she could draw her knees up against her chest. "How do the Fomorii and C-Ceithlenn—" She stumbled over the name and a brilliant white bolt of pain shot through her head. She ground her teeth before she spoke again. "How do they even know what happened to the demons and Basilisk?"

His thumb stopped moving across her knuckles. "Silver used her cauldron to scry. From what she was able to see, one demon witnessed our attack and escaped to tell the goddess. That is all we know."

"We can't sit around and wait." Rhiannon's heart beat a little faster. "How could I have slept for so long? This is too important."

Keir growled and her gaze shot to his. "You *will not* involve yourself again."

"What are you talking about?" Despite the pain in her head, Rhiannon jerked her hand away from his and almost shoved him right off the bed. "I certainly *will* be a part of this. Down to fighting the last demon."

His expression turned even more fearsome. "No, not if it could kill you—"

"What do you care?" She gripped her sheets in her fists and glared at him. "You don't even know me."

"Damnation." Keir thrust his hand through his thick black hair. "I—Rhiannon—*Damn!*" He looked flustered and angry all at once. "Ceithlenn is beyond dangerous. I will not have you in the middle of a war."

At the mention of the evil goddess's name, Rhiannon shuddered and pain shot through her head again. Something . . . Something about Ceithlenn remained just out of reach . . .

When she tried to grab at the memory, the pain only grew worse.

She held one of her hands to her forehead as she clenched her teeth. The pain was like a white-hot rod through her skull.

"You are ill." Keir's voice softened and he stood. The bedsprings creaked as they released his weight. "I will get the healing witch."

Rhiannon couldn't begin to pretend it was nothing. Her head hurt so freaking bad. "Can you tell Cassia that I have the mother of all headaches?" She scooted down and her head was on her pillow again, as she tried to get some reprieve from the pain by relaxing. Wasn't working.

He gave her a sharp nod, picked up his long coat, and turned away.

"Keir," Rhiannon called out to him before he was through her doorway. She swallowed hard. "Thank you."

He looked at her for a long moment then bowed from his shoulders and walked out of her room.

Keir was going to drive Rhiannon crazy. Since she woke from her "episode" two days ago, he'd appointed himself as her personal bodyguard whenever he wasn't off doing whatever the D'Danann did when they searched the skies for signs of Fomorii or Ceithlenn.

He didn't touch her, barely talked to her—but didn't let her out of his sight, either. She suspected he had everyone else watching out for her when he wasn't around. She'd threatened to toast his balls again, but he'd simply looked at her with that dark and arrogant expression and said nothing.

Rhiannon sat at the Formica table in the kitchen of Enchantments while her Coven sisters chattered around her. She clenched a mug of one of Cassia's healing draughts in both hands, its heat warming her cold fingers. She wasn't crazy about its taste, which included Jamaican dogwood and feverfew. She constantly smelled like lavender because Cassia insisted on rubbing it on Rhiannon's temples and the nape of her neck to help chase away the headaches.

It wasn't doing a whole heck of a lot of good. Nothing was. Each night, the Elvin witch made a sleeping brew from rose petals, myrtle leaves, and vervain, along with a good dose of her magic. It was supposed to chase away nightmares as well as help her sleep.

She'd slept okay. The nightmares, though . . . Because of the magical brew she shouldn't have had them, but somehow she was sure she had. It was driving her out of her mind not being able to remember her dreams of the last two nights. Just vague images remained when she woke.

What had happened that day she'd fallen into the vision . . . Rhiannon shuddered. It was like something had shattered her mind. Ever since, she hadn't been able to vision anything. Nothing. Nada. Zip. When she tried, her head ached so badly she had to get a mug of Cassia's healing draught. It did bring some relief—but not as much as it should have. Cassia was keeping a large pot of it brewing at all times.

Rhiannon stared at the warding bells above the kitchen door, but they blurred as she fell into her thoughts. What if she didn't take Cassia's nighttime brew? What if she let herself experience the nightmares? Maybe they were the key to unlocking whatever it was that had happened to her.

"Rhi. *Rhiannon.*" Sydney's voice barely registered as she squeezed Rhiannon's shoulder. "Are you okay?"

Rhiannon took a deep breath, then let out a slow exhale as she looked up at her friend, who was standing over her. Rhiannon shifted in her seat. "Just a headache. The usual."

A headache that made her want to puke and pass out and not wake for at least a month.

Sydney's mouth pinched in obvious concern. "I think you'd better take it easy and stop trying so hard."

Rhiannon rubbed her forehead with the heel of her hand. "I need to do something, Syd. I can't just let this go. I've got to figure out what happened, and I've got to find out what Ceithlenn is doing."

Bless it! Like always, the mention of the evil goddess's name sent a fresh bolt of pain through Rhiannon's head and she shuddered. All of this had to have something to do with Ceithlenn.

Rhiannon's hands shook as she clasped her mug again and brought it to her lips. After she took another swig, Sydney squeezed her shoulder tighter. "Come on. I think you need to lie down."

Rhiannon wanted to argue, but she just didn't have it in her. She swallowed the rest of the healing draught then let Sydney take her by the hand to help her stand. That freaking dizziness caused her to sway and she clenched Sydney's hand tighter.

Sydney held onto Rhiannon as they walked toward the doorway leading out of Enchantments' kitchen and into the café and New Age shop, which was filled with people today. The chatter and even the beep of the cash register only served to make Rhiannon's headache worse.

Chaos and Spirit followed at their heels. The Doberman put his wet nose against Rhiannon's calves as if supporting her, too. Spirit only hissed twice at the dog familiar.

"You look pale," Sydney said as she brought Rhiannon along with her through the store.

"I'm fine. Fine. Fine. Fine." Rhiannon ground her teeth. "I've got to be fine. There's too much to do."

"Let us worry about that," Sydney said as they passed a display of candles. Rhiannon caught the scents of cherry, cinnamon, and gardenia.

"I don't like this at all." Rhiannon looked at her pretty friend. "This isn't me. I'm not a weak person. I don't rely on others. I take action. I don't sit around and *wait*."

They passed two customers and Sydney pushed open the door leading out onto the sidewalk. The warding bells that usually tinkled so happily made Rhiannon's head feel like a small explosion was going off inside of it.

The afternoon light hit her full in the face and she squinted. Her skin tingled and she knew if she stayed out much longer she'd get a sunburn.

Sydney squeezed her hand. "You need rest. Then everything will come together."

Rhiannon sighed as they strode toward the apartment building. "It better. Soon."

The moment they reached the door to the building, Keir came up beside them—apparently just having returned from scouting. He folded his wings away. Even though she knew it was magic, Rhiannon was still always amazed when they did that. Fresh breezes accompanied his male scent as he stepped over to her from the opposite side of Sydney.

"Godsdamnit, woman." In a motion that caught her completely off guard, Keir swept her up in his large arms. She cried out and automatically clung to him so she wouldn't fall. "You need rest. I can see it in your face and in your eyes."

"You big jerk." She pounded one fist on his solid chest, against the soft cotton of his T-shirt. "Put me down."

Of course he ignored her. Rhiannon looked to Sydney for assistance but her friend had the hint of a smile on her face. "Get some rest, girl. You'll be okay."

"You're a lot of help," Rhiannon grumbled to Sydney before Keir carried her into the building and up the stairs toward her apartment.

When they reached it, Rhiannon used a small dose of magic to unlock the door. Keir didn't say a word, just carried her to her bedroom and laid her on her bed. He was so gentle for such a big, gruff warrior. He slid each of her sandals off, then tucked her sheets and a light blanket around her. When he finished he studied her face.

For a long moment they looked at each other. Rhiannon just didn't know what to think about this man. Powerful, possessive, arrogant, commanding most of the time. But then this softer side showed itself to her. Gentle, caring, concerned.

What was she supposed to do with a man like this?

To her surprise, he picked up a matchbook and lit the large two-wick blue candle beside her bed. Blue for healing, spirit, peace, and calm. The scent of blueberries pervaded the room as the candle wicks started to hiss and spit and melt the wax. Blueberry-scented candles were also for protection.

After Keir lit the candle and put out the match, he set the matchbook aside. He looked back to her for a long moment, and she couldn't say a thing. She felt lost in his dark eyes, eyes that held her, trapped her.

Before she realized what he was doing, he leaned close and she held her breath as his mouth neared her own. He lightly pressed his warm lips to hers then drew away. "Be well," he said as he stroked his knuckles over the scars on her cheek.

She leaned into his touch and stared up at him. His eyes held hers for several seconds. Maybe a minute. Maybe a lifetime.

He drew his hand away. After one more breathtaking look, he turned and walked out the door.

Rhiannon stared after Keir for a long time, until her thoughts blurred, her eyelids grew droopy, and darkness swept her away.

Chapter 12

Keir trudged up to the electrical room where he had continued to sleep since he had arrived in San Francisco. Unlike his normally clear mind, his thoughts were jumbled, alternately filled with fury at Ceithlenn and the Fomorii, frustration at not being able to locate them, and concern for Rhiannon.

Not to mention anger at his sonofabitch of a half-brother. Keir clenched his fists at his sides as he walked toward his room. Once again he and Hawk had ended up shouting at each other over how they should work to locate the Fomorii. If it was not one godsdamn thing it was another.

But Rhiannon . . . His thoughts turned back to her and his gut twisted. His concern for her bordered on obsession.

I must be mad.

When he opened the door to the electrical room, he saw Galia hovering in midair, curled on her side asleep even as her wings beat in time with the rise and fall of her chest.

Guilt lay like a heavy weight in Keir's gut. He had not taken her with him as many times as he should have, and he had mostly left her alone in this empty room. He had brought her food, trinkets, and tiny books from Enchantments that Cassia had given him. The half-Elvin witch hadn't said a word, just put the books into his hands along with some pretty trinkets. There was something about Cassia . . .

Galia loved the books, and the sparkling crystals Cassia

had sent delighted the Faerie to no end. With the cloths and other items Keir continued to bring her, she had made herself a pretty little place in one corner of the room to play with her things. When she was bored she begged Keir to take her places and he usually did.

But leaving her in this room so often—it brought an ache to his heart. It reminded him too much of his own childhood, where he had been relegated to sleeping in the barn when his half-brother Hawk had stayed in the family home. As the bastard son, Keir had grown up feeling lonely and he did not like the thought that Galia might feel the same way.

When he closed the door behind him, the Faerie opened her sleepy eyes and gave him a bright smile. She straightened at once. "Keir! Have you come to take me flying with you?"

He had planned to watch over Rhiannon while she slept, but it would not hurt to let the Faerie fly with him for a while. He knew exactly where he would take her this time.

"Come." He opened the door leading out into the corridor and Galia gave him a questioning look.

"You always make me hide in something," she said as she came up to hover near his face.

"No more hiding," he said in a gruff voice. "Except from humans."

The Faerie gave a delighted squeal that made Keir wince. She clasped her hands together and bobbed up and down. "Really? Truly?"

Keir did not answer, simply held the door open to allow her to fly beside him.

"I cannot believe it." She zipped to and fro, making him dizzy with her movements. "You are so sweet, Keir."

He narrowed his gaze at her and scowled. "I am *not* 'sweet.'"

She grinned. "You are. You just like to hide it beneath all that grouchiness."

Keir chose to ignore her and climbed up to the rooftop of the apartment building to the small garden. He was relieved they did not pass any of the other D'Danann. He was not sure how he was going to explain Galia's presence.

He welcomed the freedom and exhilaration of his wings unfurling from his back. With a single flap he took to the air and vanished from human sight, Galia zipping ahead of him.

It did not take long to reach the place he had never shown her before. The search for the Fomorii had been concentrated in the downtown part of San Francisco.

Ocean breezes hit him full in the face, and Galia's gasp carried to him on the wind.

Water stretched out before them, so far that no land could be seen from where they flew.

Galia seemed stunned into silence for the moment, which in itself was an amazing thing. Keir touched down on the small, sacred stretch of beach the D'Anu witches used for many of their rituals. He folded away his wings and Galia hovered beside him.

"What is it?" she said, her eyes wide with wonder. "So much water and it's so pretty."

"The ocean."

She looked at Keir. "I have heard of such large bodies of water in Otherworld, but I never thought to see anything like it." She sighed, her expression one of complete delight.

Waves crashed against the shore and the sound of the ocean was like a living thing. It smelled clean and nearly free of the pollutants that marred the beautiful city behind them. Nothing would compare to Otherworld, but this place came close.

Galia darted down and landed on the sand. She laughed and wiggled her tiny toes, then bent over and scooped up handfuls of sand and let it slip through her fingers.

"I love it!" She kicked sand into the air then plopped her naked ass onto a smooth section of the beach, close to the water's edge.

A larger wave rose, just feet from Galia. Before it crashed down on the Faerie, Keir scooped her up in his hand. Water splashed both of them and he growled as he tossed back his head to get his now-wet hair out of his face.

"You must be more careful," he told her with a scowl.

Galia grinned up at him. "Can we do that again?"

◆ ◆ ◆

Rhiannon slipped from wakefulness to dreams and back again. Strange images pervaded her subconscious that she couldn't quite reach. Whenever she came close, a flash of white light would blind her dream eyes and then it would all start over again.

But there were also the dreams she'd had since she was a child—a woman shoving her, pushing her. Falling and crying out. Then an explosion before blackness shrouded her.

Again she would go back to the strange images and flashing white light.

When Rhiannon gradually came awake, she tried to hold on to a thread of a thought, but it dissolved like every other one had.

For a while she stared up at the ceiling she'd painted bright pink. The trim was white and she liked the contrast from the yellow of one wall to the pink of her ceiling.

The blueberry-scented candle had burned low. She pushed herself to a sitting position and stared at the flame that caused shadows to dance on her walls. She looked at the dark billowy shapes in her bedroom and memories came back to her of the times she would play with the Shadows. They had been her playmates, her friends, until Aunt Aga . . .

Rhiannon's heart raced a little faster.

Shadows . . . She swallowed hard. She remembered being afraid to go to sleep at night wondering what would happen if the Shadows inside her released themselves while she slept. Right now, those dancing black shapes could well be the things that were supposed to be hidden inside her. What if they hurt someone while she was sleeping?

Right now, though, the Shadows were still inside her and those on the walls were merely a result of flickering candlelight. She could feel their presence within like dark energy balled up tight.

She rubbed her forehead and was surprised to find her thoughts clear and her head free from pain. Unless she thought of the C-word, that goddess's name, and then her head would ache. So she kept her thoughts focused on the here and now.

And right now she was hungry.

Rhiannon slipped out of bed, her stomach growling its agreement. She was still dressed in the same short purple cotton skirt and berry red top, only they were all wrinkled from sleeping in them. She glanced at the clock to see it was eleven P.M. No wonder she was hungry—she hadn't eaten since lunch. But she was pretty sure her own refrigerator was empty.

There was bound to be something in the common room, though, since Jake had installed two big refrigerators that the witches kept stocked just for the D'Danann. Could those warriors eat!

Spirit materialized from nowhere—Silver always said he was like a ghost, and Rhiannon had to agree. The cat ran circles around her ankles and meowed, and she wondered what he wanted.

She yawned, slipped on her sandals, and walked through her bedroom doorway. Her house was almost completely dark, but she could make out the shapes of her furniture well enough from what little light came in through the windows. Besides, she knew her way through her own apartment with or without light—

Her ankle hit something hard and solid. She lost her balance and pitched forward, giving a small cry as she prepared to hit the floor.

Just before her face met wood, large hands grabbed her upper arms and stopped her. Even before he pulled her onto his lap and into a chair, she knew it was Keir.

"Bless it, Keir." She tried to wriggle out of his grasp but he held her tight. She could barely make out his harsh features in the dim light as he engulfed her with his embrace.

"What are you doing up, *a stór?*" he asked in his usual rough voice.

"What are *you* doing in *my* apartment?" She had tripped over his legs. She tried to pull away from him. "You almost made me fall flat on my face."

"Where were you going?" Damn him and that possessive, commanding voice.

She narrowed her eyes. "None of your business."

He brushed his knuckles across her cheek. "You are my business, my little treasure."

His words sent thrills from her belly to that place between her thighs. The heat of his body burned through her clothing and his scent was intoxicating.

From the time she'd tripped over him she'd been tense, but now all she wanted to do was relax. She allowed herself to sink into him, to feel comfort in his embrace. She couldn't think beyond the moment and for some reason that was okay. It was the here and now that was important. Why, she didn't know.

And right now she didn't care.

She relaxed her head against his shoulder and looked up at him. His dark eyes glittered in the dim light, fierce as always, but when she tilted her head back, his features softened. He slipped one of his hands behind her head and played with the hair at the nape of her neck. With his other hand he stroked her face.

"How are you feeling?" His face was so close to hers she felt his warm breath on her lips.

Rhiannon sighed. "Right now I'm feeling really, *really* good." And bless it if she wasn't. Her whole body tingled and crazy sensations moved from her belly to her nipples, and down to her pussy.

She thought she saw the hint of a smile on his lips, but maybe she just imagined it.

Either way she wanted him to kiss her. After all this time fighting her attraction to him, she didn't want to anymore. She *wanted* him and it was time she admitted it and did something about it.

When he simply continued stroking her hair at her nape, she reached up and slid her arms around his neck. And pulled his face down to meet hers.

She felt his hesitation as she ran her tongue along the seam of his lips then gently bit his lower lip.

He groaned and opened his mouth to her and their tongues met. Thrill after thrill rolled through Rhiannon's belly. He'd kissed her three times before—she remembered every one of them so clearly that more warmth moistened her folds. Two times his kisses had been demanding and possessive, and she had to admit she'd loved the way he'd taken control, the way he'd made her feel. Those kisses had been filled with fire and excitement.

But now . . . goddess the kiss was so sweet. This one was a gentle exploration that made her body tingle from head to toes.

She felt his erection grow where she was cradled in his lap. Her nipples tightened, and her breasts ached. *Her* kiss grew more demanding as she pulled him closer to her, locking her fingers around his neck.

Keir broke away with a groan and she whimpered. She needed this. Needed *him.*

"Gods." His voice was hoarse and the look on his face was tortured. She wondered why his hands weren't roaming her body, possessing her like he had before.

"What's wrong?" She nipped at his lower lip and he groaned again.

"You have been ill," he said and his Irish brogue caused her stomach to twist. He shifted her on his lap as if to ease the pressure of her ass on his erection and she felt the sheer length and width beneath her. The jeans he was wearing had to be even more confining than the leather he normally wore.

"I feel fine right now." She slid one of her hands from behind his head to his arm and rubbed it, feeling the bulge of his biceps through the cotton of his T-shirt. She skimmed her fingers down through the hairs on his arm to his strong hand. She wrapped her fingers around his. "I feel *really* fine."

A rumble rose in his chest that vibrated against her. "Rhiannon—"

"Take me to bed." She kissed him and drew away. "Please don't wait."

"You could get with child," he said with a frown.

"I can't get pregnant because my magic protects me from

everything, Keir," she said. "So you don't have to worry about that."

Keir hesitated for all of two heartbeats. He gripped her tight in his arms and strode from the living room into her bedroom. She snuggled against his chest.

He settled her on the edge of the bed so she had her hands braced on the mattress, her feet on the floor. Looking up at him, her breathing came a little faster and her heart rate picked up.

The flickering candlelight cast shadows on Keir's face but she could see him better now. He looked so good and her body was so ready for him.

She reached out and slipped her hand into his and tugged, bringing him closer until he stood above her, in between her parted legs.

His voice was husky and raw. "You need to have time to heal—"

"Enough of that." She threaded their fingers together. When he didn't move, she tugged at him again. "Don't make me hurt you."

The hint of a smile curved the corners of his lips, just a hint, but it gave her such a thrill to know she had made the big, strong, gruff warrior smile.

"How could I ignore such a threat?" He lowered himself so he was kneeling beside the bed, between her thighs. "What else would you command of me?"

Rhiannon gave a soft laugh. "Stop making me wait already."

Keir looked down at her feet and slipped her sandals off, then began to stroke her from her heels to behind her knees and back. He did it almost reverently and she felt she was seeing yet another facet of the man who was still pretty much a mystery to her.

As his palms moved to her thighs he looked up and met her gaze. In the candlelight his eyes glittered, filled with something she couldn't read.

"You're taking too long," she whispered.

That hint of a smile flickered at the corner of his mouth

again before it vanished to be replaced by the usual dark, brooding, bad boy look he always had. He moved his palms along her thighs, pushing her skirt up with the movement. She caught her breath as his fingers reached her panties.

"Why do you wear this?" he said as he ran his palms over the silky material.

Rhiannon giggled and clapped her hand over her mouth. She *never* giggled. Keir was intent on studying her undergarment, which was obviously frustrating him from the look on his face.

"Never had sex with a human before?" Rhiannon said with a grin.

Keir growled as he found the waistband. He jerked down on the panties so hard the silk tore in his big hands. He ripped the material and tossed it aside.

Looked like she'd be making a trip to Victoria's soon.

Keir studied her like he'd found a prize. Rhiannon shivered and her belly flip-flopped at how close his face was to her folds, at the intensity of his expression, and the fire in his gaze.

He moved closer and she smelled her own musk and felt his warm breath on her folds. Her thighs began to quiver from the need to have his mouth on her. "Keir. *Please.*"

Instead of answering her, he nuzzled her curls and she heard his deep inhale. He murmured something in Gaelic. It only added to her excitement and her desire.

When he finally licked her folds, she thought she was going to come with just the one swipe of his tongue. She cried out and gripped the sheet tight in her fists to anchor herself. He buried his mouth against her folds and began licking and sucking. Small spasms caused her core to contract and she clamped her jaws with the effort it took not to come too quickly. It felt much too good to rush and she'd never felt this way with any sex partner she'd had.

She watched him lick and suck her clit and seeing his tongue flick out only brought her closer to the peak. Her whole body began to shake and then she couldn't hold back any longer.

With a loud cry she climaxed. Her thighs clenched around his head and her body rocked against his mouth. He paused and she took deep breaths as her climax slipped away. She almost let herself fall back like she was a pool of melted candle wax, when he started it all over again.

Her thighs quaked even more as he brought her to another peak, shoving her over the edge, faster this round. Her body shook and she squirmed, needing him to stop—she was too sensitive. With every lick her body spasmed. When she fell back onto the bed, he finally stopped and moved so that they lay side by side. He kissed her, this time a hungry, possessive kiss. It was different from the domination he had shown before and the gentleness they'd just shared in the living room.

He began to tug at the buttons on her shirt. She slapped his hand away. "Let me, you big barbarian. All I need is to lose more buttons."

"Do not make *me* wait," he said as he settled his palm on her belly. "I want to see the beauty of your body."

Rhiannon's cheeks heated for some reason at the thought that he was going to see all of her. She fumbled with her buttons but managed to get them undone and her shirt fell open.

Again he looked frustrated. "Why do you cover your breasts? They are so beautiful."

"It's a bra," she said with a smile. "It didn't seem to bother you the time we were in the basement."

"I want it off," he said in an impatient voice that only made her smile more.

"Hold on. No more ripping off my clothes." She pushed herself to a sitting position and shimmied out of her shirt, then unfastened the back clasp of her bra. Her heart beat a little faster as she took it off and saw the hunger in his gaze when her breasts were completely bared.

"This, as well." He pulled at the waistband of her skirt and she hurried to tug it down.

When she was completely naked, he took one of his large hands and pushed her back on the bed again. He ran his hand from the curls of her mound to the spot between her breasts and drew small circles with his fingertips. Then he slid his hand over to cup the weight of one of her breasts and pinched the nipple. Rhiannon was still in the middle of a gasp when he enveloped her other nipple in his warm mouth and sucked.

She squirmed and moaned as he eased his mouth and hands from one breast to the other. His long hair tickled her chest as he moved and his stubble abraded her skin. He slid one of his hands between her thighs.

She gave a soft cry as his finger entered her folds but his mouth took the cry from her when he kissed her, and turned the cry into a moan.

He began fingering her sensitized clit as he kissed her and in seconds she climaxed so hard, tears moistened her eyes.

When Keir drew back from the kiss he cupped her face in both of his hands. "You are so beautiful, *a stór,*" he murmured as he rubbed one of her cheeks with his thumb.

Rhiannon didn't have the breath to say a word.

Chapter 13

Keir stroked Rhiannon's flushed cheek with his thumb as he cupped her face. He wanted to smile at the pleasure it had given him to give her pleasure. He moved one hand and caressed the line of her curves from her hip to the indentation of her waist to her soft shoulder. He wanted to part her thighs and thrust into her so badly he almost shook with the need for it.

Rhiannon gave him a sated smile that warmed his heart. She brought her hand to his cheek before exploring him and touching him in much the same way—only she was naked and he was fully clothed.

She rose up on one elbow so she was above him. Her lips met his and she sighed into his mouth. A raging beast rose up inside him that he could barely control. Gods how he wanted to take her now.

Her small hand slid down his chest to the waistband of the human jeans he wore and he hissed as her fingers traveled lower.

"Mmmmmmm." Rhiannon cupped his erection through his jeans and squeezed, almost taking the breath from him at the pain and pleasure of it. "Big. I like big."

"Rhiannon—" He groaned as she moved her hand lower between his thighs and squeezed his balls.

She kissed the curve of his neck and he inhaled her citrus

and woman scent. Her musk hung in the air, only serving to make his cock harder. She moved her lips to the neckline of his T-shirt and flicked her tongue on his bared skin.

Keir shuddered at just the small contact. "You have been ill, little one."

Her grip on his balls tightened and he grimaced. "You're not going to play the self-sacrificing warrior on me." She scooted lower and he breathed a sigh of relief when she released him. "You get to see me, I get to see you. Fair's fair."

Keir remained flat on his back but slipped his fingers into the hair at the base of her neck. Her short auburn hair was silky beneath his touch and the contact made his belly tighten even more.

"You are a demanding wench," he said and she looked up at him.

"I'm not above another burst of spellfire, buddy," she said, but a teasing glint sparked in her eyes.

He winced at the thought, but when she unfastened the button of his jeans, he groaned. In short work she had his erection in her hand, running her fingers up and down his length.

"Wow." Her voice was breathless. "If all male D'Danann are this well-endowed, no wonder Silver and Copper are so happy."

Keir couldn't say anything if he tried because as soon as she finished speaking she slipped her lips over the head of his cock.

Gods, her mouth felt so warm and hot that his eyes nearly rolled back in his head. No woman had ever made him feel the way Rhiannon did at this moment. As though he would combust into a raging bonfire if she continued licking and sucking him as she was.

Her fingers moved up and down his shaft in time with her mouth as she took him deep. She made soft moaning sounds as she sucked his cock, as if she enjoyed giving him such pleasure.

She let his moist erection slide from her mouth and he wondered if his disappointment showed on his face.

"Take your clothes off." Her tone was demanding, as if she would not take no for an answer.

Who was he to refuse anything of this beautiful witch?

He eased from the bed, never taking his eyes from Rhiannon's. Candlelight flickered over her features and glittered in her eyes. There was no mistaking the desire she had for him—nor the desire he felt for her.

He undressed and Rhiannon licked her lips as if he were a tasty morsel. That only made him harder, made him want her more.

When he stood naked before her, she rose from the bed and moved so close to him their bodies melded. He gave a low growl and wanted to shout, "Mine!"

Gods, where had that come from?

Rhiannon reached up and kissed him before moving her lips away until they reached the scar on his cheek. He held his breath as she kissed its length, one slow kiss at a time. When she reached the end of his scar, she licked a trail to his ear. She gently bit his earlobe and he shuddered with need.

He was so close to picking her up, throwing her on the bed, parting her thighs, and fucking her till she screamed. And he knew she would scream.

But no. Instead he allowed her to explore his naked body with her mouth and hands.

She reached up and caressed the scar on his cheek with her fingertips. "You'll have to tell me about this." She knelt before his cock. "But we'll save that for later."

For that he thanked the gods. Fuck now, talk later.

She brushed her lips up and down his erection. "How much stamina does a D'Danann warrior have?"

He slipped his fingers into her short silky hair again. "I could take you many times over in this one night."

Rhiannon gave a soft laugh. "My kind of man."

Keir was not sure he liked that response. He did not want her to be with any other man. Not ever again.

The thought bothered him but then vanished from his mind the moment she took his cock in her mouth once more.

Keir groaned and looked down at Rhiannon as he

watched his erection move in and out of her silky mouth. She looked up at him and when her gaze met his, he thought he would climax just from the look in her green eyes.

She released his erection from her warmth and he groaned.

"I want you to come in my mouth." She blew softly on the head of his erection. "I want to taste you."

Keir thought he must be dreaming. The Faeries and Pixies must have conjured some kind of spell to make such a perfect being as this witch.

She went down on him again and his hips bucked against her face. She caressed his balls in one of her hands, alternately squeezing and fondling them. Her other hand worked his cock harder as her head bobbed up and down. With every touch, every lick, every suck Keir felt himself pitching forward into a realm he had never been to before. This witch wove magic around him. Her mouth was magic, her hands were magic. Even her eyes held magic in their depths.

His entire body began to tremble. Such incredible pleasure built in his groin that he almost could not stand.

Light nearly blinded him in his mind as he shouted. His seed burst from his cock into Rhiannon's mouth and he had to grip her hair to keep from dropping to his knees.

She continued sucking and swirling her tongue along his length until he forced her to stop by drawing her away.

"Gods, Rhiannon." He could barely get the words out as he drew her up to stand and pressed his sweat-dampened skin to her cool flesh. "Perhaps this warrior does not have the stamina it takes to please you."

She gave a soft laugh and reached up to press her lips to his. When she drew back she smiled and tugged on his hand. "I'll bet this warrior has plenty more left in him."

He couldn't have stopped her if he tried, his body was so relaxed from such a magical orgasm.

Keir eased onto the bed with her and they tangled their legs and arms as they kissed and touched one another. Their lovemaking became fiercer with every kiss, every touch, until he thought he had entered an Otherworld where nothing existed but pleasure.

Rhiannon wanted Keir so badly she was almost crazed with it. Nothing else existed for her at that moment but the big man who had her engulfed in his embrace, his thigh pinning hers down while his rock-hard erection pressed against her belly.

Their kisses grew more frantic and Rhiannon's head felt as if it was floating and she was in some other realm.

Before she knew it, he flipped her on her back so she was looking up at him. His muscular bulk pinned her down, but not so much that she was uncomfortable. Instead it was a joining of bodies that made her feel a part of him.

Only it wasn't enough.

"I know you'll feel so good inside of me." She had a difficult time talking with him on top of her. She wriggled beneath him. "Please. I want you."

That now familiar rumble rose up in his chest that thrilled her every time. It was a primal sound, a possessive sound that somehow turned her on even more.

Keir's bad-boy expression made her hotter, wetter. He knew how she was feeling. She could tell by the look on his face. Fierce male pride that made a thrill skitter through her belly.

"Spread your thighs." His commanding voice made her obey at once.

She widened her thighs and his hips settled in between them. The press of his cock against her folds made her moan and arch up to him.

He braced his arms to either side of her chest and looked down at her. In the candlelight she saw the harsh planes of his face, the wicked scar across his cheek, and the hard look of one who got what he wanted. He had wanted her and now he had her. And she had him.

A low thrill settled in her belly.

"Who do you belong to, witch?" he demanded, shocking her with his question as he held himself poised above her.

Rhiannon swallowed. "No one," she whispered.

His expression grew more fearsome. "No, *a stór*. You are *mine*."

She started to shake her head to argue but he clamped his lips to hers in a possessive kiss, and pressed his cock harder against her folds. His shoulder-length hair tickled her face and neck and his stubble rubbed her mouth until it felt raw.

When he raised his head he narrowed his eyes. "Who do you belong to?"

She shook her head but this time he captured her nipple in his mouth and bit it. Rhiannon cried out and arched her back and he moved his mouth to her other nipple. She pressed up against his cock that teased her folds. So close to being inside her, yet he was holding her back, trying to force her to say something she didn't want to.

Was she falling for him? If she was, when had it happened?

The first day they met?

That time in the basement?

When he took care of her while she slept?

When she woke and he'd spoken so gently to her?

When he insisted that she remain safe?

When he had her watched over whenever he wasn't there to do it himself?

Or was it because of the way he was making love to her now?

That was it. She was living in the moment, feeling the moment. It was nothing more than that.

He stopped sucking her nipples and raised his head again. In the candlelight perspiration glistened on his forehead. The room smelled of their sex, their sweat, the blueberry candle.

"Who do you belong to?" he demanded again.

"I can't—" She gripped his biceps and looked up at him. "Don't make me say it."

Keir gave her a surprisingly tender look. "You will admit it." He placed the head of his erection at the entrance to her channel.

"Mine," he said as he thrust his cock deep inside her.

Rhiannon cried out, almost coming off the bed. He was big, so very big. He stretched her, filled her, touched her in ways no man had ever touched her before.

He began to thrust in and out. Slowly out, then hard in. Slowly out, then hard again—over and over and over. He drove in deep enough that she felt him in her belly.

Keir continued to look at her in that way that made her feel like she was treasured, precious, and his. It should have bothered her but it didn't, oh, goddess, right now it didn't.

His thrusts gradually increased in speed. Cries of pleasure escaped her with every movement he made. She wriggled under him until she was almost out of control.

He reached between them and fingered her clit and the fire between them exploded. She screamed as her body trembled beneath his. Spasm after spasm rocked her and heat waves flooded her over and over again.

Keir continued to thrust in and out of her, his look one of sheer satisfaction, as if he had just put his mark on her.

He threw back his head and let loose a deep, rumbling shout as his hips bucked against hers. She felt his climax as if it were her own.

With one last groan he collapsed on top of her, knocking the breath from her. Then he raised himself up just enough so that she could breathe.

Keir stared down at her, his cock still inside her. "Mine."

Rhiannon woke sometime later, and saw through her curtains that the sky was just beginning to lighten.

Her stomach rumbled, reminding her of the original reason she had climbed out of bed hours ago. To her surprise she felt no pain at all in her head and her sleep had been peaceful.

Must have been the incredible orgasms. Was it four she'd ended up having? Five? Six?

She sighed then tried to move, but she couldn't even wiggle with Keir's big body draped over hers. For a moment she thought about what Keir had said. How he had insisted she was his.

A strange churning sensation rolled through her belly. Rhiannon tried to slide her way out of Keir's hold, but he had her caged completely with his body, within his embrace.

Rhiannon's pulse ramped up and a panicky sensation made her feel as if she was locked in, with no escape. She started wriggling against Keir's hold in earnest. She pushed at his thigh draped over her hip. His arms bound her so tightly she couldn't even move her shoulders.

"Keir!" The panicky sensation made her feel as if she couldn't breathe. "Let me go!"

"Sleep, *a stór*," he murmured.

"No, damn it." She ground her teeth and jabbed one of her elbows into his ribs as hard as she could.

He gave a loud grunt of surprise, loosened his hold and moved his legs. She took the opportunity to roll away and slip out of bed, even as he reached for her.

When she got to her feet, she grabbed for the robe she'd left draped on a chair. She was trembling so hard she almost dropped the garment.

"What is wrong?" Keir was already out of bed and at her side by the time she'd slipped the robe over her naked body.

She didn't say anything, just focused on tying the belt tight enough that the front wouldn't gape and expose her.

His touch was gentle as he caught her by her upper arm with one hand and used the fingers of his other to raise her chin. "Tell me."

"Nothing." Rhiannon couldn't stop trembling. "Everything!"

Keir murmured soft words in Gaelic and drew her close to him. The heat of his body, the tenderness and strength of his embrace somehow eased her trembling and calmed her racing pulse.

How she wanted to just give herself up to him. But sweet, wonderful things like this didn't last, did they? No. And where would she be when he was gone as well? Gone back to Otherworld, lost and gone in battle, or just gone because the feelings were no longer the same?

When she could catch her breath, she raised her head and pushed herself away from him by bracing her hands on his muscular chest. He was so warm, and his cock so firm against her belly that she almost thought about tumbling back into bed with him.

But the way he had insisted that she belonged to him—again that caged-in feeling caused her throat to close and she took another step away.

He looked at her with a puzzled expression as she rubbed her hands up and down her arms.

"I just need some space." She glanced toward the bathroom. "I'm going to take a shower and then I need something to eat."

Keir narrowed his eyes, but said nothing.

Rhiannon practically fled to the bathroom, slammed the door behind her, and locked it. She sagged against the door, her heart racing, her chest rising and falling as she tried to catch her breath.

For a moment she closed her eyes tight and forced herself to take deep breaths. The night with Keir *had* been magical. But . . . what had she been thinking by letting it go anywhere beyond really satisfying sex?

He had made it clear that he intended for her to belong to no one but him.

Did he think the same for himself? Had he pledged himself to her at the same time?

An ache bit at the back of her eyes and she forced herself to take deep breaths again. No good could come of this. No good for her, anyway.

Everyone left. That was just how things were.

When she was relatively calm, she opened her eyes and went to the bathtub. She turned on the shower and made the water as hot as she could handle it. Then she slipped out of her robe, draped it over the towel rod, and climbed into the bathtub.

Water from the showerhead beat down on her, pounding against her face, her breasts, her thighs. Every part of her body that Keir had touched tingled with awareness and she found herself longing to be in his arms again.

She turned, tipped her head, and water drenched her hair

and rolled down her backside. What an incredible lover Keir was. Fiery and passionate one moment, gentle and loving the next. It was as if he had a magical talent that went beyond just having sex.

She sighed at the memory of last night. They'd been so good together.

Yes, she was definitely in trouble.

Rhiannon took her time in the shower, not ready to face Keir or anyone else. She used her favorite citrus-scented shampoo to wash her hair and rubbed her scalp until she felt invigorated. She had body gel in the same scent and used a loofah sponge to scrub herself. By the time she finished, her body tingled all over.

When her fingers and toes were wrinkled, and her skin was red from the heat, she shut off the water, climbed out of the tub, and dried off with one of her bright red towels. The room was clouded with steam, but with a wave of her hand, a space on the mirror cleared so she could see herself. Her short auburn hair clung to her cheeks and her nape. Her lips were still swollen from Keir's kisses and she definitely had the look of someone who'd been completely satisfied by great sex.

But her eyes—when she leaned closer, fear clawed at her throat.

They were changing, shifting. From brown to blue to green to silver.

Rhiannon stumbled away from the mirror and hit the towel rack, barely holding in a scream.

Ceithlenn's eyes. Looking back at her!

Pain bolted through her head in a white-hot shard of light. She placed her palms to either side of her against the textured wall and took deep breaths, trying not to cry out. Trying not to lose control.

It took her more than a few moments to regain her composure—at least a fraction of it. She stepped toward the mirror, and with her heart pounding, looked at her eyes.

They were green again. Her own eyes stared back at her. Not Ceithlenn's.

Rhiannon braced her hands on the porcelain sink as she tried to breathe. She looked down at the trail of red rust that had stained the sink from the aging metal faucet to the drain.

It took her a long time to get the guts to look at the mirror again, and when she did she thanked the goddess that her own eyes still stared back at her.

For long moments she studied her pale reflection in the mirror. Could the shifting colors of her eyes—the goddess's eyes—have been her imagination?

No, it definitely hadn't been. She knew that truth with every part of her heart and soul. Even the Shadows stirred within her, recognizing what was happening.

Rhiannon squeezed her eyes shut and bile rose in her throat. The dark goddess possessed her in more ways than one.

She kept her eyes closed and willed her breathing to slow. Right now she needed to focus on the present, the here and now, and push all thoughts of Ceithlenn from her head.

When she finally willed them away, her mind relaxed and she opened her eyes.

Memories of her night with Keir replaced all other thoughts. She'd much rather think about him—that was far more welcome.

Yet disquieting, too.

Such as his insistence she belonged to him . . .

She-yeah, right.

What was she going to do about him?

She was going to do what she always did. Be strong. Be smart. Be someone who was confident and in control and wasn't going to let something said in the heat of the moment make her believe that it could be anything more than that—the heat of the moment.

With that clear in her mind, she dried her hair with her magic and wrapped herself in her blue satin robe.

She wasn't going to tell Keir what she'd just seen in her own eyes—he'd just become more possessive.

Squaring her shoulders and raising her chin, she walked out the bathroom into an empty bedroom. The door was closed.

She dressed slowly, slipping into bright green silk underwear and a matching green cotton skirt that flared at her thighs. Something really bright was in order for the day, so she chose a satiny yellow bra, a sunshine-yellow blouse, and yellow sandals. As usual she wore her gold-and-onyx pentagram ring and the matching gold-and-onyx pentagrams at her ears and at her throat.

Okay. Now she could face anything.

But could she really? Was she ready for Ceithlenn? How would she get the goddess out of her head?

She wiped her palms on her skirt, prepared to go downstairs and face whatever else she would meet today. She flung open her bedroom door and came to a complete stop.

Keir was setting her small dining table with her mix-and-match blue and red plates and the forks with the red handles. The smell of eggs, potatoes, and toast made her stomach growl, and the sight of the pitcher of orange juice caused her mouth to water.

His hair was wet. It looked like he'd taken a quick shower, changed into fresh clothing, and gathered breakfast for her while she'd taken her sweet time showering and getting dressed.

While freaking out over Ceithlenn and obsessing over Keir.

His dark gaze met hers. "You said you were hungry, so I went to the store's kitchen."

You woman, me man. I provide food, you give me sex.

She shook her head at the images in her mind, pushed her hair from her forehead, and offered him a smile as she walked toward the dining table and near him. "I'm starving."

Something close to a smile flickered across his features, making her feel good again. *She* was doing this to him. And she had the feeling that smiling was a rare thing for him indeed.

She glanced in the kitchen to see Spirit eating tuna from his bowl. The familiar glanced up, licked his mouth, and went back to eating. Keir had even thought of Spirit.

The orange juice, scrambled eggs, hash browns, and toast

were so good, and she was so hungry, that she was tempted to take thirds of everything, but she stopped herself at two servings.

She concentrated wholly on her food and hardly glanced at Keir during their breakfast. When she finally finished and wiped her mouth with a vivid green napkin, she looked up and met Keir's gaze.

He was sitting back in his chair, his arms folded across his chest and his look as intense and brooding as usual. The bad boy.

"Tell me what is wrong," he said in that demanding voice that had always pissed her off in the past. The past being only a day ago.

This time it did something altogether different. It caused her heart to melt a little because she knew he sometimes got demanding when he was concerned.

The bravado she'd coached herself on slipped, but then she sucked it up again. "Last night." She cleared her throat. "You said something you shouldn't have and I think you didn't really mean it, anyway."

He raised an eyebrow but didn't speak.

Rhiannon swallowed. "We had a really wonderful night, but it was just one night. That doesn't make me yours."

He slowly shook his head and remained unsmiling. "You are mine."

Her eyes widened and she opened her mouth to speak, then shut it, then opened it again. "It was sex. That's all it was. Sex."

He didn't change his expression. "You know you belong to me." His features almost seemed to soften as he said in a quieter voice, "As I belong to you."

Rhiannon blinked. Something in her heart shifted and she didn't know what to say.

Keir felt such a need to possess Rhiannon heart, body, mind, and soul that it bordered on pain. What had made him decide that she was meant to be his mate?

Perhaps it was the moment he recognized her from the face in the wood. Destiny had spoken to him that night, and had continued to drive him toward her. He needed her more than he had ever needed anyone in his existence.

He admired her spirit, her strength of will, her desire to protect others, and her love for her Coven sisters.

His heart nearly stopped beating when he realized that he wanted her love. It was more than possessing her, it was *needing* her.

The thought was almost dizzying and he had to focus on the here and now.

Keir uncrossed his arms, stood, and held out his hand to Rhiannon. She took it and let him draw her to her feet in front of him. He slipped his hand from hers, placed his palm on her hip, and brought her so close that her body was flush with his. With his other hand he cupped the back of her head and lowered his face to hers at the same time he drew her up to meet him.

"Mine," he said before taking her lips with his.

He gently explored her mouth with his tongue and she sighed. She tasted of orange juice and her own flavor that made him crazy for her every time they kissed.

It pleased him that she let him take control, let him draw her tongue into his mouth. She softly moved her lips with his, at his pace.

She slid her hands up his chest and threaded her fingers beneath his damp hair. Clean scents of soap and citrus filled his nostrils.

He pinned her hip tight to him and his cock was hard against her belly. Her body was so warm against his, so warm and soft and female.

When he broke the kiss he could barely breathe, much less speak. He could not fathom how one woman could steal his breath away and make him lose his words so easily. She looked into his eyes and he was unable to tear his gaze from hers.

"You are mine," he finally said. He brushed his knuckles across her cheek. "And I am yours."

Chapter 14

Rhiannon walked down the hallway side by side with Keir. Her body was still flushed and her heart wouldn't stop pounding so hard. This was crazy.

When they reached the bottom of the stairs, Rhiannon heard nothing short of an uproar coming from the common room.

"What's going on?" she said as she hurried ahead of Keir into the room.

"There you are." Sydney rushed up to Rhiannon and grabbed her hand. "Hurry. Jake and the other PSF officers have already left. We've got to make some plans."

A chill raked Rhiannon's spine as she ran alongside Sydney and came to a stop at one of the tables. A huge map of the Bay Area was spread out on it and Hannah was giving the D'Danann directions.

Rhiannon felt Keir behind her as she tried to listen in and hear what was going on.

"Since you'll be flying, you'll reach it before we possibly could," Hannah was saying as she glanced up at the warriors. She looked back to the map. "Head over the Golden Gate Bridge." She drew a line from San Francisco across the bridge using a trail of green magic from her finger. "You'll find the bus here, in Sausalito." She proceeded to give detailed instructions on where they needed to go.

"What happened?" Keir said in his authoritative voice.

Hannah looked up at him from the map. "The Sausalito Police just found a tourist bus filled with shriveled corpses. HAZMAT is there now, checking to see if it was caused by some kind of disease or chemical weapon." She paused and shook her head. "I don't think that's what we're dealing with."

"Blessed Anu." Rhiannon held her hand to her belly. "Are you thinking it's Ceithlenn?"

The moment Rhiannon said the evil goddess's name, a white-hot rod of pain jammed into her skull and her knees almost gave out. Her vision blurred. Her ears felt as if tissue paper had been jammed into them. Keir placed his hands on her shoulders from behind, as if knowing she needed to be steadied.

"We think it was." Silver sounded distant as Rhiannon's mind spun. "There are two bodies mostly eaten." Silver spoke as though the words were distasteful on her tongue. "The rest are just withered according to the police."

"As if their lives had been sucked out of them," Hannah added.

Rhiannon rubbed her temples, trying to ease the pain in her head. "Or their souls."

"That's what we think," Sydney said from beside Rhiannon.

"An entire busload of people?" Rhiannon asked to make sure she'd heard right.

The witches surrounding the table nodded. "It's off in an isolated area, but the cops are all over it. The PSF has been called in because no one's ever seen anything like it."

"We should go, too." Rhiannon's head was foggy, her mouth dry. "We can get readings off whatever energy traces might have been left behind."

"No." Keir rested his hand on her shoulder. "You all need to stay."

"As if." Rhiannon looked up at him. She blinked. She saw two of Keir. Her vision was doubling. Great, that was all she needed—two Keirs.

She swayed and Keir steadied her again with his arms on her shoulders.

"*A stór*, are you all right?" he murmured in her ear.

She gave a nod even though she wasn't okay. It was the goddess's name. Every time she spoke it or thought about it she got sick. And it was getting worse every time.

"This time they're right," Silver was saying as Rhiannon fought to clear her mind. "We'd never be able to drive there in time. The D'Danann can fly over and search the area. Jake can let them in if they can manage to land and shift without being seen."

Sydney squeezed Rhiannon's arm as she said, "We need to use our divination talents to see what we can learn."

"Yeah. Okay." Rhiannon braced her hands on the table and Keir's grip from behind her kept her steady. "This time."

The rest of the warriors had their long coats on over their T-shirts and jeans to conceal their weapons.

Just as Keir was about to run upstairs to grab his own, it floated into the room.

Floated.

"What in Anu's name?" Shock filled Silver's voice.

Keir knew and he ground his teeth as he reached for it. "Thank you, Galia," he managed to get out without snapping at the Faerie. He had promised she did not have to hide anymore, and he always kept his promises. Always.

But now was not the time to explain a six-inch, lilac-scented, pink-winged, naked blond Faerie to a roomful of witches and warriors.

The moment he took the coat, Galia darted out. He heard the witches gasp and a rumbling among the D'Danann.

"A Faerie?" Sheridan said with amusement in her voice.

"We do not have time to discuss this." Keir jerked on his coat. He strode out the door.

Galia followed just to the left side of his head, her pink dust scattering over his shoulders. "I want to come!"

Keir held back a growl. "Stay with the witches this time, Galia." The Faerie gave a pout when he glanced at her. "Now."

Galia whirled around with her tiny chin in the air and headed back into the common room.

When they were outside the apartment building, Hawk began assigning the D'Danann their duties. He ordered several of the warriors to stay and guard the witches, another group to search the skies, and five of them to go to the place called Sausalito.

Keir, Tiernan, Hawk, Kirra, and Sheridan took to the skies at once and headed across the bay to seek out the tragic scene of the crime.

The city passed below in a blur as Keir's thoughts switched alternately from their mission to Rhiannon, but as he flew over the Golden Gate Bridge, he tried to concentrate on the job ahead. The mission was of utmost importance, yet at the same time his worry for Rhiannon grew.

Wind blew past his face and ruffled his wings as it occurred to him that he was beginning to understand Hawk's and Tiernan's emotions toward their mates. Having something in common with his half-brother, Hawk, was not something he had expected.

Keir gave a great pump of his wings. He had never thought he would want one woman. To be with her. To stay with her. To keep her. To make her his.

When they located the bus, police and PSF officers were everywhere. Men and women in full white bodysuits with *HAZMAT* stenciled on the back stood off to the side with their helmets off, talking with several other police officers. The witch Hannah had explained that HAZMAT meant "hazardous materials." There were other suited and masked men and women, but they had no identification on their protective clothing.

Yellow tape surrounded the big white bus with its dark tinted windows. A crowd had gathered along the other side of the yellow tape, which fluttered in a breeze from off the bay. Officers were stationed around the circumference, ensuring no one could get through. Keir saw people with objects he knew to be cameras, while others held black things up to their mouths—microphones, he thought he had heard them called.

Officers moved in hurried but methodical movements as they went in and out of the bus, searched around it, and emptied the contents of storage compartments beneath the bus. They all wore full protective clothing and masks.

The five warriors hovered above the crowd, invisible to human eyes as long as they remained in their winged forms.

"Jake is expecting us." Hawk looked as frustrated as Keir felt at that moment.

"There." Keir pointed to a copse of large trees.

The warriors flew to the trees, climbed into the branches and shifted. One by one they eased down to the ground. When they were ready, they strode from around the trees and worked their way through the crowd to the yellow tape.

"Captain Macgregor is expecting us," Hawk said to one of the policemen guarding the area.

"Name?" the officer asked as he observed their attire—long black coats over black jeans, T-shirts, and boots.

Hawk paused and Keir said, "D'Danann."

The officer's expression was skeptical, but he turned his head and called out, "Kells, get Macgregor."

An officer in a HAZMAT suit gave a sharp nod and climbed into the bus. A moment later a suited man walked out of the bus, got closer to the D'Danann, and raised the mask he had been wearing. Jake Macgregor.

"They're part of my team," Jake said. "Let 'em through."

To keep up pretenses, Keir and his team were forced to wear full suits and what Jake called "gas masks" to avoid breathing in any foreign substance that might cause the same damage to them. The mask and clothing felt strange and uncomfortable and Keir wanted to rip it off. Not to mention he felt naked without his weapons. They'd had to change in one of Jake's big black vehicles, and leave their weapons and coats.

After following protocol, the D'Danann team was in. Hawk, Kirra, and Sheridan took the outside while Tiernan and Keir went into the bus. Even before he entered the vehicle, and despite the mask, the stench of burnt sugar hit Keir. It grew worse as he climbed in. Only Jake and one other PSF officer were inside at this moment.

"No goddamn clues." Jake's voice sounded as if it came from beneath water as he met up with Tiernan and Keir. "Two bodies look like most of their flesh was eaten right off their bones. They're in the back." He gestured as if to encompass the interior of the bus. "The rest of these look like they're mummies straight out of a sarcophagus."

Keir's face tightened as he pushed past Jake and began walking toward the back of the bus. The burnt sugar smell got worse the farther he walked.

Shriveled corpses were in various positions, most with what may have been terrified expressions. It was difficult to tell. Rhiannon had said that in her vision of the goddess, Ceithlenn had delighted in taunting her first victim, wanting him to know he was about to die. Keir would not be surprised if she had done the same to these innocents.

When he reached the back row he saw the human bones with some meat still hanging from them. The stench of the flesh and other sickening smells were enough to make him long for clean air to ease the churning in his gut.

Keir returned to the front of the bus to join Tiernan and Jake.

"Ceithlenn?" Jake asked, looking from Tiernan to Keir.

"The evidence and Rhiannon's vision tell me yes," Tiernan said,

"She sucked the souls from these bodies and ate the last two," Keir said. "I have no doubt."

"Shit." Jake braced his hands on two of the seats. "If this super-bitch isn't stopped, no telling what she'll do." His gaze roved the bus again then stopped on the driver's seat, which also held a withered corpse. "What the hell is this?"

Keir narrowed his eyes.

It looked like a black fingernail had snapped off in between the metal bar and backing of the driver's seat.

Jake dug into the pocket of his suit and pulled out a small plastic bag and a pair of tweezers. "Can't see how we missed this on first inspection," he said as he carefully pulled at the fingernail. It held for a moment as if stuck, then gave. Jake dropped it into the plastic bag.

"Ceithlenn's?" he said as he looked from Keir to Tiernan.

"We can take it to the witches." Tiernan glanced at Keir. "They might be able to divine what it is."

In an underhand movement, Jake handed the bagged finger-nail to Tiernan. "Stow this. I want it back as soon as possible after the witches check it out. Don't get any fingerprints on it."

Tiernan nodded, and Keir looked back at the shrunken bodies before returning his gaze to Jake's.

Keir let out a low growl. "I am certain we are running out of time before she strikes again."

"A Faerie?" Sydney said as she and her Coven sisters studied the diminutive blond whose wings sprinkled glittering pink dust as she stared after the departing D'Danann.

"I do not see why I could not join them," Galia grumbled.

Alyssa approached the Faerie. "Where exactly did you come from? You should be in the forest or somewhere else in nature. Not here in the middle of the Haight-Ashbury district. Did you stray from Golden Gate Park?"

The Faerie whirled, a miffed look on her features. "I came from Otherworld with Keir."

Mackenzie snorted and Alyssa giggled.

"Keir brought you with him?" Sydney said with a twitch of her lips.

The Faerie looked uncomfortable. "I . . . well, I hid in his haversack."

Rhiannon still wasn't sure whether she was glad for not swatting the Faerie like a fly for interrupting her and Keir in the basement. She hadn't been ready that day, and she wondered if she would have seen so many facets of Keir's personality if things had progressed without interruption.

"Your name is Galia, isn't it?" she asked, remembering what Keir had called her.

"Odd that he didn't send you back," Hannah said with her usual cool expression. "From what I've seen of the brute, I'm surprised he'd let something like a silly little Faerie stay."

Rhiannon bristled at Hannah's description of Keir. Anger tightened Galia's features.

"He's as much of a brute as you are a saint," Rhiannon said to Hannah with a scowl.

Haughty amusement sparked in Hannah's brown eyes as she came within inches of Rhiannon, invading her personal space. Her damned "box." Hannah smirked. "So, I was right. You *did* sleep with the barbarian."

Fury radiated through Rhiannon, causing tiny pinpricks of heat to poke at her skin and her head to hurt even worse. She clenched her right hand into a fist. This time, she really wanted to let the witch have it.

A blast of pink lightning hit Hannah in the ass.

Shock crossed Hannah's features as she went down hard, landing on her backside.

All heads turned toward the source of the pink lightning. Galia hovered, her wings beating like mad, causing large poofs of pink dust to sparkle around her. She had another tiny rod in her hand.

"Stop." Silver went up to the Faerie. "No more, okay?"

"That witch had better not call me silly or Keir a brute again." The lightning rod vanished. "Or I will make her very sorry."

Rhiannon decided she liked Galia. A lot.

As if she hadn't just been knocked on her ass, Hannah eased to her feet in one elegant movement. She reached behind her and used a bit of her magic to clean off the seat of her perfectly tailored cream slacks. She brushed the single lock of blond hair behind her ear to join her brunette hair.

"You are not the only one with magic," Hannah said in a warning tone to Galia.

"Get over it." Rhiannon's fists were still clenched. She allowed her fingers to uncurl. "You deserve to have your ass kicked."

Hannah turned her mocking glare on Rhiannon. "If I were you—"

Several men and women suddenly appeared in the large room.

Materialized. Out of nowhere.

The witches stilled.

"Fomorii!" Rhiannon cried out just as the strangers began to shift.

The Fomorii had the exit blocked.

The witches backed up in the large common room.

"Spellshields!" Silver shouted and the witches each threw up a shield, their glittering magic protecting them from the demons.

Rhiannon watched in horror as the features of the strangers melted and their bodies twisted, expanded, or deflated, morphing into demons of all sizes, shapes, and colors. Some had multiple eyes while others had one. They had any number of limbs. Some were huge while others were thin and gangly. Instantly the room filled with the smell of rotten fish.

There were at least ten of the demons in the common room.

Silver shouted, "If you're going to fight, use spellfire, and magic ropes!"

"*Gray* magic." Rhiannon's blood thundered in her ears and her vision swam from the pain in her head as she rounded up a ball of spellfire. "No mercy. We can't let ourselves get caught again. We can't kill, but we can incapacitate and bind them. These suckers need to go down. Now."

With the exception of Silver, Cassia, and Copper, every one of the witches had been caged by the Fomorii and Balorite warlocks a few months ago, just before Samhain.

And Rhiannon was going to make sure that didn't happen again. Ever.

But the witches now had their backs up against the wall.

Trapped. No way to escape.

The urge to use the dark power within her hit Rhiannon like a boulder to her chest. Black Shadows twisted in and out of her thoughts and stirred in her soul. She shook her head and almost lost her concentration on the demons.

It had to be the goddess. Rhiannon *never* lost control of her Shadows.

The Fomorii moved across the huge room toward the witches.

Rhiannon dropped her shield and flung a spellfire ball at the chest of the first demon. Dead on. The power of it knocked the creature back a good ten feet. The demon landed on one of the tables and smashed it to the floor.

A demon slammed into Alyssa's spellshield.

"Help!" she screamed, a loud scream that she must have amplified with her magic. "D'Danann! Help!"

Of course. They had to catch the attention of the warriors who were outside, guarding the entrance.

"Tegan!" Rhiannon shouted and magnified her voice magically as she flung another spellfire ball. She knew the names of at least two of the warriors who had stayed behind to guard the apartments. "Rhona!"

From her side view, Rhiannon saw Hannah and Sydney drop their shields and in a flash wound magic ropes around one Fomorii. It tripped and fell forward, flat on its face. The ropes would keep it bound as they went on to the next demon.

Mackenzie tossed her own rope of power around the neck of a demon, and the Fomorii pulled at the rope with both hands as if it were being strangled. The power of the demon fighting back jerked Mackenzie toward it. She shouted and threw up a spellshield as the Fomorii lunged at her.

Copper and Silver pitched one spellfire ball after another at the demons, driving them back. Then they whipped ropes of magic out and tried to bind those demons. Despite her foot and ankle cast, Copper was almost as agile as the rest of them.

Black Shadows flickered in Rhiannon's mind and chest as she dropped and rolled when one demon lunged for her. Even though she was flat on her back and filled with darkness and pain from her headache, she slammed the demon at its neck with a ball of spellfire. It staggered, fire whooshing up its face, and tripped over a chair.

Bolts of pink lightning struck one Fomorii after another in rapid fire. As Rhiannon scrambled to her feet, she saw

Galia flinging the bolts at the heads of the demons. The Faerie got one between the eyes and its head exploded. The Fomorii's body crumbled into black silt.

Go, Galia!

Another demon bore down on Rhiannon. Too close for a spellfire ball!

She screamed, ducked, and flung up a spellshield just in time. She felt the power of the beast as it rammed into the shield and fell back.

When she knew she had the advantage, she dropped her shield and fired another ball of magic at the head of the demon. She left charred flesh that quickly healed, but she bound the demon with a rope of magic. The witches wouldn't kill, but they would do all they could to fight them, bind them, and hope the D'Danann would come and finish them off.

Dear Anu, the demons just kept coming.

Different shouts filled the room, along with the sound of swords. Swords clanging against iron-tipped Fomorii claws.

D'Danann! Rhiannon felt a whoosh of relief, but didn't let down her guard.

She continued to fight along with her Coven sisters as the D'Danann joined the battle. The warriors didn't have the advantage of flight in the confines of the room, the close quarters making their job harder.

The only way for Fomorii to be destroyed was by beheading them or obliterating their hearts. The D'Danann preferred to wield their swords to decapitate the demons, but on occasion were forced to carve out their hearts with their daggers.

One of the D'Danann beheaded a Fomorii, but another demon jumped on the warrior's back. He shouted as he went down. Rhiannon screamed as the demon ripped open the warrior's throat and nearly took his head off with its poisonous claws.

In a mere second, the D'Danann's body sparkled and disappeared.

Dear Anu!

The warrior's death added fuel to Rhiannon's anger. She made her spellfire balls bigger, using more gray magic than ever.

The dark, the Shadows. It was becoming so hard to fight the urge to use the terrible wealth of power lurking in the corners of her soul.

She ground her teeth and flung one fireball directly at the head of the demon that had killed the warrior. Its head went up in flames and Rhona beheaded it with her sword.

The witches and Galia continued to incapacitate the demons with their magic, allowing the warriors to more easily wipe this horde of Fomorii from existence.

It seemed like the battle lasted forever, but soon all that remained were the witches, the Faerie, the remaining D'Danann, and multiple piles of black silt.

Sweat plastered hair to the sides of Rhiannon's face, her chest hurt, her head ached, and her scars burned. Her breathing came harsh and uneven.

She blinked and pinched the bridge of her nose and closed her eyes. Tears bit at the backs of her eyelids. The Shadows had never been so strong before. She'd almost lost control.

No. She could *never* do that. What would her Coven sisters think if they knew the kind of power she had inside her?

Damn Ceithlenn!

Rhiannon opened her eyes, dropped her hand from her face, took a deep breath, and immediately choked on the rotten fish stench of the Fomorii.

Everyone but the D'Danann warriors seemed exhausted and bedraggled—in other words, all of the witches looked like hell. Even Galia's hair was tangled around her and she appeared pale. The group of warriors was the younger bunch Keir had brought with him from Otherworld.

The room was a disaster. Couches slashed, grooves from claws scratched into the floor, tables smashed, one of the refrigerators knocked over, garbage strewn everywhere.

"I can't believe they got through all of our wardings," Silver said as she pushed her long silvery blond hair out of her face. "They just appeared out of thin air. How could they have done that?"

"It was probably the goddess," Sydney said as she used a broom to sweep up the Fomorii silt into one big pile with the help of Alyssa. "She could be strong enough to make them invisible and got them through. Or maybe she transported them directly into this room."

"Ceithlenn must be more powerful than we originally thought," Alyssa said with fear in her voice.

The mention of the evil goddess's name drove Rhiannon to her knees from pain.

"Rhiannon!" Sydney dropped her broom and rushed to Rhiannon's side, as did the other Coven sisters.

"Please don't say the C-word any more," Rhiannon managed to say. "Every time I hear or think that word, *that's* when my headaches start and they only get worse with each mention." She took a deep breath, holding her hand to her forehead and didn't mention the twisting of Shadows that came along with the goddess's name. "Just call her that evil goddess or the bitch from Underworld or something. Or just call her C."

"Gotcha." Sydney stroked Rhiannon's short hair in a gentle caress. "We'll be careful, honey."

"Maybe I can help her." Galia fluttered her way in between Alyssa and Mackenzie and hovered over Rhiannon. "Maybe I can see why you are getting these headaches."

Before Rhiannon could say anything, Galia held her little hands out and a wave of pink magic flowed back and forth between the two of them.

The last thing Rhiannon remembered was Galia's scream.

Chapter 15

Rhiannon snapped awake the moment someone placed smelling salts beneath her nose. Her vision cleared to see Cassia crouched before her with a concerned expression as she drew the tube away.

"Whoa." Rhiannon tilted her head back to see all her Coven sisters gathered around.

She was lying on one of the couches in the common room. She felt the shredded material beneath her from the fight with the Fomorii and a spring poked her butt. Cassia and Sydney helped her up to a sitting position and Rhiannon shifted so her ass wasn't on the spring anymore.

"I thought you were well enough to wake up," Cassia said. Her features seemed to grow more ethereal and beautiful every day. Her once short curly blond hair now rested on her shoulders in light spirals at the ends. "I sensed no damage other than what has plagued your mind."

"And that is much," came a small voice nearby. Rhiannon glanced to see Galia reclining on the arm of the couch. She had her head tilted back and held what looked like a tiny ice bag to her forehead, her wings folded beneath her. Her eyes met Rhiannon's. "We need to speak. At once."

Rhiannon nodded even though her head ached when she did. Cassia slipped her hand beneath the Faerie and lifted her up.

Galia narrowed her gaze. "You're part Elvin, aren't you?"

A smile touched Cassia's lips. "And you are Fae."

"I never thought I'd let anyone of Elvin blood touch me," Galia said, then burst into a grin. "But I like you."

Cassia laughed and raised the Faerie to her shoulder where Galia settled and began opening and closing her wings, sprinkling pink dust everywhere.

Rhiannon knew of the prejudices that ran deep between the two races, so it was a bit surprising that Galia had adjusted so easily. But then Galia appeared to be a special little Faerie. And the D'Danann warriors—most had seemed accepting enough of the few D'Anu witches who had Elvin blood.

Like Keir, Rhiannon thought and her cheeks heated.

Sydney and Alyssa helped Rhiannon to her feet. Once she gained her bearings she felt fine, and even her headache had dulled to just a throb at her forehead.

Fortunately only a few had injuries from the battle. A couple of the D'Danann had scratches that were not in areas that would be fatal. Cassia and the other witches tended to them with their magic and Cassia's potions. Mackenzie had a small gouge on one wrist, but it was taken care of and bandaged in no time.

But the death of one of the D'Danann . . . Rhiannon shuddered and her heart hurt for him. Hopefully his passage to Summerland—the everafter—would be a pleasant one, where he would join families and friends once again.

Keir and some of the other D'Danann strode into the common room. A look of fury spread across Keir's face as his gaze swept the room and landed on Rhiannon. "What were you thinking, battling the demons instead of staying behind your spellshields?"

Rhiannon rubbed her temples. *I so do not need this.*

"You expect us to just sit back and be attacked?" She moved her hands to her hips. "We're not helpless women."

"That is correct," came Galia's voice and Rhiannon saw that Galia had her arms crossed over her chest and her chin tilted.

Keir clenched his fists at his sides, but Tiernan pushed his way in front and held out a plastic bag with something small and black inside it that looked sharp.

"Jake found this on that bus." He handed the bag to Cassia. "We thought you might be able to tell if it's Ce—"

Copper slapped her hand over her husband's mouth. "Don't say the goddess's name." She let her hand slip away from Tiernan's lips as he gave her a puzzled expression. "It's what's causing Rhiannon to have those headaches."

All the D'Danann turned to look at Rhiannon, who took a deep breath. "Just call her 'C' for now."

Tiernan nodded and Keir narrowed his gaze. Cassia visibly shuddered when she held the bag Tiernan passed to her.

"It's definitely from something evil." Cassia looked at all the witches. "We need to get to the kitchen. We have protection and divination work to do."

The common room was set to rights in no time, thanks to Galia's magic. The Faerie's powers were amazing. She could make old things new, and the common room looked better than it had before the fight.

Rhiannon's Coven sisters gathered the tools of their crafts and planned to meet in the store. Rhiannon's only talent was being able to vision, and she was afraid—very afraid—that she wasn't going to be able to do anything.

Keir stopped Rhiannon as she started to head out of the common room. "Is this dangerous?" he asked in his gruff tone.

She pushed his hand from her arm and lied. "Not at all."

"I will go with you," Keir said.

With a sigh, Rhiannon looked up at him. "Listen, no one but the witches and Galia needs to be in the kitchen. We're just divining whatever we can. We've got to have some questions answered."

Which includes whatever Galia saw when she did that mind-meld thing.

Keir shook his head. "I *will* be in the room with you to ensure your safety."

Rhiannon groaned.

Keir and Sheridan escorted the witches next door to Enchantments, passing T-shirt and jean-clad guards wearing their long coats at the door to the common room as well as the entrance to the apartment building.

As usual, Rhiannon's skin tingled in what light there was in the foggy day and she squinted. Spirit appeared, and he ran circles around her feet as she walked. It was a wonder she didn't trip over him.

Once she went through Enchantments and reached the kitchen, she shivered. The encounter with the Fomorii had left her more shaken than she'd realized.

The fact that the Shadows had pushed at her mind, had threatened to come through during the fight, scared her right now more than anything.

Keir, Tiernan, and Hawk all stood a good distance from the table, obviously trying to make themselves inconspicuous so that there wouldn't be any arguments with the witches about them being there.

Soon all eight witches and Galia were gathered in the kitchen of Enchantments. More D'Danann stayed out of sight on the other sides of the doors, front and back.

The witches set all of their tools on the kitchen table while Rhiannon watched. Her pulse rate picked up as she thought about what they all were going to do. They never knew what would happen when they divined together.

Silver had her cauldron filled with consecrated water; Mackenzie, her tarot cards; Alyssa had a slender red taper candle and a dragon candleholder; Hannah was ready with her black mirror and salt crystals; Sydney arranged three candles and her silver bowl of consecrated water; and Cassia slipped her bag of rune stones from the pocket of her skirt. Copper sat between Sydney and Silver. Copper's talent was dream-visions, and Rhiannon wasn't sure if the witch had had any dreams that related to their current situation.

Everyone was standing, automatically looking to Cassia for direction. Ever since the first battle with the Fomorii, Cassia had grown more and more to be the witches' rock, the one they looked to for advice or healing.

And she baked a mean cinnamon roll.

"Before we begin"—Cassia had her hands folded in front of her as she spoke in a calm tone—"we will cast our circle to encompass the entire kitchen and weave a protection spell around us."

The witches murmured and moved into position to create a ring at the center of the kitchen. Galia hovered between Rhiannon and Sydney.

Cassia produced an athame from her skirt pocket, entered the circle of witches, and stood at the center.

With a nod to the north, Cassia turned to the east and extended her arms with the athame straight out in front of her. She began turning clockwise, deosil, moving the ritual knife from the east, continuing to the south, then the west, and ended facing north again. As she turned in the circle, she chanted.

I cast this circle as a boundary between worlds.
We ask Anu to be the protector and guardian of all who stand within.
We ask the Ancestors to add to our combined strength.
We welcome the elements. Air, Fire, Water, and Earth.
Thank you all for your protective presence as you join with us in seeking the answers to our many questions.

Once the circle was cast and the kitchen protected, the witches moved to the table, sat, and scooted their chairs close. Spirit settled himself beside Rhiannon's feet.

"We have something important to do before we begin divining." Cassia drew from her pocket the small plastic bag with the black thing in it. "We need to perform two tasks. A protection spell for Rhiannon and Galia. And," she added, "a banishing spell for Rhiannon."

Rhiannon blinked. "A banishing spell?"

"First the protection spell." Cassia's expression was unreadable. "Then Galia will explain further."

Galia sat with her knees to her chest next to a bowl of juniper berries. Also on the table were two small vials of oil; a long, tapered black candle; a match; some tiny, red-hot charcoal pieces in a fireproof bowl; and salt in a glass vial. Rhiannon felt a small wave of heat from the charcoal.

Cassia stood beside Rhiannon and Galia as she anointed the candle with the two oils then set it into Alyssa's silver candleholder that was the yawning mouth of a dragon. Rhiannon caught the scents of cypress from the oils, patchouli from the candle, and burning charcoal. Cassia lit the candle and said several words in a language Rhiannon had never heard before. Could it be Elvish? She thought she heard Cassia say "Morrigan" and Rhiannon shivered again.

The half-Elvin witch placed the juniper berries on the charcoal and the smell of the berries became sharper. Then she unscrewed the cap on the vial of salt and poured it in a circle around Rhiannon, including behind her chair. She continued to pour the salt until all the protection items and Galia were encompassed in the circle.

Cassia set the salt vial down. "Our sisters stand within the protection of the triple-goddess."

Automatically Rhiannon's hand went to her heart. "The protection of the triple-goddess lies within me."

Cassia took her seat and placed her palms on the table. "Galia, explain what you saw in Rhiannon's mind."

The Faerie took a deep breath and her gaze met Rhiannon's. "That day you blacked out, you had just visioned Ceithlenn, a warlock named Darkwolf, and a demon-woman named Junga. Not physically, but psychically you were in the room with them."

No matter the circle of protection, Rhiannon's head still ached at the mention of the goddess's name.

"Ceithlenn saw you." Galia drew her knees up closer to her chest and wrapped her arms around them. "Her magic is so powerful that she shattered that part of you that can vision. Every time you hear her name, it invokes a part of her and she delights in causing you pain for spying on her."

Rhiannon's skin went cold. "Does that mean the bitch is in *my* head?"

"In a way." Galia rocked back and forth, her wings slowly opening and closing and pink Faerie dust mingling with the salt surrounding the two of them. "That is how the Fomorii were able to penetrate the wardings and could transport into the common room. She used what essence she had stolen from you."

Rhiannon's gut churned. Ceithlenn was in her head.

In my head!

"How do we get her out?" Rhiannon's voice trembled.

Cassia settled her hand on Rhiannon's arm. "This is where the banishing spell comes in." Cassia raised the small plastic bag Tiernan had given her. Rhiannon squinted. It looked like a broken fingernail. "Thank Anu this was discovered on that bus." Cassia said. "It will help with the banishing spell."

"It's C-Ceithlenn's?" Rhiannon asked through the pain in her head, even though she was pretty sure she knew the answer.

"Yes. Through my divinations, I am positive." Cassia picked up a small mortar and its matching baseball bat–shaped pestle. Inside the rough basalt lava mortar she combined dried bay laurel leaves, black pepper, cayenne pepper, dried hydrangea blossoms, and sea salt. She ground them all to a fine powder while the witches watched. Rhiannon nearly sneezed as she breathed in some of the pepper.

When she finished grinding the ingredients, Cassia picked up the plastic baggie, unsealed it, and dumped the piece of fingernail onto the tabletop. As Rhiannon shuddered, she thought she also felt a collective shudder from all the witches.

Cassia took a small pair of scissors and snipped off a piece of the fingernail, then she produced a tiny paper envelope and a small pair of tongs. She used the tongs to put the piece of fingernail into the envelope and took the burning black taper candle to drip black candle wax onto the back flap to seal it. After she settled the candle in its holder, she placed the envelope and the tongs in front of Rhiannon.

Cassia picked up the mortar, pinched some of the ingredients between her fingers and sprinkled the powder over

Rhiannon. Some of it landed on the end of her nose and she sneezed, almost blowing out the candle.

"Burn the piece of fingernail," Cassia said in the most authoritative voice that Rhiannon had ever heard her use. "Do not stop whatever might happen."

Whatever might happen?

Rhiannon swallowed and used the little tongs to pick up the envelope. She felt the hardness of the nail as she clamped it. The tongs shook as her hand trembled when she raised the paper containing the piece of fingernail over the candle flame.

The moment the envelope burst into flame, Rhiannon heard such an incredible shrieking sound in her ears that she almost dropped the tongs.

Her eyes burned and she felt as if her heart was being ripped out. She couldn't hold back a cry of pain and held her free hand to her forehead.

The Shadows*! Oh, goddess, the* Shadows*!* Ceithlenn was taking them, releasing their blackness in Rhiannon's head. The Shadows squirmed and oozed in her mind, filling her head with dark shot through by white-hot shards of pain.

Vaguely she heard Keir's growling voice as he shouted at the witches to stop. By the sounds of the other male voices, she knew Hawk and Tiernan restrained him from intervening.

Flames continued to rise even when the envelope was long burnt away. The shrieking didn't let up. The darkness closed in on her, the Shadows ready to break free.

No! I won't let that happen!

Although her vision was clouded, she could see the piece of nail still in the tongs. Sweat poured down the sides of her face from the effort it took not to drop the tongs because of the shrieking and Shadows in her head.

Her vision grew blurry.

Rhiannon's mind swam and she felt as if something was beating on the inside of her skull trying to get out—or stay in.

Maybe both.

She struggled to focus even though she could barely see.

She ground her teeth and lowered the nail further into the candle flame.

Anu! Rhiannon cried out in her mind to the goddess for help.

Don't let the Shadows *out, Goddess, please. Don't let the* Shadows *out. Just rid my mind of Ceithlenn. Please!*

Tears streamed down Rhiannon's face as the knocking against the inside of her skull magnified. Her whole body shook but she still kept the fingernail over the flame.

She jerked in her seat. Fought the power of Ceithlenn as the evil goddess clenched her grip tighter on Rhiannon's mind, while at the same time trying to force the Shadows out.

And then what? Dear Anu. Then what?

Rhiannon brought her other hand to the tongs so that she was holding the utensil in both hands. But still she shook so hard the nail wavered. Tears flowed freely down her face.

Doing everything she could to ignore the shrieking sound, the Shadows, and the pain, Rhiannon dug deep inside herself, reaching for her faith. For the aid of the Ancestors and the protection of the Elementals. For the power of Anu that lay deep inside her. For the strength of the triple-goddess. For every bit of faith she held tight in her soul.

The fingernail crumbled to ash, falling into the pool of wax at the top of the taper. The ash vanished.

The shrieking in her head turned to high-pitched feminine laughter. Loud laughter. Evil laughter. Laughter that pounded on the inside of her skull.

Rhiannon dropped the tongs on the table. She grabbed both sides of her head and squeezed her eyes shut.

She screamed, "Get out of my head!"

But the laughter continued, and the Shadows threatened to burst from her mind and her body.

She buried her face in her hands and cried, huge wracking sobs. *No, no, no!* she told the Shadows. *Go back. Go!*

But Ceithlenn shoved and shoved. Laughed and laughed. As if it were happening somewhere outside her body—

far, far away—someone wrapped his arms around her and lifted her into his embrace. Keir. It was Keir. So far away she heard her Coven sisters speaking. Keir's growl and his harsh words.

Rhiannon gripped his T-shirt in her hands and buried her face against his chest as she cried. She was barely aware of him carrying her. The moment they left the store, light burned her eyelids and her skin tingled from what sunshine made its way through the fog.

He murmured words to her in Gaelic, words meant to soothe, but nothing would make the laughter stop or the Shadows go back where they belonged—hidden, where no one would find out about them. Where they couldn't harm anyone she knew and loved.

When they reached her apartment door she didn't have the strength to use her magic to open it. All she could do was cling to Keir.

She heard the knob jiggle and then she jerked in his arms and a cracking sound bit the air as he kicked open the door. In moments he had her in her bedroom, laying her on her bed.

Rhiannon sobbed harder and clenched her fingers in his shirt, holding him close. Her nails bit into his flesh.

Keir eased her over on the bed to lay down beside her and hold her in his arms.

Terror ripped through Rhiannon like a jagged knife.

A cry tore from her as an invisible force shoved her to a sitting position. Her back went ramrod straight and hair rose on her scalp.

Two Shadows burst from her chest.

She screamed from pain and fear.

One manlike Shadow slammed the bedroom door and locked it. Then pressed against the door as if to barricade it.

The second Shadow attacked Keir.

He gasped and clawed at his neck, right through the black Shadow that choked him.

Wheezing sounds came from Keir's throat as he struggled against a foe he could not fight with fists, sword, or dagger.

Rhiannon screamed, "No. Oh, goddess, *no*!"

The laughter in her head went on and on and more Shadows fought to escape.

Tears poured from Rhiannon's eyes as she shoved down the Shadows still inside.

At the same time she tried to draw the freed Shadows back to her.

She had to save Keir!

Banging and shouts from the D'Danann and witches came from the other side. The knob rattled. Blue and gold light bled from the spaces around the door and through the keyhole. The witches were attempting to use their magics to force their way in.

The first Shadow remained pressed up against the door. It was so powerful, it held them all back.

Keir thrashed on the bed. His face was purple, growing darker and darker. He clawed at his throat.

Rhiannon's body shook as she frantically tried to regain control of the Shadows.

"No!" She reached out her arms to call the Shadows home.

With all the strength she possessed, with every fiber of her being, she summoned the Shadows back to her.

The laughter in her mind sounded strangled as the second Shadow's hold on Keir's neck slackened. He took deep wheezing breaths.

Both Shadows fought her, but she could feel them weakening.

With one last burst of effort she yanked them to her.

The two Shadows slammed into her chest, knocking her back so hard her skull struck the headboard.

Keir was silent, his eyes closed.

He was motionless.

Heart pounding with fear for him, Rhiannon reached for Keir. She felt for his pulse, and found it. Relief surged through her. His pulse beat sure and strong.

Her head still ached but the laughter vanished.

The door to the bedroom burst open. Her Coven sisters and two of the D'Danann rushed into the room.

Rhiannon slid down the headboard so that her head was on a pillow. She curled into a ball beside Keir, exhaustion filling her from the toll the Shadows had taken by escaping. Every part of her body ached.

Silver rushed to the bedside. She held one hand to Keir's forehead and reached for Rhiannon with the other. "You— Keir. What happened?"

"I don't know." Rhiannon could barely get the words out. She couldn't tell them how the monsters inside her tore loose from her body.

"Was it Ceithlenn?" Sydney asked from behind Silver, the name causing the screeching pain in Rhiannon's head again.

"I-I think so," she said through her tears. It was partially the truth. The goddess *had* manipulated Rhiannon and forced the Shadows from her soul.

Cassia pushed through the throng and reached Rhiannon and Keir. She held her hands over Keir and iridescent sparkles swirled from his body and back—mixed with black clouds.

One of the witches gasped, but no one in the room said a word.

"I don't understand." Cassia shook her head. "Such . . . darkness." She raised her palms and the darkness rose as if she was pulling it from him.

A lump filled Rhiannon's throat and her heart pounded harder. Should she tell them?

Cassia continued to draw out every bit of blackness within Keir.

Then all that was left were iridescent sparkles between Cassia's hands and Keir's body.

Keir groaned, but did not open his eyes. Cassia lowered her hands, looking as if she might collapse herself. Rhiannon had never seen the half-Elvin witch look so tired.

Cassia came around the other side of the bed to Rhiannon. She trembled, afraid of what Cassia might see within her.

Oh, goddess, I can't lose my only family, my Coven sisters.

But what if Ceithlenn forced the Shadows forth again and they hurt one of them?

Rhiannon forced her mouth open to speak, but no words would come out. It was as if something was holding tight within her chest the words she needed to say.

"Roll onto your back," Cassia instructed Rhiannon.

She trembled. This was it, then. Her secret would be known to everyone.

Cassia held her hands over Rhiannon. Warmth traveled from Cassia's hands to Rhiannon's chest.

Blinding pain slammed into Rhiannon like a firebrand in her chest. She arched her back and couldn't stop herself from crying out. Deep black clouds marred Cassia's magic and the half-Elvin witch's eyes widened.

The more Cassia struggled to draw the darkness from Rhiannon, the more powerful the pain in her chest and head. Red-hot knives of pain stabbed her chest and made her burn. She screamed and thrashed until Cassia finally stopped.

Cassia moved her hands away from Rhiannon. Her expression was filled with shock, her voice with concern. More than concern. "The same blackness, only much, much darker than what touched Keir." Her gaze met Rhiannon's. "I can't draw it out."

Rhiannon clutched her chest with her hands. Dear Anu, how she hurt. In her mind, body, and soul.

"The—the goddess. She's still there." Rhiannon's voice sounded more like a croak. "She didn't go away."

Cassia nodded but still looked puzzled. She cast a look over her shoulder. "Someone please get Rhiannon some water."

When Cassia turned back to Rhiannon she said, "I'll get my healing herbs, potions, and oils. Maybe I can relieve at least some of your discomfort."

All Rhiannon could do was nod and close her eyes.

Chapter 16

The chill of the breeze off Alcatraz Island hit Darkwolf full in the face as he, Ceithlenn, and Junga prepared to go to the cavern beneath the island where all the Fomorii and the other creatures toiled.

After Ceithlenn loaded herself up on human protein and souls, they would join the beasts.

Darkwolf nearly shuddered.

He hoped to the gods it was only a visit and not to stay.

It was dusk and the last tour group was loading onto the cruise boat—Ceithlenn's target. He, the goddess-bitch, and Elizabeth-Junga had used transference to get to the island. Until it was time, they were staying close to the dock, but out of sight of Alcatraz's park rangers.

Darkwolf never took his eyes off Ceithlenn. She was in some kind of trance, eyes closed. Her features twisted from furious to pleased to furious again. She clenched her hands into fists, deep growls rising from her throat. Her body shook, and her lips thinned into a tight line.

Whatever was happening, it didn't look good at all.

If that wasn't the understatement of the century.

She let loose a terrible laugh that grated along Dark-wolf's spine. Like the screech of a Banshee.

Then her face turned from hideous delight to blackness.

She jerked out of her trance and gave a scream that rang in Darkwolf's ears. She thrust out one of her arms.

A bolt of magic shot through the dusk across the island.

It slammed into the last tour boat that had just pulled away from the dock.

The boat exploded.

Screams and cries rent the air. The tourists on board had been either blasted into tiny pieces or burned alive. He saw park rangers running for the boat.

Darkwolf tried not to flinch. Elizabeth-Junga stirred beside him. From the corner of his eye he saw what he thought was fear in her gaze.

Fire reached for the sky, licking at the fog like a demon's tongue. Sounds of bodies splashing into the water and constant screaming met his ears.

Not a great way to end the day with this bitch.

"So close. I almost killed her and the one she has feelings for." Ceithlenn's hair was mostly flame now, matching the fire on the water. Her eyes glowed red, her incisors dropping down so that she looked like a vampire having a serious bad hair day. "The witch shoved me out!"

Way to go, witch, Darkwolf thought but held back his smirk.

"I've got to get more souls." Ceithlenn actually sounded panicked now, her eyes wide. "I used up too much of my energy transporting those worthless demons for the attack on the witches."

Her gaze went to the tour boat. "Those souls were mine to take. Now that's all fucked up! I don't even know if I can get us back to the penthouse." Her voice lowered to a growl. "I used up my power and not one of the witches died." Her attention snapped to Elizabeth-Junga. "Your demon soldiers failed. You selected worthless scum for the attack."

The flames raging on the water highlighted Elizabeth-Junga's features. "My apologies, my goddess. I picked those who have shown the most strength as we have prepared for the great battle to come. When we will retrieve Balor."

Ceithlenn sneered and moved closer to Elizabeth-Junga.

"Obviously your soldiers need more training. Apparently you have not been doing as well as I had thought."

"Yes, my goddess." Elizabeth lowered her head, but Darkwolf saw fury on her face as she looked down. "I will go below to the cavern at once to work on their training."

Ceithlenn gave a growl that sounded like a beast from Underworld. "No."

Elizabeth's head jerked up and both she and Darkwolf stared at Ceithlenn. By the tone of her voice, he had no doubt she was up to something.

"As I have mentioned before, I have plans for the two of you." Her voice became eerily serene, her expression focused and calm.

Darkwolf's gut churned. Aided by the essence in Balor's eye, Darkwolf had participated in, even commanded human blood sacrifices to call the Fomorii from Underworld. He had influenced or forced powerful witches to become warlocks. He had corrupted, stolen, killed.

But the way Ceithlenn sucked souls from large groups of people, leaving withered husks, and the way she ate flesh from her living victims sickened him like nothing else had.

Even with Balor's eye hanging from the chain around his throat, Darkwolf regretted summoning the Fomorii and ultimately Ceithlenn. Nothing was working out the way he had planned. Not a Balor-bedamned thing.

The goddess's hair turned from flames to punk red and her incisors retracted. "I need another venue," Ceithlenn said. "A greater number of souls that I can devour in order to follow through with my plans."

Darkwolf's stomach tightened even more. He had an idea that he wasn't going to like any of her plans one damn bit.

Chapter 17

Rhiannon couldn't sleep. Images of Ceithlenn and the Shadows filled her mind. The thought that the Shadows had almost murdered Keir made her want to throw up and cry at the same time.

What have I done? She pushed herself up on one of her elbows to look down at Keir, who was still sleeping. With every rise and fall of his chest she felt both relief and remorse. She reached out to touch his stubbled jaw that felt like sandpaper beneath her fingertips.

After Cassia had used her potions, leaving them smelling of lavender, mint, and chamomile, she and the others had left to allow Rhiannon and Keir to rest.

But she couldn't rest. The pain in her head and chest was too intense.

I'm so stupid. How could I have let the Shadows escape? How could I have let them come so close to hurting, to maybe even killing Keir?

A knot formed in her throat and she had to fight back the sting of tears behind her eyes.

As Rhiannon had grown up, the Shadows had also grown in strength. They'd occasionally rattled and knocked against the lid of the mental box inside of her. Especially when she'd been in danger.

But, still, they'd remained safely locked away—

Until that day in the common room when she'd had to fight them back.

The first time they'd wanted to go after Keir.

She'd known then that Ceithlenn had been the one who'd found the key to the box . . .

And today the goddess had had the power to open Rhiannon's mental box and use the Shadows against her.

Rhiannon moved her hand from Keir's jaw to her mouth and choked back a sob. He could have been killed. The dark power inside her could have *killed* him.

Keir stirred and opened his eyes. She dropped her hand from her mouth and wrapped her arms around his neck, burying her face in his T-shirt again.

"I'm so sorry," she whispered. She turned so that her cheek was against his chest. "You could have died." He didn't say anything, but stroked her hair as she cried. "The goddess—the Shadows—too strong. I couldn't hold them back."

"Shhhh," he said and wrapped his arms around her so that he was holding her tightly. "It is all right. I am all right."

Rhiannon drew out of his embrace. He was flat on his back and she rested on one hip, bracing herself with her palm on the bed. She caressed his cheek and slipped her fingers into his dark hair. "I've always been able to control them. Since I was a small girl. Sometimes it was hard, but I made them stay inside—until now."

He furrowed his brows and gave her a puzzled expression. "What have you kept inside?"

"The Shadows," she whispered. "The one that tried to choke you and the one that barricaded the door—they came from me, not C—the goddess. She shoved them out, but they've always been there. Waiting, I think." Rhiannon shuddered and rubbed her eyes with the back of her hand. "I've never told anyone about the Shadows. No one. Not even my Coven sisters."

His dark eyes studied her. "This is some kind of power you have?"

Rhiannon wanted to look anywhere but at him, but forced

herself to meet his gaze. "I discovered the Shadows when I was a little girl, but I learned to control them." Then she whispered, "They've tried to come out. But I controlled them. Contained them. Until now."

She put a hand to her head. "I don't know what to do, Keir. I can't tell anyone. What if they're disgusted by what I really am? A witch with something evil inside her." She kept her gaze on his. "Will you tell them?" She shuddered. "How one of them almost killed you?"

Keir pulled her back into his embrace and kissed the top of her head. "No, *a stór*. That is for you to share when you are ready."

Rhiannon sniffled. Even as he held her tight and comforted her, she was afraid of what he thought of her now. "Do you think I'm a monster?" she whispered.

He rolled her onto her back so that his hands were braced on either side of her chest. His hips were between her thighs, but he held himself above her. "You are not a monster." His voice was almost a growl. "You are a woman with a good and pure heart. I know this. No matter what has become entangled deep in your soul, you are Rhiannon, my treasure."

Keir lowered his head and his lips met hers. He just brushed them lightly across her mouth. Taking nothing, demanding nothing.

Right now she wanted to forget everything else—to push it away and be with this man. The fact that she could have lost him made her chest ache in ways she couldn't define.

She wrapped her arms around his neck and pulled him down so that their lips met harder. He groaned and teased her lower lip by biting it and she opened her mouth and let out a soft moan. He worked magic as he delved inside her mouth with his tongue and and tangled it with hers. He bit her lip again, so gently, so sensuously, it made her shiver.

His cock pressed against her belly, and she wanted to feel its length and girth inside her. She wanted the healing of their lovemaking.

She whimpered as they kissed and she brought her hand between them and rubbed the jeans covering his cock. He groaned and she undid the top button of his Levi's and tugged the zipper down. He didn't wear any underwear, and his cock slid out to meet her hand and she slipped it up and down his erection.

"Make love to me now, Keir." She moved her lips along the scar on his cheek. "Please come inside of me."

With a low growl, Keir pushed up her blouse and pulled on her bra, causing her breasts to jut out. All thoughts of pain and hurt and fear fled her mind as he suckled each of her nipples. She moaned with every lick and light bite.

He tugged at her skirt so that it was around her waist. He moved his hips up and down, rubbing his cock against her belly and her drenched panties. She reached up and wrapped her arms around his neck and tangled her fingers in his long black hair.

Keir grasped the side of her panties and yanked it so that the delicate material tore. He did the same to the other side of her underwear, then tossed the scrap away.

Rhiannon could barely breathe. His look was so intense . . . and caring.

He wrapped one of his hands around his erection and pushed his cock into her core just a fraction. She shivered, knowing what was coming next. Anticipating it. He reached up and took her arms from around his neck and laced his fingers in hers. He stretched her arms way over her head at the same time he drove his cock into her core.

Rhiannon gasped, then sighed at the pleasure of having him inside of her. It felt so good, so right.

His T-shirt brushed her nipples, making them beyond hard and sensitive. She wrapped her legs around his hips and felt the powerful flex of his taut ass beneath his jeans as he took her. She fell into the pleasure of the rhythm of his movements and under the spell of his gaze as his dark eyes met with hers.

Everything else slipped away for the moment.

His cock touched that sensitive spot inside her and she felt a climax building so fast it was like a storm rising within her. A storm that matched the intensity in his gaze and the growing power of his thrusts. With her arms over her head, her fingers interlocked with his, she felt both helpless and empowered at the same time.

Keir murmured words in Gaelic. Somehow hearing him speak in a language she didn't understand made her hotter, pushed her that much closer to reaching orgasm.

She clenched her thighs tighter around his hips and cried out with every brush of his chest over her nipples, every stroke of his cock in her core.

Everything seemed to spiral inside her at once. Sensation gathered in her abdomen, deep heat grew into a blazing inferno that shot its flames through her from her pussy to the ends of her fingers and her toes. She cried out louder than she had before. Her other climaxes with Keir had all been so unbelievable, but this one was different. It rocked her in ways that none of the other orgasms had done. And, yes, it was almost . . . healing.

She was so lost in the sensations, the feelings, the fire, that she barely heard Keir's shout, barely felt the pulse of his cock inside her. She shuddered with another wave of pleasure as he released her hands and drew her close, his cock still inside her as he pulled her with him.

Rhiannon snuggled up next to him. It might be temporary, but at this moment, all she cared about was being in Keir's arms.

And forgetting the terrors dwelling inside her.

The following morning, Rhiannon made her way into Enchantments. A heaviness had settled in her belly as soon as she woke to find Keir gone.

She hadn't even had the desire to dress in vivid colors like she normally did. She'd dug out a simple white blouse, blue jeans, and blue jogging shoes. As usual she wore her jewelry, but she didn't feel as protected this time.

Her head ached and her chest hurt, and she knew Ceithlenn and the Shadows were there . . . waiting.

Spirit silently ran circles around her feet as they went to

the New Age café/store. When she glanced down at him she could swear a reproachful look was on his face, as if he didn't think she should be out of bed.

Once she was in the store, before she went to the kitchen, Rhiannon stopped at the jewelry counter, where a college student was manning the register. The witches, of course, couldn't begin to have time to run the store—certainly not while fighting evil. So they hired college students as employees. Their Coven needed the income and it gave a semblance of normalcy to what was currently an abnormal life.

She smiled at the student briefly before going to the back of the jewelry case and opening it. She withdrew a gold pagan protection-knot pendant on a long chain and slipped it over her neck. She needed all the help she could get.

After the employee had logged in her purchase on the computer, she headed to the kitchen. She nodded to another employee handling the café business then pushed open the swinging door to the kitchen with Spirit at her heels.

Rhiannon came up short as she saw that all of her Coven sisters were sitting around the table with their divination tools, and Galia was perched on the back of Cassia's chair.

They all glanced at her. "Shouldn't you be in bed?" Sydney asked, concern on her features.

Rhiannon's belly twisted and her body flushed with heat. She hoped the anger and hurt didn't show on her face. "You're divining without me?"

Cassia gave Rhiannon a look that was nonjudgmental. "If you think you're well enough to join us, then we would have it no other way."

Rhiannon raised her chin and pulled up a seat between Alyssa and Cassia.

Cassia said to all the witches, "When it's your turn to divine, put the remaining piece of fingernail near you so that it's possible to get readings from it that will help with your visions."

Rhiannon shuddered and goose bumps sprouted on her skin at the sight of the fingernail. The pain in her head and chest was almost unbearable.

"I'll go first." Alyssa used the small tongs off the table to place the nail near the red taper in front of her. She set the tongs down and adjusted the dragon candleholder. "I've chosen red to summon defense against that which threatens or opposes." Alyssa used a match to light the candle, sending a breath of the apple-scented candle as well as the smell of sulfur Rhiannon's way. Alyssa added, "The dragon is for protection, love, and healing."

Alyssa's soft brown curls settled around her face as she gazed into the dancing flame. Her talent was causmomancy, the ability to see the past, present, or future in fire. Rhiannon's heart rate picked up as she watched Alyssa's light complexion grow paler.

When Alyssa looked up at the circle of witches, her brown eyes were wide. Her throat worked as she swallowed. "I saw her. It was C—the goddess, just as Copper, Silver, and Rhiannon have described her. She *did* get on that bus and suck the souls out of all those people." Her voice trembled and a tear rolled down her cheek. "And she ate—she ate—"

Alyssa pushed away from the table, bolted for the sink, and retched. Cassia went to her and gently stroked Alyssa's curls as she helped the witch catch her breath and rinse her mouth out. When Alyssa returned to the table she stared blindly at the taper, her face whiter than pearls.

Rhiannon squeezed Alyssa's hand under the table. "It's okay, honey. We know. You don't have to think about it anymore."

Alyssa nodded, but a tear still tracked down her cheek.

The next person to go was Hannah. The matter-of-fact, *pain-in-the-ass* witch had her black scrying mirror in front of her. After she used the tongs to move the fingernail to her, she took a vial of sea salt crystals and poured some onto her palm.

Hannah held her hand high and studied the patterns of the salt crystals in the air as they trickled from her hand. When each crystal had landed on the mirror, she turned her attention to its dark surface.

Like always, the salt scattered across the surface of the black glass, but not one grain fell off its edges—part of the magic of the mirror and Hannah's divination talent. The mirror was held within an ornate frame of two dragons, each biting the tail of the other so that it was a never-ending circle.

Hannah's single chunk of blond hair swung forward as she studied her mirror and the salt crystals. With an annoyed expression she swept the hair behind her ear to join with the dark brown hair. Her talent was alomancy, the ability to analyze the grains of salt as they were tossed into the air and the patterns they made as they fell on the mirror.

That's Hannah. Always analyzing, Rhiannon thought.

Hannah's lips thinned and her brown eyes narrowed. When she raised her head, a scowl shadowed her beautiful features. "More Fomorii than we thought escaped Underworld before the door was shut. Not to mention other wicked creatures I can't define in my mirror. We're outnumbered. Way, way, way outnumbered. There aren't enough D'Danann, PSF officers, or witches to fight them all."

A sick feeling weighted Rhiannon's gut even more. "Our fight in the sewer and the one here in the common room— those battles didn't eliminate a good portion of the demons?"

Hannah's expression didn't change. "Not even close."

Sydney sucked in a deep, audible breath. "Okayyyy. With that happy news, are you ready to go next, Mac?"

"Sure." Mackenzie moved the fingernail in front of her, far enough away that she could lay her tarot cards out on the table. She used a Celtic cross spread. As she flipped cards her expression turned from confusion, to thoughtfulness, to what looked like fear.

Mackenzie looked up at her Coven sisters as she spoke. "In a nutshell, a big storm is brewing and it doesn't look good for us or humanity at large. The cards aren't giving me much to go on other than a lot of doom and gloom. I can't see the outcome—but things are about to get a lot worse."

"Great," Rhiannon muttered. "Just freaking great."

Sydney didn't say anything as she set the fingernail in front of her silver bowl of water. She used a match to light the fat pillar candles. "Lilac for clairvoyance," Sydney said as she lit it, then continued on to the next. "Orange for mental energy, purple for psychic powers."

Without hesitation, Sydney took the lilac candle, tilted it over the bowl of consecrated water, and let the wax drip into the bowl. She repeated the process with the orange and purple candles as well, and Rhiannon caught the scents of oranges and lilacs.

Sydney used ceromancy, the art of seeing the past, present, and future through the patterns of melted wax in water.

When her eyes met those of the witches around her, she slowly shook her head. "The goddess is more of a danger than ever. The more souls she devours, the stronger she becomes." She paused and frowned. "She loses some, maybe a great deal, of that power whenever she uses it. It took a lot out of her to help the Fomorii infiltrate our warded common room." Sydney adjusted her elegant glasses. "She's got something much bigger planned. I just can't see what it is."

Copper sat next to Sydney. Copper's talent was dream-visions, but she still moved the fingernail in front of her and stared at it. Her honeybee familiar, Zephyr, buzzed from where he perched on Copper's ear. "My dreams have been weird." She looked up. "I haven't been able to get a grasp on what they mean. I see flashes of the creatures that were let out before Silver and I shut that particular door to Underworld. Lots of them. In my dreams I've also seen two monstrous demon-like beings. They're hideous, but they almost seem familiar." She looked apologetic. "That's all I've got for now."

Silver grimaced as she used the tongs to move the nail in front of her pewter cauldron. She stood and leaned over to look into her cauldron, then stepped back as tendrils of fog began to rise and take shape.

Copper's eyes widened as the shapes became three-dimensional. "Those are the two monstrosities I was talking about," Copper said with a catch in her voice.

Rhiannon's stomach fell as she saw the creatures. One was hulking and blue, the other had shaggy black hair and tanned skin. Their features were twisted, mottled, and gruesome, and they both had horns.

Silver glanced at her blood sister and frowned when she looked back at the images above the cauldron before they faded away. Silver sat in her chair again. "What in the Underworld could they be?"

"A new threat." Cassia took the fingernail with the tongs and placed it about a foot from her. She tossed her rune stones onto the table and studied them.

"Yes," she said almost right away. "These two beings are created from magic—or will be. I can't tell if it's come to pass yet. They will be difficult to defeat."

"Great." Rhiannon's hand shook as she took the tongs and moved the nail until it was a few inches from her. Pain engulfed her, but she fought to keep it from showing. She had to do this.

"Here goes." She looked to each of her Coven sisters. "Everyone hold hands." Rhiannon gripped Cassia's hand on one side of her and Alyssa's on her other.

Galia fluttered down to sit on Cassia's and Rhiannon's clasped hands. The Faerie was silent and looked grim like the rest of them.

"Close your eyes." Rhiannon closed her own and tried to relax but the pain in her head made it nearly impossible at first. Spirit twined himself around her ankles. She felt her familiar's power and the energy of all the witches around her. It sizzled through her like an electrical charge. For a short moment she felt exhilarated and her mind was free— sailing through San Francisco's foggy skies and over the blue-green bay.

She mentally came to an abrupt stop over Alcatraz.

And then dived down.

Fast. Faster yet.

She almost screamed as she went through concrete, brick, and dirt.

When she regained her mental footing, Rhiannon stood

on a precipice overlooking a huge cavern that looked like it had been scooped out by a giant spoon, no matter that the walls were solid rock.

A sea of demons, three-headed dogs, Basilisks, and other creatures were in the cavern.

A sea of them.

Rhiannon's eyes snapped open.

Her heart pumped in her throat.

Pain splintered in her head.

Everyone around her opened their eyes, too.

Rhiannon squeezed Cassia's and Alyssa's hands to keep from grabbing her head in her own hands from the pain. She didn't want anyone to see how powerfully this was affecting her.

"Did you see?" Rhiannon asked in a trembling voice.

Everyone nodded.

Copper cleared her throat. "We're in deep shit."

Chapter 18

In the common room, the witches discussed their divinations with the lead D'Danann warriors and PSF officers. Spirit sat in Rhiannon's lap and the Faerie perched on her shoulder. Rhiannon felt a kinship with Galia after what they'd been through.

Cassia explained about the Coven's visions, emphasizing the sheer number of demons and other creatures they had to face.

"There's no way we can attack them where they're hiding out," Rhiannon said. "There's too freaking many of them."

"I do not remember such a large number being freed before the door was closed," Tiernan said with a puzzled expression, and Keir nodded his agreement.

Copper sat with her ankle and foot cast up on a chair. "I don't, either, but it looks like more were already here than we thought or a lot more escaped than we noticed. We *were* a little busy trying to get that door closed."

"We need more help from the D'Danann." Silver pushed her silvery blond hair from her face. "We can't do this alone."

"There may be others who can join in on this fight, too." Cassia brought her hands in front of her as she looked at the warrior leaders. "But first the D'Danann."

Hawk folded his arms across his chest. "I will go to the Chieftains."

"Nay." Keir stepped forward and glared at his half-brother before looking back to Cassia. "I must speak with them. Tiernan is in exile, Hawk still holds the Chieftains' displeasure."

Hawk growled. "I can deal with them."

A rumble rose up in Keir's chest. "You are incapable of seeing what is best for the whole."

Hawk stepped forward, fists clenched.

Cassia moved between them. "Cease this," she commanded, again in an authoritative voice that was so unlike her usual tone. She looked from Keir to Hawk. "Keir is meant to make this journey."

"The Chieftains—they have been more than conservative." Sheridan's pretty blue eyes were harsh as she spoke. "They have refused to involve too many of us in this war."

Keir pushed his hand through his hair. "I will convince them."

"Perhaps you should take the witch who visioned the great number of warriors, to explain it to the council," Kirra said, then pursed her mouth into a thin line.

Keir and Rhiannon looked at one another.

"Aye," Keir said. "I will be able to keep you safe, as well."

"No." With a frown, Rhiannon shook her head. "I need to be here, to fight. And I don't need *you* to keep me safe. I don't need anyone to keep me safe."

"Rhiannon." Cassia moved closer and touched Rhiannon's arm. "I think it will be in our best interest for you to go to Otherworld. We need you to help sway the Chieftains."

"Cassia, the timing is too crucial." Rhiannon gestured to those in the room. "Everyone here's in danger."

"Excuse us." Cassia gave a nod to the group as she turned to the hallway. Rhiannon took her cue and stood, Spirit bounding from her lap with a loud meow, then followed Cassia out into the hallway.

When they were out of hearing distance, Cassia said, "You and Keir need to go today."

Rhiannon studied Cassia. She thought of the half-Elvin witch as a friend, but also someone who was still a mystery to her in a lot of ways. "What are you talking about?"

"Not only do you need to see the Chieftains, you must go to the Great Guardian." Cassia had a solemn look about her. "You need to seek her counsel."

Rhiannon blinked, overwhelmed at the mere thought. "The Great Guardian? Why me and Keir? Why not Hawk and Silver? From what I understand, Hawk has a longtime relationship with the Guardian."

Cassia took Rhiannon's hands and squeezed her fingers. "Close your eyes, Rhiannon Castle."

Rhiannon's eyelids shut as if pressed with gentle fingers. At once her body heated and she felt a spell wrap around her body like a protective lover's arms. The only connection she had to reality was Cassia's grip on her fingers.

Rhiannon felt more than saw this vision. Colors and light swirled around her and a powerful presence touched her that must have been the Great Guardian herself. And answers. Somehow there were answers to questions she had buried deep inside. About her past, her present, maybe even her future. The future of all of those she cared about.

The colors faded, her body cooled, and she no longer felt as if she was wrapped in a cocoon of protection. She raised her eyelids and looked into Cassia's blue eyes. Eyes full of mystery and answers to questions beyond Rhiannon's understanding.

"Do you see now why you must go?" Cassia released Rhiannon's fingers and she felt a sense of loss that surprised her.

"I think so." Rhiannon pushed her short hair behind both ears at the same time, before clasping her hands in front of her. "I feel like it's important even though I'm not sure why."

Cassia smiled. She'd always had beautiful, translucent skin, but every day she seemed to glow a little bit more, as if there was a being of light hidden inside her.

Rhiannon shook off the thought and focused on what she and Keir needed to do. She frowned and looked at Cassia as a thought occurred to her. "Why Keir? Why does he need to come with me?"

Cassia said, "Keir has questions that need to be answered as well."

"It seems everyone does." Rhiannon moved her hand to the gold protection knot at her chest. "Lots of questions."

After they each had gathered together a few belongings for the trip, Rhiannon reluctantly went with Keir. He had tried to get Galia to return to Otherworld, but she'd fled and hidden where he couldn't find her.

Rhiannon and Keir walked with Cassia to Golden Gate Park. The park was beautiful, around a thousand acres, more than a million trees, several lakes and ponds. There were parts of the park that no one knew of save the witches and the Elementals. Their magic kept anyone from crossing the borders of their private realms.

The park smelled so good. Of grass, cypress, and the wind off the Pacific Ocean.

Cassia escorted them to a hidden bridge, a doorway to Otherworld that only beings with Elvin blood could pass through. They could also escort those who couldn't go without assistance.

When they reached the bridge, Cassia touched Rhiannon's arm, "You know Elvin blood runs deep in your veins. You'll be able to cross and take Keir with you."

"You've said that before, that I've got Elvin in me." Rhiannon bit her lower lip before continuing. "But I have a hard time believing it."

When she looked at Keir he was frowning. "You are part Elvin?"

"A little, I guess." Rhiannon narrowed her gaze. "Don't tell me you're prejudiced, too."

"No." He hitched his pack over his shoulder. "But the Chieftains are."

Rhiannon rolled her eyes to the treetops that waved in a soft breeze. "Well, that's just freaking great."

"It'll be fine." Cassia's words brought Rhiannon's attention back to her. "Travel well."

"That and bring back a blessed lot of warriors," Rhiannon muttered.

"Take Keir's hand and walk across." Cassia gestured toward the bridge. "Don't stop, just continue until you are in Otherworld."

Otherworld. To be honest, Rhiannon had been curious about it after Copper and Silver got to visit.

Keir grabbed her hand and she shivered as tingles radiated through her. She glanced up at him and saw the possessiveness in his gaze and she wanted to draw away. He was carrying this whole thing too far. Great sex, but too high on the maintenance side.

Rhiannon looked straight ahead as she and Keir walked onto the bridge. She'd changed and had chosen to wear blue jeans and a neon pink T-shirt, along with neon pink running shoes. Her duffle bag was the same color. She'd thought about wearing all black—briefly—just to blend in, but it wasn't her style and damned if she was going to let anyone dictate what she wore.

Keir had decked out in his leathers again. He looked so hot—in leathers or jeans, or especially nothing at all.

The wooden bridge creaked beneath their shoes and the peeling paint was rough beneath her palm as she let it slide over the railing.

When they reached the center of the bridge, Rhiannon felt as if she was being sucked into some kind of vortex.

Everything went black and she stifled a gasp.

It was like walking through cotton and it was going up her nose, in her ears, down her throat.

She couldn't breathe.

And then she stumbled out into grass and trees. Rhiannon sucked in a deep breath of pure, clean air. She drew her hand from Keir's and looked behind her. The bridge was gone and all she saw was solid rock.

Way weird.

Then it hit her. She was free of the headaches!

She took another deep mind-clearing breath. The connection between her and Ceithlenn must have been severed when Rhiannon had crossed over.

At least for now.

Dear Anu, she could just melt into a puddle of pain-free relief right here and now.

She still felt the Shadows trying to wriggle free, but the ache was less and their pull not so intense.

Rhiannon let Keir take her hand again and they walked into a large wooded area. It was beautiful. Beyond beautiful. Trees she was familiar with, others she wasn't. When she glanced up she saw a sky so blue it was like looking into a perfect sapphire.

Flowers as bright as most of her clothing and possessions at home grew in patches and birds sang and chirruped. As she listened she realized birds weren't all she heard. Faerie song was on the breeze, too.

She couldn't stop looking around. Huge trees, enormous trees, trees bigger than homes. Some looked like they had faces in them, and she swore she saw one blink—probably a Dryad, a ruler of the trees.

Dead leaves and pine needles crunched beneath her shoes, but Keir didn't make a sound. Something about being Fae, she guessed. She'd noticed before how remarkably quiet the D'Danann were on a mission.

Rhiannon came up short when she caught sight of a bunch of Faeries playing in a hollow. Children laughing and giggling—even smaller versions of Galia—and adult Faeries who were playing with them. Every Faerie had a different color of dust that glittered from his or her wings and Rhiannon caught the scents of lilies, jasmine, and roses.

Keir was a fairly good guide and pointed out various sights along the way to the village. Rhiannon saw Pixies, Brownies, even an Undine, a water nymph, when they passed a pond. Rhiannon was breathless with excitement when they reached the village.

Towering trees held homes while other houses surrounded the little town. At the far end of the village stood tall black gates just past what Keir called the Council Chambers, where the Chieftains held meetings. It looked more like a small castle from medieval times with its thick gray stone blocks and turrets.

"I must make arrangements to speak with the Chieftains in the morning." Keir released her hand when they reached the village and guided her by his hand at the small of her back. "You will wait for me at the tavern."

Rhiannon shot him a look, and he sighed. "Please."

When they walked into the village it was like stepping back in time. Street vendors, pubs, cobblestone streets, and people dressed as if they were from some point in the Middle Ages. There was laughter and chatting, and horses made *clip-clop* noises as their hooves struck the stone street.

Men and women wearing much the same garb as Keir greeted him with nods or slaps on the back, or the hand-to-elbow grip handshake. Each time Keir introduced her, the men and women D'Danann gave her curious looks. Some narrowed their eyes and she wondered if they could sense she was part Elvin. Others had teasing glints in their gazes when looking at Keir. All were more than polite.

Rhiannon breathed a deep sigh of relief when she was finally seated in the corner of the pub and Keir left her when he was certain she was okay. Smells of malt, roasted meat, and fresh-baked bread mingled with the sweat of men and women in the pub's close quarters. She looked around in curiosity and received just as curious stares. She liked to stand out, and boy was she standing out. As a stranger and wearing bright pink.

While Keir was gone, she took the time to enjoy the freedom from Ceithlenn in her mind. She felt so liberated and at ease right now. She hoped she'd severed the connection for good by crossing over. Eventually the trials of the past few days had caught up with her and she felt exhausted. But now headache-free exhausted.

When Keir returned he told her the meeting was set then ordered two ales, roast chicken, potatoes, cheese, and bread. Witches didn't normally drink alcohol because it slowed their reflexes, but right now she didn't care. She was thirsty, tired, overwhelmed, not to mention worried about the upcoming council meeting and what might be happening at this very moment back in San Francisco.

When their food arrived, Rhiannon was surprised that it was served in a long, wooden, curved platter that Keir called a trencher. The food was delicious, practically orgasmic. The ale was a different taste for her, but she got used to it. Keir drank about five pints in the time it took her to drink two.

While they ate they said few words to each other. It was so noisy in the pub that her ears rang from it. After Keir paid their tab, Rhiannon stood—and promptly sat back down. Her head spun and she had to hold onto the table to keep from toppling over.

"I think I might have had a little too much to drink," she said, but her words were lost in the pub's raucous noise.

Keir helped her to her feet and caught her to him when she swayed. He grabbed both their travel bags and kept his arm tight around Rhiannon's shoulders as they worked their way out of the pub.

When they left, it was dark outside. Rhiannon's eardrums had been battered so much by the noise she felt like they were crammed with wax.

She breathed in the clean air and glanced up at the stars. Mistake. They swirled and she would have dropped if Keir didn't have such a tight grip on her shoulders.

"What is wrong, *a stór?*" Keir held her up as they walked down the cobblestone street.

She hiccupped. "I—I've never had ale before."

Keir chuckled. He actually *laughed*. It was dark save for a sliver of moonlight, but when she looked up the corner of his mouth was quirked into the semblance of a smile.

What is the world coming to? Uh, Otherworld. Yeah, that's it.

"Come," he said in a gentle tone. "We will go where you can sit or lie down."

With Rhiannon's head on his shoulder, they walked through the woods until they came to a cabin. Keir opened the door and Rhiannon saw a basic but spacious home with chunky wood furniture, a fireplace, and a door leading to what she assumed must be a bedroom. When she glanced around the cabin again, she noticed a rocking chair in one corner, near carved figurines lining a windowsill.

"I like it." Rhiannon looked up at Keir and smiled. "It's totally you."

He gently kissed her. "You need to lie down," he murmured and Rhiannon sighed, a sense of peacefulness washing over her.

Must be the ale.

Keir escorted her into the bedroom where there was a huge bed with what looked like a pillowy mattress.

Still feeling tipsy, Rhiannon grinned, turned her back on it and let herself fall into its softness. Did it ever feel good—like the mattress was totally filled with feathers.

"You have now destroyed all my illusions." Rhiannon kicked off her pink running shoes and wiggled so that she was completely on the bed. "I figured you slept with a single blanket on a pile of rocks."

His expression was amused when he lay down beside her so that they were facing each other on the bed. He propped his head in his hand and his elbow sank into the mattress. With the fingers of his free hand, he made a trail from the curve of her jaw, down her neck, over her shoulder, and along her arm until his hand settled on her waist. His palm felt warm through her T-shirt and his eyes heated her through.

Rhiannon smiled as she looped her arms around his neck and pulled him down for a kiss.

Chapter 19

"Mmmmmm," Rhiannon said as she kissed Keir. He tasted of ale and man, pure man.

Keir moved his hand from her waist to cup one of her breasts. She drew away and looked into his dark eyes. "I want to know more about you, Keir." He cocked an eyebrow and she continued, "I don't know anything about your past, your childhood, what you do when you're not off saving people. Or beings. Or whoever."

He sighed and moved his hand back to her waist. For a long moment he looked at her and thoughtfulness filled his gaze. He finally said, "What would you like to know?"

She reached up and stroked the scar on his cheek. "How did you get this?"

Keir scowled and she knew she'd hit a big sore spot. "From Hawk, when we were children. It was not his fault, though."

"You two are brothers, aren't you?" she asked as she continued to stroke his scar.

His scowl deepened. "I am the bastard son of our father."

She brought her fingers to his stubbled jaw. "Your father had an affair?"

"Aye. With a Mystwalker. My mother left me with my father and his wife."

"They didn't treat you very well, did they." It came out as a statement, not a question.

His features darkened. "I do not wish to speak of that anymore."

"Okay." She moved her fingers to his lips and his expression softened until she dropped her hand away and said, "You were going to tell me about your scar."

Keir sighed as if facing the inevitable. "When we were very young, Hawk and I fought, constantly. He stayed in the main house while my stepmother forced me to live in the barn."

Rhiannon's heart jerked. How could they have been so cruel?

"We used to play with wooden swords," Keir continued, "but one day when we were close to the age of ten, Hawk picked up a new training sword. I went to block his blow, his sword broke my wooden one, and his blade flayed open my cheek."

Rhiannon touched his scar again. "Why didn't it heal well? You're D'Danann."

"The blade had traces of iron." He held his hand over hers and it rested against his face. "An enemy of my father planted it there to harm Hawk—my father's favored son—but he picked it up, not I. Either of us could have died. Iron is deadly even to gods in large quantities or in certain parts of the body."

"Did your father find the enemy who planted the sword?"

"Aye." Keir took her hand from his face and squeezed her fingers. "My father killed him. I think because of the threat to Hawk, not because of my injury."

"Is that why you and Hawk don't get along?"

"No." Keir laced their fingers together. "Our rivalry started when we were young. He constantly taunted me and I retaliated. Although, to be fair, I provoked him just as much and he found ways to get even as well."

"Like what?" Rhiannon asked softly.

He looked down at their joined hands, cleared his throat, and looked back at her. "I dug a pit and filled it with snakes—they were not harmful, but when he fell into the pit, the fear was too much for him. He fears snakes to this day. I regret that. And not because my father whipped me until my back was a bloody mess—like he always did—but because . . ." He shook his head and let out a low growl. "Do not mind my words."

Rhiannon's heart hurt for the little boy who had been forced to live in a barn and had been whipped by his father. "Is your rivalry with Hawk because he was the favored one, and you were treated like crap?"

Keir released her hand to pinch the bridge of his nose with his thumb and forefinger. He dropped his hand away and looked at her again. "Perhaps our rivalry extended from my jealousy of him."

"How close are you in age?" she asked, wanting to reach out to him and hold him close to her.

He shrugged one large shoulder. "A year apart. But our sparring has lasted centuries. Our rift is too far to span."

"Hey." Rhiannon leaned forward and lightly kissed him before drawing back again. "It's never too late."

Keir merely looked at her. He moved his hand to her cheek and brushed his knuckles over her own scars. Instead of feeling like the scars were on fire, they felt cooled and soothed by his touch. "Junga did this to you?"

Rhiannon nodded.

He scowled. "I will kill that bitch-demon before this war is over."

When Rhiannon pressed him, Keir told her more about his child- and adulthood. The Tuatha D'Danann had all been lesser gods, children of the goddess Anu.

To gain control of the beautiful country of Ireland, the D'Danann battled the Fomorii. At that time, the Fomorii were sea gods that served the evil god Balor.

It took many months, but finally the D'Danann were triumphant in battle.

After their defeat, the Fomorii were relegated by the greater gods to live as demons banished to a part of Otherworld. However, the demons performed more evils and were thrown into Underworld, where the god Balor and his wife, Ceithlenn, had been exiled.

Ireland enjoyed a long period of peace and prosperity under the rule of the D'Danann, but eventually that peace was shattered. The D'Danann were forced to fend off an attack by the Milesians, gods from Spain.

The D'Danann lost the great battle. Once defeated by the Milesians, the D'Danann left to live in Otherworld, no longer Celtic gods, but warrior Fae living in their own Sidhe.

"What was it like to be a god?" Rhiannon asked, finding it hard to believe she was in bed with a former *god*.

Keir shrugged one shoulder again. "It was not a lot different than it is today. We can live forever—as long as Otherworld remains our home. Before, we could have lived forever in any world."

Rhiannon moved her fingers to settle on his muscled biceps. "Does it work for anyone else who comes to live here? The living forever thing."

His dark eyes studied her. "No one dies of old age in our Otherworld."

She smiled. "That must be nice."

"When one is more than two thousand years old, years are but a blink of an eye."

Rhiannon widened her gaze. "You are more than two thousand?"

He nodded. "Aye."

"Whoa." She squeezed his biceps. "You hold up well for an old man."

Keir rolled her over onto her back so fast it was a blur. "This old man can still pleasure a woman like none other."

His long black hair tickled her cheeks and his dark eyes were filled with desire. He pressed his cock between her thighs and she wished she didn't have her jeans on. She wanted that hardness inside her, *now*.

"Take them off." Keir was obviously of the same mind as he rose up on his knees between her thighs.

She hurried to unbutton her jeans and unzipped them, but Keir had her stripped out of them, her panties, and socks faster than she could catch her breath. He loosened the ties on his leather pants and released his cock.

Rhiannon's folds grew wetter and her body ached to feel him inside her. She wrapped her bare legs around his leather-clad hips and gripped him tight, bringing them closer together. His expression was fierce as he placed the head of his erection at the entrance to her channel and she groaned as she rose up and tried to take him inside her.

What they had shared made her need to feel this closeness with him.

Keir placed his hands to either side of her shoulders and captured her mouth with his at the same time he thrust deep. Rhiannon cried into his mouth and brought her hips up as he slammed his cock into her. His leather pants chafed the insides of her bare thighs, and his balls slapped her pussy with every movement.

This was no slow, sensual mating. This was a good hard fuck that felt primal, wild, raw. She pulled her T-shirt and her bra up to bare her breasts so that she could feel his leather shirt against her nipples.

He slowed his pace long enough to help her completely out of her clothing and then resumed his hard and fast pace.

"How long can an old man like you last?" she asked as she squeezed her thighs tighter around his hips.

"How long can you breathe?"

Rhiannon would have laughed but she was too into the pleasure he was giving her.

Her breasts bounced with every thrust and his leather clothing abraded her bare skin. Cries and whimpers found their way from her throat.

When she hit her climax, it was as wild as their lovemaking had been. Hard jerks of her body. Deep spasms in her core. Heat rushing to every part of her. Hair tingling at her scalp and her cries loud and long.

Keir continued thrusting and thrusting. Taking her hard. Long. Fast.

The feel of him after having experienced such an intense climax caused another one to build and she cried out again.

"Am I such an old man?" he asked as he drew out her orgasm with every stroke.

"No." She squirmed, trying to breathe as her body vibrated. "Goddess, no."

He gave her a wicked smile then forced his hips firmly against hers and growled as he climaxed. He bucked against her and clenched his teeth as her channel squeezed down on his cock, drawing out his orgasm.

Keir remained pressed tight to her as he looked down at her. Her breasts rose and fell with her breathing and sweat trickled down the side of her face and into her now damp hair.

"Are you ready for this old man to fuck you again?" he said.

Rhiannon swallowed, not sure how much more she could take. He'd almost worn her out with that first round. "What if I say yes?"

In a fast movement, he withdrew his cock, flipped her onto her belly. "Hands and knees, woman."

Woman?

What the hell. The sex was too damn good.

She rose onto her hands and knees and he began palming her ass. He rubbed his callused hands over her, then squeezed handfuls of her flesh. Rhiannon moaned when his long hair tickled her ass. Such a sensual caress that about drove her crazy.

He bit her ass and she cried out.

"Ow!" She wriggled despite the fact he was grasping her hips, keeping her still with the power of his hold. "What did you do that for?"

"Do what?" he murmured as he licked the spot with his warm tongue. The flick of his tongue made her want to just melt.

Before she could answer his teasing question with a smart remark, his hair slid across her skin again. He bit her other ass cheek.

Unbelievably her core spasmed. It hurt, but it felt so incredibly good. This time she didn't cry out, she moaned.

"Ah, my little treasure enjoys my teeth on her." He bit her again, then licked the spot. "As she likes my tongue. My mouth. My cock."

Rhiannon groaned. "Stop teasing me and just take me."

"When I am ready." He bit her again, but this time he thrust two of his fingers into her core.

"Oh, jeez." Rhiannon was panting now and squirming. "Come on. Please."

"Mmmm." He bit her ass more gently. She felt the slide of his hair right before he found her folds with his mouth and tongue.

Rhiannon's elbows and knees almost gave out at the surprise and sudden rush of sensation. He licked and sucked her until she almost wept from the feel of it. She trembled as he brought her to the brink of orgasm. She was almost there. Ah, so close.

He moved his mouth away.

"Don't stop!" Rhiannon wiggled her hips in his hold. This time her voice was demanding. She couldn't believe he'd stopped.

He bit her ass again and a shudder traveled through her entire body. Her folds grew wetter with every touch, every bite, every lick. Goddess, she wanted him so bad.

With his hands on her hips, he pressed his cock to her ass. "Is this what you want?" He rubbed his erection against her flesh. "Do you want my cock?"

"Yes," she hissed. "That's exactly what I want."

"Hmmm." He gripped one side of her hips with one of his big hands. With his other hand he grasped the back of her neck, just below her hairline, and pushed down. He forced her low so that her cheek rested against the mattress. It was an incredibly dominant movement that both shocked and thrilled her. "Arms above your head if you want my cock."

What? "I—ooooh," she moaned as his erection rubbed between her legs and slid inside her folds. Whatever. She'd do anything to have him inside her now. "Okay. Wow."

Rhiannon obeyed and stretched her arms over her head. Keir gave something that sounded like a rumble of approval.

With his dominant hold at the base of her neck, he kept her face pressed to the mattress. Rhiannon bit her lower lip. In this position she was so vulnerable. But she was with a man she now trusted completely.

"Are you prepared to be fucked by this old man?" he said as he pumped his hips against her ass, teasing her folds with his erection, sliding it back and forth between her legs.

"Yes." Rhiannon groaned and tried to lean back against him, hoping he'd get to it. "I've been ready for ages. I don't want to wait anymore."

"Hmmmm." He made that sound again, as if contemplating whether or not he should do it.

She tried to move, but he held her motionless.

"Keir!" she shouted.

"Should I?"

"Damn it, yes!"

In the next moment he shoved his cock deep inside her pussy, hard enough to make her give a loud cry of surprise and pleasure. Now he wasn't messing around. He was taking her in earnest, his hips slamming against her ass, his cock sliding in and out. The entire time he kept one of his hands on the nape of her neck.

Her nipples brushed the mattress cover as she rocked forward and back, making her more sensitive and sending more sensation to her abdomen where her orgasm was building.

"Is this what you like, wench?" He slammed harder against her. "Is this what you want?"

Rhiannon couldn't answer. Her eyes were almost crossed the feelings were so great.

"Tell me," he said and stilled. "What do you want?"

She nearly whimpered. No, she *was* whimpering. And begging. "Take me. Please."

He gave another growl and pumped his hips even harder against her ass. Harder, harder, harder. Slamming fast and furious.

Rhiannon's orgasm exploded and she gave a cry that was muffled by the mattress. Her climax concentrated around where they were joined then shot straight to her head where he held her neck. Her breasts felt heavier, her nipples harder, and her body even more on fire.

He dragged her orgasm out as he continued to thrust in

and out. She tried to wriggle out of his hold. "No more. I can't take any more."

"Yes, you can, *a stór*," he said in his deep Irish brogue. "You can take everything I give you."

Rhiannon groaned as her core continued to spasm around his cock. This had to be the longest climax ever. He rocked against her, relentless with his every movement.

Finally, finally, he gave a growl and pinned his hips hard against hers, staying still as his semen pumped inside her. She felt every throb of his cock as her core clamped down on him.

Her orgasm came to a shuddering halt and she felt boneless and exhausted. But completely sated.

"You wore me out." She sighed as he rolled so that her back was to him, his cock still inside her. "You win."

He nuzzled her neck. "And you are my prize."

Chapter 20

Keir's cabin was located near a hot spring so Rhiannon was in heaven when she took a bath the following morning. He had already bathed and washed his hair before she woke. Now he was off doing something while she enjoyed her luxurious dip in the pool.

Delicious smells brought her out of her bathing ecstasy and her stomach grumbled. Great sex made a girl hungry.

After she toweled off, dried her hair with her magic, and scooted into some clean clothes, she made her way to the front room. She hadn't gotten a really good look last night. She'd been so tipsy and they'd headed straight for the bedroom.

A giggle almost escaped Rhiannon when she saw Keir moving around the part of the great room that served as a kitchen. He looked so *domestic* as he sliced big chunks of bread and cut off a couple of pieces of white cheese from a round. The smell that was driving her crazy, though, was from the sausage links sizzling in a pan in the fireplace. It was situated on a contraption that also had a hook on it—probably to hold pots for stew and things like that.

Keir glanced over his shoulder. "The food is almost ready."

For a moment she imagined him in an apron and she almost lost it. She snorted back a laugh and turned her attention to the room. What interested her now were the wooden figurines on the windowsill. She moved close enough to pick up a smoothly polished bird in flight. The beauty of it tugged at her heart. The carving was so life-like that the bird looked as if it could take flight. Had Keir made this?

Sculpting tools and chunks of wood were arranged in one corner and she shook her head. Whoa. This man was way more than she'd thought him to be when she first met him.

She glanced at him as he set the bread and cheese on a table near a large pantry, then looked back at the figurines as she set the bird on the sill. Incredible. Every last one of them was so detailed, down to the fine feathers beneath a ducktail.

Her gaze stopped at the small bust of a woman. A strange chill crept up her spine as she picked up the wood carving. It was beautiful and life-like, too—

And could be her mirror image.

How—when? Was it *her*?

She felt Keir move up beside her before he spoke. "I carved that piece the night before I went to Otherworld."

Rhiannon couldn't talk for a moment. She cleared her throat and said, "It looks like me, but you made it before you met me." She looked up at him, still clutching the piece. "Who is it?"

He gently pried the bust from her fingers. "I did not know who it was until I saw you." He brushed the back of his hand over her cheek. "This piece was born of the wood—as if my heart had guided my hands. It is the only explanation I can think of."

Rhiannon swallowed. "Wow. I don't know what to say."

Keir slipped his fingers under her chin and tipped it up so that her gaze was trapped by his. He lowered his mouth and brushed his lips over hers, stealing her breath. When he raised his head she looked away and took deep gulps of air. This was too weird. Way too weird.

He set the figure back on the windowsill, took her elbow in his hand, and guided her to the table. Bread, cheese, and red grapes were piled high on a platter in the middle of the table, along with another plate holding the sausage links. Wooden trenchers had been placed before two chairs.

Still feeling as if she'd been hit over the head with one of those chunks of wood, Rhiannon slipped into her chair. Like nothing had happened, Keir started filling his plate with four sausage links, two big chunks of bread, wedges of cheese, and a generous amount of the grapes—and there was plenty left.

As they had last night at the tavern, they ate their meal with their fingers. They washed down their breakfast with large metal mugs of crisp, clear, incredibly delicious water. Keir gave her a rough-spun napkin that she used to clean her hands and dab her mouth.

Rhiannon couldn't stop thinking about that figurine. Or the way Keir had looked at her when he'd said he'd recognized her from the carving the moment they'd met. The bust was too detailed, too polished for him to have sculpted it first thing this morning, and she knew he'd been in bed with her all night, holding her tightly as if afraid she might escape him.

At this moment she felt like she was a frightened rabbit and he was a wolf. She wanted to run, and to run hard. Those were feelings she didn't like, not at all. She was strong. She was just as much an alpha wolf as Keir.

She made herself take deep steadying breaths as she helped him clean up the dishes and food. They didn't talk much as they repacked their duffel bags. He seemed to sense her need for space, and he actually gave it to her. He wasn't playing the dominant male, he was simply working side by side with her.

When they finished packing and everything in the cabin was set to rights, Keir cleared his throat and came up behind her. "Would you like this one?"

She startled from the sound of his voice and turned to meet his gaze. "Like what?"

He held the carving of the bird she had first picked up and fallen in love with. Tears burned the back of her eyes. She didn't know why the gesture meant so much to her, but it did. Without thought, she flung her arms around his neck and kissed his cheek.

"I would like it very much," she whispered.

• • •

Keir focused his thoughts on the meeting with the Chieftains as he walked with Rhiannon through the woods to the Council Chambers. As much as his mind wanted to stay on Rhiannon, he needed to concentrate on the business at hand.

She strode quietly at his side, her thoughts seemingly far away. For the first time, he found himself wondering what a woman might be thinking when she was with him.

He shook his head to clear the notion, to focus his mind.

When they reached the Chambers, they climbed the steps, past the Council guards, and into the building, which smelled of the passage of time. To the left was the huge gathering hall. To the right was a hallway that led to the Chieftains' quarters and several other rooms.

Today Rhiannon had on a bright blue shirt and jeans, along with the gold-and-onyx pentagram earrings, necklace, and ring that she always wore. Her pink shoes squeaked on the stone floor, her short auburn hair bobbed around her face, and her sprinkling of freckles stood out across her nose. She was beautiful. And she was his.

The thought sent a spear of pride through his chest and invigorated his senses.

At the door to the Chieftains' quarters stood two green-robed guards. Each gave a bow from their shoulders.

"The Council awaits you," the female guard said.

She and the other guard pushed open the great wooden doors and held them until Rhiannon and Keir passed through, then closed the doors once again. Two more guards stood to each side of the door inside the chambers.

The Council of thirteen highly esteemed male and female D'Danann were seated behind a half-moon-shaped raised dais. Each was garbed in royal blue robes and sat in high-backed chairs carved from the finest woods the Dryads would allow. All of the Chieftains were older than Keir, but most did not look so.

Rhiannon's shoes continued to squeak and Keir held back a smile. The noise echoed in the chamber and it was a sound probably never heard in this room. When they stood before the High Chieftain, Chaela, Keir bowed. Rhiannon stood straight and met Chaela's gaze. Keir was torn between elbowing Rhiannon into a bow and laughing at her defiance.

The High Chieftain pulled her hood away from her face and let it fall to her back. Chaela was a stunning woman with blond hair and eyes almost as green as Rhiannon's. Chaela pursed her lips and studied Rhiannon.

"Welcome," the High Chieftain said with a slight nod to Rhiannon, which surprised Keir.

Even more of a surprise was when Rhiannon smiled brilliantly and returned Chaela's nod. "Thank you for speaking with us on such short notice."

Gael, a Chieftain seated beside Chaela, frowned. "I sense this being is of Elvin blood," he said. "No Elves are allowed in the Council Chambers as you know, Keir."

Keir scowled and Rhiannon eyed the Chieftain head-on. "I am Rhiannon, a D'Anu witch, and, yes, I recently discovered I do have some Elvin blood in my veins. However, I'm sure such an incredibly intelligent being as yourself would hold no prejudices against me and will listen to what Keir and I have come to discuss with the Council."

Gael looked taken aback, as did many of the other Chieftains, and Keir almost smiled again. This high-spirited woman surprised him at every turn and the knowledge filled his chest with warmth.

Chaela folded her hands atop the carved wooden table. Emerald rings that matched her eyes glittered from each of her fingers. "Speak, Keir, D'Danann, and Rhiannon, D'Anu witch."

By second nature, Keir bowed from his shoulders again. When he rose he addressed the entire Council, his gaze moving from the first Chieftain to the thirteenth.

"The battle in the San Francisco Otherworld grows more deadly every day," he began, "now that the Fomorii have freed Ceithlenn. Balor's wife has become an eater of souls, and with every soul she steals, she grows in power."

Chaela's face was an expressionless mask even as she nodded for him to continue.

"Not only has Ceithlenn found a way to seize human souls, but we have discovered there is a force of Fomorii so massive the D'Danann are greatly outnumbered. We ask for a large host of our brethren to join us when we go to war."

A stirring of unrest whispered through the Council.

"How do you know this?" Gael said with narrowed eyes. "Have you seen this host of demons for yourself?"

"*I* have." Rhiannon's voice rang high and clear. "I'm a seer and I visioned not only the enormous number of Fomorii, but also Basilisks and three-headed dog-beasts. Other creatures I can't name are there, as well. They're hiding beneath a rock island known as Alcatraz."

Gael made a scoffing noise and Keir fought to keep from clenching his hands into fists.

"This is merely a halfling witch," Gael addressed Keir. "What evidence do we have that her vision is true?"

"She is a talented seer." Keir's voice came out harsher than he intended. "She has foreseen much of what has happened in the past, what occurs in the present, and what may come to pass."

Rhiannon's voice had a hard edge to it. "I can see the direction the wind blows. Right now it's blowing in favor of Ceithlenn and the Fomorii."

"We must see proof of this." Chaela's features were placid, but her tone was not. "You cannot expect the Council to send more warriors to the San Francisco Otherworld without it."

"It isn't exactly a Kodak moment," Rhiannon said. Keir did not understand the word "Kodak" but he had the feeling she was trying to rein in her temper. "We can't just sneak into a cave of demons with a camera and take photographs."

Gael thumped his palm on the table. "This is not our war to begin with. We should not have sent *any* of our forces."

Rhiannon's fair features turned a shade of pink and her green eyes sparked with fire. "I know you are a neutral race of beings and you choose only to aid those in need if you believe it to be the natural order of things. But haven't you already determined this is the case in San Francisco?"

"The D'Anu witch is correct." Keir kept his voice steady and moved his hands behind his back so that he *could* clench them into fists. "Whether or not we are to be involved in this war is no longer a debate. What is important now is that the Council approve a larger contingent of our warriors to be readied for the oncoming war."

Silence reigned for a long moment.

"The Council will discuss the matter." Chaela's emeralds glittered on her fingers as she motioned for the guards to open the doors. "Return after the noon meal. We will give you our answer then."

Keir ground his teeth but kept his expression steeled as he gave another short bow.

"Thank you," Rhiannon said, and turned with Keir to head out the chamber doors.

Rhiannon kept her temper in check until they were a good distance from the Council Chambers so they wouldn't be overheard—at least, she *hoped* they were far enough away.

"Do they have to be so damn pigheaded about everything?" she asked. As they continued walking through the forest, she looked up and met Keir's stormy gaze. "Millions of lives are at stake. Look what Ceithlenn did to that busload of tourists. What if she gains enough strength that she can wipe out a city full of people?"

Keir took her by the shoulders and held her still. "No matter their decision, we *will* persevere. We will strike where they are most vulnerable—their leaders." His face held dark promise. "We will get that goddess-bitch."

Instead of feeling relieved by what Keir had said, a sense of hopelessness gripped Rhiannon. She moved away from his grasp, plopped down in the grass at the foot of one of the larger trees, and rested her head against its trunk.

"What if we don't, Keir?" She looked up at the leaves above her that were splashed with sunlight. Her skin tingled from the sunshine and her eyes burned a bit. "Ceithlenn is strong. So, so very strong."

Keir eased down beside her. He sat with one knee bent, his forearm resting on his knee as he studied her. "Have faith, *a stór*."

Rhiannon looked at him. "I have faith in you. I have faith in all our people who fight this war. I just don't know if faith is enough."

"It may have to be." He squeezed her thigh with his big hand.

With a sigh she leaned her head against his shoulder. Right then she needed his support, needed the closeness.

He tugged a lock of her hair. "It is your turn."

"For what?"

"To tell me about you. I answered your questions last night. You should now answer mine."

Keir's muscles flexed against her cheek as he shifted to a more comfortable position against the tree and draped his arm over her shoulders. Rhiannon felt like she was burrowing in a comfortable blanket. He felt so good, smelled so good.

"What do you want to know?"

He nuzzled her hair. "Your childhood."

She stiffened. His turn to hit a sore spot. Well, fair was fair. "When I was a kid my parents dumped me on the doorstep of my aunt because I wasn't . . . what they wanted. I was just a little girl, maybe two. And they left me. When I was five, Aunt Aga made it clear that the power . . . the Shadows in me was why I was sent away from my parents," she finished in a whisper.

She was afraid of his response when she mentioned the Shadows, but he only squeezed her closer to him.

For a moment she did feel wistful. What would it have been like to know her parents? If she met them today, how would she react?

Did she inherit that dark power from one of them?

She sucked in her breath. *They left me. That's all there is to say.*

"Aunt Aga wasn't exactly the warm and fuzzy type." Rhiannon started picking at the grass, letting the blades slip through her fingers without pulling them from the ground. "The old hag treated me like crap and kicked me out the moment I turned eighteen."

As she spoke, Keir tensed beside her. "So," she continued, "my childhood isn't something that's fun to talk about." She sighed. "At least I didn't have to sleep in a barn."

"You were mistreated." Keir's voice had that rumbly growl that it got when he was passionate about something, whether it was from anger or during sex.

"It's been a while." She sighed again. "I really should get over it, but I don't think I can."

Rhiannon's words gave Keir some pause. For centuries he had never forgiven his father, stepmother, or brother for his treatment. Was it far beyond time for him to "get over it?"

He ground his teeth. "What did you do once your aunt forced you to leave home?"

"There was a nice elderly couple who I always called my stepparents." Rhiannon gave a little smile. "They let me live on their houseboat for a time until Silver took me in and hired me to work in the D'Anu Coven's metaphysical store."

Rhiannon continued, "I guess I do have to thank Aunt Aga for teaching me the ways of the D'Anu and allowing me to serve as an apprentice. She died not too long after she kicked me out."

"Do you remember anything about your mother and father?" he asked.

"Not really." Rhiannon paused. "I always wondered about my parents. Why they left me like they did.

"Anyway"—she sounded as if she was trying to make her voice brighter—"I've had a good life since I moved in with Silver and since progressing from apprenticeship to full D'Anu witch. When all this is over with and we get rid of Ceithlenn and the Fomorii," she said, "I want to open my own shop. I've saved up a lot of money over the years, invested it well, and pulled out of the stock market before it crashed. Since then I've been a little more conservative, but I'll be able to do it."

"I am certain you will do anything you wish to," Keir said. And with all his heart and soul he prayed to the gods that one of those things would be to stay with him.

After a filling lunch in the tavern of baked beans, corn bread, and roast beef, Keir escorted Rhiannon back to the Council Chambers.

Rhiannon's heart beat faster as they ascended the stairs and worked their way to the big Council room itself.

The Chieftains were waiting for them when they arrived. The High Chieftain, Chaela, was so beautiful. Rhiannon had expected a bunch of old farts, but she should have realized in Otherworld people didn't age like they did in her world. Hell, maybe she and her friends needed to move here.

"Keir." Chaela nodded to him after he gave a short bow, then turned to Rhiannon. "D'Anu witch."

Keir remained silent with his hands behind his back, his stance wide. Rhiannon didn't know what to do with her hands, so she clasped them in front of her.

"We have determined," Chaela said very slowly and clearly, "no more D'Danann will be sent to the San Francisco Otherworld." Rhiannon's ears began to ring. "We have lent enough of our warriors to this cause and will provide no more."

"You can't be serious." Rhiannon couldn't believe what she'd just heard. Everything felt surreal, as if she were standing outside herself watching these people make a decision that could cost them everything. "Millions of lives are at stake."

"How can the Council turn its back on the very world we once lived upon?" Keir's hands were at his sides now, clenched into fists. "For the gods' sakes, we were born in that world, made in that world. That was where we fought the Fomorii nearly two millennia ago. We once destroyed the threat to mankind. We *must* do it again."

Every Chieftain remained stone-faced. "We have made our decision." Chaela motioned to the door guards. "You have our well wishes in defeating the Fomorii and Ceithlenn with what forces you have at your disposal."

Rhiannon wanted to scream, cry, rage. But all she could do was stand there and shake, heat flooding her face as these thirteen people determined the fate of everyone in her home world.

Keir pivoted, took Rhiannon by the hand, turning her around, and marched ahead of the guards. His stride was so long he practically dragged her through the doorway and out of the Council Chambers. They went into the bright afternoon sunshine that caused the burn of anger beneath her skin to feel hotter.

"How could they?" Rhiannon was close to tears as she doubled her steps to keep up with him. He was heading in the direction of his cabin.

"The Chieftains are fools," he said under his breath once they were out of the village. "They have grown complacent and indifferent to the needs of Otherworlds."

A tear made its way down her cheek and Keir brought them both to an abrupt stop when he glanced at her. He moved one of his hands to her face and rubbed the tear away with his thumb in a gentle movement.

"We *will not fail*." Determination filled his tone. "Whatever we must do, we will do. But we *will* find a way."

Chapter 21

After Rhiannon and Keir grabbed their duffel bags, they stepped outside the cabin door. As Keir closed the door behind them, Rhiannon came to a stop.

A lavender-winged Faerie flew up to them, lavender dust spilling from her wings. Like all the Faeries Rhiannon had seen, this one had a perfect body and features, and was absolutely beautiful. She had long black hair and lavender eyes. The difference between her and other Faeries was that she had such a regal look about her that she had to be some kind of royalty.

"Keir, D'Danann," the Faerie said, then looked at Rhiannon. "Of course you are the D'Anu and Elvin witch."

Keir gave a slight bow. "Queen Riona."

Rhiannon studied the Faerie, not surprised she was a queen. "I'm Rhiannon," she said. "Nice to meet you, Queen Riona."

"Of course you are," the queen said, "and it is my pleasure to meet you as well."

Keir hitched his leather pack higher on his shoulder. "What brings you to us?"

"The Great Guardian." She looked from Rhiannon to Keir. "You have been summoned."

Keir raised his eyebrows, obviously surprised. Apparently Cassia hadn't shared that part of their trip with him.

"It would be my pleasure to see the Guardian," he finally said.

The fact that it was a Faerie, and a queen at that, relaying the message from an Elvin woman surprised Rhiannon.

"Do you know the way to the transference stone?" Riona asked.

"Aye."

"I will accompany you as I need to return to my own Sidhe." The queen flew up to Keir and settled on his shoulder. She crossed her legs at her knees and began swinging one foot. "I have had business here of my own."

Keir linked his fingers with Rhiannon's as they trudged through the forest. Handfuls of sunlight spilled through the leaves and pine needles.

A knot formed in Rhiannon's belly. What would it be like to meet such an esteemed being, a powerful Elvin woman of Otherworld? Rhiannon had heard of her from Copper, but never expected to meet the Guardian.

They finally reached a small meadow where the sunshine was bright enough to make Rhiannon squint and she felt more of a burn on her skin.

At the center of the meadow was a circular platform made of stone that looked like gray marble, but different. Around the circumference of the platform, strange symbols had been carved into the stone and she wondered what they were. Runes, perhaps?

A narrow footbridge spanned a small stream. The sound of running water trickling over stones and the breeze through the ancient trees made her shiver as if spirits had caressed her skin.

She gripped Keir's hand tighter and looked up at him. "What do we do now?"

His face was all seriousness as he shook his head. "I do not know."

Riona fluttered from Keir's shoulder. "I have more business to attend to. I will see you again, D'Danann and D'Anu witch," she said before she darted into the forest, leaving a trail of lavender dust in her wake.

A glow brightened the small meadow and Rhiannon turned her attention toward it. The glow intensified until it was almost too bright to see.

When the light settled into a pale glow, Rhiannon's eyes widened as she stared at the most stunning woman she'd ever seen. The Elvin woman was much taller than she, almost as tall as Keir. Her white-blond hair hung straight and glossy all the way to her bare feet. Her skin was smooth, perfect. Her pointed ears peeked through strands of her hair and the long fingers of her delicate hands were laced together in front of her.

Rhiannon caught her breath at the ancient wisdom in the woman's eyes—yet she appeared so young.

Without thought Rhiannon knelt with Keir, as if she and the D'Danann warrior were one. She hadn't noticed Keir unsheathe it, but his sword lay on the stone in front of him, the metal glittering not only from the sunlight, but also from the glow that came from the Elvin woman.

The Great Guardian, whispered her mind.

In her heart she felt she should lower her eyes so she did. "My lady," she said as if it was the most natural thing to do.

The Elvin woman gave a sweet laugh. "Rise, Rhiannon D'Anu and Elvin, and Keir D'Danann and Mystwalker."

Keir gripped Rhiannon's hand and together they stood to face the woman. Rhiannon's gaze met the Elvin woman's eyes. Eyes so blue and clear and beautiful . . . eyes that reminded her of someone from another place, another time. But she couldn't quite grasp who it might be.

To be part Elvin meant she was related somehow to this beautiful being, and it made her warm inside.

"You really are the Great Guardian," Rhiannon said, a sense of awe filling her to the brim, bubbling over and making her almost giddy.

The incredible power of the being flowed over Rhiannon, yet a feeling of utter safety as well. And Keir—he seemed completely trusting of the Guardian. She never expected him to lay down his weapon for anyone.

"It is good to see you again, Rhiannon," the Elvin woman said as she extended one of her hands. "Come to me."

"We've met before?" Rhiannon released her grip on Keir's fingers as a wave of confusion washed through her. "I'm sure I would have remembered it."

"You were but a small child." The Guardian kept her hand extended and motioned for Rhiannon to approach.

She trembled as she moved closer to the Great Guardian. They had met when Rhiannon was small? The Guardian must have known her parents!

Rhiannon raised her hand and the Elvin woman clasped it in her own.

Warmth rushed through Rhiannon like never before, an electrical feeling that zinged to every part of her body. The fine hair rose on her arms and her scalp prickled. Her heart beat faster, lodging in her throat as her gaze locked with the Great Guardian's. The Elvin woman's scent of wildflowers, fresh breezes, of all that was good and pure, swept over Rhiannon.

"You wish to know more of your family," the Guardian said in a voice so light and fair it was like the caress of the wind over Rhiannon's skin. The Guardian took Rhiannon's other hand in hers. She had never felt so much power and strength as she did through that connection.

Rhiannon barely knew how to talk, being so close to this beautiful Elvin woman. Behind her she was aware of Keir in an amazingly intense way. As if he were a part of her and connected through this woman.

The Guardian looked into Rhiannon's eyes, causing her to feel like she'd been found after being lost for a very long time.

Before she could stop herself, the words burst from Rhiannon as if from a dam. "Why was I here as a child? Why did my father send me away? Why did they both leave me?" The last question came out in a painful cry and Keir moved closer to her in support though he didn't touch her. "I hate them for leaving me the way they did!"

The Guardian studied Rhiannon. "I believe you have the ability within you to forgive your parents if you understand why you were sent away from your father." The Guardian's face was a mask, an expression that told Rhiannon nothing. "Your father is fully Elvin," she said.

"*Is?*" Rhiannon stared at the Guardian. "Does that mean he's still alive?"

"In darkness and shadow." A sad look crept across the Guardian's face. "He is Drow, one of those unable to walk in the light, forever banished to the underground."

Rhiannon's eyes widened. Her mouth opened, then shut.

The Guardian reached out her hand and cupped the side of Rhiannon's face. "You are the daughter of a king. A Drow king who took a D'Anu witch bride of the light. He loved her so much that he helped her to travel freely between worlds so that she could still feel the sun on her face, the warmth on her body. He wanted her to have what he could not have for himself."

Rhiannon couldn't breathe as the Guardian spoke. She was the daughter of a king? The daughter of the king of the Dark Elves?

The Guardian smiled at Rhiannon. "One day you will see him. One day soon. And he will explain all."

A mixture of emotions whirled through Rhiannon and she stared off into space. Did she even want to meet this king of the Dark Elves?

"You inherited some things from your father," the Great Guardian said, snapping Rhiannon's attention back to her.

Rhiannon blinked. "I—what?"

The Great Guardian clasped her hands in front of her. "Your skin—does it not feel sensitive to the sun?"

As if in response to her words, Rhiannon's skin tingled and felt hot from sunlight shining on the meadow. Rhiannon swallowed and nodded.

The Elvin woman had a spark in her eyes—amusement, maybe? "Your temper, definitely from your father."

Rhiannon felt additional heat rush to her face. "Well, I guess we can't all be perfect."

The Guardian let out a soft laugh, then sobered. "And the Shadows, dear Rhiannon. Those Shadows within you, that you fight so hard to keep inside, are Drow powers."

Rhiannon's lips parted and she took a step back. She felt a little dizzy, as if she might drop right there in front of Keir and the Elvin woman.

"So what's inside me *is* evil." Tears bit the backs of Rhiannon's eyes and she looked away from the Guardian. "I'm part of an evil race with terrible powers. That makes *me* evil."

"No, sweetling." The Guardian took Rhiannon's chin in her hand and forced their gazes to meet. "Your father is not evil, nor are the Drow, and especially not you."

The Guardian released Rhiannon's chin as Rhiannon narrowed her brows. "The Dark Elves *are* evil."

The Great Guardian slowly turned her head from side to side. "The Drow use powers that are unacceptable in our world. They manipulate and use magic against beings who do not wish it. But that does not make them evil."

"I don't believe it." Rhiannon also couldn't believe she was arguing with this powerful Elvin woman. "The Shadows inside me *are* evil. They tried to choke Keir to death, for the goddess's sake! Not to mention my Aunt Aga."

The woman remained so blessed serene-looking that Rhiannon wanted to rage and scream. She no longer felt at peace. She felt as if she were being torn inside out.

"Too long have the Shadows been held captive within you," the Guardian went on. "If you stop fighting them, they will help you. You need to trust yourself, and in turn the Shadows will answer to you." The Guardian's features were perhaps more stern now. "When the Shadows attacked Keir, they were reacting only to Ceithlenn taking control of them through your mind. The Shadows can and will fight for purposes that serve the greater good so long as you believe in them."

Rhiannon folded her arms across her chest and stepped back. "I don't know if I can believe that."

"Make peace within yourself." The Guardian's gaze never wavered. "Take time to consider the possibilities, Rhiannon D'Anu and Drow."

Rhiannon felt like she'd been slapped at being called

Drow. How could this woman believe the Dark Elves were not evil? Weren't they banished to live underground because of that very reason?

The Great Guardian turned her gaze on Keir.

Keir's gut clenched as the Guardian moved her intense blue eyes to meet his. "What question of the heart would you have answered, Keir D'Danann?"

He tightened his grip around Rhiannon, needing her closeness. He looked down at her before returning his gaze to the Guardian's. "I have none."

The Great Guardian folded her hands. "What of your birth mother?"

"What is there to say? I was left a bastard to be raised by my father and stepmother." Keir scowled and couldn't hold back his words from coming out as a low growl. "My mother is a Mystwalker. My father made it clear she made the choice to leave me with him so that she might return to the Shanai."

Rhiannon looked from Keir to the Guardian. "What's a Mystwalker? Or a Shanai?"

"Mystwalkers are beings of mist," the Guardian said, her gaze now resting on Rhiannon. "They take human form when they wish, but must stay away from saltwater as much as possible. If they are touched by it, they cannot hold their mist forms without being cleansed in fresh water."

Keir ground his teeth. "Mystwalkers are little more than slaves to the Shanai." A sudden wash of anger slammed him with the force of a tidal wave. His mother a slave. And willingly so.

Again the Guardian smiled. "There is a great faction who are not 'protected' by the Shanai. Your mother is one of these rebels."

Keir's muscles tightened and his thoughts whirled. His mother a rebel? *Not* a slave?

Rhiannon said, "You haven't told me what Shanai are."

"They are shape-shifters who live near our Otherworld ocean, far from here," the Guardian said. "Many years ago they offered the Mystwalkers a trade. Protection from evil forces for the Mystwalker talent at lovemaking."

Keir's mind still reeled even as Rhiannon looked at him and raised one eyebrow, the corner of her mouth quirking. "Lovemaking talent?"

The Guardian gave a slow nod. "An agreement the Myst-walkers entered into willingly."

Keir found his voice. "They are banded so that they cannot take their mist form. That makes them naught more than slaves."

The Great Guardian continued as if Keir had not spoken so roughly. "Your mother would have taken you with her if you had inherited her gifts, but you were born with only the traits of a D'Danann warrior.

"Your father forbade her to see you, ever," the Guardian went on. "However, she lives close and has watched over you all these many years. She has cried countless tears about the way you were raised, but she had no say. Mystwalkers cannot stay long from freshwater, as you well know."

The revelation should have come as no surprise because of his father's abuse. Yet shock still sliced Keir like a dagger to his gut. His father had lied. Had made Keir think his mother had chosen the life of a slave over caring for her own son.

Keir's chest tightened and he felt as though the dagger twisted deeper inside him. He could not find words to express the intense feelings ripping through his belly like a blade hot from the forge.

He wanted to rage, he wanted to shout and yell and hack at something with his sword. Pound his fist into a wall. A battle with his half-brother Hawk would be his heart's desire at this moment.

The Great Guardian turned her gaze from Keir to Rhiannon. "It is imperative you each meet with your other people, the Drow and the Mystwalkers. As the Chieftains have failed to support you in this tragic war, new alliances must be made."

Keir and Rhiannon looked at each other. He saw pain in her eyes that matched the pain in his chest.

"I—I don't know if I want to see him." Rhiannon shook her head and frowned. "No—no. I'm sure I don't."

The Guardian retained her placid expression. "The pain in your heart must be set aside for the good of the many. These alliances must be forged or your world will be lost, Rhiannon D'Anu and Drow, and Keir, D'Danann and Myst-walker."

Rhiannon leaned against his shoulder and wrapped one of her arms around his waist. In turned he squeezed her tight to him with his arm on her shoulders.

"I don't know if I can do it," Rhiannon whispered.

"You have the strength within you." The Guardian turned to Keir. "You are aware that you do as well."

He rubbed his free hand over his face. *Godsdamn.*

"For now you must return to the San Francisco Other-world where you are needed," the Great Guardian said.

Rhiannon straightened. "Has something happened?"

"Step on the transference stone." She gestured toward the round, flat platform with the runes etched on it. "I will send you back, now."

He and Rhiannon obeyed, both giving slight bows before stepping onto the stone.

The Guardian added, "I will send word when it is time to return."

"Okay," Rhiannon said, her words sounding rough, as if she needed a drink of water.

Keir nodded. "Aye."

As the transference began, Keir's thoughts tumbled through the revelations.

Gods. His Mystwalker mother not allowed to spend time with him because of his sonofabitch father. He easily believed his father to be so callous.

His woman half-Drow. He almost laughed at the thought of a D'Danann/Mystwalker/Drow/D'Anu witch child should he and Rhiannon have one.

The thought truly did not bother him. For Rhiannon to have his babe would be his second greatest wish. His first was to have Rhiannon as his own.

Chapter 22

As she studied them in the penthouse suite, Ceithlenn felt the heated thrill of conquering Darkwolf and Junga. Both had strong wills and had mentally fought submitting to her, but she had broken them.

"Leave us," she ordered the Fomorii in human shells who were in the room. Ceithlenn waved the demon-men and women off to the left hallway where their rooms were when they were in the penthouse. These were the Fomorii she would replant throughout San Francisco to replace those killed in the sewers.

When all the demons had left the room, Ceithlenn returned her attention to Junga and Darkwolf.

One more task and they would serve her in a way that neither could begin to imagine. That no one would expect—least of all the D'Danann and witches.

Her fangs elongated as she looked from the warlock to the Fomorii Queen. "I've devoured ten more souls and their flesh, and it will give me the strength to accomplish today's task. A task that involves you both."

Darkwolf, as always, masked his feelings, his features blank. She narrowed her gaze as he said nothing. Perhaps she hadn't broken him enough.

Junga gave a low bow but her expression had a hint of anger. Ceithlenn would soon change that.

Satisfaction charged through Ceithlenn, enhancing the beginning of her Change. She tilted her head back and closed her eyes. Heat boiled the blood in her veins, worked its way up from her toes through her body until it reached her hair. Flames licked her scalp as her fingers stretched, turning into talons, and her already long nails lengthened.

A hiss spilled from her lips as her leathery wings pushed their way through her clothing. When they had stretched out and she felt the pleasure of her full transformation, she lowered her gaze and looked at Junga and Darkwolf. She no longer saw in full color as she did in Sara form. Instead, her vision was a mixture of gray and red—but she had the ability to see a being's soul. The Fomorii Queen and the warlock both had strong souls. A rumbling grew in Ceithlenn's mind and her belly.

"Be prepared for my return." She hissed again. Her voice had changed to a different pitch than the host body she shared with Sara. Lower. Thicker. Lustier.

She wrapped her arms and wings tight around her body and readied herself for transference. Tingling sensations radiated through her body as she focused on her destination, a location Elizabeth-Junga had shown her earlier.

The penthouse suite spun out of sight until she was in a void of fire and ice. She pressed her mind onward and arrived inside the theater behind the very back row, close to the doors.

She smiled at all the life she saw before her. Life that would soon be her own. Interesting how some souls were strong and pure where others were dark and soiled. She cared not which kind she devoured, so long as she had many to draw from.

Ceithlenn took a deep breath, inhaling the smells of sweat, popcorn, spilled sodas. She heard many hearts beating and blood flowing through veins, as well as explosions and car chases in a movie playing on the big screen at the foot of the rows of delicious people. All that noise was convenient.

As she slowly unfurled her bat-like wings, she smiled at

the irony. Her Sara host told her what was playing on the screen was a *Batman* movie.

The blood she heard and smelled called to her belly, the souls called to her own black soul. She needed the flesh and blood to quench the hunger in her stomach, the souls to fill her with powerful magic.

With a mere ripple in the air, she made herself invisible to human sight. Then she worked her way down one of the aisles. An electric feeling bolted through Ceithlenn and she almost roared. She would be so fast she would steal as many souls as she wanted without anyone realizing what was happening. In time.

She stopped at the front, turned, and sucked deeply of air and human essence from an entire row at once. Soft gasps were the only sounds the humans made as she stole their souls. She watched in fascination as bodies withered until dry skin clung to bones.

She swept row after row, faster than anyone could react. She drew in and savored every single bit of the human essence that became hers. The more she gathered, the stronger she became, the faster she could steal what was now hers—what would give her the power she needed to perform her next task.

Ceithlenn relished every moment, enjoyed everything about her feat. It almost seemed as if she was finished too soon. A theater employee entered and made a small cry, but in seconds Ceithlenn had her soul, too.

When all but the four humans in the last row were taken, Ceithlenn's growling stomach made her lick her lips. She dropped her shield so that the humans could see her, then focused on her meal.

With a smile, she raised her hand and sent a burst of energy to the four people. All became instantly motionless, but dropped whatever they were holding. A bag of popcorn tumbled over a man's lap, its contents scattering. Two drinks slipped from grasps and crashed to the floor. The rush of soft drink rolled and trickled over the steps.

Ceithlenn walked to the first human and tapped her shoulder. The woman came out of her stupor, looked up and screamed. The sound echoed throughout the theater but could barely be heard over the squealing car chase in the movie.

Ceithlenn showed her fangs as she grabbed the human by her shoulders. The woman screamed again as Ceithlenn sank her fangs into the woman's throat. A gurgling cry bubbled up and blood rushed over Ceithlenn's tongue. She savored the flavor as the human slumped. Ceithlenn tore the woman's flesh from her bones with her teeth. It was so sweet, so delicious, so satisfying.

When she had taken the flesh, blood, and souls from her last four victims, Ceithlenn wrapped her wings around her body and began the rush of transference.

She arrived back in the penthouse in moments. Elizabeth-Junga sat regally on one leather couch, but her fingertips tapped on the couch's arm in a nervous rhythm. Darkwolf was pacing the length of the room.

Darkwolf paused mid-stride, his gaze riveted on Ceithlenn. Junga stopped tapping her fingers.

Ceithlenn licked the blood from her lips and smiled.

Chapter 23

Darkwolf's body went cold when he saw the look in Ceithlenn's eyes. Whatever the bitch had in mind, he knew he wasn't going to like it one damn bit.

Ceithlenn drew up to her full height. She was not a tall being whether in her goddess form or in her Sara body, but the flame hair and black wings made her appear taller and, he had to admit, more frightening.

The stone eye at Darkwolf's neck heated against his chest and pain seared his head. He fought to keep his face expressionless. The lidless eye on the metal chain glowed a brilliant red, which matched the intensity of Ceithlenn's own red eyes.

Ceithlenn's gaze rested on Elizabeth-Junga, and she said, "Shift."

The demon-woman got up from the couch and approached the center of the penthouse's enormous living room. The once beautiful woman's hands and fingers turned into ham-fisted hands with hideous claws. Her body slowly morphed, bones shifting, her body elongating and thickening, until she was at least the size of a gorilla. Her arms hung down to the floor, and she had bulging eyes and an earless head.

Seeing her like that . . . Darkwolf turned his head away and focused on Ceithlenn.

The goddess smiled and stretched her arms out, her palms facing Junga. Darkwolf's attention jerked back to the demon. A black light streamed from the goddess, striking Junga in the chest, then spreading over her body like a black fog. The demon began trembling—

And then she grew. *Grew.* Darkwolf watched, trying to keep from his face what would surely be a look of horror if he allowed it. Right before his eyes, the demon's body pushed up to the ceiling and her girth tripled. The pop and crunch of bones and ligaments moving made his blood ice-cold.

Junga's teeth became longer, wider, and looked as if they had been filed to sharp points. A pair of horns thrust up from her head. Her snout expanded and looked like a pig's, only larger, and her now crimson eyes grew until they were large and round.

He held his breath as Ceithlenn turned her satisfied smile on him. It was a lot harder to maintain his expressionless mask when he knew what was coming. He had no doubt in his mind what she was going to do to him.

He couldn't stop the *"umph"* that came from his mouth as her magic slammed into him. It was a living thing, crawling over him like a million black spiders. His body shook and trembled and he lost control and shouted from the pain as he began to morph. He looked down at his hands, which widened and thickened, and nails burst from his fingers.

The pain!

It was so intense as it ripped through his body. He felt as if his skin would tear as he expanded. He felt his features shift. His hair lengthened and hung over his face, lank and stringy. Smells became sharper and his vision turned so that everything was red and gray. He thought it was likely the chain holding the stone eye would break, but when he looked down, the chain links were thicker, longer.

And the eye was bigger.

Horns exploded from his head and matching pain burst in his mouth as he felt his incisors lengthen until they were outside his lips. He tried to shout his fury at Ceithlenn, but it came out as a powerful roar.

Like Junga, he had been fully changed into something inhuman. An enormous monster.

The goddess lowered her arms and shifted easily back into her Sara form. When she was completely transformed she sank into a nearby chair, slouching down in the seat and appearing exhausted, as if she had used up so much of her power that she couldn't stand, much less sit up.

Now he should kill her. Darkwolf roared again and clenched his massive fists.

Ceithlenn's gaze narrowed on both of them. "Kneel."

Darkwolf let a fierce rumble rise out of his chest and Junga growled.

The goddess's features changed to one of fury. "You will always bow to me. Kneel *now*!"

She straightened in her chair and focused first on Junga. The demon's knees dropped to the floor and she prostrated herself.

Just as Darkwolf was wondering if Junga operated under her own volition, he felt Ceithlenn's magic ram into him like a telephone pole pounding on his head. He barely contained a shout as his own knees gave out and a force like a gigantic hand pushed him so hard his torso slammed to the floor, his arms straight above him so that he was positioned exactly like Junga.

He raised his eyes. Ceithlenn reclined in her chair again with a satisfied smile. Her gaze met Darkwolf's. "Now that's much better."

Chapter 24

By the time they'd left Otherworld and made it back to the apartment building, Rhiannon had worked herself into a major snit. It would have been so satisfying to throw a spellfire ball at each Chieftain's ass.

A Drow king was her father! One of the Dark Elves. And she was supposed to embrace the Shadows and allow them to help her. The Drow and the Shadows were nothing short of evil, no matter what the Great Guardian said.

The fact that she'd inherited such perverted dark magic lay in her belly like a heavy weight. The Shadows were evil, just like her birth father.

She couldn't tell her Coven sisters about the Shadows, and she certainly wasn't ready to tell them about her father being Drow.

On top of everything, the head-splitting pain returned the moment they crossed over from Otherworld. The thought of Ceithlenn being in her head made the weight in Rhiannon's stomach heavier.

When Rhiannon and Keir arrived in the common room, her jaw nearly dropped and her eyes widened.

High Priestess Janis Arrowsmith, of the white magic D'Anu Coven, stood in front of most of Rhiannon's friends, who were all members of the gray magic D'Anu Coven. None of the PSF officers or D'Danann were in the room.

Janis's frosty eyes still had that you're-scum-beneath-my-feet look as she met Rhiannon's gaze. Her gray hair was pulled back so tight it stretched the skin around her eyes and made her look like she'd had a face lift. She was tall, taller than Rhiannon and all of her Coven sisters, and had a way of looking down her nose that made Rhiannon want to slap her. Since she couldn't singe a Chieftain's ass, maybe Rhiannon would get Janis with a good spellfire ball to her backside.

Mackenzie and Alyssa stood beside Hannah, Sydney, and Silver. Cassia and Copper weren't in the room. Most of the witches didn't look too pleased to have Janis there.

Silver, though, maintained a polite expression—despite the fact that she had been the one who had been thrown out of the D'Anu white magic Coven for using gray magic. Rhiannon, Cassia, Sydney, Mackenzie, Alyssa, Hannah, and Copper had left with Silver, and the eight of them had formed their small gray magic Coven.

Mortimer, Janis's mouse familiar, peeked out of the High Priestess's forest green robes and Spirit hissed from across the room. Rhiannon's gaze snapped to her familiar, who perched on the arm of a couch, his tail twitching.

To her immense surprise, Galia was sitting on Spirit's back, her small fingers clasped in his hair, as if he were a horse. The Faerie was studying Janis with a frown on her petite face.

Spirit turned his head to glance at Rhiannon in a way that let her know he was ticked at her for leaving him behind when she went to Otherworld. His gaze returned to Mortimer and he crouched, looking ready to pounce the first chance he had. Galia patted Spirit's side and the cat relaxed his position a little.

"What can we help you with?" Silver said in a calm tone that reminded Rhiannon of Silver's and Copper's mother. Moondust was one of the fallen in their battle against the Fomorii on Samhain.

Apparently Janis had just arrived. "I had a vision." Janis focused her attention on Silver. Her voice was strong, yet her lips twitched in an almost nervous manner. Was the High Priestess a bit shaken up over something?

"Go on," Silver said quietly.

Janis cleared her throat. "I visioned a great host of demons. I saw a being with hair of flame and the wings of a bat gather the souls of many, many people. That evil creature freed a force even more powerful than she."

The room was entirely quiet.

"I saw panic as well as riots when people started to learn of mass murders being committed by this creature," Janis said in a shaky voice. "People of the city thought it to be a terrorist attack.

"I saw more death." Her hands actually trembled at her sides. "I saw San Francisco's devastation."

Goose bumps rose on Rhiannon's skin. Janis was a more powerful visionary than she. It didn't mean the vision would necessarily come to pass. The outcome could be changed.

But Janis having this vision—it wasn't good. It *really* wasn't good.

All of the witches in the room looked as stunned as Rhiannon felt. Everyone knew how powerful Janis's visions were.

"This future can be prevented." Janis met Silver's gaze. "All my D'Anu Coven can do is pray and meditate, chant and heal what damage has been done or comes to pass. We can use the white magic we have at our disposal that does not venture close to the gray. You know this."

Rhiannon took a step toward Janis. "What exactly are you saying?"

The High Priestess raised her chin. "I can only tell you of my vision. I can only warn you. I cannot and will not ask anything of you."

"Because we use gray magic." Copper pushed her way past Rhiannon and Keir into the common room, obviously having just come in from the outside. Her walking cast thumped as she moved forward to confront the High Priestess.

Janis's eyes widened. "Copper?"

"Alive and kicking." Copper looked down at her ankle cast. "More or less."

"You were missing so long . . ." Janis said, a shocked expression still on her face.

"Took gray magic to get me out of the mess." Copper narrowed her eyes. "And then I get back to learn you kicked my sister out of the Coven."

Janis straightened and her expression became steely again. "As I expressed, I came only to share this vision with you." Her robes swished as she turned and walked past Rhiannon and Copper. When her gaze landed on Keir she narrowed her eyes. "D'Danann."

"One who helped save your ass on Samhain, from what I was told," Rhiannon said.

Janis raised her chin and swept out the common room door and out of their sight.

"Whoa." Sydney looked at her Coven sisters. "I can't believe Janis told us about her vision."

"She did come to me not long before Copper made her way back home," Silver said. "Only Janis didn't make any dire predictions."

"I remember you telling me about that." Copper took an audible breath. "So just how deep are we?"

"I'd say pretty deep." Rhiannon moved from the doorway to drop her duffel on a couch. She plopped down beside it. "The Chieftains said no. They won't send any more help."

The witches stared at Rhiannon.

Galia's little face twisted with fury. "Those idiots!" She stood on Spirit's back. But then a puzzled expression replaced the anger. "I will be back," she said before she zipped out of the room in a poof of pink dust.

"What are we going to do?" Alyssa asked in a trembling voice.

Rhiannon clenched her hands on her thighs. "The best we can, and it's going to have to be enough to get the job done."

At this moment she couldn't talk about her heritage. It was too raw, and still difficult for her to believe. Maybe she and Keir would seek help from the Mystwalkers as the Great Guardian suggested. But Rhiannon didn't want to go near the Dark Elves.

She squeezed her hands into tighter fists. She had to set those thoughts aside and concentrate on the here and now.

A pink flash startled her. Galia came to a stop right in front of the witches and Keir.

The Faerie wrung her little hands. "It happened." More pink Faerie dust and the scent of lilacs poofed from her wings. "I went outside and heard Jake talking to the other officers and D'Danann."

"What's going on?" Rhiannon's brows pinched with confusion.

Galia turned to Rhiannon, her long blond hair flying over her shoulders. "Ceithlenn struck again."

A collective gasp went around the room. Rhiannon's blood chilled and she gripped the arm of the couch with one hand.

"Explain," Keir said in a harsh tone.

The Faerie looked a little green. "A whole theater filled with people. Jake said they are all wrinkled up, except for a few who were . . . eaten."

Nausea swept through Rhiannon's belly as her thoughts returned to her vision where she had been inside the goddess and had felt and tasted everything C—the goddess had.

Keir tossed his pack on a couch as he looked at Galia. "Where?"

"Someplace called the Grand Theater."

"By the Ancestors," Silver said as Rhiannon got to her feet again. "That place is huge."

Galia wrung her hands so tight they were pale. "They are afraid she has gained much power from this."

Keir jerked the long black coat more snugly over his weapons in order to conceal them better. He was still wearing his leathers and sword since they'd just returned from Otherworld, and had worn the coat to cover them. He turned to Rhiannon. "Can you tell me where this theater is?"

"I'll show you." She held up her hand when he scowled. Before he had a chance to say anything, she stated, "I'm not staying behind."

For a moment it looked like she was going to get his usual argument, but he gave her a sharp nod. "Come."

"Can I?" Galia asked.

"No." Keir tossed a glance over his shoulder. "This will be no place for a Faerie."

Behind her, Rhiannon heard the other witches chatting and making their own plans to hurry to the theater.

Rhiannon had to jog to keep up with Keir's long strides as he exited the apartment building. "I forgot my keys," she said.

"We do not need your car. It would take too long." He grabbed her around the waist with both hands. "Hold me. Tight." Keir unfurled beautiful black wings and Rhiannon gasped. She'd never seen his wings. Even when they went to Otherworld he hadn't flown.

He spread his wings like a great eagle. Before she had time to think, he pumped his wings and they were airborne.

She cried out in surprise and fear as she threw her arms around his neck and wrapped her legs around his hips. Her stomach lurched and her breath wouldn't come easily to her. Wind rushed past her face and made her hair stand on end. They were flying in the fog and everything was gray.

Her voice trembled and she did her best not to look down. "I didn't even have time to pull a glamour."

"We cannot be seen." His powerful wings moved with incredible grace for such a harsh man. "So long as I hold you, my cloak will envelop you as well."

Rhiannon thought about how Superman flew with Lois Lane over the city and how Lois had enjoyed the flight and the city at night. Well, it wasn't night, Rhiannon wasn't Lois Lane, and she wasn't looking down.

"Where is it?" Keir asked.

Crap. So much for not looking down. She peeked over her shoulder, grew dizzy, and thought she might pass out from fear. She wrapped her body tighter around Keir's.

"Farther. Head northwest." She pressed her cheek to his chest and for some reason thought about what she'd learned of her birth parents.

"Keir," she said above the rush of wind over her ears. "Finding out about my parents—it's so confusing. And meeting my father—I can't see myself learning more about that part of me."

He pressed a kiss to her forehead. "Aye. It will be difficult for me as well to meet my mother and her people." He held her impossibly tighter. "We will face this together."

Rhiannon shook her head. "I can't believe we're on our way to a horrible tragedy and I'm thinking about all of this."

"It is difficult not to." He began to descend. "Are we close now?"

She looked over her shoulder and again thought she was going to lose her lunch. "There. By that hotel with the red awnings. The place with the huge crowd of people in front of it." She immediately put her face against his black shirt again. She *was* going to throw up if they didn't get on the ground soon.

When Keir landed, he had to pry Rhiannon away from him.

"You are all right, *a stór*," he said.

"That's what you think." She released the vise hold her thighs had on his hips, and let him remove her arms from around his neck. She met his gaze as her shoes touched the asphalt and her legs trembled. "Let's not do that again."

They had landed in an alleyway, but the roar of a crowd could be heard from where they stood. Keir retracted his wings, took her hand, and led her toward the noise.

News vans, reporters with cameramen, and countless other people stood outside an area that had been cordoned off with yellow tape. Police stood two feet apart all the way around the circumference to ensure no one could get into the theater. Countless emergency vehicles were parked out front and red and blue lights flashed nonstop.

"I'll pull a glamour." Rhiannon glanced up at Keir. "It's been a while since I've used one but it should work to get me past the police. I'll get Jake to let you in."

Keir opened his mouth then frowned when Rhiannon ran her hand in front of her face. Glamours didn't always work with nonhumans like the D'Danann and the Fomorii, but humans were easy to get past.

"I can see you," he said.

"Yeah, but they can't." Rhiannon walked up to a man and tapped his shoulder. The man glanced behind him and appeared confused, as if he couldn't see anyone. "Adios," she said to Keir when the man turned back to view the spectacle before them.

It took some maneuvering and some puzzled expressions from people being pushed aside by an invisible witch, but she managed to get to the tape. She crawled under it, between two police officers, and hurried into the theater. In the lobby she saw theater employees being interviewed. They looked pretty shaken up.

Countless emergency personnel were in the lobby wearing HAZMAT suits, and she recognized two PSF officers who did not have their protective masks on. She stepped aside where she couldn't be seen when she ditched her glamour, and then she walked up to the PSF cops. They found protective gear for her, along with a mask, and let her into the theater.

Immediately, the smell of burnt sugar slammed into her along with the putrid odor of death. Her stomach clenched. When she made it through the doorway, into the theater, she was almost certain she was going to be sick.

Corpses filled the red velvet seats in the old-fashioned, one-screen theater. The bodies were withered, most shriveled beyond recognition.

She looked away and searched the enormous room for Jake and the D'Danann who were bound to be here. The lights were on and she was able to see everything clearly.

The D'Danann and PSF officers were scattered throughout the theater, wearing protective gear and masks, no doubt searching for clues.

Even with their protective gear on, Rhiannon recognized a few members of their "team." By the screen, Jake was talking with Tiernan, Hawk, Sheridan, and a couple of officers. Rhiannon made her way down the aisle until she reached them.

"There's no way to keep a lid on this kind of mass murder," Jake was saying, anger and frustration in his voice. "Shit. All I can think of is to have a statement made to the press that it was a terrorist attack."

"This is going to cause some serious problems," Rhiannon said, thinking of Janis's prediction about panic and riots.

"Of course that's the understatement of the last twenty centuries."

Jake acknowledged her with a nod. "Things are going to go to hell in a hurry."

"News of the Chieftains?" Tiernan asked Rhiannon.

Rhiannon scowled. "They said no."

"Godsdamnit!" Tiernan clenched his hands. "This war will be over before the sun rises if the goddess uses her powers against us."

"Ceithlenn will be very strong now." Sheridan gestured to the theater full of bodies.

Rhiannon rubbed her forehead above the mask as pain spiked her head—as always—from the mention of Ceithlenn's name. Her head ached and she felt exhausted to her bones. Keir's promise that they would find a way to defeat Ceithlenn rolled through her thoughts, but right now she had a hard time believing in his words. "Jake, Keir is outside and more of the D'Anu are on their way. Can you send someone to give them gear and let them in?"

Jake gave the order to one of his officers who hurried out of the theater. He turned back to them. "With or without more help from the D'Danann, we've got to kick this bitch's ass."

"You've got that right," Rhiannon said.

The D'Danann and Jake talked about what they'd found. Pretty much nothing but four sets of bones with meat and blood still on them, and a whole auditorium full of mummies.

Rhiannon took a deep breath but that was a mistake. She just sucked up more of the smell of death and burnt sugar. She coughed, almost choking on the stench.

Keir came up beside them and rubbed Rhiannon's back until she stopped coughing.

They brought him up to speed on their conversation and Keir pushed back his coat and placed his hand on the hilt of his sword. "We need to strike her first and strike her hard."

"Now to find the bitch so we can do just that." Rhiannon

shoved her hair out of her face and looked around. "The bad vibes in here might be enough to give me a good vision."

"Are you certain that is wise?" Keir's voice was both gruff and concerned.

Rhiannon nodded. "When they get here, I'll combine my strength with that of my Coven sisters'. We'll find something. I just know we will."

Jake and his officers continued searching for clues as Rhiannon waited for her Coven. It wasn't long before they arrived. Silver, Alyssa, Hannah, Sydney, Mackenzie, and Copper joined Rhiannon. Cassia always stayed behind to tend to matters there. Hawk didn't even want Silver in the room because of her pregnancy, but she was wearing protective gear like the others and there wasn't much he could do since she was already there.

The D'Danann gathered around, and so did the PSF.

Rhiannon motioned for them to step away.

After everyone gave them some space, the seven witches joined hands. Rhiannon gripped Sydney's hand on one side and Alyssa's on the other. With the scene being so fresh and reeking of Ceithlenn, Rhiannon had a gut feeling she was going to be able to get some kind of vision.

As she lowered her eyelids Rhiannon told her Coven sisters to close their eyes.

For a long time, all Rhiannon saw was blackness, and her head ached bad enough that she wanted to drop to her knees. The burnt-sugar-and-death smell was so strong she had a hard time blocking it out. When she finally did, the blackness behind her closed eyelids began to lighten until she was no longer in darkness but wrapped in fog.

She found herself on a sidewalk in front of a tall brick building of penthouse suites. She recognized it towering above its shorter neighbors between the Embarcadero and the bay.

This time it wasn't Ceithlenn she saw in her vision. She recognized Junga in her human form—Elizabeth. Anger flared through Rhiannon and the scars on her cheek burned. She had to struggle to pull herself back into the vision.

She mentally followed Junga as she walked up the concrete steps in front of the building and through the door that was opened for her by a security guard.

Junga went through the marble and brass lobby and into one of two elevators. Rhiannon entered with her and stood beside the Fomorii Queen, who slipped in a key card then pushed a button for the fourteenth floor.

Rhiannon's heart began racing. Could this be it? Could this be the time she would find out where Ceithlenn's lair was?

Rhiannon could smell human perspiration and perfume. No fish smell because Junga inhabited a human body. The person Junga had taken over had been a wealthy woman named Elizabeth, and the host body was graceful, elegant, stunning looking. But Rhiannon would never forget the demon inside that human body. Horrid, twisted features and a blue hide. Long claws tipped with iron.

When the bell dinged and they reached the fourteenth floor, Junga stepped into a semicircular foyer, then used her key card to enter a penthouse.

It was sumptuous. Rhiannon had never been in a place that exuded so much wealth.

But then she realized she'd been here before—when she'd watched Ceithlenn, the time the evil goddess had broken her mind. Just the thought made Rhiannon feel like she would go up in flames.

At the same time, excitement burned through her belly. She knew where their lair was! She didn't see any sign of Ceithlenn, but this was the place. She smelled burnt sugar and the odor of rotting fish so she knew the Fomorii came here as well.

The scene fast-forwarded through her head with Ceithlenn-Sara coming into the room, turning into her horrid goddess form and leaving, then returning. For some reason, the goddess didn't sense Rhiannon's presence this time, thank Anu.

And then Ceithlenn turned Junga and Darkwolf into those hideous creatures Copper had dreamt about and Silver had scried in her cauldron.

Rhiannon's stomach churned.

The vision faded.

Gray fog wrapped her again, until she slipped back into her own body. Her eyelids snapped open and she saw her friends with their eyes still closed. Rhiannon's breathing came harsh and fast.

"I'm back." Rhiannon let go of Sydney's and Alyssa's hands and pressed her fingertips to her throbbing forehead. "You can all open your eyes."

Everyone complied and looked at Rhiannon, who dropped her hands to her sides and tried to keep her features calm. "Did you see the vision?" she asked her Coven sisters.

All of the witches shook their heads. Alyssa said, "Not a thing."

Rhiannon sucked in a deep breath. "You want the good news first, or the bad?"

Chapter 25

In the common room, Silver shoved her daggers into special sheaths in her boots while Rhiannon shrugged into one of the Kevlar vests Jake had given each witch for the attack on Ceithlenn's lair.

Spirit stood at her feet and meowed, as if telling her to be safe . . . or warning her.

Keir, of course, had argued against the witches being involved in the mission, and Rhiannon had threatened to spell-fire his ass. The threat hadn't worked, but neither had she given in.

Keir wasn't the only one who was being overprotective. Hawk was flipping out that Silver was going, despite her pregnancy, Tiernan was furious when Copper insisted on being included, ankle cast and all. Even if she did get around pretty well, considering.

Jake and his officers tugged on their own protective gear, along with kneepads and tactical gloves. The gloves were thin, with nonslip material to pull a trigger and hold weapons. Gloves were useless to the witches since they needed their hands to perform any kind of magic.

Galia fluttered out of nowhere, pink dust scattering all over the common room floor and the smell of lilacs following in her wake. "May I go with you?" she asked Rhiannon with a pleading expression.

Rhiannon almost laughed. She had no idea where the Faerie got the clothing, but she looked like a pint-size, pink-winged version of the D'Danann when they were in their leather warrior gear. Galia wore a tiny set of skintight leather pants and a leather tunic. She even had a sword strapped to her side.

Might be useful if she wants to poke out a demon's eyeball.

Doing her best to keep a straight face, Rhiannon said, "Why not? As far as I'm concerned you proved yourself in battle the day the Fomorii broke through our wardings and attacked us." She smiled. "Those pink lightning bolts of yours come in pretty handy."

Galia clapped her hands together and bounced up and down in the air in front of Rhiannon. "Thank you! Keir was so awfully grouchy when I asked him if I might go. But then he's grouchy about you going, too."

"No kidding." Rhiannon shook her head. "He's really got to get over it. All of these guys are too possessive when it comes to their women." She clamped her mouth shut. Good goddess, she wasn't Keir's woman, that was for sure.

"Let's hope the goddess is *really* weak after using her powers to create those monsters," Rhiannon said. "Right now I'd be happy to just eliminate *her.*"

Sydney finished strapping on her body armor that she'd put on over another shirt, then pulled her hair out of the neckline. "If only it can be that easy."

Jake stuffed a handgun at his back. "The PSF has specialists working around the clock to develop firepower that just might give us a fighting chance." Another handgun and a dagger were sheathed in his weapons belt. "We have a couple of things that might help us for now."

"What's that?" Rhiannon asked.

"These are fucking expensive, so we've got a limited amount and every shot has to count." Jake handed Rhiannon a bullet with a red point. "They're designed with a special microchip to listen for and detect a demon's heart—a human heart, too, for that matter. After hitting its target, the microchip sends a powerful electric current straight to the beating heart, zapping it so hard it explodes."

Rhiannon looked at the bullet closely, feeling the cool metal of the dangerous ammo between her fingertips.

Jake showed her something that looked like a big gun. "We've developed these high-powered tasers that'll help us fight the demons off long enough to put one of those bullets in its body."

"What'll the PSF use for guns?" Rhiannon asked. "I wasn't here when you fought them at Samhain."

Jake grabbed a rifle off one of the tables and started loading some of the special bullets into its chamber. "Automatic rifles for one. They're compact and lightweight. Instant response, good for speedy deployment, mobility, and heavy firepower as close as twenty feet." He set the rifle down and drew out the handgun he had slipped behind his back. "I use a .357 semiautomatic as a backup weapon and for close-quarter combat."

He withdrew a canister from his weapons belt. "This is like pepper spray, but it's far more potent—a special formula that we hope will help fight the Fomorii. The idea is for the spray to work as an irritant to the demons' mucous membranes, buying us more time when needed."

In past battles, the PSF had been at a disadvantage because the standard-issue weapons did nothing to the Fomorii. The demons' bodies immediately healed if a bullet pierced their thick skin and flesh. The only way for the demons to be destroyed was by cutting off or blowing up their heads, or completely destroying their hearts. A simple bullet wouldn't do it because the heart would heal. It took blasting the beast's heart out of its body, cutting, or ripping it out of their chests.

The witches relied on their magic and chose not to kill, but did their best to incapacitate the Fomorii and let the D'-Danann and PSF take the demons out. Like white witches, the gray witches didn't want to kill any living thing. Unlike white witches, gray witches believed that if evil could be stopped it was their responsibility to do what they could—without crossing the line themselves.

Galia settled on Rhiannon's shoulder. Sydney braided her hair to keep it out of her face while Silver used a Celtic knot clasp then put her thick hair up under her black cap. The rest of the witches were ready and waiting.

The D'Danann had already left and were stationed on top of and around the building where the penthouse suite was located. They were handling surveillance until the team of PSF officers and witches arrived.

Rhiannon clasped the Celtic knot necklace she was wearing for additional protection. "Ready," she said as she released the necklace and jerked on her black cap.

It seemed as if everyone took a collective deep breath then headed for the door. Spirit meowed again and followed them as far as the apartment entrance.

The witches, along with the PSF officers, climbed into the unmarked trucks that looked like a cross between a SWAT vehicle and a Hum-V. Jake shouted commands and his team looked prepared for action. He glanced at Galia, who was still perched on Rhiannon's shoulder, and Rhiannon shrugged. Jake shook his head and smiled.

When they finally arrived at the penthouses, everyone poured out of the PSF vehicles. Jake flashed his badge at the bewildered security guard, got the key card to access the penthouse from the stairs, and another card to get to it by the elevator. Jake ordered some of his officers up the stairs, while stationing others at the bottom floor entrance. The D'Danann would take care of the rooftop and the stairs leading to the rooftop.

Galia chose to fly and disappeared from sight.

Jake spoke into his wireless earpiece that connected him to his officers and the D'Danann captains and informed the D'Danann of their positions.

Rhiannon's heartbeat picked up as she stepped into the elevator with her Coven sisters and PSF officers. More PSF officers took the other elevator. Rhiannon glanced at each witch who looked nervous, stoic, or—in Hannah's case—expressionless. Alyssa, who tended to be more on the sensitive side, appeared to be scared spitless, yet she was there.

She never gave up. Never gave in. And Rhiannon admired the hell out of her for that.

When they reached the fourteenth floor and the elevator dinged, Rhiannon held her breath. What if Ceithlenn heard it and was prepared for them?

They filed out of the elevator to an empty foyer. It was exactly as Rhiannon remembered it from her vision of Junga. Now there was just a door standing between them and Ceithlenn—

And the two monsters the goddess had created.

The other elevator arrived. The officers poured out and got into position.

Jake and another officer stood ready at the door.

"Now!" Jake said into his transmitter.

At the same time, two of his officers used what they called a "slammer," a small battering ram. With one strike it ripped the door right off its hinges.

The door smacked up against the wall, and the officers aimed their rifles into the room.

No Ceithlenn. No Junga or Darkwolf. No monsters.

Only a group of men and women, near the windows at the far side of the enormous room. They looked like they might have been mingling at a party.

There were maybe twelve, fifteen at the most.

All had startled looks—

Then their expressions changed one by one, and they shifted into their hideous Fomorii forms.

With roars and shrieks the demons charged the officers and witches who were pouring into the room.

The officers immediately fired their rifles and handguns at the demons.

The room lit up with an explosion of spellfire balls and magic ropes.

Galia appeared and started throwing one pink lightning bolt after another at the demons.

Windows imploded behind the Fomorii and D'Danann warriors swooped in, tearing down the blinds at the same time. Glass sailed everywhere and wind whooshed into the penthouse.

The D'Danann drew their swords and went after the Fomorii from their backsides.

Jake fired his .357 and a demon's heart exploded out of its chest. The demon crumbled to the floor into a pile of dark silt on the white carpet.

Silver hit one Fomorii square in the chest with a spellfire ball, and the D'Danann named Sheridan lopped its head off. The demon crumbled.

A PSF officer screamed as a demon raked its claws down the officer's face and chest. As one, Sydney and Hannah flung magic ropes at the beast and bound it so that it fell to the floor. Keir beheaded it with one swing of his sword.

Alyssa threw a spellfire ball at a charging demon and screamed as the Fomorii swiped at her. One of the PSF officers shot it in the heart, disintegrating the demon on the spot.

Rhiannon and Jake looked at each other. She cocked her head toward one of the hallways and he nodded. With Silver, Sydney, and two PSF officers following, they skirted the edge of the battle, shooting and flinging spellfire balls as needed to keep the demons off their backs.

By the time they reached the far end of the living room, where halls split off into two opposite directions, the battle in the living room was over. Nothing was left but piles of silt and the lingering stench of rotten fish. Mixed with that was the burnt sugar smell Rhiannon recognized from the theater, along with a hint of jasmine. She remembered the jasmine as Sara's scent.

Rhiannon, Jake, Keir, and several others took the left hallway, while another group went to the right.

Glass crunched under their boots from the broken window. The hallway had twelve-foot-high ceilings and was at least six feet in width. Jake gave the all-clear, and they moved into it to check each room.

Before they reached the first closed door, Ceithlenn materialized in the hallway in front of them.

Flame-haired, bat-winged, a wild look in her crimson eyes.

With a terrible shriek, she let loose bolts of black fire that slammed into Rhiannon's and Jake's chests.

Rhiannon flew back into the arms of several PSF officers.

Dear Anu, the pain! It felt as if flesh had been seared from her breastbone.

Gunshots echoed in Rhiannon's ears and the clang of magic against swords rang out as D'Danann blocked Ceithlenn's spells. The bullets never touched Ceithlenn. They just bounced off her shield like pennies.

Then Ceithlenn smiled and held out her arms.

Instinct grabbed hold of Rhiannon and she threw up a protective shield.

A powerful force of magic caused the shield to reverberate and waver.

"She's trying to suck up our souls!" Rhiannon shouted to everyone around her. "I've got a shield blocking this entire hallway."

Okay, now Rhiannon was way pissed. First the mind-shattering thing, then she'd nearly had her heart burned out of her chest, and now the bitch was trying to take her soul.

Heat expanded from the burn and through her body as Rhiannon shoved away from the officers.

Ceithlenn looked as angry as Rhiannon that she was being stopped from taking their souls.

Rhiannon's fury was so great her vision blurred and incredible power rose up within her.

The Shadows charged from her body.

Straight through Rhiannon's magic that protected them all from Ceithlenn.

Stunned, Rhiannon almost dropped the shield.

It felt as if her body was an electrical storm as the Shadows whirled out like tornados.

The goddess screamed as the Shadows slammed into her and forced her back. The Shadows—indistinct shapes—crawled all over Ceithlenn, driving her to her knees.

Head-splitting pain shot through Rhiannon's skull as she

felt Ceithlenn try to gain hold of her mind. The goddess was trying to control both her and the Shadows!

The Great Guardian's words flowed through Rhiannon's mind—

"If you stop fighting them, they will help you. You need to trust yourself, and in turn the Shadows will answer to you."

Rhiannon ground her teeth, focused on the Shadows, and—let it all go. She stopped fighting and allowed the Shadows free reign over Ceithlenn.

She glanced at Jake and nodded. He returned her nod and held his .357 in both hands, his stance wide, and pointed it at the goddess.

Rhiannon dropped the shield.

"Now, now, now, now!" Jake shouted.

Shots rang out in the hallway as bullets went through Rhiannon's Shadows and pierced Ceithlenn's flesh. Spellfire ripped her wings as Sydney and Rhiannon flung fireballs.

The goddess let out a shriek that tore at Rhiannon's eardrums.

Ceithlenn's unholy red eyes met Rhiannon's. The goddess snarled, wrapped her wings around her battered body—

And vanished.

The Shadows immediately shot into Rhiannon's body.

She stumbled backward at the force of their entry. It felt strange and awful, like her body was made of electricity and someone was walking inside of her. Several someones.

Yet at the same time, it felt right. Like they *belonged* inside her.

She swayed, suddenly feeling tired and worn—like the Shadows had taken so much energy from her, worse than when they had attacked Keir.

"Fuck!" Jake motioned to his officers and they checked every room, kicking the doors in, grasping their rifles or handguns and sweeping the room.

The D'Danann kept their swords readied and the witches were prepared with their magic and their shields.

Nothing.

No more Fomorii. No Junga or Darkwolf monsters. No Ceithlenn.

Rhiannon stood where she was for several moments. She'd lost control of the Shadows, but they'd helped her fight Ceithlenn.

They'd *helped* her fight.

Another thought jabbed her heart hard. Those involved in the fight had to have noticed that the Shadows came *from* her. Returned *to* her.

Exhausted, Rhiannon felt her stomach twist as the Shadows stirred within her, retreating back to the place where she kept them hidden—only not as deep as they had been before.

She wrapped her arms around her belly and felt sick, like she might throw up. Dear Anu, how could such evil be good? And how could it come from her?

But her headache—it had been lessened, as if somehow the Shadows had weakened the goddess's hold.

Sydney touched Rhiannon's arm, startling her. "We've got to get you bandaged up," Sydney said. "You're injured."

Something else was in her eyes as her concern warred with a frown. After a pause, Sydney adjusted her glasses and added, "It looks like all of the Coven sisters are going to have to have a talk when we have a chance. I don't know what just happened, but I think you do."

Rhiannon's heart sank and she squeezed her arms around her waist tighter.

Sydney didn't say anything more. Instead she took Rhiannon by the arm and led her to the penthouse living room with the other fighters. The team that had taken the right hall were already there.

"Not another damn Fomorii to be seen," Tiernan said, his expression tight with anger. "What did you find?"

"The goddess bitch." Jake holstered his handgun and winced. "But she got away."

Rhiannon looked at Jake's chest. A smoldering hole in his T-shirt and the Kevlar exposed burnt flesh. The hole was about the size of an orange.

"You're hurt, Jake," she said and almost moaned as she touched her own chest and felt the pain of a burn. "Let one of the witches examine you," she managed to get out through gritted teeth.

"It's just a burn. Nothing serious." Jake braced his hands on his thighs and glanced up at her. "Looks like she got you, too."

Her own wound wasn't as bad as she expected when she checked. Like Jake, a large hole had been seared into her black body armor and the T-shirt beneath it. The Kevlar had a hole the size of a golf ball melted into it, right below her breastbone.

The body armor had saved her life, as well as Jake's.

And the Shadows . . . Goddess. They had saved *all* of their lives.

In the next second, Rhiannon was jerked around by her upper arms. Keir's gaze traveled the length of her, as if assessing her for damage.

"You fool of a witch!" His expression was furious when his gaze met hers. He shook her a couple of times. "Ceithlenn almost killed you."

Rhiannon scowled and started to tell him off only to have Keir's mouth take hers. She fought him, but his kiss was harsh, punishing.

Rhiannon bit his lower lip hard, trying to get him to stop, but he didn't. Instead his kiss only became more intense.

She started to kiss him just as fiercely. And before she knew it, he had her backed up against a wall and she'd wrapped her arms around his neck. His stubble chafed her face and his body was hard against hers.

When he finally tore his mouth away, she could only stare into his dark, furious eyes. His voice was low and harsh. "She. Almost. Killed. You. *Never* get close to the goddess again."

Rhiannon slid her arms from his neck, down to his biceps, and to his chest. She didn't have the strength to push him away. The shot of magic from Ceithlenn, the power of Keir's kiss . . .

She looked him in the eyes. "We all came here to do a job." Rhiannon straightened her spine. "Sometimes the job comes with danger, but that's something we all have to face."

"Not *you*." Keir reached up and cupped her cheek. "Not you."

Rhiannon shivered at the power of the tenderness in his touch and in his eyes. He'd gone from fury to a gentleness that tore at her heart.

She grabbed his shirt in her fists and rose up to brush her lips over his before drawing back. "You've got to understand, Keir. This is my fight just as much as it is anyone else's." She brought her hand to her cheek and touched the Fomorii scars that burned even now. "It's not only this, it's the fact that my friends' lives are at stake. Countless other people's lives are in danger. And if this entire city could be blown off the map, then who knows what's next?"

Rhiannon brought her fingers to his lips when he started to speak. "This is not going to change. Instead of fighting me, fight *with* me. I'm a strong witch, but together, as a team, we'll really kick some ass."

Keir wrapped his arms around her so tightly that he smashed her face against his shirt. She inhaled his comforting male scent. "*A stór*," he whispered and pressed his lips against her head. "Now that I have found you, I do not want to lose you."

Rhiannon closed her eyes when she felt the pinprick of tears. Oh, how she wished this could last forever.

She pushed away and avoided his gaze. "I think there's probably work to be done now."

He let her slip away from him. When she turned to face the room, some of the witches, in addition to Hawk, were staring at her and Keir. Heat rose in her cheeks, but Rhiannon walked over and stood next to Sydney. "Find anything?" she asked.

"No." Sydney fingered the burnt edges of the hole in Rhiannon's T-shirt. "You and Jake could have bought it. You could have died."

"Hey." Rhiannon looked to everyone who was watching

her. "This isn't just a bunch of small skirmishes that we're involved in. This is outright war. The only way we're going to win is if everyone works together. It's the risk we all have to take."

Silver flung her arms around Rhiannon's neck. "I didn't save your butt months ago just to lose you now. Be more careful."

"Okay." Rhiannon drew away from Silver, who had tears in her eyes. "We'll *all* have to be more careful."

Silver rubbed Rhiannon's arm and gave a small smile. "That means everyone here. All we have is one another."

Rhiannon hugged each of her Coven sisters until she came to Hannah, who glanced at the hole in Rhiannon's vest and back to her face. "We need to get you and Jake to Cassia." Hannah cleared her throat. "To make sure you're properly healed."

Rhiannon sighed and nodded. "You're right."

Hannah raised her hand until her palm was level with Rhiannon's wound. "Sorry about invading your little box." Hannah's voice took on her usual sarcastic tone. "But this time just shut up about it."

Rhiannon opened her mouth then closed it as green sparkles radiated from Hannah's hand to the wound on Rhiannon's chest. Immediately, the burning sensation eased and she took a breath of relief.

"Go on." Hannah backed away. "Get to Cassia."

Rhiannon nodded. "Thank you."

She turned and shook her head. What was the world coming to now? Hannah was concerned about her?

And Keir . . . she couldn't even begin to think about his part in all of this. And exactly how she felt about it . . . about him.

Chapter 26

Ceithlenn burned with fury.

In the cavern beneath Alcatraz, she crouched on a ledge with her palms braced between her thighs. Far below her was the army of Fomorii, Basilisks, and three-headed dogs from Underworld.

Ceithlenn growled as she thought about what had happened only hours ago. She had come face-to-face with the bitch who had invaded her mind and her sanctum. *Rhiannon.* Her mind should still be broken, and she should have died from the blast of Ceithlenn's magic.

"Why isn't the bitch dead?" Ceithlenn said aloud.

Her own wounds had healed, the tears in her wings mended with her regenerative powers. The only reason she had suffered any damage at all was because she had drained herself transforming Darkwolf and Junga into her special weapons. Too bad she had already transferred them here, to this rock of an island, or those who had dared to attack her would have suffered a sure defeat.

No matter. Her lips curved into a smile and she licked her fangs. She would defeat the human law enforcement, D'-Danann, and those *witches.* She had devised a plan to lure them out in order to do so. And she had come up with the perfect venue. One where she could draw on many souls before the battle was finished, allowing her to bring Balor back. There were relatively few of her enemies in comparison to her legions that it would not take her entire force to defeat them. She would save the bulk of her army to devour San Francisco.

Below the ledge where she perched, the demons of her army sharpened their nails, which they all had dipped in iron heated until it was a fiery liquid. Before today, only a few of the Fomorii had iron-tipped claws. But now all the demons would.

Her gaze landed on Darkwolf and Junga. She had put the pair to work commanding her legions.

Ceithlenn flapped her great wings and pushed herself from the ledge. Air rushed past her now-healed face. She soared above the legions, her gaze taking in all who served her. From one end of the cavern to the other, she assessed the demons.

Her eyes narrowed as she honed in on the bodies of multiple dead humans being dragged into the cavern by a group of Fomorii.

She dove toward the leader of the group. Paa, Ceithlenn thought her name was.

She landed before Paa and the Fomorii demon immediately bowed her scaly, hideous orange head. "How may I serve you, my goddess?" Paa asked in the guttural language of the Fomorii.

Ceithlenn's hair flamed higher, burning with the force of her anger. "Where did these humans come from?"

"One of the tour boats, my goddess." Paa raised her head. "We found much flesh to feed the Fomorii."

"You idiot!" Ceithlenn held out her hand. A burst of magic shot out and slammed into the demon's chest.

Paa was flung back several feet and struck its head on the stone wall. The demon held its hand to its chest, where it was seared so badly the heart was exposed.

"I did not give you permission to harvest humans!" She stalked toward the demon. "We cannot have too many humans missing. Yet. Only I may take their lives and their flesh."

Paa trembled, and its three eyes were wide with fear.

When Ceithlenn stood directly in front of Paa, she reached out, grabbed the demon's pulsating heart, ripped it from Paa's chest, and sank her teeth into the organ. She ate as she watched Paa die.

The demon screamed, but the sound faded away as it crumbled to silt on the cavern floor.

Ceithlenn turned to the demons that had gone quiet as she punished the legion leader. Blood dribbled down the goddess's chin, and she took another bite of the heart. The heart of a Fomarii did not turn to silt if it was ripped from a living demon's chest.

With the D'Danann it was much the same. Their bodies would vanish, but their hearts would remain if torn from their chest before they died.

"No eating humans," Ceithlenn shouted to the legions. "Harvest only fish. No more whales. I do not wish to have a trail left that might expose us before we are ready to attack."

"Yes, my goddess," came the replies, the roar of voices equal to the roar of the ocean.

Ceithlenn swallowed the rest of the heart.

Using great nets, her demons had been capturing fish and other sea creatures from the bay and as far out as the ocean for food. When she had been in her penthouse lair, the Sara part of her had listened to what was called a television. It pleased Ceithlenn to hear the frantic concern about the gradual depletion of the bay's creatures. Once the Fomorii had brought in a whale, and several times sharks and octopi.

Ceithlenn soared over the heads of the demons and shouted out commands to the remaining legion leaders. "All beings in this sanctuary must train each waking minute of every day."

Her creatures bowed so low their faces touched the cavern floor and she smiled.

The Fomorii practiced using speed to get to their enemies and jumps to snatch D'Danann warriors from the sky. They would dig their nails into the warriors' flesh and destroy them with the iron on their claws.

Basilisks and the three-headed dogs of Underworld were worthless to train, but very useful in battle.

She would gain massive power from devouring the souls from the San Francisco Giants' exhibition game in the baseball stadium.

Ceithlenn glided back to her ledge, landed, and crouched again with her palms on the rock's bumpy surface. She smiled. She would soon call forth Balor.

When her beloved arrived, she would take the eye from Darkwolf's throat. She would present it to her love, her husband. Without his eye he was blind. With it, he could kill legions with just one look.

He had lost his single eye when a prophecy came to pass and his own grandson, the sun god Lugh, had shot the eye from Balor's head.

But the eye, all these centuries later, had been retrieved.

Once Balor had his eye, all within his line of sight would perish.

Chapter 27

Strange sensations twisted Keir's gut as he stood in Rhiannon's apartment and watched Cassia treat Rhiannon's wounds with creams that smelled of chickweed, aloe, and comfrey. Blue sparkles radiated from Cassia's fingertips. The burned area lightened and no longer looked charred, yet remained red and blistered.

The feelings inside him—gods, he had never felt this way about anyone in his lifespan. Centuries had passed and suddenly one woman arrived in his life who practically wrenched his heart in two by almost being killed.

"It won't completely heal for a couple of days." Cassia taped a pad to Rhiannon's chest, covering the burned area. "But it should feel better."

Rhiannon's chest rose and fell as she took a deep, audible breath. Keir found himself taking a breath with her.

"Who's treating Jake's wound?" Rhiannon asked as she leaned back in her bright blue overstuffed chair.

"Silver and Hannah have him covered," Cassia said.

Spirit kept twining himself around her ankles and making soft mewling sounds. Keir went to Rhiannon's kitchen, used a can opener, and put cat food in Spirit's bowl. The cat immediately ran into the kitchen, rubbed against Keir's leg, and purred.

"The wound on my chest is already beginning to feel like

it's not there," Rhiannon was saying as she started buttoning a bright pink blouse over that thing she called a bra. She had showered and her hair was damp. He thought about the ruined T-shirt and the strange body armor that human law enforcement used. He thanked the gods for that armor or his treasure would have been lost.

Cassia gathered the small vessels she had brought with her then paused to look at Rhiannon. "You must speak with your Coven sisters soon," she said, and Rhiannon's face fell from a smile to a look of sadness as Keir watched her. "I know of the power within you, and it's time your sisters know, too. And of your heritage."

"I'm not ready," Rhiannon said in a husky voice and Keir moved behind her and gripped her shoulders as he studied Cassia.

The half-Elvin witch's voice lowered. "You must be ready. They need to know."

Rhiannon nodded and Cassia smiled at her, then Keir.

"Take care of her, Keir," she said before walking around them both.

He barely heard Rhiannon mumbling, "I don't need to be taken care of."

His gaze landed on the carved bird he had given her in Otherworld. She had set it upon a small table at the end of her couch and it pleased him to see it there.

After Cassia slipped out of the apartment and closed the door, Keir massaged Rhiannon's shoulders for a bit and she sighed and let her head loll forward.

When he believed she was a bit more relaxed, he let her go and moved in front of her, crouched on one knee, and pushed her thighs apart to get closer. She wore a short article of clothing she called a skirt, and it showed a great deal of her beautiful legs. It barely hid the soft flesh beneath the material.

"What are you doing?" she whispered as he took her face in his hands.

He captured her mouth in a swift kiss, the only answer he needed to give. Rhiannon moaned into his mouth as he brushed his lips over hers.

Keir rubbed his thumbs over her cheeks as he slipped his tongue into her mouth. She tasted sweet. Like apples and cinnamon from the tea she'd been drinking as Cassia tended to her wound.

Rhiannon moved her hands to his chest then slipped them around so that her palms were on his back. She clung to him like one might cling to a tree limb when being swept down a river. He bit her lower lip softly and she moaned again.

Gods, the feelings inside him had already stolen his breath and swept him down the same river. He could get lost in this woman. A sense of being off-balance, almost dizzy, had him spinning into a whirlpool of desire.

He moved his hands slowly over her body, tracing her curves. She shivered and raised her chest, offering herself to him as he drew small circles around her nipples with his thumbs. He took great care to not touch her wound.

When his palms rested at the indentations at her waist, he drew away from the kiss. Rhiannon's eyes were heavy-lidded, her mouth moist, and her lips swollen from his kiss.

"Don't stop." She gripped him tighter and wrapped her legs around his waist.

"I want to bed you, *a stór*." He stroked her from her waist, past her skirt, to her bare thighs and knees. "I want to be inside of you." He needed the closeness, needed to know she was alive, to feel her alive. But he said, "I fear for your injury."

"I'm okay." Her green eyes grew to a shade of emerald darker than the ones on the High Chieftain's rings. "We can avoid touching my burn. Just take me to bed."

Keir kissed her hard again, then slipped his hands under her ass while she continued to cling to him with her arms and thighs. He rose up with Rhiannon cradled in his embrace, taking care not to hold her too close. It was but a few strides to make it to her bedroom, where he pushed aside her tangled sheets and blankets with one hand then carefully laid her on the center of the small bed with her head on a pillow. She smiled up at him, and his heart twisted again.

Rhiannon began unbuttoning her blouse as he pulled off her skirt and tossed it aside. She was already barefoot. He went back to draw down her undergarment but saw she'd finished unbuttoning her blouse and helped her shrug out of it. She had shown him how to unclasp the undergarment that hid her beautiful breasts. If he had any say in the matter, she would wear nothing beneath her clothing. But with Rhiannon . . . she was so stubborn he did not know if she would do as he requested. Perhaps if he used that word "please" that she seemed to like so much.

When he removed her bra and other undergarment, for a moment he could only look at her. He studied her lovely body from her short auburn hair, to her breasts and the hard peaks of her nipples. The bandage just below her breasts caused a tightness to squeeze his chest.

Keir forced himself not to linger on it and instead swept his gaze from her belly to the full flare of her hips and the auburn curls of her mound. He could already scent the musk of her desire and his cock grew even more painful against his breeches.

"Your turn." Her smile made his gut turn inside out.

He shucked off his boots, untied his leather breeches, and stepped out of them, then practically ripped his shirt over his head. When he was naked she studied him as he had studied her.

"You are so beautiful," she whispered.

Taken aback, he paused. He certainly had never been called beautiful before. A great lover, aye, but not beautiful.

Lise's comments came to the forefront of his mind as he knelt beside the bed and stroked Rhiannon's hair from her face.

"I wonder what kind of woman it would take to tame you?" Lise had said.

Was he tamed? The warrior inside him wanted to say no, but his heart said yes.

Keir slipped onto the bed beside Rhiannon, propped his elbow on the mattress, and touched her face with his free hand. He trailed his fingertips along the scars on her cheek and anger flared through him again at the thought that the Fomorii Queen had done this to her.

His anger faded, however, as she brought her hand up to his head, and ran her fingers through his hair. She made him shiver with longing and need from just the touch of her fingers on his scalp and the brush of her hand on his shoulder when she reached the ends of his hair.

He cupped her cheek and brought his mouth to hers. He wanted to take his time and explore every inch of this precious woman. Gods, he could have lost her today. Every time the thought crossed his mind, it made him feel as if a boulder was weighted in his gut.

Those thoughts vanished when she moaned and slipped her fingers around his cock. It jerked in her hand and he bit her lower lip with the promise of passion. She slid her hand further to cup his balls and gently fondled them, making him groan. The need to part her thighs and drive into her was so great that he thrust his tongue hard into her mouth and plundered it like he wanted to plunder her tight channel with his cock.

She gave a sigh as he moved his lips along her chin to her earlobe and bit it. He darted his tongue into her ear and she shivered in his arms. At the same time he moved his hand from her face, exploring the curves of her neck and shoulder to her waist and the flare of her hip. He cupped her ass and drew her closer to him so that his cock was against her belly, his hips tight to hers. But he was ever aware of her burn, and careful not to let their chests touch.

"You are mine, *a stór*," he murmured as his lips moved from her ear to the softness of her neck.

Rhiannon gave soft sighs and moans as he touched her, kissed her, made love to her. She had yet to admit that her heart and soul belonged to him, but he was certain it was only a matter of time. She was his.

He slid down her body so that he could move his lips to the hollow of her throat. "Has anyone ever told you what a wonderful lover you are?" she murmured.

Keir simply continued his gentle lovemaking with Rhiannon. He had been told many times what a skilled lover he was, but he had never made *love* before. He'd fucked countless women, but he had never wanted to explore a woman so thoroughly, to become part of her, to cherish her, to please her in a way that would steal her breath and his.

Her fingers slid up his cock to the head, where she stroked the slit at the top with her thumb. "Maybe you're such a good lover because you're part Mystwalker," Rhiannon said in a teasing voice. "Didn't the Guardian say something about Mystwalkers being known as incredible lovers? Maybe I'll keep you around for a little while."

Keir grunted as his lips moved over the curve of one of her breasts. He would keep her a long while—an eternity. He licked her nipple in gentle strokes and Rhiannon gripped his cock more firmly as she cried out and tilted her head back. He almost couldn't breathe from the hold she had on his erection and he sucked her nipple hard in response. That only made her grip him tighter and her cries grew louder.

Keir moved his mouth to her other nipple and licked and sucked it. She sighed, she moaned, she made soft mewling noises. All the sounds made his urgency for her even greater than before.

Rhiannon raised herself up and pushed at Keir's shoulder. He let her force him onto his back as she straddled him, her folds slick against his cock.

"I want to taste you, *a stór*." He gripped her hips with both hands. "You steal from me what I most want."

Rhiannon smiled. "You can have your turn next. But first I get to taste *you*."

With a groan he allowed her to slip between his thighs, her body brushing over his painful erection as she moved lower. When her mouth was level with his cock, she looked up at him and smiled again. With her eyes fixed on his, she slipped his erection into her mouth.

His hips bucked up in reaction. "Gods above," he managed to get out.

Her mouth was warm and moist and when she softly sucked he let out a loud groan. She fondled his balls with one hand while using her other hand to move up and down his shaft in tandem with her mouth.

He gripped his hands in her short, silky hair and held her while his hips bucked up to meet her. She took him so deep. And the way she watched him while she slid his cock in and out of her mouth . . . he knew he would climax soon.

"I am going to spill my seed," he said in a voice so rough he almost didn't recognize it as his own. Rhiannon sucked harder and pleasure radiated around his cock and balls. The intensity of the pleasure grew within him until he felt as though his eyes had crossed and his mind had fled.

His orgasm arrowed through him, to every limb of his body, to every hair on his head. She drew his seed from him until he was so sated he thought he might never move again.

She grinned as she crawled up to lie beside him. "Is my warrior tired?"

His lips twitched and he rolled her so that her head was on the pillow again. "This warrior is always ready for a good battle."

Rhiannon's head spun with the quick movement as he moved her onto her back. She still tasted him in her mouth. What he was doing to her now. Good goddess! He knelt between her thighs and slowly made his way down her body. He stopped to suckle her nipples and she sighed with pleasure. It felt so good. Beyond good. Freaking out of this world good.

Keir suckled her nipples so hard they grew almost sore from the attention, becoming even more sensitive. His rough palms cupped her breasts, kneading them at the same time his lips and teeth paid attention to her nipples.

She raised her hips in an invitation for him to move to where she wanted his mouth. He bit each of her nipples, then kissed the spot between her breasts. He skirted the bandage on her chest and moved his lips to her belly button. When he darted his tongue inside, she moaned and more moisture flooded her folds. It felt as if her navel was connected to her pussy, and she felt a small spasm in her channel.

He tangled his fingers in the curls of her mound then moved his lips to it and darted his tongue to the soft skin beneath the curls.

His callused hands slid beneath her ass and he raised her

up so that his mouth was level with her folds. She held her breath as she watched him close his eyes and inhale. *Just lick me,* she cried out in her mind.

He looked up at her with an amused expression and she wondered if he had just heard her thoughts. After all, he could talk in her head.

But then she could no longer think. She could only feel. Soft growling noises rose up from his throat as his tongue stroked her folds. He delved into her channel then swiped his tongue back up her folds to her clit. She squirmed and cried out as he paid special attention to that hard, swollen nub. He swirled his tongue around it and softly bit.

This time Rhiannon's cry was more of a shriek when she came. Warmth burst through her body, waves and waves of it as he continued to nip at her clit. Her orgasm caused goose bumps to break out over her skin and her heart to thump like crazy against her breastbone.

Just when she was going to beg him to stop because the pleasure was too much, he rose up and braced his hands on the bed to either side of her breasts.

"Are you ready for me to make love to you, *a stór?*" He pumped his hips so that his already hard cock slid back and forth in her folds.

More shivers passed through her. His rich Irish brogue made her even hotter.

She reached around him and scratched her nails across his back. "I can take anything you can dish out, warrior."

Keir kissed her hard and she tasted her own musk and the flavor of pure male. He raised his head and sat back on his haunches between her thighs. He moved close enough to place his cock at the entrance of her channel, just sliding in a tiny bit and causing her to groan for more.

He slipped his arms under her knees and moved her legs so that her ankles were around his neck. This was one move she'd never experienced before.

Keir drove his cock inside her. She gasped at the power of his thrust and how deep he'd buried himself inside her.

Incredible. It felt so incredible.

Still holding her ankles around his neck, he began to pump his cock in and out of her channel. His balls slapped against her pussy and his hips were tight between her thighs.

"Jeez, Keir." She could barely talk.

She cried out in frustration when he stopped. "Did I hurt you?" he asked.

"No." She thrust her hips up, trying to take him inside her. "The way you're taking me. It just feels so good. Goddess, it feels good."

His expression was one of satisfaction as he began pumping in and out of her, harder and deeper yet. Her skin was slick with perspiration and she saw a droplet of sweat roll down the hollow of his throat and splash onto her belly.

"Look at how I am taking you." His voice was like sandpaper over wood.

Her gaze traveled to where she could watch his cock slide in and out of her core. The sight of him taking her like this made the sensations in her belly intensify, wind tighter and tighter.

"Now look at *me*," he said.

She slowly swept her gaze from his six-pack abs to his muscular chest, strong shoulders, and to his harsh features. Her eyes met his dark ones and she caught her breath at how he was staring at her. That possessive expression he had whenever he was with her, yet something more. Like his feelings for her went beyond merely wanting to possess her.

The look in his eyes was enough to hit Rhiannon hard where they were joined. Her already sensitive channel clenched down on his cock at the same time a whoosh of heat shot through every fiber of her being. Her cries came with deep pants as she struggled to breathe. The orgasm was so intense it stole the breath from her.

He raised his head and groaned—more of a growl—as his hips rammed against hers, hard, several times before he stopped and held himself still. He shut his eyes and she felt the pulse of his cock inside her as he came.

When the last spasm had passed, along with the last throb of his cock, he rolled them over onto their sides so that they were looking at each other. He still took great care not to touch her chest.

Keir's lips met hers in a gentle kiss. He drew away from her and said something softly in Gaelic that gave her chills.

Her eyes met his. "What did you say?"

A smile actually formed on his lips. "One day I will tell you, *a stór,* but not yet."

Chapter 28

The Great Guardian stood in a garden in Otherworld, a beautiful place filled with roses, pansies, poppies, daffodils, tulips, orchids, and other flowers Rhiannon had never seen before. At this moment the Guardian was tending to a single, large purple bud that looked as if it would flower soon. The lone bud perched atop a great, thick stem, and the bud almost had a sparkle to it.

A breeze tugged at the Guardian's diaphanous white robes and tendrils of her long hair. Sunlight touched the Elvin woman's features causing her celestial glow to radiate from her so much so that her expression was difficult to make out.

"It is time." The Guardian didn't part her lips, but Rhiannon heard her clearly in her mind. *"Arrangements have been made. You and Keir must come at once."*

The Elvin woman stretched out her arms and the glow became so intense Rhiannon couldn't see the Guardian's form any longer. The brightness faded away until all Rhiannon could see was the bridge and the meadow.

Rhiannon blinked as the vision faded away, and reality came into focus. She had her palms flat on the scarred Formica table in the kitchen of Enchantments and she was staring at one of the walls.

She shook her head to clear the fuzziness in her mind.

"Vision?" Hannah said in her cultured voice. "Or daydreaming about that barbarian D'Danann warrior?"

Rhiannon turned to look at Hannah, who sat on the other side of the table, just off to the side. She wore her usual arrogant expression. Of course she looked perfect from her glossy brown hair with the shock of blond hair framing her face, to her expertly applied makeup, to her tailored clothing. No one else was sitting at the table but her, and she hadn't been there when Rhiannon fell into her vision.

"It doesn't concern you," Rhiannon said, before glancing across the kitchen to see Cassia look at her.

The half-Elvin witch raised an eyebrow.

Rhiannon took a deep breath. "In my vision, the Great Guardian told me it's time for me and Keir to go."

"Where?" Hannah asked, tapping her perfectly manicured nails on the table. The noise always irritated the hell out of Rhiannon and she was sure Hannah knew it.

Rhiannon fought to keep from making a smartass remark. "To Otherworld."

"Really." Hannah leaned back in her chair and folded her arms across her chest. "Just the two of you?"

"Yes," Rhiannon snapped. "Why do you care?" she said and then felt childish. She took a deep breath. She *was* acting childish.

"My divining has told me that I'm to go to Otherworld in the near future." Hannah unfolded her arms and got to her feet in a graceful movement. She reminded Rhiannon of a tigress. "But I don't think it's to go with you on this journey."

Thank the Ancestors. Rhiannon didn't say a word as Hannah pushed open the door to the shop. For a moment sounds of customers in the café and store carried into the kitchen, then vanished when the door closed behind her.

Rhiannon sighed as she stared at the doorway. "Why does Hannah drive me crazy?"

"I think one day you'll grow to value your Coven sister more than you can imagine." Cassia's voice drew Rhiannon's attention as the half-Elvin witch walked over to her. "We're not all what we appear to be on the outside."

"I suppose," Rhiannon rubbed her palms on her skirt. "But Hannah loves to push my buttons."

Cassia's expression became more serious. "I think it's time we gather everyone together to talk about—"

"Later. When we get back from Otherworld." The legs of Rhiannon's chair scraped the floor as she got to her feet as fast as she could. "I'd better get Keir."

"What guidance have you, Guardian?" Keir said as he and Rhiannon rose from a bow.

They had just walked over the bridge in Golden Gate Park and had appeared on the transference stone in front of the Great Guardian. It appeared as if she had been waiting.

The Guardian glowed from inside, like in Rhiannon's vision, and like she had the first time Rhiannon met her.

"Now that you have performed the tasks you needed to, it is time to meet with the Mystwalkers and Drow." A breeze picked up and caused flowers at the Guardian's feet to lean as if pressing kisses to her bare toes. "The Mystwalkers and the Dark Elves take family bonds seriously, and they will battle to protect their own."

"Mystwalkers, perhaps." Keir scowled. "But the Drow? They do nothing that does not benefit themselves. And the war between Elves and Fae—it runs too deep."

The Guardian gave a gentle smile. "Our peoples have been divided for far too long. Perhaps with a new alliance some of these prejudices will be lessened."

"I bet it's hard when you all live so long." Rhiannon sighed. "You can't simply forget something that's been ingrained in you forever."

With a nod, the Guardian said, "This is true. But the time will come when differences must be set aside for the greater good."

The Guardian turned her peaceful gaze on Keir. "You, Keir D'Danann and Mystwalker, must speak with your mother and her rebel faction and ask them to fight in any way they can."

Keir shook his head. "They cannot come in contact with saltwater and must be near freshwater to survive. All that surrounds this San Francisco and the island where the Fomorii and other beasts hide is the ocean and the bay."

"Yes," the Guardian replied. "However, they can create weapons of much use to you."

The thought of meeting his birth mother caused a strange ache in Keir's chest. Who would this woman be when he met her? Would her people help him, a half-D'Danann bastard they didn't even know?

Rhiannon studied Keir and the conflicting emotions on his face. She knew the feelings he was experiencing right now—because she was feeling the same way.

It didn't take a rocket scientist to figure out what was coming next. "You, Rhiannon D'Anu and Elvin, must go to the Drow King," the Great Guardian said as she turned her attention from Keir to Rhiannon.

Rhiannon's heart beat faster and her throat was dry. "What do I say? 'Hi, Dad. Nice to meet you. Can you help me and a bunch of friends in a war we're fighting against an evil god and a goddess, and a bunch of demons that you happened to have helped set free?' "

The Guardian smiled. "You will find your way."

Rhiannon just couldn't get used to the idea of her father being one of the Dark Elves. A bunch of them had betrayed Copper when the door to Underworld was opened, setting loose Ceithlenn.

And they had bluish gray skin, for the sake of the Ancestors. *Blue!*

"What's his name?" Rhiannon asked.

"King Garran."

Rhiannon's heart stopped and her eyes widened. "Oh, wait a minute. No way. Garran? *He* was the betrayer. He helped set loose that bitch of a goddess. My father is evil!"

"No, he is not." The Guardian stroked Rhiannon's upper arm with her fingertips, and her beautiful wildflower scent floated on the breeze to Rhiannon. "Yes, at the beginning he worked with Darkwolf to open the door under the promise that he and his people would be able to walk in the light again. A promise Balor made through the essence of the eye."

The Guardian's voice was kind despite the words she spoke. "When he saw the manner of evil that was being released, Garran ordered the Drow to fight against Darkwolf and the Fomorii. Garran had his people side with Copper, Silver, and the Tuatha D'Danann, and lost his own brother to protect them."

"The fact that he was on Darkwolf's side at all is unforgivable." Rhiannon clenched her hands into fists, her heart clenching just as hard. "I won't have anything to do with him."

The Guardian raised her fingers to caress Rhiannon's face, and some of her tenseness slipped away at the Guardian's touch. "Like the D'Danann, the Drow are a neutral race. They do what they think is right for their people but do not involve themselves in the concerns of others if they do not believe it to be the natural order of things." Rhiannon shivered as the Guardian cupped her cheek. "Garran chose what he thought was right for his people. When he realized he had chosen wrong, he tried to right that wrong."

"But he didn't." Rhiannon's tone was bitter. "It's not right at all. Everything's so screwed up I don't know if it'll ever be right again."

"Give him the opportunity, Rhiannon D'Anu and Elvin." She smiled. "He is a good being."

Rhiannon closed her eyes and felt the warmth, the magic of the Great Guardian's touch. Could she forgive her father for so much?

"He saved Copper's life," the Guardian said softly.

Rhiannon opened her eyes and swallowed. "He did?"

The Guardian let her hand slip away from Rhiannon's face and simply gave her gentle smile that warmed Rhiannon through. "Indeed. And did it occur to you that if he could walk in the sun, he could finally see you, and get to know his own daughter? Darkwolf could scarcely have chosen a more beguiling—and cruel—promise with which to tempt Garran."

Rhiannon pressed her fingertips to her forehead. "So much. There's just so much to think about. Too much."

"Rest, Rhiannon D'Anu and Elvin, and Keir D'Danann and Mystwalker." The Guardian stepped back. "I will send you directly to Keir's home using the transference stone upon which you arrived. Tomorrow the Faerie Queen Riona will guide you back to me. She has ties of sorts to both Mystwalkers and Drow."

"Thank you, Great Guardian." Rhiannon bowed from her shoulders, as did Keir, who also thanked her.

Keir and Rhiannon washed the morning's dishes. He felt such pleasure having her at his side as they ate breakfast and took care of the morning chores. They had made love through the night and Keir was certain he would never get enough of her.

"I'm scared, Keir," she said as she looked up at him. "I don't know if I can do this—meet my father."

He rested his arm around her shoulders and squeezed. "You will do what your heart tells you to."

"What about you?" Rhiannon clenched a drying cloth. "What about your mother?"

He sighed and moved his arm from around her shoulders and braced his palms on the countertop. "I do not think I will know until I meet her."

A light rap at the door caught Keir's attention and he dried his hands on a rough cloth.

"The Faerie Queen?" Rhiannon asked as she set down her own drying cloth.

"Most likely." He strode to the door and opened it to see Queen Riona.

Her long black hair was behind her shoulders, baring her naked breasts, and her tiny hands were propped on her hips. "You took long enough."

"My apologies," he said, and she looked surprised before she fluttered into the cabin, her lavender wings sprinkling purple dust as she traveled through the living room and approached Rhiannon.

"So you are King Garran's daughter, Rhiannon D'Anu and Elvin," Riona said, her lips pursed and her arms now crossing her chest.

Rhiannon didn't know what to think of this tiny being. "Does everyone know?"

"I do not believe Garran is aware that his daughter is here, in Otherworld." Riona smiled. "When you do meet him, hearing of the Drow King's surprise will be a pleasure to all of us."

Rhiannon wasn't sure quite what to think about that statement. And did she want him to expect her or not? "You won't be there?"

"It is unfortunate that I cannot." The queen flew to perch on Rhiannon's shoulder, crossed her legs, and began swinging one of her feet. "The D'Danann are the only Fae who can survive the Drow realm." She shuddered. "It is not a place for the rest of us."

Rhiannon had to crane her neck to see the Faerie who sat so regally on her shoulder, yet swung one of her feet in a relaxed manner. "What's he like?" Rhiannon asked, half afraid of the answer.

The queen gave a smile that met her lavender eyes, an expression that could only be described as mischievous. "You will see, Drow Princess."

Rhiannon blinked. That was the last thing she expected to be called.

Keir brushed her cheek with his knuckles. "Come, princess."

She slugged his upper arm. "Don't call me that."

"Aye, princess," he said with a grin and ducked out of reach when she took another swing at his shoulder.

After they grabbed their packs and left Keir's cabin, Riona took the lead.

She guided them in a direction he hadn't expected. It was not far before they reached a large crystal blue pond surrounded by wildflowers and thick grass. Heavy mist lay close to the ground around the pond. Some of the mist moved and Keir's heart thumped as he realized what it must be. *Who* it must be.

Rhiannon gave a startled gasp as the mist rose. Keir watched as the being grew to be almost as tall as Rhiannon. Slowly it began to take shape until a beautiful woman stood before Keir.

The woman wore almost sheer clothing that shimmered in the gentle light shining through the trees. She had a soft smile, and the telltale flaxen hair and shifting gray-blue eyes of the Mystwalkers. Her long hair floated in the breeze and exposed a gold band around her throat.

The Mystwalker held her hand to her chest and stared at Keir. She looked as if she wished to speak, but nothing came from her lips.

"Keir," Riona said softly, "this is your mother, Keaira."

Keir's chest seized and he couldn't breathe. The longing combined with anger that had been inside his heart all these years felt like a fist in his throat.

The anger faded as he looked upon the woman, leaving only a sense of pain and loss.

He gave a bow from his shoulders. "Keaira, it is my pleasure to meet you."

The Mystwalker woman's lower lip trembled. Tears glistened in her eyes. She rushed the few steps forward and wrapped her arms around Keir's neck.

Keir froze, not knowing what to do. He raised his stiff arms and touched her shoulders.

"So much time," Keaira said against his chest. She stepped back and looked at him. "For so long I have wanted to touch you, to know you as my son. But I could not. Your father forbade it and I could not have survived long enough from freshwater to tell you everything I wanted to." Tears rolled down her cheeks. "I was uncertain you would want to know me."

The thought that his father had forbidden his mother to come to him sparked a different kind of anger with Keir. All these centuries he had believed his mother had abandoned him to be a pleasure slave for the Shanai. He would have words with his father and it would be soon. As harsh as his father had always been, Keir had no doubt this woman spoke the truth.

Keir still had a grip on Keaira's shoulders and met her blue eyes. "I am very delighted to meet you, my true mother."

More tears slipped from her eyes and she sniffed. "Too much time has passed."

"It has," Keir said softly as his gut tightened at actually meeting his mother.

He turned to Rhiannon, who was slightly behind him, her hands clasped in front of her. Riona fluttered near Keaira.

Keir released his mother's shoulders, took one of Rhiannon's hands and drew her next to him. "This is Rhiannon, D'Anu and Elvin."

Keaira gave a brilliant smile and clasped Rhiannon's free hand. "To meet you is a pleasure."

"I'm so glad to meet you, too." Rhiannon gave Keaira the beautiful smile that turned Keir's heart inside out. "Keir must be named after you."

Keaira nodded. "His father gave him that part of me, at least."

Keir's Mystwalker mother released Rhiannon's hand and turned to face him. Her expression became serious. "I understand you seek council with the Mystwalkers."

"We do." The overwhelming feelings of meeting his mother had all but discarded thoughts of war from his mind.

Shapes rose around them until six men and women formed from the mist, Keaira being the seventh. Each Mystwalker wore the same type of misty clothing and had a rune-engraved gold band around his or her neck. None wore a ring that would declare them a pleasure slave of the Shanai. To Keir's immense surprise, one of the Mystwalkers had dark hair and green eyes—unheard of for a Mystwalker.

"This is the council of the free Mystwalkers." Keaira gestured to the other men and women, drawing his attention from the green-eyed Mystwalker. "They have joined me to summit with you and discuss what it is that brings you to us."

Keir took a deep breath and focused on the reason he was

meeting with the Mystwalkers, and not the unsettling thoughts of seeing his birth mother.

"We are at war with the Fomorii in an Otherworld called San Francisco," Keir said. He proceeded to explain the part the D'Danann, the D'Anu, and the human Paranormal Special Forces played in the great battle, a fight that had grown increasingly worse since Samhain.

"There are far too many Fomorii to fight alone," Keir said as he looked to each blond-haired, blue-eyed Mystwalker, and the one dark-haired woman of the mist. "And now Ceithlenn." A rumble rose in Keir's chest. "We fear she is too powerful to battle without the aid of our allies."

"Mystwalkers have never been allies of the D'Danann." The dark-haired woman folded her arms across her chest and tilted her chin. "The D'Danann have chosen to not free our sisters and brothers who are kept as pleasure slaves by the Shanai."

"I was not aware any request had been made to the Chieftains," Keir said.

The woman narrowed her eyes. "We should not have had to ask for aid. Our people are being kept as slaves to pleasure the Shanai, for the gods' sakes!"

"Alaia." Keir's mother turned to look at the dark-haired woman. "It is truly the people of San Francisco and not the D'Danann who make this request. The Chieftains have failed to fully support this fight for freedom. Do we ignore the plight of these peoples simply because of our displeasure with the D'Danann?"

Alaia's green gaze met Keir's. "I believe the free Mystwalkers need time to discuss this matter."

" 'Tis true," one of the males said. "A decision cannot be made without careful consideration."

Keir gave a slow nod. "When may we hear of your decision?"

"Three days' time," the Mystwalker called Alaia said, surprising Keir. Perhaps she was their leader?

Keir gave a deep nod. "We thank you for listening to our plea."

As the other Mystwalkers vanished into mist, Keaira smiled and caressed his cheek. "I will see you again, my son."

Before Keir could respond, her form wavered and she slipped into mist and shadow and vanished with the other mist into the forest.

Rhiannon squeezed Keir's hand and he looked down at her. "Your mother is beautiful. And she seems very kind."

He nodded and looked back to where his mother had disappeared. A knot formed in his throat and he raised his chin. It was time to move on.

Rhiannon felt a keen need to hurry as they walked to the transference stone. There was so much to do. What could be happening in San Francisco? Could Ceithlenn have struck again so soon?

The thought wrenched her stomach in two. She and Keir had only spent one day in Otherworld, but it seemed like a lot more.

When they reached the transference stone, the Great Guardian was already waiting for them. Again they bowed to her.

"Riona will now take you to your next destination," the Great Guardian said. "The entrance to the Drow kingdom is where Riona's Sidhe resides, but above ground."

Nervousness and anger warred within Rhiannon, heating her belly, as they prepared to meet her father.

What would she say? How would he respond?

Not only did she feel abandoned, but he was the reason she carried such a dark secret—the Shadows she kept locked inside.

Although the Shadows had helped her. Maybe they weren't so bad after all?

Rhiannon shook her head. *Yeah, right.* They'd almost hurt Keir. She was lucky they hadn't turned on her friends, too.

She and Keir walked onto the stone and Riona perched on Rhiannon's shoulder. "I will focus on where we must be, and we will arrive in moments," the queen said.

The Great Guardian folded her hands in front of her. "I will see you upon your return."

The same wild feelings overcame Rhiannon as the meadow whirled around her until everything was a complete blur. She stumbled again as they came to a stop but Keir caught her to him.

They were in a beautiful meadow with an apple tree. Flowers and bushes were arranged in an almost perfect circle along the outskirts of the meadow. To the north side of the apple tree was a large outcropping of rocks with a waterfall that trickled down into a couple of basins.

"This is where Copper trapped us all," the Faerie Queen said. "By accident, when her magic backfired."

"When she was missing for so long?" Rhiannon looked around her. "It's beautiful." Her gaze landed on the apple tree. "No wonder she won't eat apples anymore—I imagine she got pretty tired of them."

Riona laughed, a soft tinkling laugh. "Come."

Rhiannon's belly felt hotter and hotter as she and Keir followed the Faerie whose wings sprinkled lavender dust in her wake. When they were on the backside of the rock outcropping, beside a pine tree, Rhiannon saw a flat, rectangular, rock surface. It was the shape and size of a large door and surrounded by dirt, no grass. The flat stone had strange markings scratched into the stone along all sides.

"Stomp on the door five times," Riona said.

Keir moved in front of her and his boot thumped against stone as he did as the queen instructed.

Rhiannon's heart beat like crazy as the stone jerked and trembled. It made a noise that grated on her nerves as it started sliding to the left. She took a step backward. "I don't think I'm ready."

Keir took her by the hand and she could do nothing but follow him down a set of stone stairs.

Chapter 29

The stairs smelled of damp soil and minerals as Rhiannon slowly walked down to the Drow realm. Fine dirt and small rocks crunched beneath her shoes as they made their way and a rush of cool air from below swept over her.

The door above them scratched closed and Rhiannon shivered. It went completely dark, then torches along the walls sputtered to life, giving enough light to see by.

It took some time, but when they reached the bottom of the stairs, they entered a great, circular hall. Carvings of warriors graced the walls, highlighted by torches lit around the room. Despite the fact that it was underground and dim, and not colorful like Rhiannon's apartment and belongings, she felt it was almost . . . homey.

At that thought, she frowned.

Four warriors met them at the bottom of the stairs. Rhiannon was surprised at how sexy the Drow were. Their blueish gray skin actually looked good on them. Their long hair fell to or past their broad shoulders, and their muscular bodies were well defined. The hair color of the four warriors ranged from black to steel gray to silvery blue, and they were as tall as Keir.

Instead of shirts the Drow men wore metal shoulder and breast plates and snug breeches of dark gray or black. At their backs were quivers with arrows that looked as if they were made of pewter.

"Who may we have the pleasure of meeting this day?" one of the warriors said.

"I—I'm Rhiannon, D'Anu and Elvin." She gestured to her companion. "This is Keir D'Danann."

"Ah, yes, Keir, the warrior who assisted in the fight at the Underworld door." The Drow male gave Rhiannon a long, appreciative look, causing Keir to scowl. "I will escort you to the king. I'm sure he will be pleased to see you both."

Rhiannon gave a slight nod. "Thank you."

"The throne room," the Drow warrior said as they reached the entrance and Rhiannon's jaw dropped. Every wall sparkled like clear-cut crystal, including the ceiling. To the back was an obsidian door. To the left crouched a black granite table surrounded by padded granite chairs. At the center of the room was a huge black granite throne with a padded back, and to one side of it was a matching smaller one.

Reclining on the larger throne was a man she assumed to be the Drow king.

Her father.

The king had sculpted muscles, a massive chest, and a very fit body. He wore leather straps crisscrossing his bare chest along with shoulder plates. His long silvery blue hair was loose around his shoulders and his pointed ears peeked through the strands. He didn't look any older than Keir.

King Garran had one elbow resting on the arm of the chair and a shocked expression on his features.

"This is—" their guide started.

Before they could be introduced, the Drow king pushed himself to his feet, held his hand up for the guard to be quiet, then stood completely still for a moment.

Rhiannon was looking at her father.

He was staring at her.

"Anna?" he finally said in a deep, hoarse voice filled with emotion that sounded like longing.

She cleared her throat. "I'm Rhiannon."

He stepped down the dais and took slow steps toward her. "My daughter?"

Rhiannon couldn't move her feet if she tried. She nodded. He stepped closer. She held her breath.

When he reached her he stared for a long time. "You look so like your mother." He reached up and caught a strand of her hair in his fingers. "Everything about you, down to the fire in your green eyes."

Rhiannon swallowed. The accusation in her tone was strong when she spoke. "You're talking about someone I never knew. Just like I never knew you."

Garran closed his eyes for a moment, letting his fingers fall away from her hair. When he opened his eyes again, his chest rose and fell with a deep breath. "There is nothing I can say that will change the past. You were meant to be a child of the light like your mother. That is why we parted and she took you to live in your Otherworld."

Rhiannon swallowed back the hurt. "Then where was she when I was growing up?"

Pain reflected in his eyes as he spoke. "Did not your aunt tell you? Anna died saving you and Aga during a car accident in your world."

Rhiannon's heart pounded. The images she'd seen so often in her dreams . . . that woman—could she have been Rhiannon's mother?

"No," Rhiannon whispered. "Aunt Aga told me that neither of you wanted me because of—" She stopped herself short, not ready to talk about the Shadows.

The Drow king said some harsh words in a language she didn't understand and looked furious as he shook his head. Then he spoke in her language. "Anna and I—we loved each other and loved you beyond words. But we chose for Anna to take you to the light where she watched you, while I could not."

Rhiannon's heart pounded. "She was truly with me?"

He studied her. "Until you were two human years of age."

A mixture of emotions swirled through Rhiannon. Aunt Aga had lied all this time?

It would have been just like her.

The pain of growing up without a mother and father

reared through her like a horse's hoof against her chest. "When my mother died, you could have come for me."

He slowly shook his head. "As much as I wished to, I could not."

She swallowed back other words she wanted to say. Hurtful words borne of the pain of all the years spent with an old woman who had turned her out when she was only eighteen.

She stepped back into Keir's embrace.

Garran looked over her head at the men who had accompanied her. "Keir, welcome. I am glad to have you join me with my daughter."

His daughter.

My father. Not Garran. Not the king. My father.

She shook her head. How could she think of this man as her father? He had abandoned her, and not to a good childhood.

Garran's liquid silver eyes returned to Rhiannon to study her. Without looking away from her, he said to the men, "Leave us."

"Yes, my king," one of the Dark Elves said.

Rhiannon tore her gaze from Garran's to look behind her and saw the warriors who had accompanied them retreat.

"Please allow me time with my daughter—alone, Keir D'Danann," Garran said.

Rhiannon glanced up at Keir and he scowled. He looked down at her and after a brief moment she nodded. She needed answers from her father, and right now she'd rather do it alone.

When it was just her and Garran, Rhiannon shoved her hands in the front pockets of her jeans because she didn't know what else to do with them. She glanced around the sparkling room, then back to meet her father's gaze.

She jumped when he cupped her elbow with his palm and led her to the granite table. "Would you like something to drink? Eat?"

Rhiannon jerked her hands out of her pockets as Garran helped seat her at the right side of the large chair at the head of the table. The seat she settled in was surprisingly comfortable but she couldn't relax as Garran took the head chair.

They studied each other for a long time, neither saying a word. Her father was so handsome despite the fact he had light blueish gray skin.

She fiddled with a fold of her T-shirt. "How did you and my mother meet?"

He closed his eyes and tilted his head back for a moment, as if remembering that day. After a few seconds of silence, his gaze returned to Rhiannon. His expression seemed somewhat wistful, as if he wished he could turn back time.

"She was so beautiful, your mother." His mouth curved into a smile that any woman would probably find sexy if he wasn't her father. "When I saw her strolling through the forest, beneath the moonlight," he continued, "I knew I had to have her."

Rhiannon leaned forward in her chair, waiting for him to say more.

"I slipped through the trees and watched her until she came upon a pond where she settled on a rock." His eyes looked distant as he spoke. "She leaned back and tilted her face to the night sky. I could see every perfect feature from the outline of her face, to her full lips and the curve of her neck, to—"

Garran cleared his throat and his gaze came more into focus as he looked at Rhiannon. "I went to her and saw that her eyes were closed as moonlight spilled on her features. I knelt on one knee beside her and she opened her eyes and looked at me. There was no shock, no surprise at seeing a stranger at her side. She smiled as if she had been waiting for me."

"What then?" Rhiannon asked softly.

"We talked. She told me a little of the world she came from, and I spoke of mine." He sighed. "But I did not tell her I am Drow. In the moonlight it would have been difficult for her to see the true color of my skin.

"When I sensed night was nearing its end, I kissed Anna and told her I had to go, but that I wanted to see her again."

"Did you enchant her?" Rhiannon asked. "I remember Copper saying that the magic of the Dark Elves can cause a human woman to fall in love with a Drow male."

"No." Garran shook his head. "Anna . . . she was special." He continued, "She agreed to meet me at that same pond when darkness fell. Every night we met and I can recall every word we spoke, every one of her smiles, her every touch—"

Garran broke off, looking a little uncomfortable, and Rhiannon figured out pretty quick that he felt a little off-kilter telling his daughter about having sex with her mother.

"One night when she came to me, brimming with joy, she told me she was with child." Garran shook his head and smiled. "We were both filled with such happiness."

He paused and the pleasure in his eyes faded.

"That's when you told her you're Drow," Rhiannon said, the thought coming to her swift and sudden.

The smile on Garran's lips had turned to one of sadness. "She left, angry with me. She had spirit, that one."

With a heavy sigh, he continued, "Night after night I returned to the pond, and it was as if my heart had been crushed between two great boulders when Anna didn't return."

Rhiannon's own heart felt heavy and she found herself wanting to reach over to her father, to touch him, to comfort him. Instead she squeezed her hands together in her lap.

"I never gave up." He raked his hand through his silvery blue hair. "It seemed an eternity passed—until one night I found her there. She looked even more beautiful than before, and for a long moment I could not speak, such a lump crowded my throat."

Garran's throat worked as he swallowed, as if that lump was still there. "Anna turned and looked at me, and I saw she held a small bundle." His gaze met Rhiannon's and goose bumps rose on her skin. "She was holding you."

Rhiannon couldn't say a word as she looked into her father's liquid silver eyes.

"It was as if she had never left, my love for her was so strong." Garran shifted in his seat and stared into space. "And you—I could not bear it when she said she was taking you back to the San Francisco Otherworld, that you could only be a child of the light. I knew she was right, but I did not want to let you go."

Again he looked at Rhiannon. "Your mother did come to me every full moon and would stay a week at best. She would go back to your Otherworld and my heart ached for her until we could see one another again."

Rhiannon thought she saw Garran's eyes glisten as if with tears, but that vanished so quickly she had probably imagined it.

His voice was hoarse as he spoke. "One full moon she did not come—and I knew something terrible had happened."

Rhiannon bit her lower lip and barely held in the sudden desire to throw herself into her father's arms and hug him. All this time. All this time.

At that moment she couldn't think of Garran as anything but her father and the man who'd loved her mother.

"I went to our pond again and again, but she never returned." Garran clenched his fist that was resting on the armrest of the chair. "The Elvin witch came one night instead."

"The Great Guardian?" Rhiannon asked.

He shook his head. "No. Cassia is her name."

Rhiannon's eyes widened and she sat straighter in her chair. Cassia? No. She couldn't have known all this time and not have told Rhiannon. She couldn't have.

But Garran continued. "Cassia told me of your mother's death. How she saved you and your aunt in a tragic accident." He held one of his fists to his chest as if the ache in his heart was too much to bear.

"I wanted you here with me, to watch you, to see you grow," Garran went on, pain in his voice, "but the Elvin witch said that was not your path."

Rhiannon's scalp began to tingle. Could it have been the Cassia she knew? Could she be that old? And had she made such an important decision in Rhiannon's life?

"I finally agreed." He rubbed his hand over his face and she wondered if he was struggling to keep his emotions hidden. "You were meant to be a child of the light, not of the dark. Like your mother wanted for you. And," he added,

"Druid blood runs strong in you from your mother's side and you needed to train to become D'Anu."

Garran dropped his hand away from his face and gave a heavy sigh. "Now you know the truth of it." He studied her as if trying to judge her expression. "I wanted what was best for you. What Anna would have wanted."

Rhiannon closed her eyes for a moment and clenched her hands into fists. She really didn't know how she felt right now. Years of hurt and anger had been balled up inside of her so tightly she wanted to explode. But what her father said changed everything.

And she didn't know what to do about it.

Rhiannon opened her eyes and looked at Garran. He leaned forward in his chair. "I want to know more of you, my daughter."

There was that word again. *Daughter.* Did she have half-brothers and half-sisters running around? "Do you have any other children?"

"No," Garran said. "After Anna . . . I have never taken a wife. There has been no other woman who has *truly* touched my heart." He glanced toward the door and back to her. "Are you bonded to Keir D'Danann?"

Heat rose within Rhiannon and she shook her head. "No. We, ah, just have a kind of relationship." Hell, what kind of relationship *did* they have?

Garran gave a knowing smile. "Again, tell me of yourself."

She shrugged. "I don't know what to say." She looked around at the monochrome room that she liked despite herself. "This is nice, but I like color," she said. "Lots and lots of bright colors. I play video games, I love to shop, and I've devoted my life to being a D'Anu witch. I run the Coven's café/metaphysical store." She frowned and her mood blackened. "When we're not fighting demons, that is."

He studied her intently and a hard expression came over his face. "Now tell me of this Aunt Aga."

Rhiannon sucked in a deep breath and told him about her childhood—minus the part about the Shadows. She shared how cruel her mother's sister had been and how she had turned Rhiannon out when she was eighteen with nothing. Not a cent to her name.

The only thing Aga had done that was not hurtful or hateful was have Rhiannon trained as a D'Anu witch. Rhiannon had put everything she had into becoming a more powerful witch than her aunt. Aga was furious when she saw just how powerful Rhiannon had become.

Garran looked angrier and angrier as she spoke. When she stopped he banged his fist on the arm of the chair. "If I had known, I would have taken you from her, light be damned."

That statement gave Rhiannon some pause. It warmed her insides that her father had reacted so passionately, but at the same time, would it have been the right thing for her—to grow up as one of the Drow?

It came crashing down on her. Her father was king of the *Dark Elves*. He was *Drow*.

She raised her chin. "I have a power. A power that no witch should have. Dark magic."

Garran didn't look surprised and some of the anger in his expression faded. "What is it?"

It was harder to say to her father than she'd expected. Aunt Aga had been the only person in the world who knew—until recently—and Rhiannon had hidden it ever since.

"Shadows," she finally said. Her father cocked an eyebrow. "When I was little they would slip out of me and play. But my aunt caught me with them once. She yelled at me. Told me it was black magic and the reason my parents sent me away."

Rhiannon's throat felt thick as she spoke. "The Shadows attacked her, hurt her. I screamed at them to stop and they came back inside me." Her chest ached and she felt the Shadows stir within. "I never let them out again . . . until recently. And even then it wasn't intentionally."

Garran leaned forward, and braced his forearms on the granite table, his features harsh. "Your aunt lied. You were not sent away because of any powers. I have told you the story of how you came to live with your aunt." His jaw clenched. "And if she were before me today, I might let the Shadows have her."

Rhiannon straightened in her seat, her heart pounding. "So the Shadows *are* bad. They're evil—like the Dark Elves."

Her father's expression was no less harsh when he answered her. "Drow are not evil. At times we might have dealings with those that are, but *we* are not evil beings."

"What's the difference?" Rhiannon shot back, feeling heat flush her face. "If you work with evil then that makes you just as bad as they are."

Garran clenched his fists on the table. "Drow are neutral beings, like the D'Danann."

"Only the D'Danann do not *ever* side with evil," Rhiannon said, her tone rising. "But the Dark Elves do."

Garran's chest rose and fell as he took a deep breath. "We choose to aid whatever side might benefit our people."

Her chair scraped against the floor as Rhiannon forced it back and stood. "Even if that side is evil. You don't care about anyone but yourselves."

Garran pushed himself to his feet. His chair fell and slammed against the granite floor, the sound echoing through the chamber.

Immediately Keir strode into the room, followed by two guards.

Garran studied her for a long moment, as if trying to read her. "You did not come to meet me," he finally stated.

"No." The word came too fast and abrupt, and an expression of hurt flashed across his features. Immediately a warrior's mask replaced the look.

Rhiannon hardened her own expression and narrowed her eyes. "I didn't want to come. I was told I had to." Her voice was filled with accusation as she said, "I need to help the D'Danann and D'Anu fight the Fomorii and other creatures *you* helped set free. Our city in our Otherworld will soon be overrun with them."

Garran turned his back to her and walked to the dais. He climbed up and sat in his throne. He had a casual way of sitting in it, his long legs stretched out as he leaned on his right elbow and stroked his chin with his fingers. He looked deep in thought, as if contemplating her request.

She held her breath, waiting for his answer.

"No." The word came out of his mouth as sharp as her own had.

Rhiannon fought back the tide of tears. She was too overwhelmed. And to be told no once again—goddess, it was too much.

She turned her back to Garran, pushed her way past Keir and the Drow warriors. She headed toward the stairs that led up and into the sunlight.

Chapter 30

It was late afternoon when Rhiannon and Keir made their way back from Golden Gate Park. She wasn't sure what time it was, but when they reached Enchantments, it was open.

The pain in her head had instantly returned when they arrived back from Otherworld, but it seemed as if the Shadows had weakened the goddess's hold on her during the fight at the penthouse because it wasn't quite as bad. But it still hurt like hell.

How can I go from thinking the Shadows are evil to believing they were helping me? she thought as Keir reached for the store's door handle.

Warding bells tinkled as he opened the door, then stepped back to let her in. She saw the college students busy helping customers in the front and in the café. Rhiannon tried to smile at the employees, but had a hard time as she made her way to the kitchen.

When Keir pushed open the swinging door to the kitchen and she walked through, she was surprised to see all of her Coven sisters gathered together seated at the table, as well as the Faerie. Galia perched on Mackenzie's shoulder.

After everyone said hello, Cassia pointed toward an empty chair for Rhiannon to sit in. "I thought you would be arriving any time," Cassia said. "I called everyone together so that we can discuss what happened in Otherworld."

Rhiannon took the chair and tensed as everyone turned to her. Keir moved behind her, rested his hands on her shoulders, and squeezed, and it gave her some comfort.

She didn't want to look anyone in the face but she forced herself to meet her Coven sister's eyes as she looked from one to another.

Rhiannon cleared her throat. "When we went to Otherworld the first time, when we were trying to get the Chieftains to give us more help, we met with the Great Guardian." She took a deep breath. "The Guardian told me about my—my birth parents."

Silver gave her an encouraging look that said, "Go on. We're here for you."

Rhiannon swallowed, her stomach suddenly feeling queasy. "I found out that I'm half D'Anu . . . and half-Elvin."

Copper drew Rhiannon's attention when she said, "Really? A full half?" She grinned. "That's too cool."

"I'm half Drow," Rhiannon said, looking at Copper. "I'm King Garran's daughter."

A stunned silence filled the room. Even Galia looked at her with wide eyes.

"You're what?" Hannah finally said, her voice incredulous. "You're the daughter of that traitor?"

Rhiannon clenched her fists and glared at Hannah. Before she could fire back a response, Copper said, "Garran was doing what he thought was right for his people."

"And look who we ended up with." Hannah folded her arms across her chest. "Ceithlenn. Bitch of the Underworld."

Rhiannon winced and gritted her teeth at the pain caused by hearing the goddess's name.

"I was there." Copper's jaw was tense. "Don't you think I know that? But I also know that Garran started to help *us* once he figured out what was happening."

Hannah scowled "A little too late, don't you think?"

Copper stood and her cast clunked on the floor as she faced Hannah. "He. Saved. My. Life."

Hannah stared at Copper for a few moments longer, then turned her attention to Rhiannon. "What does Daddy being the king of the Dark Elves have to do with this whole conversation?"

Rhiannon thought about letting Hannah have it, but Cassia caught her eye. Rhiannon clenched and unclenched her fists on the table. "On this second trip, I met him and asked him to become our ally."

Silver reached across the table and rested her hand on top of Rhiannon's. "And?"

"I basically told him he could shove it, as far as being my father." She looked around at her Coven sisters. "And in return he said no to helping us."

Hannah flung her hands up. "Well, isn't that just perfect."

Rhiannon got to her feet, drawing her hand away from Silver's. "First you carry on about my father being a traitor and now you act like I should've played nice. Why don't you get yourself together?"

"If your father is the king of a bunch of warriors who could be on *our* side because he's related to you, then yes, you should have played nice." Hannah stood, too, and placed her hands on her hips. "Better having him on our side than against us."

"Oh, for Anu's sake." Silver touched Hannah's arm. "Let's sit down and discuss this, all right?"

Copper shook her head and grinned. "I can't believe the same Garran who came on to me is your father."

"TMI," Rhiannon said, unable to believe her father had the hots for one of her closest friends. "I don't need to know that about my father."

Hannah's features returned to their normal sophisticated calmness as she seated herself across from where Rhiannon was now standing. Hannah turned her attention to Cassia. "We need to send a more *neutral* contingent to the Drow."

Before Rhiannon could come back with anything, Cassia said, "That will have to wait for now." Her gaze returned to Rhiannon's. "There's more you need to tell your sisters."

Rhiannon sat back in her chair and resisted squirming in her seat.

Sydney nodded. "She's right. It's time you told us what

happened in the penthouse. That black fog that came from you and helped us to fight off Ceithlenn."

"Black fog?" Copper said, Silver echoing her. Galia's wings beat slower as she braced her hands to either side of her on Mackenzie's shoulder and leaned forward.

"You all didn't see it because it happened when we were in the hallway," Sydney said to her Coven sisters. "It was like they burst out of Rhiannon's chest and went after Ceithlenn. If it wasn't for that foggy stuff, I'm not sure all of us would have made it."

Rhiannon's heart and head hurt more now that she had to tell everyone. "They're Shadows," she whispered.

"Shadows?" Silver studied Rhiannon. "Tell us everything."

The Shadows wanted to come out—Rhiannon felt it chest deep—it was like the Shadows wanted to socialize or something.

Slowly she began her story about the power, how she had first come upon it and how she'd hidden it because she knew it was bad.

"That's why I never told any of you," she said quietly. "I was afraid you'd reject me."

"Oh, honey." Silver got up to go around the table. Keir backed up as Silver put her arm around Rhiannon and squeezed. "You're our Coven sister, and our friend. We would never reject you."

"We want to hear more," Mackenzie said from across the table, looking particularly interested as she rested her elbow on the table and her chin in her palm.

Rhiannon told them about the fight in the penthouse with Ceithlenn. She moved on to how she had confronted her Drow father about the "ability," and how that confirmed in her mind that they *were* evil.

"But they're not," Copper stated emphatically. "Not only did they help us fight Ceithlenn, but they're a part of *you* and *you* are not evil. So don't even go there."

Galia still had an undecided expression on her face, but to Rhiannon's surprise everyone else seemed to accept it with no problem. They talked a little more about how—according to the Great Guardian—the Shadows would likely help battle the demons and Ceithlenn if Rhiannon freed them.

Rhiannon's friends and Coven sisters were emphatic in the fact that they felt Rhiannon should allow the Shadows out. If the Great Guardian told her the Shadows would help, Silver remarked, then they would help.

By the time the Coven finished discussing the subject, Rhiannon's heart had lightened. She should have trusted her Coven sisters all along.

The witches helped Cassia straighten up the kitchen and helped her make more food for the D'Danann. The way Cassia managed to keep up with the warriors' appetites was beyond magical.

Rhiannon's Coven sisters insisted that she leave and get some rest since she'd had a long day. Even though she was tired, she argued, but lost when Keir steered her out of the kitchen. Galia stayed behind with the other witches.

When Rhiannon and Keir reached her second-floor apartment, she used a brief flare of her magic to unlock the door and let them inside. A pair of lamps brightened the room as soon as she flipped the switch by the door. The rooms normally looked so cheerful to her and made her feel better sometimes when she was down, but did nothing to change the way she felt right now as her thoughts turned to her father again.

Spirit appeared out of nowhere and started rubbing himself against her jeans and gave meows that told her that he sensed her pain and was trying to support her. And that he was hungry.

"Sorry, guy." She dropped her duffel on one of her kitchen table chairs as she eased out of Keir's hold. "I'll get something for you to eat, Spirit."

She made her way to the kitchenette side of the apartment. Her arms ached—for some reason her whole body ached—as she drew a can of tuna out of a cabinet and a can opener and a spoon from a drawer. After she finished plopping the tuna into a bright blue bowl, she set it down at her feet. Spirit mewled, his gaze fixing on hers, before he turned his attention to the tuna and began eating it.

Rhiannon looked at Keir and gestured toward the fridge. "I'm not up to entertaining right now so you'll have to fend for yourself."

After dropping his pack on the floor with a thump, he shrugged out of his long coat and laid it over the back of a chair. Instead of heading for the fridge, he came up to her and surprised her by taking her into his arms.

He pressed her head against his chest with one hand while wrapping his other arm around her waist. At first Rhiannon felt stiff, the disappointment and pain of the day almost too much to bear. But then she allowed herself to sink into him, to enjoy the feel of being in his embrace and letting him comfort her.

"One thing after another." Rhiannon's voice was tight as she spoke. "First the Chieftains, and now my—the Drow King—telling us that he won't help us either. Who do we have left to go to?"

Keir pressed his lips to her hair and just held her close.

"I didn't know what to expect when I met my father." Rhiannon swallowed, hard. "I didn't expect it to hurt so much. Especially when he said no." The backs of her eyes stung. "It feels like he abandoned me as a child, and he's abandoning me now."

"I believe he hurts, as well," Keir said, his voice soft and low. "I believe he reacted from that pain."

"Damn it, Keir." Rhiannon drew away from his embrace. "He's the one who left me. I've done nothing to him."

"I know, *a stór*." He grasped her upper shoulders and massaged them as she looked up at him. "His decision regarding helping our cause was impulsive. He did not give time for thought."

"Because I rejected him," Rhiannon said and rubbed her hand over her eyes. "He expected me to just forgive and forget and to embrace being part Drow. Well, it wasn't that easy!"

But . . . now that she'd talked it over with her Coven sisters, could she find it in her heart to accept who her father was, to forgive him, and to ask his forgiveness for the way she acted? Could she accept that part of her that was Drow?

Rhiannon took a deep breath. "I didn't even ask you how you felt about meeting your mother."

A pang gripped Keir's chest as he let his hands slide away from Rhiannon's shoulders. His thoughts turned back to the blond woman with the beautiful grayish blue eyes. Keaira. His mother's name was Keaira.

"I am not certain how I feel." He stared over Rhiannon's head at the brightly colored kitchen wall. "If what Keaira says is true, then she had no choice. I do not doubt her words, as there is no love lost between my father and me. He is powerfully controlling, and he treats concubines like cast-off towels."

Free Mystwalkers. His mother, forced to stay away from him. His father being the dark curtain between him and the other half of his own heritage.

One myth he had heard time and again, was that a man or woman should never kiss a Mystwalker. Fuck them, yes, kiss them, no. Legend had it the Mystwalker kiss could be deadly, yet his father had taken a Mystwalker as a bed partner.

Keir brought his thoughts to the present, and to Rhiannon, who had pressed herself into his arms again.

"It must have been hard for you, too," she was saying. "Yet you did what I couldn't. You accepted your mother and I rejected my father."

"I do not think it is as simple as that." Keir cradled Rhiannon's face. "Let us speak of this no more tonight." Rhiannon sighed again, this time a deep, heavy sigh. "You are tired and need rest."

She nodded and he pressed his lips to her forehead. He brushed her hair from her face before taking her hand and leading her to her bedroom. Her hand felt small in his and her body had been so soft in his embrace. No matter what might be happening around them, her mere presence made him want her in every sense of the word with a fierce ache in his heart and in his loins.

When they reached the bedroom, Rhiannon switched on a pair of lamps to either side of the bed. She let go of his hand and began stripping out of her clothing, starting by kicking off her shoes and tugging off her socks.

With fascination he watched her pull her T-shirt over her head and toss it aside. It had ruffled her hair and he held back a smile at how adorable she looked.

His gaze dropped to the burn on her chest from Ceithlenn's magic and he tamped down the fury that rose up in him.

Instead he focused on her breasts as she reached around her back and unclasped her bra, freeing her soft white mounds and baring her taut berry-red nipples.

He should let her rest, but gods how he needed to be inside her and to have her wrapped around him. He needed to possess her, to brand her again and again. Fierce pride rose within him. Rhiannon was his woman. *His.*

The low rumble in his chest caught her attention and she raised her gaze to meet his as she dropped her undergarment on the floor. A spark lit her eyes and she continued to watch him as she unfastened her pants and pushed them down along with her panties.

His mouth salivated as she stepped out of the rest of her clothing and kicked it aside. When nothing remained but the pentagrams at her ears, throat, and finger, she walked toward him. The goddess Anu could have been no more beautiful than Rhiannon.

Golden light from the bedside lamps highlighted her mussed auburn hair. The sprinkling of freckles across her nose made him want to kiss each and every one of them. The auburn curls between her thighs hid the treasure his tongue and fingers ached to find.

To his surprise his entire body trembled, his need for her was so great.

When she reached him she tilted her face and studied him, her eyes searching his as if asking a question he did not know the answer to.

It took great pains not to take her now, like this. It would be so simple to lay her on the bed, free his erection from its bindings, and drive his cock into her.

He toed off each of his boots and they thumped on the wood flooring as he kicked them out of the way, then he shrugged out of his tunic and tossed it aside. While she watched she moistened her lips and brought her gaze to his hands as he undid the ties on his breeches, pushed them down to his feet, and stepped out of them and toward her.

They were now so close he could feel the heat of her body join with his. His nostrils flared at the scent of her musk and the clean citrus smell of her skin.

For some reason he waited. As if knowing Rhiannon wanted him to let her take control. Right this moment he was certain she truly needed him as much as he needed her.

She melded her body flush against his, wrapped her arms around his neck, and brought her lips to his. Keir groaned as his erection pressed against her belly and her tongue darted into his mouth.

Her kiss was filled with sweetness and a sense of longing. He returned her kiss, keeping his slow and deliberate.

She drew away. "Lie on your back, Keir."

He took the few steps to the bed and settled onto his backside, his gaze never leaving the beautiful woman who was nothing short of a goddess.

Rhiannon's belly flipped a little at the way Keir was looking at her. She tried not to tremble as she moved closer to him and climbed onto the bed.

A sigh rose up within her as she straddled his hips and her folds settled on his thick cock. She bent forward and braced her hands to either side of his chest before brushing her lips over his. He nipped at her lower lip and another sigh slipped from her as he grasped her hips in his big hands and his tongue delved into her mouth.

It was a long sweet kiss, but she needed more. Needed to soothe the ache inside her. And she needed Keir.

She reached between them and wrapped her fingers around his thick cock before rising up and breaking their kiss. She raised herself just enough that she could plant the head of his cock at the entrance to her core.

She slammed herself down, driving his cock deep inside her. She shouted out at the sudden shock of him filling her so fully and deeply. Keir groaned and grasped her hips tighter.

Rhiannon began to ride Keir. She was so wet and slick,

and he was so big. She tilted her head back and brought her hands to her breasts and pinched her nipples. The sensations traveled from her breasts to her belly button to her pussy.

She closed her eyes, seeing only Keir in her mind, feeling only him between her thighs and inside her. He felt so good, so good, so very good.

A storm rose within her and she rode him harder until the clouds burst open. Lightning sparked behind her eyelids and thunder rumbled in her ears.

Her body jerked and trembled and her cry sounded distant as if not her own. She shuddered with every strike of her orgasm, as if lightning bolted through her time after time.

Finally she collapsed on Keir's chest and heard his pounding heart beneath her ear. Her skin was sticky with perspiration and her own heart was beating like crazy.

He eased them both over so that she was on her back and he was on top. Her head spun a little with the movement. She looked up at him as he began to drive himself to his own climax. His gaze fixed on hers, his long black hair tickling her cheeks.

Every thrust of his cock made her core spasm, forcing her closer and closer to another orgasm. Tears came to her eyes and she cried out when she climaxed again.

Keir shouted and she felt his cock throb inside her as he dropped and held himself tight to her. He was so heavy she could barely breathe, but it felt so good as he continued to pump his hips until he came to a shuddering stop.

He rolled so that she was half on him and he trapped her upper leg with his thigh. He seemed to enjoy holding her like this, and she loved how it felt to be in his arms.

Goddess, how she had needed this. Needed to feel a part of something special and that she was wanted.

Sleep came easily and a smile was on her lips as she thought about Keir.

Chapter 31

Late the following afternoon, Rhiannon fixed sandwiches for herself and Keir in her kitchenette. The bright colors in her apartment almost always had a calming effect on her. Her sanctuary was something in her life that remained constant and made her feel good.

Sometimes it was the small things that mattered when one's world was falling apart.

She felt little sense of accomplishment as she and Keir fixed a late lunch. All morning, the leaders of the D'Danann, the PSF, and all of the witches—not to mention Galia—had met in the common room.

For several hours they had discussed their best battle strategies. No matter the sheer size of the goddess's army of demons and other creatures, they had to figure out a way to strike first, and strike hard.

A big problem was that they knew some Fomorii had infiltrated areas of law enforcement, which caused some serious problems—like who could they trust? If they asked for help, and it happened to be a Fomorii that had taken over a human's body, they'd tip their hand.

Rhiannon sighed as she drew a pitcher of iced herbal tea out of the refrigerator. The team was also beginning to worry that the witches' additional magical wardings weren't going to hold up much longer against Ceithlenn. If the goddess became strong enough, all hell could break loose. Ceithlenn could attack again—worse than when the demons had been transported through all the prior wardings and battled the witches.

Through their divinations, the witches knew Ceithlenn had used a great deal of power to transport that host of demons. It had sucked out her magical strength, leaving her weak until she was able to steal the souls of more humans.

Would she waste that soul-sucking power on attacking the headquarters of those who battled her? Or would she concentrate on bringing Balor to this world?

Rhiannon and the rest of the team were betting on Balor.

As she and Keir set the table with the mountain of sandwiches—most of which Keir would eat—Rhiannon couldn't help but churn over what the team had finally decided. The witches, D'Danann, and PSF officers needed to find a way to attack all of the demons in their lair beneath Alcatraz.

The team couldn't trust anyone in the city. They were going to need help from Otherworld to do it.

Keir and Hawk actually agreed on this point. Strange, but true. Representatives for the witches and D'Danann needed to go back to Otherworld and see what weapons the Myst-walkers could provide, to see if the Drow would change their minds and fight with them.

Rhiannon managed to smile at Keir as they started to sit down at the table, but that quickly vanished as intense pain made her head feel like it was going to explode. She felt as if worms were crawling beneath her skin.

Something was going to happen today.

Something horribly, horribly wrong.

A vision hit Rhiannon hard and fast before she could take her seat at the table.

She stumbled backward and landed on one hip on the hard floor. The vision spun through her head as if she were on a merry-go-round. Vaguely she heard Keir calling her name and felt his heat as he moved close.

Her eyesight swam and her heart pounded like it was going to come out of her chest. She held her hands between her breasts and struggled to breathe.

Keir's voice was urgent, concerned. "What is wrong, *a stór?*"

Rhiannon's heart continued to pound beneath her hands as she held them tighter against her chest. Her eyes were wide and dry and she couldn't blink. She saw only the images in front of her and couldn't answer him.

Keir murmured soft words in Gaelic, and Rhiannon slowly came back to the present.

"I had a vision," she managed to get out.

He held her closer. "What did you see?"

Rhiannon took a deep breath. "Something really bad."

"Tell me." Keir's voice was edged with concern.

Rhiannon took another deep breath and then another. Some of the images were vivid in her mind while others were hazy.

"Ceithlenn." A very familiar shard of pain jabbed her mind. "There were so many people around her." Rhiannon squeezed her eyes shut, trying to get a better grasp on the vision. "It was all a blur but there were thousands of people. I couldn't tell if they were near or far. They wavered in and out. But I saw bright colors—pennants or banners. From what little I could hear, people were shouting and cheering."

Keir wrapped his other arm around her so that she was surrounded in his embrace.

"The goddess spread her arms and wings wide." Rhiannon's scars burned like crazy and she rubbed them with her fingertips. "Souls started shooting toward her like pale missiles. Hundreds. Maybe thousands. Some like white puffs of clouds and others as dark as thunderheads."

Rhiannon tried to fight down a sense of rising panic. "The goddess sucked them all into her body. They came to her so easily—all she did was utter a command and it was done.

"And the corpses." Tears burned behind her closed eyelids. "Dead. Everyone was dead. Bodies littered the ground all around her. As far as I could see with my vision eyes. But I couldn't tell *where* she was. Or how many people."

Keir's body tensed next to hers, steel beneath hard flesh, and she opened her eyes. "We had best tell the others," he said.

Rhiannon's eyesight swam but she finally regained her focus.

"When do you believe this will happen?" Keir gripped her upper arms and started to stand.

"Today." A sense of panic kept Rhiannon's heart beating fast. "I don't think we have much time. But I have no idea where it's going to happen!"

"I will summon my brethren through our mind-link, and they will gather the others." Keir said. Only a moment later he said, "It is done."

When Rhiannon and Keir reached the apartments' common room for the second time that day, most of the witches had arrived, along with Galia, as well as representatives of the D'Danann. Several of those present asked Rhiannon what was going on, but she said she'd explain when everyone else arrived.

It took a while before Jake and a few of his key PSF officers jogged into the room. A few minutes later, Sydney followed by Hannah made it back to the apartment buildings from their homes.

Cassia was the only person not in the room when Rhiannon was prepared to speak, and she wondered where the half-Elvin witch was.

"I had a vision." As Rhiannon spoke, she stroked Spirit, who was nestled in her lap. "It was a vision subject to interpretation, but I believe what I saw will happen *today*. It is what will come to pass unless we find a way to prevent it.

"It happened in a huge crowd. I couldn't tell if the people were right beside her, or far away. But there were thousands of them."

"Crowds . . ." Jake frowned. "The SFPD has got its hands full with the Giants playing their first exhibition game of the season." Jake glanced at his watch. "Starts around ninety minutes to an hour from now. That doesn't give us much time. We've got to figure out what the hell we're going to do."

"It's a weekend." Sydney frowned as her eyes met Rhiannon's. "Attendance is going to be high at the game."

Rhiannon gripped Spirit's fur and he gave her a warning sound that she ignored. "There were so very many people."

Silver rubbed the snake bracelet on her wrist. "Did you see any demons with Ceithlenn?"

Rhiannon shook her head and shuddered at hearing the C-word. "Just the goddess. But that doesn't mean the Fomorii won't be there."

"Either event will be a tactical nightmare." Jake braced his hands on the back of a chair. "I'll get with the SFPD chief of police, along with other areas of law enforcement. But—shit. It's like what we talked about this morning. Who the fuck do we trust?"

"Can the event be canceled? A terrorist threat or something?" Alyssa piped up from the corner.

"I can try." Jake glanced at his watch. "But it's already loading up with spectators. What we don't need is mass hysteria."

A flash of the vision came back to Rhiannon. "My gut tells me it *is* the game."

Silver spoke up. "My senses tell me she's right. It's the perfect venue to steal a massive amount of souls."

Most of those in the room nodded in agreement.

As Jake took his cell phone out of its holster, he said, "I'll have every available PSF officer guarding the field before the game starts." He punched in a couple of numbers and brought the phone to his ear. "Providing we can't cancel the game and evacuate."

Everyone was quiet as he tried several phone numbers and was shot down each time. His face was grim as he punched the off button at the end of the fifth call. "We are so screwed," he said. "They've got us by the balls. And now they'll know we're on to them."

"Dear Anu," Rhiannon said as she held Spirit closer to her. "What if we can't stop the goddess?"

Jake's muscles flexed as he crossed his chest with his arms. "We'll see what we can come up to use against the bitch. We have equipment available for outside use that we weren't able to take advange of in the penthouse."

"Wait." Rhiannon held her hand up. "We were lucky at the penthouse. The goddess could have taken the souls of the PSF officers and witches if I hadn't thrown up the shield. Maybe even the D'Danann. What if she does it at the game?"

"Shit," Jake said again and shook his head. "Goddamnit."

"Wait," came Cassia's voice from the doorway. Rhiannon had to tilt her head to see the witch make her way through the crowd until she stood at the center. She was holding what looked like a water flagon made from red clay. It had a pot belly, a long, long neck, and a handle that spanned the distance from the back of the pour spout to the widest part of the flagon.

Rhiannon frowned. Something about Cassia looked different, but she couldn't quite place it. By the Ancestors, it seemed like Cassia changed daily. She no longer resembled the bumbling D'Anu apprentice she had pretended to be before the battle of Samhain.

"The Great Guardian has sent a precious gift." Cassia held up the large flagon as well as a tiny chalice with a bowl about the size of a big thimble. "She has made this elixir from the rare Amarant of Otherworld, the exceedingly powerful forbearer of our world's Amaranth.

"Have every one of the PSF officers, the D'Danann, and the D'Anu drink from this and their souls will be protected from Ceithlenn." Cassia raised the small cup. "Only drink what fills this chalice."

Rhiannon winced from the name, but at the same time remembered her vision of the Great Guardian tending to the purple flower in her garden. A bud that sparkled with magic.

Everyone was silent for a moment. "Wow." Copper thumped her cast onto the floor as she stood and walked toward Cassia. "Solves that little problem."

"We've got to get the hell out of here." Jake glanced at his watch again. "Pass that thing around."

While everyone was taking their share of the potion, they continued strategizing.

Mackenzie's gaze darted from one witch to the next. "If she brings her friggin' army, I don't think there will be enough of us to take care of them all."

"We need to ask for Anu's and the Elementals' assistance." Alyssa visibly swallowed and Rhiannon could tell her friend was afraid of going into a big battle. It didn't take seer's skills to be sure of that.

Galia took the tiniest of sips at Cassia's direction. Rhiannon drank her share of the potion from the tiny chalice. It tasted like blackberry syrup.

When she passed it on, she took a deep breath and addressed the whole room, hoping Alyssa would listen to her words. She wouldn't and couldn't order her friend around, because Rhiannon herself didn't like to be told what to do. But she tried to get her to take another option. "We can't leave our headquarters and store unprotected." Rhiannon said. "Some D'Danann and perhaps a witch or two need to stay behind."

The witches argued that all of them needed to be at the stadium. Cassia could guard the store as she usually did— her magic was the strongest out of them all.

Rhiannon looked at Alyssa. "I'm going, too," Alyssa said, and Rhiannon sighed.

"She's bound to be ticked off after our attack on her place. Not to mention she was weakened." Sydney adjusted her glasses. "We know she has an agenda. If she collects a huge amount of souls she'll be strong enough to bring Balor to San Francisco and that would *so* not be good."

"One question," Mackenzie said. "If Ceithlenn does bring a portion of her army, or even all of it, how is she going to get them inside undetected?"

"Host bodies." Silver rubbed her arms with her hands as if she had chill bumps. "No doubt the demons will be in the stands, posing as spectators."

Rhiannon slowly nodded. "They could already have infiltrated stadium security. They could attack us at any time."

Jake raked his hand through his short hair, ruffling it. "We'll have to handle this without informing security. They're not going to be happy about it."

"None of us like any of this." Rhiannon clenched her hands into fists. "What about the public's reaction to finding out that an evil goddess bitch from Underworld is responsible, if she's successful?"

"They'd laugh the local law enforcement out of the city if we come out with that kind of statement." Jake shook his head. "People won't believe it until the city is overrun with demons—which is exactly what's going to happen if we don't take Ceithlenn down."

Rhiannon twisted her gold-and-onyx ring. "They could even think *we* are terrorists when we try to stop her, if we're not successful."

"We'd better get it right the first time," Jake said with a determined expression."

Sweat rolled down the side of Rhiannon's face during the trip to the stadium. It was cramped in the PSF truck—one of several that were on their way to the baseball park. The witches and their familiars—all of the animals had been temporarily protected by glamours—stayed together because they believed they worked better as a team. Their goal was to get to Ceithlenn while the others fought off any attacks. They had no doubt the goddess wouldn't be alone.

Jake had worked out their covert operation with select friends in the SFPD and other law enforcement agencies, trying to keep things undercover best as possible so that they'd have backup that wouldn't be blocked by a Fomorii in a host body in a position of power. Rhiannon hoped none of Jake's contacts were now demons.

After what happened at the theater, the mere mention of a potential attack would have every law enforcement agency scrambling if they spread the word everywhere. But what could they do against the goddess? At least Rhiannon's team was prepared to fight, and protected against getting their souls sucked dry.

Rhiannon flexed her hands, ready for a spellfire attack, and Spirit gave a meow from where he sat on her lap. She concentrated on her magic, still feeling infused with power from the earlier ritual. Spirit's magic enhanced her own, but she worried about the familiar being in the middle of the battle. But they could use their familiars' strengths and magical powers.

The public, of course, had no idea what had truly happened to the people in the theater, or those on the tour bus. The taste of fear in the city was strong and grew more so as each day progressed. Everyone continued to wonder what had shriveled the bodies so badly their families and friends would never be able to recognize their remains? The only thing that had identified most were forms of ID in their possessions.

Already a rally for sometime during the week had been organized, and talk shows and news programs around the world were speculating over what was now being called the Movie Theater Massacre. Speculation on news radio and on television was that it must have been a biochemical terrorist attack using some kind of virus or gas even though HAZMAT had found no airborne threat.

Only the PSF, the witches, and the D'Danann knew the truth of it.

Everyone in the truck was quiet. The PSF officers were armed to the teeth, from the rifles they carried to weapons belts. The belts held extra magazines containing the special bullets Jake had shown her, as well as knives, handguns, and other things she wasn't sure about.

The PSF officers also wore riot gear and along with their protective clothing, they wore Kevlar vests, kneepads, and gloves. The witches wore as much protection as the PSF officers with the exception of the gloves.

They arrived at the stadium about fifteen minutes before the scheduled start of the game. The unmarked PSF trucks each backed up to one of seven side entrances around the ballpark that the public didn't have access to. With the truck doors opened directly into the entrances, the witches, familiars, and officers were able to unload into the stadium and make their way to their stations. Rhiannon clutched Spirit close to her chest.

Every time Rhiannon passed a security guard or other stadium employee, she couldn't help but wonder if the person was actually a demon in a host body. Unfortunately, when in their host bodies, they couldn't be scented. They just smelled like the person's body that they inhabited.

When they arrived at their stations, Rhiannon gripped Spirit tight to her. Chaos, Sydney's Doberman, sat quietly at her side. He had a Doberman's protective instincts and would viciously attack when his mistress was faced with danger. He was just a goof when not in a serious situation.

Rhiannon had a good vantage point as they waited against the walls of entrances that led onto the field. The players were warming up but her heart chilled to think any of them could be murdered by Ceithlenn. That any single person here could be taken by the goddess.

She glanced up at the sky and saw some D'Danann circling over the stadium. Others would be perched strategically throughout the ballpark. As long as their wings were exposed they could remain invisible to human sight if they chose to. Unfortunately, like the witches when they pulled glamours, the D'Danann stayed visible to magical beings, including the Fomorii.

She held one hand to that place on her breastbone where Ceithlenn's magic had struck her. It felt only slightly sensitive to the touch beneath her T-shirt and Kevlar vest. The wound was healing quickly due to the fact she was a witch.

A wiggling in Rhiannon's jacket made her jump. When Galia's little face peeked out of Rhiannon's pocket, she almost bopped the Faerie on her head for scaring her. Spirit, who was still in Rhiannon's arms, hissed and batted at Galia with his paw, but she ducked.

"I didn't even know you were here," Rhiannon whispered.

"I sipped the potion." Galia looked up at Rhiannon and edged far out of Spirit's reach to the opposite end of the pocket. "Everyone fights. Including me."

"Of course." Rhiannon peered back at the ball field before looking at Galia again. "I just didn't know you were in my pocket. Like I said before, it isn't fair to ask you to stay behind when the rest of us insist we have the right to kick that goddess's ass."

"Exactly." Galia climbed out of Rhiannon's pocket and flew up to her shoulder. The Faerie was wearing her skintight black fighting outfit.

The PSF officer next to Rhiannon blinked and squinted at Galia. "Is she a Faerie?"

Galia fluttered her pink wings, spilling pink dust and hints of lilac. She snorted at him. "I am most certainly not a demon."

Rhiannon turned her attention back to the field. It was an unusually warm San Francisco day and it caused her skin to tingle, which only reminded her of her father and her failure to get the Drow to help them.

Only a few clouds streaked the cerulean blue sky. The scent of freshly mowed grass carried on a light breeze, along with the plastic and metallic smells of the weaponry and clothing the PSF officers wore and carried. Rhiannon almost wished for one of their ballistic shields, but she knew it would hamper her magic, and she could throw up a spellshield whenever she needed it—as long as she wasn't caught off guard.

Her breathing rate picked up as she waited. Waited for a sign. Waited for Ceithlenn.

A popular rock singer sang the national anthem and Rhiannon automatically stood straighter with her hand over her heart. Her gaze roved the stadium. She wanted to cry at the thought of all of these people being taken away from their families, their friends. Age, race—none of that would matter to Ceithlenn. She would take every soul she could.

We have to stop her! We have to!

Team pennants waved in the crowd. The State of California flag snapped in the breeze next to the American flag. People were shouting, whistling. A huge Trinitron flashed pictures of people in the crowds and the spectators would cheer when they saw themselves on the big screen. Vendors walked up and down aisles selling popcorn, peanuts, hot dogs, ice cream, and cotton candy. Even from where she was standing, Rhiannon could smell it all.

The governor of California walked out onto the field to make the first pitch. Rhiannon's heart nearly stopped beating.

Not her, too!

Rhiannon held her breath from the time the governor pitched the ball until she left the field with the roar of the crowd following in her wake.

By the time all the players from both teams were on the field, Rhiannon was trembling. This was *so* wrong. Dear Anu, this was wrong. None of this should be happening.

The Giants' pitcher finished conferencing with the coach and the catcher and started to make his way to his position.

The scars on Rhiannon's cheek burned, pain spiked through her head, and her heart thrummed against her breastbone.

Ceithlenn materialized on the pitcher's mound.

Chapter 32

A collective gasp rolled through the stadium when the flame-haired, red-eyed, bat-winged goddess became visible.

Pain screamed through Rhiannon's head and her heart beat in her throat as she readied herself to run onto the field as boos, jeers, and hoots came from the crowd. Ceithlenn looked like a Halloween reject.

"On my mark," Jake said through the transmitters in their ears. Like a football quarterback throwing a pass to his receiver, he lobbed what he called a flash-bang. It arced through the air and landed in the grass only feet from the goddess.

Rhiannon closed her eyes and covered her ears with her hands just as the 170-decibel object, with intense flare, detonated. Jake had said it would temporarily blind and deafen anyone within close range and might buy them some much needed time.

Despite the fact she'd had her hands over her ears when the flash-bang exploded her ears rang and spots flashed in front of her eyes.

Her gaze immediately went to the goddess.

Ceithlenn was still standing there.

The goddess stretched out one of her hands and rotated on the mound. All of the players, coaches, batboys, and umpires froze in whatever positions they had ended up in as a result of the flash bang.

They looked like wax dummies out on the playing field.

"Dinner for my army." Ceithlenn's voice echoed throughout the stadium as if she were speaking with a microphone. "And you all are dinner for my soul. Your sacrifices will bring my love back to me."

A rumble of disbelief, anger, and fear traveled through the crowd.

"We'll give her an appetizer," Jake growled through the earpiece. "Archer. RPG, go!"

A thunk and a hiss as the rocket-propelled grenade launcher sent one of its deadly missiles right at Ceithlenn.

A force field shimmered around the goddess as she whipped her gaze toward the oncoming danger.

The grenade hit the shield and exploded—and did nothing to the goddess.

She dropped her shield and pointed her fingers right at Jake and the witches. Rhiannon's heart jumped. She felt as if something was trying to suck her through some kind of vortex. But then she felt nothing.

The goddess screamed with fury on her face and turned back to the crowd that seemed confused. Rhiannon could almost hear their thoughts. Was this some kind of pregame show?

"Move, move, move!" Jake shouted in Rhiannon's earpiece. Spirit bounded from her arms as Rhiannon bolted from the entrance.

Ceithlenn spread her arms and her wings wide as she stared at the crowd.

PSF officers holding their ballistic shields charged onto the field, the witches right beside them with their familiars.

At the same time, countless people swarmed from the stands—

And shifted into Fomorii as they bounded onto the field with shrieks and roars.

Rhiannon's gut churned. They had to get to Ceithlenn! Had to stop her!

But the pitcher's mound was far from all the entrances the PSF and witches were charging from.

And the Fomorii were so damn fast. They scampered, ran, bounded—so many different types of beasts. Red, orange, yellow, blue, green. Some had single eyes, others had many. The demons had anywhere from two to six arms and their bodies were all twisted and malformed. Their claws glinted in the sunlight.

They were tipped with iron.

The field smelled of smoke, sweat, burnt sugar, and the demons' rotten fish stench. And death. It already smelled of death.

Screams came from the now panicked crowd, but the sounds started to die away. Rhiannon glanced up into the stands. She could see the people closer to the field slump in their seats and wither as white, gray, and black puffs of smoke rushed to the goddess.

Other people higher up screamed and started to stampede from the building. Some escaped, but others froze in their places like mummies. The stands grew quieter and quieter. Still screams and shouts, but everything was gradually becoming silent.

Dear Anu, how had Ceithlenn done it so quickly?

"No!" Heat flushed Rhiannon and she gathered a huge spellfire ball while she bolted toward Ceithlenn. She dug into her gray magic and felt the power of Anu within.

Rhiannon stopped short as a demon landed in her path.

She flung the spellfire she was carrying at the Fomorii's face. The orange demon screeched as its head went up in flames. In the next second a sword sliced the head from the demon's body. Rhiannon met Keir's eyes and saw the intense, furious look on his face.

"Help me!" she shouted over the fighting. "Together we can work toward getting to Ceithlenn."

Keir gave a sharp nod. In almost perfect choreography, they fought off one demon and then another and another. Spirit did his part by jumping on the heads of attacking demons and clawing their eyes completely out just long enough for Rhiannon and Keir to do away with the beast.

Beside them, Jake took a two-fisted stance with his handgun

and with a single shot blew a mammoth hole in the chest of a Fomorii, obliterating its heart. No sooner had the beast crumbled to silt than Jake took down another demon.

One Fomorii came at Jake from his back and Rhiannon flung a spellfire ball that caused its feet to fly out from under it. Jake whirled, planted his foot on the demon's chest, and fired at its heart with his handgun.

From behind their ballistic shields, other PSF officers fired off rounds of the special heart-seeking bullets at the Fomorii. Rhiannon saw one officer go down on his back when a demon pounced on his shield. It swiped its fierce claws at the downed man, but another officer shot the demon, wiping it out.

Other officers used the enhanced tasers, dropping some of the demons long enough to shoot them, or giving a D'-Danann warrior time to behead the beast.

But there were so many Fomorii. As Rhiannon fought she saw PSF officers and D'Danann go down at the claws of demons. Blood splattered from the officers' bodies, and the D'Danann twinkled and vanished as their souls traveled to Summerland.

Rhiannon's heart sickened and her fury magnified. She put more and more of her gray magic into her spellfire balls as her determination grew to take down as many demons as she could.

Nearby, her Coven sisters flung spellfire balls and used magic ropes to bind and incapacitate demons. The air crackled with the power of their magic and different colors lit up the air like fireworks. Their familiars did what they could, adding strength to their mistresses' magic.

Chaos buried his teeth into the flesh of a demon's leg and Sydney bound the beast with her ropes of magic, allowing another D'Danann to take it out.

Hannah's falcon, Banshee, was using the same tactic as Spirit and going for the eyes.

As planned, all the witches were trying to work their way toward Ceithlenn. But the tremendous number of demons held them back.

D'Danann charged Ceithlenn from the air, but their swords bounced off some kind of invisible barrier. The D'-Danann were the only beings able to get close enough to the goddess, yet they couldn't touch her.

A pink-and-black blur sped by Rhiannon, straight toward Ceithlenn.

"No!" Rhiannon shouted. The Faerie couldn't take on the goddess alone. "It's too dangerous, Galia!"

As soon as she reached the goddess, Galia started flinging pink bolts of lightning. The Faerie's magic actually pierced Ceithlenn's shield! The goddess's clothing burned every place a bolt struck and the leather seemed to melt against her skin. Galia's magic even tore holes in Ceithlenn's wings.

A look of intense fury crossed Ceithlenn's face. For a moment, souls stopped making their way toward her. In a movement so fast Rhiannon almost didn't see it, the goddess swung her hand. She slammed her magic at Galia, knocking the Faerie from the air.

Galia dropped to the ground and didn't move.

"Galia!" Fear followed by fury for her little friend rose up in Rhiannon's throat. She put so much of her gray magic in the next spellfire ball she gathered, she nearly blew up the closest demon's head before Keir could lop it off.

Spirit bounded toward Galia, arched his back, and took a protective stance over the Faerie's little body.

From the air, D'Danann sliced and hacked at demons with their swords. Metal clanked against the iron-tipped claws of the Fomorii. Blood splattered the field as D'Danann swords made contact with demon necks and chests.

PSF officers and D'Danann were covered with blood, too, some their own. Claw marks grazed arms, ripped through clothing. The officers' bodies were protected by their armor and helmets, but it wasn't enough. Flesh was flayed open and throats torn out.

There were so many demons. Every time one Fomorii dropped it was replaced by another.

And the people in the stands—no more screaming.

Nothing. They were frozen by the power of Ceithlenn's magic and she quickly sucked the souls from one human after another.

Rhiannon flung spellfire after spellfire and Keir swung and sliced with his sword. Demon blood coated Rhiannon's and Keir's shirts and streaked their faces.

When Rhiannon missed the next demon, she had to drop and roll away from the beast as it lunged for her. Keir took the demon out and Rhiannon scrambled to her feet. Her breathing had become harsh and ragged and her arms sore from throwing spellfire balls. But the adrenaline pumping through her kept her going.

After battling two more demons, another beast got close enough to rake its claws across her chest, ripping her shirt. Thank Anu, the Kevlar vest protected her. Keir gave a mighty roar and lunged for the demon. He cut its heart out with a skillful movement.

But another demon came up from behind Keir and gouged its iron-tipped claws down his bare arm. Blood flowed. Rhiannon screamed and flung spellfire. Keir whirled and cut his sword through the air, decapitating the demon.

Dear Anu, don't let that wound have enough iron in it to hurt Keir! Her heart nearly crumbled at the thought and she barely avoided dodging the claws of the next demon.

While she continued to fight, Rhiannon noticed that Sydney and Hannah had each teamed up with a D'Danann warrior. They each used their magic ropes to bring a demon down. The D'Danann finished the Fomorii off, turning them into piles of silt.

Silver worked with Hawk and Copper with Tiernan. Silver not only had her magic, but used a pair of silver stiletto daggers as she fought. She had developed a knack for flipping the knives through the air and into a Fomorii's heart at the same time she flung a spellfire ball. The knives didn't kill the demons because they didn't destroy their hearts, but it slowed them down.

Copper had been the lead pitcher on the California Bears team at U. C. Berkeley during her undergrad years. Despite her broken ankle, she maneuvered easily and fired off one spellfire ball after another with nearly perfect precision.

Alyssa bit her lower lip as she flung spellfire balls and one of the D'Danann stayed by her side. When a Fomorii got too close, she would throw up a spellshield, protecting herself from attack. But Rhiannon saw Alyssa's clothing had been shredded and her arm was bleeding.

Rhiannon glanced toward the pitcher's mound after she took down another Fomorii.

Ceithlenn was still drawing souls from the crowded stadium. The goddess radiated power. The cloudy wisps came faster and faster to her, and her body soaked them in like a sponge.

A sick feeling weighted Rhiannon's belly, almost driving her to her knees. All those people. All those people! Men, women, children.

Everyone.

Rhiannon clenched her teeth. She threw everything she had into fighting the demons harder.

She and her Coven sisters had to get to Ceithlenn.

Keir roared, fury giving him even more strength.

His fear for Rhiannon mingled with admiration for the way she fought. She was a true warrior in every sense of the word.

Sweat streaked her cheeks, along with Fomorii blood. Her black cap had fallen off and her short auburn hair was wild about her face, her green eyes burning with fire.

Keir's fellow warriors fought from the air, using their advantage of speed and flight. Rhona and Tegan attacked Ceithlenn's shield time after time, as did Kirra and Sheridan. When they struck her shield the warriors were flung backward and had to catch themselves in mid-flight to keep from crashing to the ground. Yet they went after Ceithlenn again and again.

So many Fomorii and so few of the D'Danann, witches, and PSF. Godsdamn the Chieftains for not sending more aid!

When he saw two of his comrades go down, along with PSF officers, Keir's rage magnified and his strokes grew harder and faster.

Keir lopped off another demon's head, making way for yet more Fomorii. He ground his teeth and jabbed at the next demon. Whatever the case, Keir and their team *would* win this battle against the Fomorii.

Ceithlenn was another concern altogether.

Rhiannon missed a demon with her spellfire ball and the Fomorii lunged for her. She whirled, turning her back on it and dropping. Instead of catching her in her face with its claws, it raked its nails across the body armor on Rhiannon's back as it dove for her. The demon gripped her clothing in its fist.

As the Fomorii jerked Rhiannon backward, its jaws set to bite her neck, Rhiannon screamed.

Keir roared and chopped off the demon's hand, releasing Rhiannon. In another powerful swing, Keir beheaded the beast.

His rage grew beyond the heat of fire from a forge. His anger was insurmountable as he witnessed more PSF officers dropping to the grassy field, either lifeless or injured. And he felt it in his heart each time a D'Danann went down at the claws of a demon and moved on to Summerland. At least three of his warriors had passed.

With a quick glance at Ceithlenn, Keir saw her satisfied expression as she sucked in more and more souls. The screams and noise from the stadium had quieted as she took life after life.

How were they going to destroy such a powerful and evil goddess?

Despite the fact they had outnumbered the forces of good at the beginning, the Fomorii ranks began to thin. Countless piles of silt littered the field along with the bodies of PSF officers.

After Keir beheaded another demon and another, he realized the tide had turned.

Their team had destroyed most of the Fomorii.

He and Rhiannon looked at each other. He gave a sharp nod, and in silent agreement they both started toward Ceithlenn. Keir from the air, Rhiannon on foot. The other witches and their familiars began flowing toward the goddess, too, while still fighting.

The ground shook.

Rhiannon cried out as she fell and landed on her backside.

Great pounding noises, like monstrous footsteps, sounded on the field.

Keir whirled in the air. Two giants headed toward them. Both swinging great spiked clubs.

One of the creatures was hideous and blue, with horns sprouting from its forehead. The monster roared and swung its club back and forth like a great elephant's tusk. Its arms were long enough to hang down to the grassy field.

The other monster was just as revolting, including the massive horns—but almost human looking. Its skin was tanned and it had long, lank black hair. But what captured Keir's attention was the large, glowing crimson eye hanging from a chain around its neck.

Balor's eye.

Keir knew it as sure as his heart beat in his chest.

Silver and Rhiannon had visioned these two giants—Junga and Darkwolf, distorted by Ceithlenn's magic.

The giants charged them, swinging their spiked clubs in huge arcs.

PSF officers regrouped behind their shields and fired rounds of ammunition at the beasts.

The bullets bounced off the monsters' flesh. No matter where the bullets hit, they did not harm the beasts. Even a shot to an eye did nothing, as if the beasts were made of impenetrable steel.

Then the monsters were upon the PSF.

Officers screamed as the clubs slammed into their shields. The clubs knocked the men and women into the air like fall leaves blown from a tree in a sharp gust of wind.

Zephyr, Copper's honeybee familiar, zipped through the air toward the human-like monster and attacked. The giant roared and brought his free hand to his face. The bee was actually hurting the giant! Because he was magical, the honeybee never lost his stinger and his sting was more potent than a common bee.

From where he hovered in the air, Keir assessed the rest

of the situation. The witches were binding the last of the Fomorii with their magic, or incapacitating them with spellfire
and their familiars helped them.

Ceithlenn still drew in souls. The more she absorbed, the
more powerfully she glowed. She even seemed to grow
taller, her wings wider.

His heart lurched when he saw the tiny body of Galia just
feet from Ceithlenn, guarded by Spirit. Keir growled. He
would get his revenge on the goddess bitch.

The D'Danann trying to get through Ceithlenn's magical
shield continued to fight to no avail, but they had not given
up. They attacked over and over again, looking for some spot
of weakness in her shield.

"Take out the monsters!" Keir shouted to his fellow warriors.

He and most of the D'Danann charged the creatures that
continued to bash their clubs into anyone within reach.

The D'Danann flew through the air and zeroed in on the
monsters. Keir aimed his sword at the beast that looked
somewhat like a man—only the monster was four times the
height, ten times the width, and malformed. Its face was red
and swollen in spots, no doubt from the bee stings.

The beast roared and swung its club up in the air at Keir.
He dodged and went for the giant's throat with his sword.

Instead of piercing the monster's flesh, Keir's sword hit
what felt like cold iron. The impact and force of the rebound
flung him back. He caught himself and barely dodged the
spiked club again as the beast cried out. It was almost a human cry.

With a flap of his wings, Keir charged forward. Other
D'Danann helped to fight the man-like monster, while additional warriors battled the blue giant.

The D'Danann only served to distract the beasts from
hurting the rest of the humans and witches. The monsters
swatted at the D'Danann like flies, using their great clubs.
Three times the monsters caught warriors with their clubs.

Keir was almost blinded by rage. More than two thousand

years of training made keeping his focus and fighting as natural as breathing.

Nothing the D'Danann did seemed to hurt the monsters in any way. Not a scratch, not a pierce, not a drop of blood. They did nothing but incite the monsters into a more intense frenzy. Only the honeybee had any kind of effect. It was obvious the giant was distracted and angered by the stings.

His frustration mounting, Keir struggled to come up with some solution to harm the monsters, to destroy them. They had to find a way to stop them. The monsters were as invincible as Ceithlenn appeared to be.

From out of nowhere, magical ropes snaked around the ankles of the giants.

Keir jerked his attention to see the witches working together to take down the monsters. All seven witches used their ropes of magic to bind the giants from head to toe. Their ropes wound around and around the monsters.

Rhiannon's face was a mask of both fury and concentration as she held on to a gold magical rope that continued to loop around the blue giant. Silver and Copper aided her, while the other four witches tackled the man-like monster.

Because its entire body was bound by the ropes, the blue monster dropped its club with a shriek and a tremendous crash. It lost its balance and fell onto its back, striking its head on the ground. The earth thundered from the force of the giant's fall, as though an earthquake had struck. The monster struggled against its bonds. It screamed and shrieked and fought the magical ropes.

A few moments later, the other giant fell forward, landing on its chest and covering the great crimson eye. The witches stumbled backward and three of them fell as another quake rocked the ground. The monster roared and tried to get out of its bonds.

Keir took a quick glance at the goddess.

Ceithlenn had lowered her wings and her arms.

She smiled and the very air around her began to pulsate.

All attention turned to Ceithlenn.

Keir's heart thrummed harder. He brushed sweat and blood from his face as he stared at the goddess.

Something was about to happen.

Whatever it was, Keir had no doubt it could mean nothing but more devastation.

Chapter 33

Ceithlenn took a deep breath of sweat and blood, human and Fomorii. She smiled, her body filled with so much heat that the flames of her hair crackled and hissed. This was it. This was the moment she would finally bring her lover, her husband, back from exile.

It didn't matter that all the Fomorii around her had been destroyed—she had only brought a fraction of her army. Once Balor was here, once the eye was taken from around Darkwolf's throat, Balor would kill the witches and D'-Danann with the power of his eye. One look from him and each victim would turn to ash.

Just as the witches finished binding Darkwolf and Junga, Ceithlenn had taken almost every soul in the stadium. The richness of the souls ran through her veins, pounded in her heart, throbbed in her body. The magic built up within her was so heady she shook with it. She had never felt so invincible, so immortal.

Now it was time to focus on bringing Balor to her. "My love," she said, holding out her arms as if to embrace him. "It is time to return."

She concentrated on Balor, focused on bringing him to her. Everything around her sparked. Crackled. Glimmered.

The air folded, distorted. Became blurry, wavy.

From her peripheral vision she saw her attackers fall

from the sky or where they stood. Her magic was so powerful the force of it kept her enemies from moving. It pinned them to the ground.

She smiled again as she drew on her image of Balor as she had last seen him. The richness of his brown hair, the angular lines of his face, the tone of his body. She had missed her lover, had missed having him between her thighs, having him inside her. The memory of the last time they had been together now drew him closer to her.

With his eye missing all these centuries, he had been unable to see her beauty. Countless times she had cursed her grandson, the sun god Lugh, and one of the Tuatha D'-Danann for taking Balor's eye and sending him to Underworld.

Ceithlenn had been exiled with Balor. After she escaped from Underworld, she never doubted that one day they would be reunited. Stronger. And able to make this Otherworld theirs again.

Together they had planned and planned before her escape.

Part of Balor's essence had remained in the eye. They had developed their magic so well that when Balor's eye washed ashore, they knew at once. And they were ready. When the right being was near, one who wanted power, they were able to influence him through the essence and drive him to pick it up.

Then he belonged to them.

Once the eye was in his hands, the being became known as Darkwolf. In Balor's name, Darkwolf had performed blood rituals and human sacrifices, had killed, stolen, and kidnapped. He had summoned the Fomorii to herald Balor's and Ceithlenn's way to this Otherworld. Through the eye, Ceithlenn and Balor had driven Darkwolf to do everything they wished.

And now, finally, *finally,* it was time to bring Balor back to this Otherworld.

Ceithlenn's body vibrated from the magic emanating from her. She felt the pull of Balor, felt him unite with her soul. She felt it in her heart, her body, between her thighs.

"Yes. Yes!" Ceithlenn held out her arms for her husband. "Come to me, love."

In the distance, through the blurred and folded air, time, and space, she saw him. Balor's carriage was proud despite the missing eye in the middle of his forehead. His muscles bunched and flexed as he strode toward her through the tunnel now connecting them. He wore only a loincloth, showing his body to perfection.

Ceithlenn's heart beat faster. Her smile grew broader. Heated pleasure rushed through her body the closer Balor came to her.

She gasped and grabbed her belly.

Her magic began to slip away.

Her power was dwindling!

"Hurry, love," she cried. Bringing her husband to her was taking every ounce of the power she had.

She was fading. Fading.

No! She had to bring him to her. It was time!

"Balor!" she cried, and he moved toward the sound of her voice.

She held her hand out to him. "Ceithlenn!" he shouted as he stretched out his arm.

Their fingers brushed.

The air around them exploded like a mirror shattering into a million fragments.

Ceithlenn shrieked as she flew backward, away from Balor. She landed on her ass, her palms braced on the ground. She rose as her lover fully formed on the field.

Her heart leapt. She had done it!

But now she was weakened.

From her peripheral vision she saw Darkwolf and Junga deflate. Slowly their bodies shifted, squirmed, and returned to their normal forms, the magic ropes loose around them.

Her heart pounded as only a human's could. The Sara part of her recognized what was happening. Her magic that had enslaved them, and kept them in their monstrous shapes, was now broken and she could no longer maintain control over them.

The magical ropes the witches had restrained Junga and
Darkwolf with were now too big. The Fomorii and the warlock scrambled out of their bindings.

Balor's eye glowed so brilliantly from Darkwolf's throat
the air surrounding them was red. Darkwolf shouted something to Junga that Ceithlenn couldn't hear. Then for some
strange reason, Junga morphed to her Elizabeth form. Her
more vulnerable form.

"Give the eye to Balor!" Ceithlenn shouted to Darkwolf
as she pushed herself to her feet. "Hurry!"

Darkwolf brought his hand to his chest and grasped the
eye. The red of it bled through his fingers. He looked at
Balor, who headed Darkwolf's way despite his blindness.
Balor could sense his own eye.

Ceithlenn shouted again, "Give him the eye, Darkwolf!"

The warlock hesitated.

He grabbed Elizabeth-Junga by her upper arm.

And vanished.

They both vanished.

Ceithlenn shrieked. "No! You bastard, no!"

She cried out to Balor, "Leave this place, my love. Hurry.
You must find Darkwolf!"

The god roared so loud it shook the stadium. He started
toward Ceithlenn then came up short, likely sensing the D'-
Danann flying his way.

Balor's voice boomed throughout the stadium. "I will
come for you, my Ceith."

And he disappeared.

Chapter 34

Rhiannon's fury mounted as Ceithlenn turned her rage on the witches and their allies. The flame-haired being flung out her arms and the two PSF officers closest to her were hit with her magic and flung back, across the stadium.

"*No!*" Rhiannon shouted through the pain in her heart, drawing Ceithlenn's attention.

The goddess pointed one finger at Rhiannon.

You need to trust yourself, and in turn the Shadows will answer to you, came the Great Guardian's voice in Rhiannon's thoughts, through the incredible pain that Ceithlenn was inflicting on her mind. *They can and will fight for purposes that serve the greater good so long as you believe in them.*

Ignoring the head-splitting pain of being near Ceithlenn, Rhiannon set her jaw.

Through all the pain, anger, hope, and fear, she freed the Shadows.

Again she felt as if a thunderstorm filled her body. Shadows whirled out of her like small tornadoes and Rhiannon felt an electrical charge with every single one of them.

The black, almost human-shaped Shadows converged on the goddess. She screamed and struggled as they trapped her arms, her legs, and even had her by the neck.

Ceithlenn focused her stare on Rhiannon and she felt as if

her skull would burst from the pain. She dropped to her knees, her vision blurring as the goddess continued to grasp at Rhiannon's mind despite the Shadows.

Rhiannon's entire body shook. Blinding white light flashed in front of her eyes.

She raised her hands, clenched her fists at the sides of her skull, and shouted, "You bitch. Get. Out. Of. My. Head!"

With a powerful mental shove, Rhiannon slammed her magic against Ceithlenn's hold. A harsh struggle took place inside Rhiannon's skull. The battle for her mind was almost enough to make her pass out.

Then she gave another mental shove with everything she had.

Ceithlenn reeled back and the Shadows fully tackled her to the ground.

The pain vanished and Ceithlenn's hold on Rhiannon's mind shattered.

The goddess looked furious and shocked all at once.

And the pain from Rhiannon's head was gone. Ceithlenn's name no longer had power over Rhiannon!

The Shadows seemed to read her mind and tightened their hold on the goddess as she struggled to a sitting position.

Magical ropes snaked around Ceithlenn from Rhiannon's Coven sisters.

The ropes drew the goddess's arms tight against her sides and pinned her wings to her. She dropped from her knees to her haunches. The witches' familiars stood by, shrieking, growling, hissing.

Ceithlenn hissed back, her hair flaming, her eyes glowing evil red. The stench of burnt sugar and rotten fish was so strong Rhiannon wanted to gag.

Slowly Ceithlenn's wings and fangs retracted. The fire of her hair faded.

The goddess wavered. Sara appeared in her place and slumped onto her back. The smell of Jasmine mingled with the other stenches.

Still wrapped in the Shadows and the other witches' magical ropes, Ceithlenn-Sara screamed again. It was an inhuman shriek, but Rhiannon could tell the goddess didn't have the magical energy to struggle. Ceithlenn had used most of her power in bringing Balor to this world.

Chaos pounced on Ceithlenn-Sara's chest, pinning her down. The Doberman had his jaws open, poised above Sara's jugular, ready for the command to finish her off. The Shadows ignored Chaos and clung to Sara like a thick black fog, surrounding the Coven sisters' magic ropes

Even through her shock of losing Darkwolf, Junga, and Balor himself, Rhiannon kept her resolve firm. She didn't exactly have control over the Shadows, but she knew they served her will.

Rhiannon wasn't about to let this bitch live.

But, dear Anu. Balor is here! Ceithlenn set Balor free!

Yet, Darkwolf had left with the eye—as if he couldn't give it up to the god.

Or wouldn't.

Did he have other plans?

How did he escape the god's powers?

Rhiannon had to thank Anu that Darkwolf had not given the eye to Balor—yet. If mythology and history had any merit, Balor regaining his eye would mean devastation for all.

Right now Rhiannon didn't have time to dwell on that. At this moment her attention needed to be entirely focused on Ceithlenn-Sara and the Shadows.

Sara, the traitorous witch turned warlock. Whether by her own plan or by Ceithlenn's, Sara had absorbed the goddess's soul into her own so that they were one.

Keir jogged toward Rhiannon, his sword gripped in his fist. Blood and sweat streaked his rage-filled face and blood poured from the slashes on his arm. Chaos saw Keir and backed away, obviously recognizing that Keir was going to finish Ceithlenn-Sara off.

When he reached the bound and Shadow-covered Ceithlenn-Sara, Keir readied his weapon, his muscular biceps bulging with the motion.

A rush of relief for her friend swept over Rhiannon when Galia zipped up. She wasn't hurt! Just knocked unconscious.

The Faerie looked a little woozy, but she shouted, "Finish her off, Keir!" Her little wings beat like crazy and she hovered beside him. She held another pink lightning bolt in her hand, the magical fire aimed at Ceithlenn's heart.

"Stop!" came a powerful voice Rhiannon recognized at once.

Keir paused in his swing and Rhiannon looked up at Janis Arrowsmith. The sight of the High Priestess pricked Rhiannon's skin like needles.

Janis of the white magic D'Anu Coven stared at Sara in shock. "Sara was once a D'Anu witch. You cannot kill her."

"The Underworlds, I cannot," Keir growled and raised his sword high again.

"No!" Janis's voice was high and sharp-pitched. "I'll not see it!"

Sword still held high, Keir bent so that his face was close to Janis's before he said, "Then do not look."

So fast that it was almost a blur, Janis flung her body over Ceithlenn-Sara's, protecting her neck.

"Shit," Jake said as he jogged up. "Get that old lady away and finish Ceithlenn off."

Keir grabbed one of Janis's arms, while Jake grasped the other, but she didn't move a fraction.

"My magic will not allow you to move me," Janis said as she raised herself just enough to look into Ceithlenn-Sara's face. The goddess was still bound by the Shadows and magic ropes, and Janis was lying on top of them and the goddess.

The goddess's fierce expression turned softer as she stared up at Janis with pleading eyes. "I couldn't stop her. She took over my body—everything." Sara bowed her head. "I can't get her out of me."

With most of the people in the stands likely dead, the only other sounds that could be heard were the moans and groans of the injured PSF officers and D'Danann, and Alyssa's small cries as her arm was cared for.

To Rhiannon's further surprise, when she took a quick glance around, she saw members of the white magic D'Anu Coven. They were attending to those who still lived, using their white magic to heal what wounds they could. By silent agreement, some of the gray magic witches and their familiars turned to help the other D'Anu Coven, leaving Copper, Silver, and Rhiannon to ensure Ceithlenn's containment with the Shadows and magic ropes.

Confused conversation came from people on the field itself. From what Rhiannon gathered, when Ceithlenn first spoke from the pitcher's mound, the goddess had merely "frozen" the people on the field for her demons to eat after the fight. Her control over them must have failed, too. The governor and some members of the baseball teams were among those who had survived.

"We will perform a ceremony with Sara and banish the demon-goddess from within her," Janis Arrowsmith announced, her voice ringing through the almost silent stadium.

"What?" Rhiannon's word of incredulity was echoed by several of the other witches, including Copper and Silver. "There's no saving her," Rhiannon stated. "No banishing Ceithlenn from her. She's a willing host, and she's murdered thousands of people. She needs to be killed."

Janis's gaze grew icy. "We will banish the evil from Sara's soul."

"I can't believe this." Even though Rhiannon was exhausted from releasing and manipulating the Shadows—not to mention the battle—she mentally yanked harder on the Shadows holding onto Ceithlenn-Sara. It caused the goddess-bitch to yelp. "You want to take the chance of Ceithlenn escaping? What if she jumps from Sara's soul to someone else's?"

Janis's look hardened, her face like lined white marble. "The goddess will be sent back to Underworld."

Rhiannon widened her eyes, a what-the-hell-is-going-on? expression on her face. "That's gray magic. You don't go there, remember?"

Janis cleared her throat. "But you do," she said in a voice that was tight with both distaste and resignation.

Rhiannon glanced from Janis to Ceithlenn-Sara, who maintained an innocent expression.

Innocent, my ass.

Janis brought her palm to her throat before her hand fluttered to her side again. A vulnerable gesture. Janis wasn't vulnerable to anything that Rhiannon knew of.

"Sara was my apprentice," Janis finally said, her voice filled with barely restrained emotion.

Rhiannon just stared at Janis, incredulous. "You can't be serious."

"I'm sorry." Sara bowed her head. "Darkwolf wove such black magic around me. And then the goddess . . ." She shuddered. "I can't get her out of me."

"This isn't the Sara you knew. The goddess is tricking you." Rhiannon's heart pounded faster. "Look around you. Look at all the dead people in those seats up there. *Thousands* of dead people!"

Sirens blared and the sounds of screeching vehicles came from outside the stadium, cutting across Rhiannon's words.

She looked up at Keir. "The cameras. Even if everyone is dead, there were still television cameras all over the place. Everything's been seen, including the D'Danann and the D'Anu."

Keir lowered his sword and his eyes met hers.

Jake looked worn from battle, but as pumped as if he could take on ten more demons. "You need to go," Jake said to Keir. "Now. With your help we'll take care of Ceithlenn and the rest, but the D'Danann need to get the hell out of here."

"I will not leave Rhiannon or the other witches," Keir growled. Tiernan and Hawk came up beside him and agreed.

"You guys are allergic to lead, right?" Jake said. "The truck interiors are lined with it."

"Godsdamn," Keir said with a furious glare. "Then they will fly with us."

Rhiannon shook her head. "We've got to keep our bindings on her or she'll get away."

"You are part Elvin," he said, his face furious.

"Only part," Silver said. "We've got to try."

"Do not free her." Keir glared at Janis Arrowsmith. "Your apprentice is gone. What you see here is an evil being controlling the shell that was once your apprentice. She must be destroyed."

Shouts and orders of "Put your weapons down!" rang through the air.

"Go, Keir. All of you." Rhiannon poured more of her own magic into the Shadows surrounding Sara and met Keir's gaze. "I'm not going to let the bitch free."

Keir gave one look at the law enforcement officers approaching them from all sides. He glanced at the other D'Danann and gave a short nod. Those who already had their wings spread launched into the air and vanished, some carrying their wounded. Almost as fast, the rest of the D'Danann unfurled their wings, took to the sky, and disappeared from human sight, too.

"Holy shit!" one of the players on the field cried out.

"What the fuck?" an umpire shouted.

"I don't think I'll ever get used to seeing that," Jake murmured at the same time he held his hand and his credentials up for the oncoming law enforcement officers to see.

"Macgregor." A San Francisco Police Department officer with a blond crew cut and hard look in his blue eyes jogged closer to them. "What the hell is going on, Jake?"

"Here we go." Jake shook his head at Rhiannon before heading toward the cop to fill him in the best he could considering the situation.

Rhiannon fought a wave of nausea, fought to keep from becoming sick. Some of the officers were beyond magical healing. Dead or mortally wounded. All the blood! So much of it. The piles of silt littering the battlefield gave her no satisfaction. If the damned Chieftains had sent more D'Danann to help fight, many lives would have been saved.

Fire trucks, ambulances, and more cop cars began making their way onto the field. Lights flashed, sirens shrieked. The stench of battle and Fomorii were almost more than Rhiannon could handle. Just the screaming sirens were enough to make her dizzy.

She turned back to Ceithlenn-Sara, who was looking up at Janis now. Tears filled the being's eyes.

Rhiannon blinked. Those strange, shifting eyes . . . they weren't Sara's at all.

"The chief says we've got to cuff her." Jake came up beside Rhiannon and she looked up at him. "This magic stuff—I don't think anyone's getting it."

Panic rose up in Rhiannon. "Cuffing her won't be enough!"

Jake jerked his head to one of the black PSF trucks now on the field, backing up to them. "We'll get her in the truck and out of this zoo." He glanced around them. "You *all* need to leave and fast."

"Have your officers cover us." Rhiannon looked at Copper and Silver, who were watching her intently. "We'll get Ceithlenn in the truck and keep her contained."

In the back of her mind, Rhiannon realized she'd truly kicked the goddess from her mind, and saying or hearing Ceithlenn's name no longer hurt.

Jake nodded and within moments his officers surrounded them in an arc around the rear door of the truck. All officers but Jake and three others had their backs to Ceithlenn and the witches, a human barricade.

The witches' magical ropes and the Shadows held as Ceithlenn was carried by one of the PSF officers into the truck. Jake and the two officers by his sides kept their rifles pinned on Ceithlenn as they ushered the witches and their familiars into the truck, including Janis.

Rhiannon shuddered. The truck's walls wanted to close in on her. But she could do this. She could do this.

Copper and Silver looked pale from the battle.

"What about the rest of my Coven?" Janis asked as they all crowded inside the vehicle.

Silver paused and looked back. "And ours?"

"They're being taken out in another truck," Jake said before backing up and hopping out of the vehicle. "I have to stay. My officers are taking you to PSF HQ and putting Ceithlenn into a holding cell."

"*A holding cell?*" Rhiannon said with incredulity. "No damn holding cell is going to keep her contained."

Jake was already shutting the back doors of the truck and spoke into his microphone. "Pull out."

Rhiannon had forgotten all about the earpiece, and she startled. She was so wound up that she felt like she could rip off her skin. Everything had been so intense, so loud, so frightening on the battlefield, that she couldn't remember if anything had been spoken through the transmitter or not.

The tank-like truck began to rumble and bounce along the field. Still keeping her focus on her Shadows, Rhiannon stared at Ceithlenn-Sara, a young woman in a revealing cat-suit with punk-red hair and eyes that shifted like reflections rippling on the surface a pond.

Ceithlenn-Sara now sat between two armed PSF guards, magical bindings still around her upper body. One additional guard trained a gun on Ceithlenn.

The Shadows covered the goddess, still, along with Copper's and Silver's ropes.

Utter and complete exhaustion overcome Rhiannon. The Shadows fell away from Ceithlenn and shot back into Rhiannon with an electrical charge.

"No!" Rhiannon shouted, trying to get them to go back to the goddess. But she felt their energy depletion down to her bones.

Rhiannon had seated herself directly across from Ceithlenn-Sara, and held Spirit in her lap. She pushed her hand against her chest where she still felt the entry of the Shadows. No matter how much they needed to be recharged, she still tried to get them to come back out.

The being's gaze met Rhiannon's. Her eyes flashed red and her lip curled into a wicked grin.

"*I* will *get you*," Ceithlenn's voice came loud in Rhiannon's thoughts. "*You are mine.*"

Rhiannon jerked back, her face stinging and the claw marks on her cheek burning as if she'd just been slapped. She opened her mouth to say something to Janis when both guards to either side of Ceithlenn gasped.

Spirit hissed.

The guards slumped. Their rifles clattered to the floor.

The officers' bodies began jerk. To shrivel. Their hands went to their faces. Their mouths opened wide in obvious terror before their features lost all recognition and their eyes became sightless.

Two wispy white puffs slipped from the guards to Ceithlenn.

Horror ripped through Rhiannon. "No!" she screamed and tried to force the Shadows out again. At the same time Copper and Silver threw spellfire balls.

A blinding flare caused everyone to shout as the spellfire exploded where the goddess was sitting.

When the sparkles faded, Ceithlenn was gone.

The magic ropes that had bound her vanished.

For a moment the entire group in the back of the truck was stunned into silence. All that could be heard was the roar of the truck that now smelled of death and that constant smell of burnt sugar.

"Oh, my God." One of the other PSF officers, a Lieutenant Landers, put her hand over her mouth. "Graves and Monson. Oh, my God."

"How did she take their souls?" Rhiannon said, beyond horrified and feeling the urge to puke.

"The potion should have saved them!" Silver said.

"What potion?" Landers managed to get out.

"Dear Anu." Rhiannon looked at the PSF officer. "There was so little time that it must not not had time for it to get to you."

Janis's face had gone beyond marble white. She was pale with a tinge of green to her features.

Rhiannon glared at Janis. "These men are dead because of *you*. If you had let Keir finish her off, they would still be alive." Rhiannon clenched her fists at her sides. "Now Ceithlenn's free to kill more people! And who knows what she and Balor will do together."

"But Sara . . ." Janis continued to stare at the bodies.

"Don't you get it?" Copper said. "Sara is as good as dead. She has to be destroyed."

"Sara would never—" Janis shook her head. "No. She was a good girl. She would never."

"She went with Darkwolf willingly." Rhiannon's voice was calm, controlled. "You know she did. Of her own free will."

Janis looked dazed, and she wavered from side to side. "To save herself from the Fomorii. She did it to save herself from the demons."

"And she became worse than the demons." Rhiannon clenched her teeth. "Sara is *gone*. This being is a monster. A goddess bent on nothing but destruction and death."

Janis shook her head, still in denial. "No. I will *not* believe she cannot be saved."

Rhiannon braced her elbows on her thighs and buried her face in her hands. After all they'd been through. After all those deaths. After seeing two men killed right before her eyes, Janis couldn't see the horror in front of her.

The backs of Rhiannon's eyes stung. Her face burned and she felt filthy and sticky from sweat and blood. She could barely breathe from the stench in the truck.

They'd had Ceithlenn. They'd *had* her. And the goddess had been weak enough for them to destroy.

Maybe it's my fault, Rhiannon thought. *I should have had the strength to keep the Shadows on her. The battle shouldn't have made a difference. The Shadows were what controlled Ceithlenn, not the magic ropes. I should have practiced with the Shadows—something! But time—dear Anu, everything has happened so fast.*

After one of the officers transmitted what had occurred, they were ordered to continue course. Everyone in the truck was silent the rest of the ride to the PSF HQ. An ambulance would meet them there—not that there was anything that could be done for these poor officers. Silver, Copper, and Rhiannon were exhausted and covered with stinking Fomorii blood, but had no scratches from the demons' ironclad claws, thank Anu.

When they arrived at the PSF headquarters, everyone

spilled out of the truck and into the abnormally warm day. Rhiannon barely felt the tingle of the sun on her skin.

It was all so surreal, as if this had happened in a movie instead of real life. Once the other truckload of witches arrived and the bodies of the two officers were taken away in an ambulance, all of the witches were asked for statements.

Rhiannon looked at the officers in amazement as they were asked to come in through the back of the nondescript building that housed what *had* been the highly secretive PSF Department.

"How can you ask us for statements?" Rhiannon asked. "What can we possibly say? That we duked it out with a bunch of demons and a soul-sucking goddess with the help of some winged Fae warriors?"

She looked at Lieutenant Landers. "And not only is there a massive amount of demons hidden beneath Alcatraz, prepared to go to war on San Francisco, and a goddess-bitch on the loose again, but now we have a one-eyed god here, too? Although—if Darkwolf is keeping the eye from Balor, maybe he can't find it just yet?"

"I know it doesn't make sense, but we have to do it." Landers sighed as she ushered them into the building. "Millions of people saw it all happen on national television. Thousands were killed in that stadium and thousands more will be affected by the deaths of their loved ones." Landers shook her head. "Most won't be able to accept what happened, even though they *saw* it happen. But we have to come up with something."

"They'll think it was some kind of horror movie." Copper threw her thick braid over her shoulder and spoke with her hands as they walked down a narrow hallway. "This has to be the single most devastating thing to happen to the United States since 9/11. And it was because of demons and a goddess? I can hardly believe it myself."

"I sure as hell am having a hard time with it." An other officer named Marsten spoke briskly as he guided them into what looked like a large classroom. "But the PSF has been fighting these demons since Halloween, and we've all seen a lot of serious shit."

Rhiannon shoved her hair away from her face. She could barely hold back tears.

Sydney came up beside Rhiannon as they came to a stop in the room. Sydney put her arm around her as she said, "It wasn't your fault she escaped."

"I should have been able to force the Shadows to keep her down," Rhiannon whispered. Her head felt so heavy she rested it on Sydney's shoulder. "I should have told Keir to take her out before Janis even got close. Instead we let her hold us back a fraction too long."

Her gaze met Janis's stone cold one as the High Priestess said, "Is it so easy for you to kill now, Rhiannon Castle? Have you turned to black magic?"

Rhiannon pushed away from Sydney and marched up to Janis. "It's not black magic to get rid of something so foul, so evil, so deadly. It would have been the most humane thing we could have done. Now thousands more will probably die.

"You could be next." Rhiannon swept out her arm as if to encompass the room. "We all could be next and we're the only ones who can fight her. Can't you see that? Can't you open your mind long enough to understand what we're up against?"

"Save it." Copper took Rhiannon by the hand and led her to one of the seats. "You'll never get her to see past her own prejudices."

Rhiannon gave a weary sigh and slid into a seat as Landers handed her a form and a pen and Spirit rubbed himself against her ankles. More exhaustion was setting in and she barely had the strength to hold the pen, much less write.

Where did one start when the world as they all knew it could be coming to an end?

Chapter 35

The rush of transference faded as Darkwolf arrived in the now closed hotel where he had first met Elizabeth. His grip on her arm failed and his legs gave out. He dropped to the marble floor of the lobby and landed on his hands and knees.

Elizabeth collapsed near him, striking her head on the marble. He managed to move to a sitting position and scooted over beside the demon-woman. Her eyes were closed and her breathing shallow. He held his hand to her heart. It beat strong and sure.

Darkwolf sighed with relief. He didn't know why it mattered that Elizabeth survived, but it did. He didn't even know why he had taken her with him when he escaped Balor and Ceithlenn.

The eye burned at his chest, hotter than ever, now that Balor was here. And it felt heavy. So, so heavy. The shields Darkwolf had thrown up in his mind were all that kept Balor from finding them.

Something had changed in Darkwolf, making him strong enough to escape both Ceithlenn and Balor. Could it have been the magic the goddess had used to turn him into that monster? Or had his magic grown strong enough from wearing the eye for so long?

He had no idea.

But now he knew he could never return the eye to the god.

Darkwolf had been *used* to bring forth the Fomorii, Ceithlenn, and now Balor. He had never truly wielded the power he'd thought he had.

In a frustrated motion he clenched his hand into a fist so hard his nails dug into his palm. Gods. If only he had never picked up this eye off the shores of Ireland.

He closed his own eyes and fought back the pain, the hell his life had been since then. He had been taken over so easily and he had reveled in the power. He'd killed, he'd sacrificed, he'd summoned evil, all in the name of Balor.

Darkwolf took a deep breath and sat back on his ass. He pushed his hand through his hair and caught his reflection in a mirror. He looked like hell. His face burned and was red where that damned honeybee had stung him. He felt a little sore from all the bullets that had pelted him when he was in his monster form, but none of those at least had pierced his flesh.

Thank the gods he and Elizabeth had returned to their natural states and were no longer within Ceithlenn's magical hold. It had been a living hell being under her control.

But the eye. What was he going to do with the eye? His gut told him he couldn't take it off, couldn't take the chance that Balor would get his hands on it. But Darkwolf would be on the run forever until Balor was sent back to Underworld.

If he was sent back.

How in the fuck would that be done?

A shrouding spell would help him in blocking the eye's essence. Now that he had made the decision to fight Balor, his mind was clearer.

He avoided touching the eye with his palm. That had always drawn Balor to him. Instead, he held his hand away from the eye and let his power radiate from within him. The purple glow of his magic surrounded the eye.

White-hot pain stabbed his head as he felt Balor's essence fighting the shrouding. But Darkwolf increased his magic, wrapping the eye over and over again until the purple magic was so thick the eye could barely be seen through the glow.

He collapsed onto his back, the eye heavy against his chest as his breathing grew harsh and ragged. He could still feel Balor shouting in his mind, but the pain was receding as Darkwolf shoved at it and tightened his mental barriers.

He held his hand to his forehead and grimaced as he rose back up to a sitting position.

"That godsdamn bitch." Elizabeth pushed herself up so that she was standing. Her jaw worked and her eyes literally flashed as she clenched her fists at her sides. "I am now no longer Queen of the Fomorii. I have lost everything I have worked for. *Everything*."

"Oh, yeah?" Darkwolf stood and faced her. "You're not the only one who's lost. I worked my ass off to be the most powerful warlock in the country. To bring *Balor* here—only to have that bitch ruin it all."

"We must get our revenge on her." Her gaze met his.

Darkwolf took another deep breath, his scowl so fierce his face ached. "No fucking kidding."

Chapter 36

Ceithlenn materialized on the ledge above the army of Fomorii and other creatures. Once she had fed on the souls of the two PSF officers, she'd had enough strength to return to her full goddess form and command her army.

She sniffed the air and reached with her senses to see if Balor had found his way to their lair.

Nothing. No sign of her husband.

With a scream of fury, frustration, and the pain of missing her lover, Ceithlenn swooped from the ledge and over the demons and beasts filling the cave. They looked up at her and she could see the wariness in their gazes.

Good. They should fear her. She was their goddess and all should pay homage to her.

Her fury mounted as she thought of Darkwolf's betrayal. The bastard had kept the eye! And somehow he was shrouding it, keeping it out of her mental sight. Where had he gained such power?

Balor could have killed all of their enemies if Darkwolf had turned it over. They had prepared him for that moment from the time they used the essence in the eye to compel Darkwolf to pick it up.

Ceithlenn landed on the bumpy floor of the cavern beneath Alcatraz. She braced her hands on her hips and her hair flamed higher with her anger. Darkwolf had taken the

Fomorii Queen, Junga, too. Now she would have to make one of the legion leaders the commander over all of the troops.

"Silence!" she shouted in her magically enhanced voice. The room went completely quiet at once. "Bow to me."

All of the demons and other beings prostrated themselves until she could see all of the cavern and the backs of her demons. The cavern reeked of fish, dog breath from the three-headed hounds, and feces.

"Tryok!" her voice echoed throughout the silent cavern. "To me."

A hulking, six-armed, one-eyed orange demon rose and made his way from the middle of the cavern. He bowed at her feet when he reached her.

"In what way can I serve you, my goddess?" Tryok asked in the guttural language of the Fomorii.

"Stand," she commanded.

"Yes, goddess." The six-armed demon scrambled to his feet and looked at her with his single eye.

"You will now be the commander over all the legions," she shouted in a voice loud enough to be heard in every corner of the cavern. "Junga will no longer be your queen."

Sounds of surprise rumbled through the cavern. Tryok's lone eye blinked and he appeared confused.

"Silence." The enormous cave immediately went quiet at her command.

She scowled at Tryok and felt fire burn in her own eyes. "Are you up to this position?"

"Yes, my goddess." His voice and his expression were clear, definite.

"You will select a demon from your legion to carry out your duties as legion leader." Ceithlenn braced her hands on her hips. "All legion leaders will report to you."

Tryok bowed low.

When he raised his head again, she said, "See that they are prepared to go to war on my notice."

"Yes, my goddess."

Ceithlenn flapped her wings and rose in the air. She

clenched her fists at her sides and said to herself. "As soon as we locate Balor and retrieve the eye, we will go to war on San Francisco. And then the world."

She narrowed her own eyes until they were mere slits. "And *I will* find Darkwolf."

Chapter 37

Darkness was nothing new to Balor. Nor was the hatred pumping through his heart.

He felt his way down a sewage tunnel, his palms running along the rough surface of the stone-like walls. His bare legs and feet splashed through filth that reminded him of Underworld.

He was sick of Underworld.

For centuries he had plotted and planned with his Ceith, and for one glorious moment they had come so close to realizing their goals.

To be the only gods of the old world to rule this Otherworld again.

Balor let out a roar that echoed through the sewage tunnel.

Then he paused, his entire body going tense.

He felt the presence of his eye.

Darkwolf.

Somewhere . . . near.

Balor smiled.

Chapter 38

By the time Rhiannon reached her apartment, she was ready to drop into a pile of complete and utter exhaustion. Her arms ached, her legs ached, her head ached. Actually, she didn't think there was a place on her body that didn't ache.

And her gut hurt so bad to know that they'd lost the battle. Oh, they'd defeated the Fomorii that were there, but Ceithlenn, Balor, Darkwolf, and Junga were all free. Not to mention all of those people dead. Thousands of them.

Her heart jerked with pain. They hadn't saved all those people.

And if her visions were right, there was a whole army of Fomorii ready to swarm her city.

Some of the D'Danann, because of the iron-tipped claws, their wounds would never heal. A few had been killed and passed on to Summerland. Then the PSF officers—so many dead. And too many wounded to count.

No sooner had she shut the apartment door behind her than she heard a loud knock. More like a thunderstorm. *Dear Anu.* She really didn't want to deal with Keir right now.

Rhiannon turned the knob and opened the door just a crack to see the big warrior in the hall. "Listen, I'm tired and—"

Keir pushed his way into her apartment and caught her by her upper arms when she stumbled back.

She was too tired and upset to be angry. "Not now, Keir."

He slammed the door shut with his boot, jerked her to him, and gave her a hard kiss that made her head spin.

When he drew away, she widened her eyes at the look of tenderness on his face. Then he brought her to him, crushing her to his length with his embrace. "I do not know how I will be able to accept you putting yourself into danger any further."

"But you will," she said against his chest. "You have to."

For a long time he held her, his big, rough hands stroking her face and hair. She allowed herself to sink into his embrace. It felt so good being in his arms. Letting him comfort her, letting him make her feel like everything would be all right—

Even though she knew it wasn't. It wasn't going to be all right at all.

In the hour before dawn, while it was still fairly dark outside, Rhiannon tugged on a lime green T-shirt and turquoise jeans before fluffing her hair and studying her face in the mirror. The sprinkling of freckles across her nose and cheeks stood out in sharp relief against her pale features. Yesterday had taken a toll on all of those who'd fought, and she could see it in her own eyes and on her face.

She wore her gold-and-onyx necklace, earrings, and ring as usual, and somehow they made her feel a little more secure.

Yet her thoughts continued to turn to the dangers they all faced.

Without help, how could the D'Danann and the D'Anu possibly defeat Ceithlenn *and* Balor? Never mind the horde of Fomorii still loose in the city.

Rhiannon stuffed her feet into socks and then lime green running shoes. When she got up this morning, Keir had been gone, and she'd found herself disappointed not to have his arms around her when she'd woken. He'd just held her last night after she'd taken a shower. It had soothed her enough that she'd been able to fall into a deep, exhausted sleep.

Rhiannon walked out of her bedroom and Spirit jumped out of his cat bed, meowed, and began running circles around her feet.

The TV caught her attention, black and silent where it was positioned in the whitewashed entertainment center. The last time she had turned it on she'd been playing a video game and fighting spiders with a hobbit.

In this war she felt like a little hobbit fighting a giant She-lob with only a small sword for defense. What was it that Frodo had on his side that she needed to defeat Ceithlenn?

Intelligence. Fortitude. Determination.

But she needed a whole hell of a lot of help against her giant spider.

She thought of Keir being her Sam. Not exactly a good comparison. He was more like Aragorn but with a few—a lot—rougher edges.

The moment she flipped on the TV her gut sickened she felt as if she was going to puke.

Rhiannon flipped from station to station. On one channel a reporter spoke as a camera panned the rows and rows of the stadium. The fact that it was barely dawn didn't keep them from seeing shriveled corpses and people with gas masks carrying the bodies to waiting trucks.

Another channel showed a reporter talking about the "San Francisco Stadium Slaughter," her features tight and drawn. ". . . a terrorist attack using biochemical warfare is what law enforcement agencies are disseminating to the public.

"This despite what was caught on camera during what should have been an exhibition game between the San Francisco Giants and the San Diego Padres. Footage that some have called nothing more than a poorly made sci-fi flick used to trick people into believing the attack was *not* by terrorists."

While Rhiannon's mind reeled, the newscaster went on about panic. Riots. Curfews. Tight security. Martial Law. The Red Cross and other emergency response teams coming to the city to help with the devastation. Military units being deployed from all over the United States. Responses from foreign countries.

It was all coming down like 9/11.

What else could she have expected?

Rhiannon's knees gave out and she sank down onto her couch as the battle they'd fought yesterday was shown from one angle to another. It felt like she was standing outside herself as she watched the battle play out.

Ceithlenn appeared on the mound. Bizarre and terrible all at once. When the witches and PSF officers charged onto the field, so many Fomorii flooded from the stands that it became hard to make out anyone. But then the D'Danann arrived, those who became visible when they folded their wings away and battled the Fomorii on the field. The D'-Danann fought with swords that glinted in the afternoon sunlight.

Rhiannon couldn't stop herself from watching the news program. Demons crumbling, D'Danann vanishing to Summerland, PSF officers dying. More fighting. Witches flinging balls of light and glittering ropes.

Seeing it on television felt completely surreal. And when she spotted herself and Keir fighting, it seemed even more so.

All seven witches had been caught on film.

Rhiannon swallowed. They weren't safe. They would be recognized and either blamed for what happened or hounded by news reporters and people from all walks of life. The terror in the city would be so high their lives would be in danger.

Out of morbid curiosity, she flipped to another station.

The camera was focused right on Enchantments.

Her jaw dropped as she saw the store and apartment building cordoned off with yellow police tape and police barricades—and hundreds of people yelling and shouting. Some carried signs.

Rhiannon nearly jumped off the couch when her cell phone rang. She grabbed it off the end table and flipped it open. "Pack a duffel with some clothing and get to the back door to the kitchen of Enchantments right away," came Jake's voice. "And use one of your witch's glamours when you leave the building. I'm calling everyone else. The D'Danann have already been notified. Hurry."

Rhiannon's throat constricted. "I'll be right there."

After she snapped her cell shut, she rushed to stuff some jeans and T-shirts, and underwear and socks into her pink duffel bag. She scooped up Spirit, who gave a loud meow, as she headed for the front door.

The television was still blaring when she locked the door behind her and hurried down the hallway. Even before she made it all the way downstairs she heard the roar of a crowd. She grasped her belly and nearly doubled over.

Oh, my goddess.

A touch on her shoulder startled her so badly she almost dropped her duffel and Spirit. Rhiannon straightened to see Mackenzie, who was pale-faced and gripping an overstuffed backpack. Draped on one of her arms was her ferret familiar.

"What are we going to do?" Mackenzie asked as she glanced behind them.

Rhiannon followed her gaze to see Silver with a backpack in her hand and her python familiar curled around her shoulders.

"We're going to get the hell out of here, that's what," came Copper's voice from the stairwell. Her honeybee familiar buzzed around her head, then settled on the curve of her ear.

As the four witches made their way down to the first floor, they were joined by Alyssa and her owl familiar, Alyssa carrying her own traveling bag. Her arm was bandaged from the battle at the stadium.

Cassia was the only other witch who lived in the apartments. Hannah and Sydney had their own homes in San Francisco. How were they going to get here?

The noise was almost deafening when they stood just inside the apartment doors. Through the foggy windows, Rhiannon saw just what she'd seen on TV—police officers had cordoned off the street from the apartment building all the way to Enchantments' front door. Law enforcement officers were wearing riot gear and carrying rifles.

Jake slipped into the doorway dressed for battle. "Are you ladies ready?"

Rhiannon sucked in her breath as they nodded. "Let's do it."

Each witch ran her hand in front of her face, drawing a glamour. They could see one another, but humans couldn't see them. Their gear, clothing, and even their familiars were protected by the glamour.

"Works," Jake said. "I sure as hell can't see any of you now."

He pushed open the doors and the noise was nearly deafening. Shouts and cries came from the crowd that was filled with news reporters and cameras.

"Witches!" someone cried. "Burn the fucking witches!"

Now didn't that take one back in time.

They must have guessed they were witches by the shop they owned. Possibly by what they'd seen on TV. That might be a dead giveaway.

What about Janis's Coven? Had their place remained a secret in the chamber deep below Janis's home? Rhiannon knew that at least that place was well protected with powerful wardings, and she was glad for them.

But this—this was *so* not good. It wasn't good at all for *any* Pagan witch when what they worked for was harmony and good in the world and the universe.

Instead Ceithlenn had brought this upon all of them.

The crowd and the noise were ten times as bad as what had been outside the theater. Jake strode to the back of the store, the witches following.

When they slipped inside the shop, Hannah and her falcon were there, along with Sydney and her Doberman, and Cassia and her wolf. Several D'Danann warriors—including Keir, Hawk, and Tiernan—were also in the now very crowded kitchen.

Galia fluttered over Keir's shoulder, sprinkling pink Faerie dust all over him and probably making him smell like lilacs again. Another place, another time, Rhiannon would have thought it funny to see Keir covered in pink Faerie dust.

His arm had been rebandaged, and she noticed bandages on a couple of the other D'Danann as well.

Everyone, including Cassia, had a bag.

"Where are we going?" Alyssa asked.

Rhiannon knew exactly where before Cassia even said it. "Otherworld." Cassia's features had her normally calm expression and Rhiannon wanted to yell at her for not showing any kind of emotion. Their entire world was falling apart, for Anu's sake!

Cassia continued, "We will stay there until we find a new stronghold here in the city. But for now we need to go. We'll think of some way to keep in contact with Jake."

It was still barely dawn as they slipped out the back door with the D'Danann. Goddess, the noise from the crowd was deafening.

Rhiannon expected to walk to the park with her glamour for cover, but was surprised when the D'Danann each held on to a witch and took off into the sky.

"Oh, no." Rhiannon tried to back up as Keir wrapped his arms around her waist. "I'll walk, really." She had Spirit in one arm, her duffel slung over her opposite shoulder.

"I will get you there safely," Keir murmured in her ear just as he flapped his wings.

It was all Rhiannon could do not to scream as she buried her face against his shirt and squeezed her eyes shut. She held Spirit so tight he yowled, but he didn't struggle. She managed to cling to him with her other arm and keep her duffel over her shoulder.

The roaring of the crowd gradually faded as they traveled farther from it. Rhiannon felt the rush of wind over her body and took deep gulps of air to try and calm her racing heart.

Finally, they touched down in the park's thick forest where the bridge to Otherworld spanned the small creek. She heard the voices of her Coven sisters and the D'Danann, but it still took her a few moments to pry her eyes open and step away from Keir. Her legs trembled just as badly as they had the first time they'd flown together.

Rhiannon looked at the rest of the group. Everyone was solemn-faced.

"This is it," Copper said as she hitched her pack up higher on her shoulder. "Life as we've known it is truly over."

"I'll escort those without Elvin blood, first, and the Faerie." Cassia started by taking Hannah, Tegan, and Galia over the bridge. Next went Sydney and a D'Danann warrior Rhiannon didn't know. After taking across Alyssa and another warrior, Cassia didn't return as it wasn't necessary since those witches left at the park did have Elvin blood. Of course their familiars all went with them.

Copper and Tiernan crossed alone, as did Silver and Hawk—with their familiars. When it came time for Keir and Rhiannon to take their turn, they were the last. They looked at each other, then walked across the bridge as Rhiannon held Spirit tight in her arms.

The now familiar sensations of crossing to Otherworld still made Rhiannon almost claustrophobic. She didn't feel like they could breathe until they stumbled out into the sunshine. Spirit jumped from her arms and Keir steadied her.

None of the other witches or warriors were around.

Where was everyone?

Rhiannon and Keir were standing on the transference stone. Rhiannon looked at Keir again, and he began to bend on one knee.

She sensed the Great Guardian before she saw her.

Rage spiked Rhiannon's heart. She didn't want to kneel. She wanted to yell. Scream. Tear out her hair and tear her clothing to shreds. How could she talk to this creature of peace when so much war crowded her mind?

And yet, Rhiannon felt her knees bending. Felt her head lowering.

"Rise," came the serene voice of the Guardian.

Rather than the calmness that being around the Elvin woman usually invoked in Rhiannon, what came out was all anger.

"Why are we here?" she demanded as she straightened. "What do you want with us now? Nothing you suggested worked. We're getting help from nowhere, and now we've even been kicked out of our home world. Everything is wrong. All wrong!"

The Great Guardian looked at Rhiannon for a long moment. She didn't seem angry at Rhiannon's words, but her eyes held a blaze of urgency Rhiannon found unsettling. "Rhiannon Castle, D'Anu and Elvin, for you to gain the aid of others, you will have to learn how to open your heart."

"You've got to be kidding . . ." Rhiannon gestured wildly with her hands. "There's a freaking war going on in my world with a bunch of demons and a soul-sucking goddess. What has opening my heart got to do with anything?"

The Elvin woman moved closer and grasped Rhiannon's hands. "Tell me your greatest burden, and all else will flow from that confession."

Rhiannon opened her mouth to talk about Ceithlenn, the devastation, the horrors they were facing, and the fact that they were no longer safe from even their own people.

But that wasn't what came out of her heart.

"I don't know if I can love." She couldn't believe the words that came pouring through her lips. What did they have to do with anything? But she couldn't stop. The Guardian's touch seemed to draw it out. Things that she was sure couldn't relate to the war, but words she couldn't stop.

"The only love I know is what my Coven sisters have given me, and they mean everything to me." Her heart felt as if it were tearing in half, pain squeezing her chest. "After being abandoned by my aunt, my parents, ex-lovers, my old Coven . . . I don't think I'm capable of letting anyone else into my heart."

"You already have." The Great Guardian smiled and released Rhiannon's hands and motioned to Keir to step forward.

When he was beside Rhiannon, the Elvin woman pressed their hands together. Rhiannon looked up at Keir and saw the warmth and caring . . . the love in his eyes. Her heart beat faster and a lump crowded her throat. Dear Anu, what were these feelings welling up inside her? The fierce ache in her heart and soul?

"Rhiannon D'Anu and Elvin, what is your heart telling you now?" The Guardian's words washed over Rhiannon like a sudden wave of confidence.

"It's telling me . . ." She licked her dry lips as her eyes met Keir's. "It's telling me that I love you, Keir. Everything about you from your arrogance to that gentle side you try to keep tucked away."

He smiled and it wasn't one filled with arrogance or supreme satisfaction. It was a smile from deep in his soul. He said a phrase in Gaelic, the same one he'd said to her before but wouldn't tell her what it meant.

"It means I love you, *a stór.*" He brought his mouth close to hers and his warm breath caused her to tremble. "I think I always have." He kissed her, a gentle brush of his lips, a soft meeting of their mouths.

Rhiannon's heart fluttered, the release of emotions almost causing her to break into sobs.

When he drew away he let go of her fingers and caught her face in his hands. He rubbed his thumbs against her cheeks.

The Guardian drew her attention again when she said, "Rhiannon D'Anu and Elvin, keep a place open in your heart for your father and for his people, too. *Your* people." She raised her hand and gently touched Rhiannon's face. "Garran is finding his own way, as are you. Judge not your father so harshly." The Guardian let her hand fall away from Rhiannon's cheek.

The Great Guardian's expression returned to that which Keir could not read, and he stilled, his arm remaining around Rhiannon. Late afternoon sunshine created a halo around the Guardian's head.

She closed her eyes a moment before opening them. "It is as my visions told me. Balor has been freed."

"Yes." Rhiannon's voice came out in a husky whisper. "We couldn't stop Ceithlenn." Her tone grew stronger. "Now Balor and her huge army are ready to storm my city. And the power Ceithlenn wields—she's already taken thousands and thousands of lives."

"She must be stopped." Keir rested his hand on his sword and gripped the hilt tight enough to cause his knuckles to ache. His anger mounted. "Yet we do not have a force large enough to face the goddess, the demons, and Balor."

The Guardian's eyes never left his as she spoke. "Should Balor retrieve his eye from the warlock known as Darkwolf, the tide of battle will turn far darker than any could imagine."

Keir felt Rhiannon shudder beside him before she said, "Darkwolf took off with the eye when Ceithlenn asked him to give it to Balor. We think he's decided not to turn it over and he's in hiding."

With a nod, the Guardian said, "That is good."

Rhiannon propped her hands on her hips. "Maybe the idiot finally understands what he's done. What he's turned loose on our city."

"Perhaps." The Guardian studied Rhiannon. "Go now. You will need to regroup and seek your answers with your Coven sisters and the D'Danann. And in your heart."

"Yes, my lady," Rhiannon murmured, and Keir bowed.

They straightened and moved to the center of the transference stone. Spirit bounded into Rhiannon's arms.

Immediately, all that surrounded them whirled around Rhiannon and Keir—the sky, grass, trees, flowers, the waning sunlight . . . it was like colors of an oil painting spilling and merging together.

Until everything disappeared from sight, including the Great Guardian.

Chapter 39

Dizzy, Rhiannon clung to Keir and Spirit. In moments the whirling came to a stop and they stood outside of his cabin's front door. It was Otherworld, so instead of dawn, the sun peeked low over the horizon.

The spinning in her head eased, too, but she leaned against him. Spirit bounded from her arms and immediately started stalking something in the grass. Probably a Faerie.

Rhiannon breathed in Keir's pure male scent that mixed with the forest smells of pine and loam that surrounded them. "I love you," she murmured against his leather shirt and knew that she meant it with all her heart.

He pressed his lips to the top of her head. "As I love you, *a stór.*"

She sighed as he drew away and she looked up into his deep, dark eyes. She still felt the man had mysteries yet to be discovered.

"What Lise said has come to be," he said, his expression serious.

"Lise?" She scrunched up her nose. "Who's that? What did she say?"

"So many questions." He caressed her cheek with his knuckles. "Lise said, 'I wonder what kind of woman it would take to tame you?' And she added that one day a woman would bring me to my knees."

Rhiannon's heart thudded as he bent with one knee on the ground and took her hands in his. Those dark eyes never left hers.

"Will you bond with me, Rhiannon Castle?"

Rhiannon wasn't sure she'd heard right. Even though Keir was down on one knee.

His voice was clear and strong as he repeated, "Will you bond with me? Come sunset tomorrow?"

Her mind spun. "Do you mean *marry* you?"

"Through all that has yet to come, I want to know you are mine." He gently squeezed her hands. "And for you to know I am yours."

Rhiannon's legs trembled and her thoughts whirled until she came to a decision. She lowered herself so that she was facing Keir, and felt the soft pine needles and dark earth beneath her knees.

"If the world as we know it was to end tomorrow, I would want it to happen as your—your mate. Your wife." When a smile began to curve the corner of his mouth she said, "I belong to you." It felt right, it felt good. Her voice was stronger when she said with her own smile. "And you are *mine.*"

Keir grinned. He actually *grinned.* Goddess, he looked sexy. "Perhaps we should do so this eve."

"I—I. Wow." Rhiannon almost couldn't talk. "Tomorrow—we can wait one more night. I can't believe we're really going to do it." Sunlight barely peeked through forest branches. She reached up and kissed him, then drew away.

He grasped her hand and brought her to the cabin. "There is little daylight and I have matters to attend to."

"I'll go with you. I need to talk with my Coven sisters." Rhiannon looked over her shoulder to see Spirit cleaning his whiskers, and she hoped he hadn't eaten a Faerie. "I need to get Spirit settled."

"Aye." Keir opened the door to his cabin and let them in. He located some hard sausage and cheese, and cut them into chunks before putting it into a wooden bowl for Spirit. Then he put out a bowl of water, too.

Rhiannon smiled up at Keir as he drew her to the door

and out into the twilight. His strides were so long she had to walk double-time to keep up with him. Butterflies went berserk in her belly and she felt giddy and scared all at once.

When they reached the village he stopped at a beautiful two-story building made of white marble. "First I would like to invite someone special to witness our bonding. Wait for me."

Rhiannon rubbed her arms with her hands as she stood outside the building. She didn't question for a minute that she was doing the right thing. Keir was her soul mate in every sense of the words.

He came out moments later, following a beautiful woman with blond hair and fair, perfect skin. She was scantily clad, just enough to hide her, er, perfect assets. Her clothing reminded Rhiannon somewhat of a skimpy harem outfit.

"Rhiannon, this is Lise," Keir said as he took his place next to Rhiannon.

"So you are the one." Lise gave a delighted smile as she grasped Rhiannon's hands and kissed both of her cheeks. The woman smelled of warm vanilla. She gave Keir a teasing glance. "As I told you."

Keir bowed from his shoulders. "As you did, Madame Lise." He took Rhiannon's hand. "I wish for you to witness our bonding."

"I will summon others," Lise said with another smile and released Rhiannon's hands. "So many hearts will be broken."

Great wings spread from Lise's back, wings that matched the golden color of her hair. She took to the air with a graceful flutter and Rhiannon heard her bubbling laughter that sounded like she was taking extreme pleasure in Keir having found a mate.

Rhiannon would have liked to have questioned the woman more about Keir, but she disappeared into the trees.

Keir practically dragged her through the village.

"Where are my Coven sisters?" Rhiannon asked. *They're going to think I've lost my mind.*

Galia flew up to them so fast that Rhiannon stumbled back in surprise.

The Faerie clasped her hands, her eyes wide. "Is it true? You two are to be mated tomorrow?"

Rhiannon blinked. "Boy does news travel fast here."

Galia grinned and fluttered around in circles, her lilac scent following in her wake. "I knew it. I bet the witch Hannah that it would be so. She thought he would only 'get in your pants,' as she said, but I knew you would fall in love."

Rhiannon narrowed her gaze. "Get in my pants?" She was going to kill Hannah.

"I will let the witches and others know at once to meet you in the village." The Faerie giggled and zipped away.

Keir took her in to stand front of what appeared to be a different tavern that looked far more quiet than the one he had taken her to the first time she was here.

"One moment." Keir brushed his lips over hers. "I must speak with the tavern-keeper."

Rhiannon's heart wouldn't stop pounding as she waited for him. Wow. She was getting married. Her mouth quirked into a grin. And to the guy whose nuts she'd zapped the first time she met him.

People walked the streets of the village, some casting curious glances her way. Funny how normal everything looked—if one could consider standing in an Otherworld medieval-like village normal.

A horse pulling a load of hay trundled by, the *clip-clop* of the horse's hooves ringing through the dusky evening. The smell of the hay mingled with smoke from chimneys and warm scents of roasted meats and baked breads.

In only moments Keir returned. "Wait for your Coven sisters here. I will be back soon."

As she watched Keir walk away, Rhiannon knew then that she'd lost her mind. If she was feeling like she'd seen Copper and Silver acting, she'd truly gone and lost it.

She smiled. And she loved it.

Silver was the first to come running up from around a corner and straight to Rhiannon.

"Oh, my goddess!" Silver flung her arms around Rhiannon. "I can't believe it. You're marrying Keir!" She leaned back, tears glistening in her eyes as she smiled. "And to think that makes us sister-in-laws since Keir is Hawk's half-brother."

Silver hugged Rhiannon again before backing away and it was Sydney's turn to hug Rhiannon. "Congratulations, Rhi." Sydney leaned back and smiled. "I think you two make the *perfect* match."

"Unbelievable," Copper said with a grin when Sydney moved out of the way. "If you and Keir can settle down and bond with somebody, that's proof that miracles *can* happen."

"The bonding ceremony is wonderful." Silver wiped a tear from her cheek. "I wish you and our Coven sisters could have attended mine and Copper's bondings to our men. Now with all of us in Otherworld, every one of our Coven sisters will be able to share in the celebration."

One by one the rest of the Coven sisters converged, along with Galia. Everyone hugged Rhiannon, although she felt a little stiff with Cassia. She and Cassia—they had to talk, after what Garran had told her about Cassia's involvement in the decision to keep her in San Francisco.

The half-Elvin witch had a look in her eyes that said she knew there was unfinished business between them.

When Hannah was the only one who remained, she and Rhiannon looked at each other. Everyone else went quiet. The corner of Hannah's mouth curved into an amused smile. "You finally let someone into that little box of yours. About time."

Rhiannon rolled her eyes then grinned when her gaze met Hannah's. "Guess so."

Laughing and giggling, the eight of them pushed into the tavern. They found a long table with benches and took their seats. To a one they were wearing T-shirts and jeans—even the normally always elegantly tailored Hannah and Sydney. Fleeing from one's own world kind of put a damper on dressing up.

When they were seated, two women started putting food

in front of them along with mugs filled with something that smelled of apples.

Before Rhiannon could tell the servers they had no way of paying for this, one of the tavern women said, "Master Keir has ordered up a fine meal for you ladies."

Rhiannon's belly rumbled. She couldn't argue with that.

The drink was an apple-flavored ale that went down well with the fresh-baked fish that had an unusual paste of wine, saffron, cinnamon, and cloves. Only Copper refused to drink the ale—she said she'd had more than enough apples when she was trapped in Otherworld.

Heavy wheat bread, peas, and baked pears were served with the fish, and the meal was topped off with egg custard.

The conversation went from chatter about the wedding, to the seriousness of the situation they were in.

When it started to get a little depressing, Mackenzie lightened things up by bringing the conversation around to the gorgeous D'Danann warriors they'd been seeing around the village. "Oh, my goddess," Mackenzie said. "I don't think I've seen one who isn't hot."

When the topic moved on to when Silver's baby was due, Rhiannon's eyes met Cassia's across the table. By silent agreement they got up and moved to a table a distance away from their Coven sisters.

"You have questions," Cassia stated as soon as they were seated.

"You're damned right I have questions." Rhiannon studied Cassia, who had changed so much since the battle on Samhain. "It's all been an act from the start. You played the bumbling apprentice witch until Silver started realizing you're not who you appeared to be. And Hawk knew it right away."

Cassia smiled. "This is true." She looked so different now. Long, blond curls, clear blue eyes, and a delicate quality to her features that gave away her Elvin heritage.

"Why?" Rhiannon asked. "Why the act?"

"I was sent to protect Copper, Silver, and you. All of

Elvin blood. Copper and Silver were the last of their line. And you—you had no awareness of your heritage and no one to watch after you."

Rhiannon scowled. "It *was* you who brought my mother across from San Francisco to meet my—my father, wasn't it? And *you* decided not bring me back to live with him once my mother died." Rhiannon's voice rose with her anger. "What right did you have to make that kind of choice for my life?"

Cassia simply studied Rhiannon. "Are you embracing your Drow heritage now? Do you wish that you had not been raised D'Anu and had grown up among the Dark Elves?"

Rhiannon shoved her fingers through her short auburn hair. When she drew her hand away, the ends tickled her cheeks as they swung forward. "Goddess. I—" She swallowed hard and clenched her teeth before speaking in a voice that was almost a whisper. "I don't know. Life with Aunt Aga . . . Would being raised by my father have been worse than her?"

"Would it?" Cassia asked softly.

Rhiannon rubbed her hand against her chest. "After meeting him, inside me I do think with Garran that maybe I would have known a father's love . . . But I would be a different person than I am now." She glanced at her Coven sisters, who were still chatting, and placed her palm on the table. "I wouldn't have the people in my life that I *do* love. And I would have been raised to embrace what I now believe is wrong."

Cassia put her hand over one of Rhiannon's. "What is wrong with your father's way of life?"

Rhiannon felt the warmth of Cassia's touch, a calming warmth, almost like the Great Guardian. "He's one of the Dark Elves, Cassia." *Duh.* "He's *Drow.* That means he's evil." Rhiannon felt resignation to her toes. What was she even arguing about? "You're right, I wouldn't have wanted to be raised that way. As much as I hated her, Aga was the only choice."

"I never said your father is evil." Cassia folded her other hand over Rhiannon's and squeezed. "Garran is what he is. He's Drow. But he is not *evil*. Few of the Dark Elves truly are."

Rhiannon drew her hand away. "Then why were they banished and forced to live beneath the ground?"

"The Drow simply chose a darker path." Cassia straightened herself on the bench. "They choose to use dark magic their kinfolk refuse to. The Drow made their choice. Now you must make yours—will you or won't you accept that part of you?"

Rhiannon couldn't think of anything else to say. Cassia gave her a soft smile, then got up and went back to sit with their sister witches.

For a long time Rhiannon sat in the same spot, alone, staring into space as her thoughts churned.

What would be her choice?

Keir strode to the only home he had known as a child. When the D'Danann had been forced to leave Ireland for their own Sidhe, everything they possessed and had known went with them. So perhaps he had not grown up *here,* but he still felt that little boy in him cower at the thought of going up those imposing stairs to his father's home.

Keir let out a low growl at his weakness. He had not been a youth for centuries. Why did the memories cling so tightly to him? Or did he cling to the memories?

He growled again.

A horse whinnied as he passed the barn he had slept in and he walked up to the great door of the house. It was a magnificent place, but he had only been allowed inside to do chores. His meals had been brought out to him in the barn by the one servant other than himself. He'd always eaten alone. He was used to being alone.

But Rhiannon. By the gods he never wanted to be without her.

He pounded the great door knocker against the door. It

was with some satisfaction that he did so—he had never been allowed to as a child, and as an adult he never bothered.

The imposing door opened, its hinges creaking.

He stood face-to-face with his father, Niall.

Keir paused as they studied each other. Keir and Hawk had Niall's dark looks, but Niall's face was more seasoned with lines around his mouth and a touch of gray at his temples. Even gods aged when not in Otherworld, and the Tuatha D'Danann had been gods for more than two millennia in Ireland. Niall had aged during his years in Ireland, but had stopped once they came to Otherworld.

"So, you are to take a half-Drow bride." Niall's expression was one of superiority and disdain as he looked at his son.

"Rhiannon," Keir said as he fought to rein in his temper, "my mate's name is Rhiannon."

With a slight wave of his hand, Niall brushed his words aside like one might a fly. "I understand you have met your Mystwalker mother, Keaira."

"Why did you keep her from seeing me all these centuries?" Keir's voice came out low and harsh. "Why did you tell me she didn't wish to know me? And that she willingly went to serve as a pleasure slave to the Shanai?"

Niall shrugged as though it was of no concern. "It was in your best interest. There is no living between worlds. One is either D'Danann or Mystwalker."

Keir ground his teeth and the heat in his gut grew. "I should have been the judge of that. At the very least when I came of age."

"It is of no matter now."

"Niall?" came Keir's stepmother's reed-thin, high-pitched voice. "Who is at the door?"

"I must get back to your stepmother." Niall cast a glance over his shoulder before turning back to Keir. "She would not be pleased to see you."

Keir struggled to keep his anger in check and said nothing.

"Well wishes," Niall said, then turned and slammed the door in Keir's face.

He sucked in his breath. He wanted to rage, to beat down

the door. To go back to the San Francisco Otherworld and fight every demon single-handedly.

Niall wasn't worth his fury. Keir clenched and unclenched his fists at his sides. He let out the breath of air he'd been holding and tried to calm his mind and his body. No, his father wasn't worth the anger that Keir should have released long ago.

When Keir turned, Hawk was standing at the bottom of the stairs.

Keir's body immediately tightened, wary of his foe. Aye, at this moment he would be happy to take his half-brother on in a fight.

In just a few steps, Keir stood before Hawk and glared.

Hawk was frowning, but did not look angry as he usually did.

"I never truly realized until this moment how badly our father treated you," Hawk said. "It is not a wonder you hate me as you do."

Keir spat on the ground to get the sour taste out of his mouth. "How could you not know? For the gods' sake, we are twenty centuries of age."

Hawk pinched the bridge of his nose with his thumb and forefinger. When he dropped his hand away he met Keir's gaze.

"Father always told me you *wanted* to sleep out there." Hawk gestured to the barn. "That you did not like my mother and chose to eat your meals alone."

Keir made a scoffing noise. "You think eating cold rations, sleeping on straw, and smelling horseshit was preferable to a soft bed and a hot meal?"

Hawk let out a loud sigh. "I always thought your defiance was what made Father angry with you. But now I see differently. I never stopped to consider that things may not have been what they seemed."

For a long moment they studied each other.

Keir growled. "You put spiders in my straw bed."

"What about you?" Hawk narrowed his eyes. "Destroying my favorite wooden practice sword."

"Telling Father lies and getting me into trouble."

"Putting syrup in my shoes."

"Chopping off a chunk of my hair with shears as I slept."

"Putting a burr under my horse's saddle."

"Stealing Molly from me."

"Breaking my nose."

"Shoving me down the manor stairs."

"The snake pit."

At that, both Keir and Hawk grew silent. Keir had sought revenge on Hawk for pushing him down the stone stairs. Keir had dug a pit and filled it with hundreds of harmless snakes. Hawk had fallen into the pit and ever since that day he'd had an intense fear of snakes. A fear that he blamed for the loss of his first mate.

Keir pushed his hair from his face and sighed. "I have long regretted that action. Not from the whipping Father gave me but because I caused you to have such fear."

Hawk lifted his brows, surprise on his features.

"All the rest—" Keir shook his head. "Childish actions that we allowed to let us to continue to fight over the centuries."

With a slow nod, Hawk said, "You are right, brother."

For a long moment they stared at each other.

The corner of Hawk's mouth quirked. "The syrup in my shoes was especially brilliant."

Keir struggled to keep a straight face. "Spiders in my straw was well conceived."

Hawk snorted. Keir coughed.

First one let out a chuckle, then the other. Before they knew it, they were laughing hard enough that Keir had a difficult time catching his breath.

Hawk wiped tears from his eyes. "The time you pushed me into the swine pen before my outing with a girl. Whatshername."

Keir's face hurt from grinning. He never grinned. "You should have seen how you looked, head to toe in mud."

"I took you down, though."

"Aye." Keir shook his head. "It was a good fight."

Hawk quieted. "That it was."

"Rhiannon and I are to be mated." Keir had sobered. "Would you stand by my side to serve as witness to our joining?"

Without pause, Hawk said, "Aye."

He extended his hand and Keir took it in the hand-to-elbow grip of their people. Then Hawk surprised Keir by embracing him as a brother and slapping his back.

Hawk drew away and they released each other's arms. "I will see you at the hall tomorrow eve."

Keir gave a low nod. "I will see you then . . . brother."

Hawk returned Keir's nod and jogged up the steps to the manor and let himself in.

Keir shook his head and started back to the village where he'd left Rhiannon with her Coven sisters.

Chapter 40

Keir didn't let up on his grip of Rhiannon's hand until they reached the Chieftains' place, which she recognized from her last visit. It was evening and a cool wildflower-scented breeze caused her hair to stir about her neck and cheeks.

Rhiannon wore a beautiful dress of vivid yellow beaded with clear crystals, which touched the top of her matching beaded slippers. Lise, along with Galia, had brought the dress to the cabin that morning as a gift for Rhiannon's and Keir's joining day. It fit beautifully, a straight-cut style with a princess neckline and a short train.

Keir looked handsome in what must have been his dress leathers. She barely kept in a grin. He looked basically the same as always—incredibly yummy.

Her belly did a double twist as Keir escorted her up the stairs and into the castle-like Chieftains' building. This time they went to the left, through the biggest pair of doors she'd ever seen, and into a huge room that reminded her of pictures of a great hall in King Arthur's court.

To her surprise the room was filled with people, mostly D'Danann warriors dressed in black and wearing their weapons belts with their swords and daggers. But there were other beings, too, including Faeries, Pixies, Brownies, and what Rhiannon thought might be Dryads.

Light flickered from sconces, casting shadows on the

faces of the people and beings gathered in the hall. Tapestries of D'Danann in flight, in battle, as well as couples and children, decorated the walls. The room smelled of wildflowers and roses.

With her arm tucked to his side, Keir escorted her along a velvety green carpet to the front of the room. All the people stood on either side of the carpet. Whispers and conversation followed in their wake and he received many pats on the back from his fellow warriors. Yet some seemed distant, others looked almost angry.

They didn't approve of a D'Danann marrying a woman with Elvin blood, Rhiannon was sure of it. And did they know the Elvin in her was Drow? Would they care? But at least many beings in the room didn't seem to have a problem with the fact that she was half Elvin.

The next thing she knew her Coven sisters were flooding the room with Galia buzzing behind them. The seven witches and the Faerie surrounded her. Again they hugged Rhiannon and exclaimed their happiness for her.

Then Cassia said, "We have the joining of not two but four races in peace. Perhaps it will turn out to be a beginning of true and powerful alliances."

"I think you could be right," Sydney said with a broad smile.

Keir tugged Rhiannon's hand and drew her from her Coven sisters toward the front of the great hall.

All around them was laughter and chatter, but Rhiannon was certain she heard some grumbling, too.

When they reached the huge dais at the front of the room, she wasn't sure her legs would hold her up. She still didn't doubt her decision, but it didn't make her any less nervous.

More people flooded the hall. She'd never have guessed Keir had so many friends, as gruff and as unsociable as he came across. Maybe some of them were curiosity seekers.

A hush settled over the crowd. Along the emerald green carpet, the High Chieftain, Chaela, slowly made her way toward Rhiannon and Keir. Chaela's royal blue robes were long enough to trail behind, and her hood almost kept Rhiannon from recognizing her.

Chaela stepped up the few stairs onto the dais and pushed back her hood. She was so beautiful with her long blond hair and bright green eyes.

Silver came up to Rhiannon, a smile on her lips. She pressed a bright bouquet of brilliant blooms of red, pink, yellow, and blue into Rhiannon's shaking hands.

Great. Now she had trembling flowers, too. Not that she wasn't appreciative. And the fact that Silver hadn't chosen anything plain like white was pretty cool.

Silver placed a circlet of colorful flowers on Rhiannon's auburn hair, stepped back, and smiled. "You are so beautiful, Rhiannon."

She smiled at her best friend. "Thank you, Silver."

More tears glistened in Silver's eyes and Rhiannon's felt a little watery, too.

Silver moved behind Rhiannon, and she was surprised to see Hawk standing just behind Keir. Would wonders never cease?

Chaela cleared her throat. From her position above them on the dais, the beautiful woman looked like a golden-haired goddess.

The High Chieftain motioned for Keir to climb up one side of the dais, and Rhiannon on the other.

Damn. Her legs were shaking so badly, Rhiannon was afraid she would trip and sprawl across the dais. But thank Anu she made it.

Chaela stood behind them so that Keir and Rhiannon were closest to the crowd. They slowly walked up to each other and stood maybe an inch apart. The flowers she held were probably tickling him.

"Why are you willing to participate, when my mate is half-Elvin?" Keir asked so low that those gathered in the room likely couldn't hear.

The High Chieftain said, "You have suffered enough at the hands of your father's people. The least we can do is seal your chosen bonding properly."

"You have my gratitude." Keir gave a deep nod, then smiled down at Rhiannon as Chaela began to speak. Rhiannon's face felt frozen. She hoped not in an expression of terror.

Keir took the flowers from her, crouched, and gave them to one of the younger women near the dais. When he straightened he took Rhiannon's hands and linked his fingers with hers, and she felt a thrill at his touch.

Chaela placed her hands over theirs. Her emerald rings glittered in the low lighting from the sconces throughout the room.

"Keir, D'Danann and Mystwalker," Chaela started and Keir shot her a look of surprise, "do you wish to soul bond with Rhiannon, D'Anu and Elvin?"

His gaze returned to Rhiannon's and he smiled in a way that made her want to melt into him, become a part of him.

"With all my heart and soul," he said so clearly that she was sure it could be heard in every corner of the room, "Aye."

Chaela gave a slight nod and turned her bright green eyes on Rhiannon. "Rhiannon, D'Anu and Elvin, do you know what it is to be soul-bonded in the D'Danann tradition?"

Rhiannon swallowed. "It is a marriage of two people who love one another."

The High Chieftain kept her steady expression. "It is more than that. A soul bond is something that can never be broken. You will feel each other's pain, each other's joy. Should this bond be broken by either of you, it would slowly drive you mad. Only death can sever the bond."

Rhiannon shivered and her heart gave a little lurch. Okay, so Keir hadn't told her about this part. Even Copper and Silver had neglected to mention it.

But she knew this was the man she wanted to be with forever. She had no intention of ever being separated from him.

She straightened her stance. "I understand."

Chaela gave a nod and a smile of approval. "Rhiannon, D'Anu and Elvin, do you wish to soul-bond with Keir, D'Danann and Mystwalker?"

"With all my heart and soul," Rhiannon replied as she gazed into Keir's dark eyes, "yes."

Chaela released their hands.

A sudden vibration traveled throughout Rhiannon's body. Her head spun a little as if she had an onset of vertigo and the trembling that had already wracked her body became more intense.

In the next moment she felt as if something was being sucked from her body. Keir caught her to him as iridescent sparkles danced and intertwined between and around them. A tightening sensation caused her to feel like she had just become a physical part of Keir, and he had just become a tangible part of her.

When the vertigo and vibrations died away, the sparkles cleared and she found herself locked in Keir's embrace. He crushed his mouth to hers and she felt a connection unlike anything she'd ever experienced before. He slipped his tongue into her mouth and she tasted his maleness, his wildness, all that made him Keir.

Applause and cheering broke out in the room and Keir drew away from the kiss and smiled against her lips.

Pink fireworks exploded around them and Rhiannon grinned when she looked up to see Galia laughing and shooting bolts of her magic at the ceiling and the pink glitter raining down on everyone in the room. Her lilac scent joined the fireworks.

"Your soul-bonding is complete." Chaela's voice rang throughout the room and over the cheers of the guests.

Rhiannon didn't need Chaela to tell her that little fact. She could feel the bond locking her to him and him to her.

But the soul-bond didn't feel suffocating or like she was chained down. It felt freeing, as if she was more alive than she'd ever been in her life.

"Mine," she said against his lips. "You're all mine."

Chapter 41

As Keir and Rhiannon walked down the dais, she noticed the room had gone completely silent. She thought she heard the scrape of metal against leather scabbards, as if D'Danann were unsheathing their swords.

Tension was thick. Everyone was looking to the back of the room.

The moment Rhiannon and Keir reached the long green carpet and had a clear view of the doorway, Rhiannon saw why.

At the other end of the carpet stood her father, accompanied by several armed Drow.

Rhiannon swallowed, hard. The train of her dress dragged slightly against the carpet as she moved with Keir toward Garran. She felt numb and had a hard time believing her eyes.

The Drow were dressed much as they had been when she'd visited them—breastplates and leather straps crisscrossing their bare chests, leather breeches. Their black, silvery blue, or steel-gray hair shone softly in the light from the sconces, and they were tall and imposing.

Their features were hard and unyielding, almost arrogant as they stood at the end of the carpet.

Except for Garran. He looked . . . proud.

Rhiannon's heart rate picked up the closer she got to

Garran. Keir held her tightly to his side and she felt the tension in his body against hers.

When Rhiannon stood directly in front of Garran, she tilted her head up to meet his liquid silver eyes. They showed a certain hesitancy, like he was unsure. Rhiannon was uncertain, too, but her heart—it seemed to know what to do.

She slid her arm out of Keir's grip, flung her arms around Garran's neck, and hugged him. With no hesitancy, he hugged her, too, his grip firm. Rhiannon felt tears slipping down her cheeks and onto her father's warm skin. He smelled earthy, mossy, fresh, clean scents that felt somehow homey.

When she drew away, she realized people in the room were murmuring, whispering, talking. But she didn't care. This was her *father.*

He gripped her hands in his. "I wanted to share this day with you, my daughter. I hope you do not mind. Forgive me for my actions when we first met."

"Forgive *me.*" Rhiannon squeezed his hands in return and offered him a smile. "I shouldn't have judged you so harshly."

Garran gave her another fierce hug. "We will talk soon, you and I. For now, enjoy your bonding."

She let her hands slip away. "Are you going to stay?"

His mouth quirked into a smile. "We are not welcome here."

"You're welcome as far as I'm concerned." Rhiannon reached for his hand again, but he stepped back.

"I will see you soon, daughter." With that, he turned his back and strode along the break his warriors made for him to pass through. They turned and followed him out of the room. Rhiannon watched until she couldn't see him anymore.

The buzzing in the room had taken on a harsher quality, but Rhiannon ignored it. If they didn't like that her father was Drow, tough.

Gradually, everything settled down, and Keir took her around the room, introducing her to his friends and acquaintances. Some were very friendly, others barely, but she made sure she maintained her poise. Hell if she was going to let them ruin her wedding night.

Bonding night.

The celebration had lasted far too long as far as Keir was concerned. He wanted to take Rhiannon home to his bed—their bed. As he took another swig of ale, the thought warmed him and his chest filled with pride.

This beautiful woman was his. Her fiery green eyes drew him to her, the sprinkling of freckles across her nose and her fair complexion made him want to caress her, he desired to hold her sweet curves in his arms.

She was his.

Keir kept Rhiannon close as they mingled with the witches, D'Danann, and other Fae from all walks of his centuries of existence. The fact that these comrades, these friends accepted his half-Elvin—half-*Drow*—mate made his jaded heart melt a little bit more, as Rhiannon had done from the first moment he met her.

He almost grinned as he watched Galia zip around the room, creating havoc in her wake. She sprinkled pink Faerie dust over the merrymakers, went skating on the buffet table, and with the help of two Pixies, made rows of braids in Tiernan's long blond hair when he wasn't paying attention.

Keir did chuckle when Queen Riona flew up to Galia, grabbed her by the hand, and pulled her from the room. "You will work in the kitchens for a month!" the queen was saying as she passed by with Galia in tow.

Galia wailed as she was dragged from the great hall. "But, Aunt Riona, I was just having fun!"

Keir shook his head and brought his attention back to his mate.

The air still carried the smells of the roasted beef, bread, potatoes, cakes, and ale that had been brought in. Laughter and chatter filled the large gathering hall, enough to make his ears ring.

Another fellow warrior slapped Keir on his back with words of congratulations and Keir sloshed his ale onto his boots. He nodded and mumbled words of thanks and kept trying to work his way to the exit with Rhiannon in tow. Perhaps they could make their escape soon.

He set his tankard of ale on a table and started to hurry Rhiannon through the room.

They pushed their way further on until they ran into his half-brother. Silver, Hawk's mate, stood beside him.

Hawk smiled and held out his hand. "Congratulations, brother."

Keir paused then grasped Hawk's arm and slapped him on the back.

When they released each other, Hawk turned to Rhiannon. "I am proud to call you my sister." He looked down at Silver and kissed the top of her head. He touched her belly that still showed no signs that she carried his child.

Silver grinned and flung her arms around Keir. He stiffened in surprise before relaxing. "I think it's awesome that you and my best friend tied the knot. I can't wait for you to have children of your own!"

Keir glanced at Rhiannon to see her cheeks flush as she said "Er, let's not be in too much of a hurry, 'kay?"

Silver released Keir, turned to Rhiannon, and hugged her. "I love you, Rhi."

"I love you, too." Rhiannon smiled. Silver gave another quick hug before she took Hawk's hand and they wandered over to a table laden with desserts.

"Phew." Rhiannon looked up at Keir. "Things went well at least with your brother."

"Aye." He and his brother had come to an understanding. Perhaps for the next two thousand years their rivalry would fade.

"Think we can get out of here?" Rhiannon said in his ear, her warm breath stirring his desires to be alone with her even more. She still wore the flowers on her short auburn hair but the wreath was skewed to one side. She pushed it up with one hand while she squeezed his fingers with her other.

She gave him a mischievous grin. "I think we can do a little celebrating of our own. Alone."

The thought of carrying Rhiannon straight down the hall to the Chieftains' chamber, then taking her on the great dais crossed his mind and he nearly groaned aloud. He could push up her dress, tear away her undergarments, release his cock from his breeches and drive into her.

His erection grew painfully hard against its constrictions and he lowered his head and gave a soft growl in her ear. "I want to take you now, *a stór*. I do not know if I can wait much longer."

Her tongue darted out to touch her lower lip and this time he did groan out loud. She grasped his biceps and raised herself on her toes to whisper in his ear again. "Think anyone would notice if we made our escape now?"

A rumble rose up in Keir's chest and he tugged her with more purpose toward the door. No matter how they tried to make it through the crowd with a hurried pace, they were waylaid every step.

Lise stopped them just at the door. She and Rhiannon were the same height, and Lise took Rhiannon by the shoulders and kissed each of her cheeks again. Lise gave Keir a sly look before she turned back to Rhiannon.

"This one will need much work to keep in line," Lise said to Rhiannon with a grin.

"Don't worry about that." Rhiannon returned a grin of her own. "He's all taken care of."

Lise laughed, reached up and kissed Keir on each cheek, then melted into the crowd.

"I like Lise." Rhiannon watched as she disappeared into the crowd. "How do you know her?"

Their eyes met and he had the good sense to give her a general reply. "I have known many beings during my two thousand years of life."

Rhiannon seemed satisfied with his reply and he gave an audible sigh of relief as they made their way from the great hall into the empty foyer. He could breathe again—the air didn't seem stifling in here and the sounds not as loud.

He whirled her around, pressed her up against the wall, and took her mouth, claiming her as his. The soul-bond intensified the kiss and he felt the pull of her soul within his own. The feeling made his cock so hard he was certain it was near to bursting the seams of his breeches.

She tasted of sweet wine and her own special flavor. He delved his tongue into her mouth, and she returned the kiss with just as much fervor. When he nipped at her lower lip, her body vibrated beneath his and she wrapped her arms around his waist. In return, she bit his lower lip with her small white teeth and he groaned.

"Now." Rhiannon was breathless, her face flushed as he drew away from their kiss. She ran her hands from around his waist up to his chest. "I want to be with you. Fully. I want you inside me now. I don't want to wait."

Keir grabbed one of her hands, gave her another kiss, then turned to check the hallway to the right. Thank the gods it was clear. He slid his hand to the back of her waist and guided her.

They slipped down the hallway toward the Chieftains' Chamber. The doors remained unguarded once the Chieftains had left. He grabbed the handle of one of the big heavy doors and swung it open—

To see the High Chieftain, Chaela, on her back on the dais being fucked by one of the D'Danann warriors—a large blond warrior by the name Conlan.

Chaela's robe was spread open, revealing her large breasts and her mound. Conlan stood as he drove his cock in and out of the Chieftain. He still wore his leather breeches, opened just enough to fuck Chaela as she lay back on the dais. The low lighting from twin torches on the walls were bright enough that Keir could see her flushed features. Her cries echoed in the room, as did Conlan's grunts.

Keir glanced down at Rhiannon to see her eyes wide, her mouth open. Chaela cried out and Conlan shouted. Keir was just about to step out of the doorway when Chaela rose from her prone position to wrap her arms around Conlan's neck.

She saw Rhiannon and Keir.

Chaela gasped and jerked her robe tight around her and Conlan threw a look over his shoulder. The big warrior showed neither embarrassment nor surprise. He turned back to Chaela and brought her close to him, hiding her nakedness.

"Um, sorry," Rhiannon said as she backed away.

"My apologies, High Chieftain," Keir added with a slight bow.

They closed the door and looked at each other. Rhiannon clapped her hand over her mouth, only minutely smothering her giggles, and Keir could not hold back a snort of laughter. "Conlan and the High Chieftain. One never would have thought."

Rhiannon giggled all the way down the hallway as they moved further away from the Chieftains' chamber to a smaller room used for private interviews. It had a table in the middle with four chairs around it.

He drew her into the empty room and closed the door behind them. He would have barred it if there was a way to, but none of the rooms in the Chieftains building could be barred.

Keir and Rhiannon looked at each other and Rhiannon's giggles died away. He shoved her up against the smooth wood of the door, grabbed her ass, and pressed his cock tight against her belly. She gasped and grabbed his biceps.

"I need to be inside you now, *a stór.*" He pushed up her long dress, then slipped his fingers over the silk of her undergarment. The cloth was soaked when he rubbed his fingers between her thighs against her folds. He pressed hard and rubbed her clit through the material.

Rhiannon moaned. "Don't make me wait." She slid her arms around his neck and wiggled against his hand. The wreath of flowers tumbled off her head and onto the floor.

Keir added his groan to her moans, and with a hard tug ripped her delicate undergarment away from her body and tossed it aside. She hooked her thighs around his hips as he rubbed her slick folds with his hand. With every stroke of his fingers, she made small cries that served to make him want her more.

Unable to control himself any longer, he held onto her with one hand while he untied his breeches with his other. As soon as his cock and balls were freed, he placed the head of his erection at her entrance, slipping a little into her channel, teasing both of them. He grabbed her ass with both hands and drove himself deep.

She cried out and he groaned at the feel of her tight, slick core around his cock. With extreme control, he held himself still so that they would both enjoy the moment. "Gods, you feel so good."

Rhiannon felt so full, so incredible with Keir bound to her like this. He was thick and long, filled her, and touched her so deep it was a wonder she didn't come with his first thrust. "I love you inside me," she managed to get out. "And I want more. More, more, more!"

Keir kissed her hard and she felt a small contraction around his cock. He started to pump his hips, slow at first, but then picked up his pace until he was taking her hard and fast. Their kisses grew more frantic and heat rose in Rhiannon like a firestorm.

Their soul-bond intensified and iridescent sparkles surrounded them. Rhiannon felt not only full with him buried deep in her body, but filled with Keir's soul, too.

In one moment she was feeling what it was like to have him thrusting in and out of her. She gasped as in the next second she felt as if their positions were switched and she was Keir and knew how it felt to him to be inside her. The feelings whirled and she had such a deep connection to him that it was as if his fire was her own.

Their heat joined and they became one burning bonfire. Wild sensations centered where they were connected, building like an inferno, a volcano, until they both exploded.

Keir threw his head back and shouted and Rhiannon's cry met with his. She felt the power of his orgasm as if it were hers, along with the intensity of her own climax. It was almost too much, yet not enough.

He continued to thrust, driving out their orgasms until she collapsed against his chest and the sparkles around them faded. Her breathing was hard and the scent of their sex was heavy as it surrounded them. He was still inside her and she wasn't ready to part.

For a long moment he held her, then let her legs slide down over his hips so that his cock slipped out of her and her feet touched the ground. She raised her head to look up at him and he kissed her hard again, setting off more spasms in her core.

She could barely find her voice. "That was unbelievable," she whispered as he drew away from their kiss.

Keir crushed her to him and pressed his lips to the top of her head. "It is only the beginning, *a stór,* only the beginning."

After Rhiannon tugged down her dress and ran her hand over her hair so that she wouldn't look like she'd just been taken up against a door, she moved her palms up and down Keir's arms. He tucked his cock and balls back into his leather pants and she thought she felt him shaking.

The idea that she affected him so much made her smile. He hooked one of his fingers under her chin, tilted her face up, and brushed his lips over hers.

"I love your smile," he said, his expression serious.

"You should smile more often, too." She brought her hand up and stroked her fingers over his lips. "You are even more gorgeous when you do."

He gifted her with the smile she asked for and raised her up and spun her around. She laughed and braced her hands on his shoulders until he set her onto her feet. Her beaded dress swirled around her feet.

Keir brought his hands up to hers and laced their fingers together. "Come. Let us return to our home."

"Our home. Wow." Rhiannon swallowed down the lump of wonder that had risen in her throat. "But we'll have a home together in San Francisco, too." She frowned. "We just have to find one."

"Aye." He kissed her again and released one of her hands and opened the door with his free one. "We will have two homes and we can travel freely between both as we wish."

"I like that." She smiled. "I like it a lot."

They hurried down the hallway, back toward the gathering hall where she heard raucous laughter and chatter. It would probably go well into the night—a D'Danann excuse to party, no doubt.

Rhiannon thought they would be able to slip out into the night, but in front of the doors they met up with the warrior who'd been with the High Chieftain. Rhiannon's cheeks heated at the memory of what they had seen and the fact that she and Keir had found a room to do the same thing. She wondered if she and Keir smelled of sex, then decided she really didn't care.

"Conlan," Keir said with a nod.

"Keir," Conlan returned with a nod of his own.

Conlan was a huge D'Danann warrior with broad shoulders, green eyes, and a dimple in his chin. He was taller even than Keir but his eyes held a certain glimmer that told her he was definitely a ladies' man.

Conlan said to Keir, "I am to accompany you to the San Francisco Otherworld to aid you in the fight against the Fomorii."

Keir raised an eyebrow. Through their soul-bonding, Rhiannon sensed he believed the same thing she did. Conlan was being sent away because they'd caught him fucking the High Chieftain.

For a moment Keir didn't reply. Then he said, "Aye. It will be good to have you fight with us."

"I will wait for your summons in the training yards." Conlan bowed from his shoulders and exited the Chieftains' building without a glance back.

Rhiannon looked up at Keir and grinned as she said, "Well, that's one more for our side."

He chuckled and guided her out the doors with his hand at the small of her back. "We could not have a fiercer warrior join us than Conlan."

This time they escaped without being seen. Rhiannon laughed as she doubled her steps alongside Keir's. He seemed rather determined to get back to the cabin. As a matter of fact, so was she.

When Keir let her into the cabin, she saw that Spirit had curled himself onto a cushion on one of the chairs. He gave a sleepy meow, then closed his eyes.

Instead of heading toward the bedroom, which she was pretty sure was his destination, she went over to his carvings and touched each one again. His warmth surrounded her, his breath soft against the back of her neck as she picked up the bust of herself.

She stroked the smooth, polished hair of the carving. It was chin-length, like her own. "Amazing that you created this before we met." He pressed his lips against her own hair as she spoke. "It's missing something, though."

"What is that?" he murmured.

"My scars." She rubbed the burning marks with one hand.

"What scars?" he said, sounding serious.

She turned to face him, the bust between them. She pressed her hand to her cheek. "These, of course."

He held his hand over hers. "They are a part of your beauty. I would have you no other way."

"You are an incredible man." She reached up on her tiptoes and kissed his own scar. "I wouldn't change a thing about you either." She drew away and gave him a serious expression. "Except your griping about my going to fight with everyone else every time there's a battle."

For a long moment he looked at her. "You are a great warrior. You have my promise that I will never hold you back in any way. I will fear for you, and protect you with my life. But I trust you to make the decisions that you feel are right."

Rhiannon set the bust of herself down on the windowsill then turned back to Keir and flung her arms around his neck. "I love you, Keir. Everything about you."

"You have my love for all time, *a stór*." He scooped her up and she gave a surprised laugh. With determination in his steps, he strode away from the carvings, through his small living room, and down the short hall to his bedroom.

He laid her on the bed and looked at her with such gentleness it tugged at her heart. Slowly he began to take her dress off as if he were unwrapping a treasure. The thought choked her up, causing her eyes to tear a little. That was what he always called her, his treasure.

After he slid off her slippers, he looked upon her for a long moment. "You are so very beautiful."

She swallowed and held out her arms. "Come to me."

With every movement he made as he stripped out of his clothing, Keir's well-defined muscles rippled. She hungered for him beyond words as he toed off his boots then tugged off his shirt and tossed it aside. She lowered her arms and her mouth watered. She couldn't wait to caress all those muscles and dig her fingernails into his fine ass.

When he was naked, she sighed as she gazed upon his luscious cock that would soon be inside her again. Their first lovemaking after being bonded had been hard, wild, exciting. She knew this would be even more precious. Her soul-bonded mate, her husband.

Keir moved onto the bed beside her and stroked his finger gently down her side, to the indentation at her waist and over her hip to her thigh. His dark eyes held hers the entire time. "I never doubted that one day you would be mine," he said with a serious expression. "Yet now that it is true, now that we are soul-bonded, I feel such wonder that you belong to me."

"Don't forget that you happen to be mine, too." She traced the Fomorii scars on his neck, then lightly touched the bandage from the battle at the stadium. "Even if we weren't soul-bonded, I would never let you go."

He caught her hand in his and lowered his mouth. His lips hovered just above hers. "You are the most precious gift a man could have."

His kiss was so tender, so sweet. His tongue gently danced with hers and she again tasted his flavor that she loved so much. Incredibly masculine and uniquely Keir.

He pushed her raised shoulder down to the mattress, then knelt between her thighs. Butterflies darted in her belly as he lowered his head and licked and sucked each of her nipples.

She slipped her fingers into his long, black hair as it tickled her skin.

The way he suckled her nipples caused her to grow wetter between her thighs and the ache inside her to spiral tighter and tighter. He said nothing, only looked at her with eyes that spoke volumes. His love for her, and so much more, shone in their depths.

She was going to cry from the power of the emotions building within her. He braced his forearms on the bed as he lowered his head and brushed his mouth along the length of her scars. He kissed one at a time and the burning somehow lessened with every tender touch of his lips.

"Please be inside me now." She shivered as his lips trailed the last scar. "I need to feel us become one."

Keir rose and braced his palms on the bed. He took his cock in one hand and moved it into the opening of her channel before returning his palm to the bed.

Ever so slowly, he slid inside her. Rhiannon sighed from the deep connection that made her feel a part of him again. His strokes weren't hurried or rushed, but long and deliberate.

Their soul-bonding gripped her and the sparkles grew between and around them. The intensity of everything she felt did cause tears to trickle down her cheeks. A tear rolled from each eye down her face.

"Why do you cry, love?" He bent and licked away one of the tears down the path it had taken.

"Because this is so beautiful." She linked her hands behind his neck. "Everything is so beautiful."

"That it is, *a stór*," he murmured as he kissed the trail of the other tear.

His thrusts continued at a deep, even pace, and she felt that swirling feeling again. That he was part of her and she was part of him. She felt what he did at the same time her own climax spiraled in her belly. Together they were rising, rising, rising. His jaw tensed as he neared the peak with her and his eyes seemed impossibly darker.

So close, so close . . . she felt both their climaxes build and build until neither of them could hold back any longer. Their cries mingled as sensation burst from where they were joined. She felt his heat as it exploded from him and rushed to every part of his body. Her own fire rushed like flames licking her from head to toe.

When they were both sated and exhausted from their mating, Keir rolled over with her in his arms and held her tight.

She snuggled closer to him and he murmured in his sexy Irish accent, "My treasure. All mine."

FOR CHEYENNE'S READERS

Be sure to go to http://cheyennemccray.com to sign up for her PRIVATE book announcement list and get FREE EXCLUSIVE Cheyenne McCray goodies. Please feel free to e-mail her at chey@cheyennemccray.com. She would love to hear from you.

*Keep reading for an excerpt
from Cheyenne McCray's next novel*

ᴍOVING TARGET

Coming soon from St. Martin's Paperbacks

Without glancing down, Daniel slid his cell phone out of its holster on his belt. As he drove, he flipped the phone open and punched the speed-dial number for Ani without taking his eyes off the road. He'd pushed that button so many times he didn't have to look at his phone to call her.

He brought the phone to his ear as he caught up to a pair of red taillights and switched lanes to pass the vehicle, then moved back into the right lane. In moments he came up on the exit to Benson. If he was going to do any kind of fast driving through the small towns from here to Bisbee, he'd have to use his lights.

A ringing tone started on the other end of the line, but immediately the generic recording came on telling him to leave a message. Looked like she was listening to him in one regard—he'd told her not to talk with anyone.

When he took the exit, he slowed down but switched on his flashing red, blue, and white strobes. He went a bit faster than he should have through the forty-five, thirty-five, then twenty-five mile-an-hour zones. All of the small towns on this stretch of highway were speed traps, and he couldn't waste time being pulled over.

From the three small towns was a long stretch of highway and a good thirty-minute drive to Bisbee. It felt as if he was steering a boat against a current.

When he finally reached the Mule Pass Tunnel, he should have felt some relief, but he remained as tense as a coiled spring.

Ten more minutes and he'd be there.

Agonizing minutes.

Daniel finally reached the police department. He pulled

out his credentials, shut off his flashing lights, then stepped from his SUV and strode into the department building.

"U.S. Deputy Marshal," Daniel said to the officer manning the front desk and showed the cop his creds.

After checking them out, the cop motioned him on.

Daniel strode to the back of the building where he'd been directed. In one glance, he saw Ani wasn't in the room. Only one woman was there, other than a female police officer. The civilian woman was talking with a paramedic.

What the hell were paramedics doing here?

And where the hell was Ani?

His voice came out in a growl, carrying over the discussions in the room. "Where's Ani Carter?"

"I'm right here, Daniel." The familiar feminine voice came from the left of him—from the woman sitting next to a paramedic.

"Ani?" He narrowed his eyes, taking in the slender woman who looked so unlike the Ani he knew that he hadn't recognized her. But her crystalline blue gaze, her dark brown hair, small nose and fair complexion were familiar, even though her face was much thinner. What clinched it for him were her full lips. Lips he'd wanted to kiss way too many times.

Goddammit. He had to get those thoughts out of his head and now.

She offered him a nervous-looking smile, and he pushed his way past the officers in the room and past the paramedic. He crouched in front of her, wanting to take her in his arms, but he couldn't. "Are you all right?"

"I'm fine." She looked down at her hands in her lap. "I'm so sorry."

He hooked his finger under her chin and forced her to look at him. "Everyone makes mistakes, honey," he said in a low voice that likely couldn't be heard by anyone but her. "But yours could get you killed. You can't take chances with your life."

A tear trickled down her cheek. "I just had to help that boy."

The desire to take her into his arms and hold her was so strong he found it difficult to restrain himself. He dropped his hand away from her face. "We've got to get you out of here."

"All right," she said quietly. "What do I need to do?"

"Wait here for a few moments." He couldn't be mad at her, no matter what had happened. "I'll be right back."

Daniel rose from his crouched position and turned away from her. He talked with a couple of officers before heading out to his SUV, then drove up so that the passenger-side door was next to the rear door of the police department. He brought in an extra set of body armor for her to wear for protection. If he could, he'd make her wear a helmet—anything to protect every inch of her.

After she had the Kevlar vest on, over her blouse, he took her by the arm and, with the cover of several police officers, hustled her into the passenger seat of the SUV and slammed the door behind her.

He sucked in a deep breath of relief as he went to the driver's side. They'd gotten her this far. He'd never let anything happen to her.

When he climbed in and shut the door, he paused to look at her. "It's good to see you again, Ani."

She'd been staring at her lap, but her head jerked up when he spoke. "You're not mad?"

"Hell, yes, I'm mad." He reached over and gripped her forearm. "Because I was worried about you."

He shouldn't have touched her. A jolt traveled through him and he removed his hand. Her eyes widened, as if she felt the same electrical feeling he had.

Daniel forced himself to look away from her and turned his keys in the ignition. "Let's get out of here."

The drive back through the small towns and on to Tucson was less hurried, but the tenseness in his muscles wouldn't let go.

They were both quiet for a while before Daniel said, "I've been looking forward to seeing you for a long time."

"You have?" She sounded so shocked that it surprised him.

"Ani, we've been talking to each other nearly every week for a year now." He glanced at her. "Don't you think I'd like to see you?" Daniel clenched the wheel tighter. What the hell was he saying?

"I guess," she said as he focused his gaze on the road, and he frowned. "I mean, I feel the same way," she continued, "it's just the circumstances—"

"Are behind us now." He shifted his hold on the steering wheel.

This time when he glanced from the road to look at her, she was smiling. She was so beautiful. He'd always thought she was, no matter what she looked like. It might take him some time to get used to this toothpick version of the woman he'd—

Daniel clenched his teeth.

Don't even go there.

After a moment's silence, she asked, "Where are we headed?"

"After we stay the night in Tucson, we'll take a puddle-jumper to the Phoenix airport in the morning." Daniel guided the SUV into the passing lane. "We've booked a direct flight out of Sky Harbor to New York. Our plane leaves at noon."

She shuddered. "The trial. It's time."

Daniel gave a slow nod. She stared at his profile that was illuminated by the red dashboard lights. She'd memorized his features down to the shadow of a beard on his jaw. But now her heart was pounding like mad.

"Oh, jeez." She leaned her head against the headrest. "I can't believe it. So much time has gone by that it doesn't seem real now."

"It's real, honey," he said in his deep voice. "We've got to do everything we can to protect you."

Ani's belly did a little nosedive when he called her honey, the endearment he'd used so many times on the phone. Maybe he said it to all women, but it made her feel special somehow.

"Have you had anymore of those bad flashbacks from

your PTSD?" he asked quietly. "You sure had me worried the last time."

"Not since then." Ani paused, then remembered that she nearly did this evening. "Well, I almost had one while I was waiting for the cops, but I pulled out of it."

He glanced at her. "Did something trigger this one or did it just come on?"

She shivered before she said, "I saw a man outside the window, watching the store. He dropped his cigarette butt and it reminded me of the fire—how it started."

Daniel's jaw was hard when he looked at her. "That could have been one of Borenko's men. They could already be on to you."

Ani took a deep breath. "The doorknob to the back room jiggled just before I heard police sirens."

Daniel cursed again. She saw him look at the rearview mirror as he said, "It's dark, and with the amount of traffic— it might be hard to see a tail."

"I'm sorry," she said, but this time Daniel didn't answer.

They were quiet most of the trip to Tucson. On the way, Daniel had Ani use his secure cell phone to call the hotel and make a reservation. Her stomach dropped to her toes when he said one room, no smoking, double beds.

Her voice shook as she made the reservation. Daniel and her sleeping in the same room?

That thought drove away her worries about the danger from the Russians.

Daniel. Her.

In the same room.

So that he could protect her, of course. That was it.

After she made the reservations, Ani could hardly think straight the rest of the way to Tucson. She didn't know what to do with her hands, so she clenched them in her lap. Every now and then, Daniel would glance her way, and she felt heat in her belly that traveled downward, and it wasn't to her toes.

When they arrived in Tucson, Daniel drove up and down several streets and said if they did have a tail, he hoped they shook him off.

At the hotel, Ani walked beside Daniel up to the front counter, her high heels clicking against the stone-tiled floor in the large lobby. It was a nice place with a restaurant and a gift shop.

She had absolutely nothing with her but what she was wearing, which now included a plain navy-blue windbreaker she had zipped up over the body armor. Daniel hadn't even let her bring her purse, her cell phone, and definitely not her credit cards. He'd forced her to leave them all at the police station. Now that the location where she worked had been exposed, her identity had been compromised.

Daniel had brought in a duffle bag with him, and she wondered if he kept one packed in his SUV for emergencies.

Like helping a dumb protected witness who gave away her true identity to someone from her old life.

He'd put on his Stetson before heading into the hotel and that just about made her melt. Between that bod, the tight Wranglers, Stetson, and boots, she'd been a goner from the first time she met him.

Once Ani and Daniel checked in at the front desk, they took the elevator up to their floor. Daniel swiped the key card in its slot to let them into the room. It smelled of new carpeting and starched sheets when they walked in. She blinked in the darkness and Daniel switched on a light.

The first thing she noticed was that there was one king-sized bed in the room. Not double beds.

She could barely breathe and stood still. He tossed the duffle on the bed, laid his hat on a vanity table, and shrugged out of his plain dark blue windbreaker, which he discarded by draping it over a chair.

"I've got to take a shower." Exhaustion was evident in his voice and he rubbed his eyes with his thumb and forefinger. It was well after one in the morning. "Mind if I head into the bathroom first?"

"Uh, Daniel?" She swallowed hard when he turned to face her. "There's only one bed."

He cast a tired glance over his shoulder at the bed. "Yeah, there is," he said just before continuing into the bathroom.

Ani stared at his back and then the bathroom door as he closed it. She was standing in the same spot when she heard the shower start.

She closed her eyes and imagined water running in rivulets over his hard, naked body. Her breathing elevated and her heart pounded a little harder at the images. She knew his body would be perfection. Picturing his muscled form caused her nipples to harden and she ached between her thighs like she'd never ached before.

Ani opened her eyes and shook her head. In her fantasies she didn't have a scarred back or an equally ugly pit from a large bullet wound in her shoulder. Even if there was a chance of them getting together—a chance in hell—she couldn't handle him seeing the mess her lower back was now.

With a sigh, she kicked off her high heels. When she went to the mirror over the vanity, she ran her hand through her thick, brunette hair. She'd lost the clip long ago. She sighed at her appearance. Tired, red eyes stared back at her. Mascara smudged one cheek, her makeup pretty much gone from crying. Her black slacks were wrinkled and her white silk shirt limp and clinging to her skin.

This was all she had to wear and she was flying with Daniel to New York tomorrow. She sighed again as the weight of the day settled on her shoulders. She was so, so tired. She pushed out of the windbreaker Daniel had loaned her, and tossed it on the chair by his.

The door to the bathroom opened, sending wafts of steam into the bedroom along with the clean scent of soap. Suddenly she didn't feel so tired.

Instead, her mouth watered and she could feel the ache in her nipples as they pressed against her bra. Daniel was rubbing a towel over his head and wearing another towel low around his hips. She'd never seen him in anything but jeans and shirts, and *oh, my God,* did he look delicious.

Fortunately, he didn't seem to notice her panting or her tongue hanging out. Instead he went to his duffle bag, pulled out a T-shirt, and tossed it to her. "Will that do to sleep in?"

She caught it and he went back to towel-drying his hair.

A little more and that towel around his waist would just slip off . . .

"The bathroom's all yours if you want it," he said in his smooth drawl.

"Um, yeah." She gripped the T-shirt tight against her chest. "Thanks."

She darted into the bathroom, closed the door, and leaned against it. Crap. Daniel was bound to see how attracted she was to him, and even if he *was* interested in her, they couldn't do anything about it. And she wouldn't want him seeing her—or touching the twisted flesh on her back.

Daniel's clothing and body armor were lying on the floor in a heap with the rest of his clothing and boots. She paused to look at the armor. This was what protected him when he was out on the job.

Ani fumbled with the vest Daniel had given her for protection. When she managed to get it off, she put it on top of his. She slipped out of her clothing and folded them on top of the marble vanity.

She climbed into the shower and let the warm water ease her tired muscles and relax the tendons at her neck. The hotel's almond-scented shampoo, conditioner, and soap were all relaxing.

Ani felt almost human again when she climbed out of the shower and toweled herself off. The hotel hair dryer was handy, so she used it to get her hair mostly dry. The shirt Daniel had loaned her to sleep in had "U. S. Marshal" emblazoned on the back. When she slipped it on, his masculine scent surrounded her. The shirt was so big on her—or she was just so small now—that it hung to mid-thigh. It was one of the most erotic sensations, to be wearing his T-shirt with no underwear. Nothing had happened, and nothing would, but she always had her imagination.

After hand-washing her bra and panties, she hung them over the shower curtain and picked up her blouse and slacks from where she'd left them on one end of the marble vanity.

She slipped into the bedroom, her heart thumping like mad. This was going to be so awkward.

But when she saw Daniel she had to stop and smile. He was passed out cold on one side of the bed, on his back on top of the bedspread. He wore a T-shirt that matched hers and a pair of jogging shorts, and one of his arms was resting across his eyes. She shook her head and went to the closet to hang up the blouse and slacks. She'd just have to iron out the wrinkles in the morning.

Before turning off the light beside the bed, she had to study him. He was even better looking than she'd remembered. All those muscles, sinewy forearms and carved biceps. She was so in lust.

And so in love.